We All
Live Here

We All Live Here

JOJO MOYES

PAMELA DORMAN BOOKS | VIKING

VIKING
An imprint of Penguin Random House LLC
1745 Broadway, New York, NY 10019
penguinrandomhouse.com

Simultaneously published in hardcover in Great Britain by Penguin Michael Joseph,
an imprint of Penguin Random House Ltd, London, in 2025

First United States edition published by Pamela Dorman Books, 2025

A Pamela Dorman Book/Viking

The PGD colophon is a registered trademark of Penguin Random House LLC.

VIKING is a registered trademark of Penguin Random House LLC.

Designed by Cassandra Garruzzo Mueller

LIBRARY OF CONGRESS CATALOGING-IN-PUBLICATION DATA
Names: Moyes, Jojo, 1969– author.
Title: We all live here : a novel / Jojo Moyes.
Description: [New York, New York] : Pamela Dorman Books/Viking, 2025.
Identifiers: LCCN 2024037389 (print) | LCCN 2024037390 (ebook) |
ISBN 9781984879325 (hardcover) | ISBN 9781984879332 (ebook)
Subjects: LCGFT: Novels.
Classification: LCC PR6113.O94 W4 2025 (print) |
LCC PR6113.O94 (ebook) | DDC 823/.92—dc23/eng/20240816
LC record available at https://lccn.loc.gov/2024037389
LC ebook record available at https://lccn.loc.gov/2024037390

Printed in the United States of America
1   3   5   7   9   10   8   6   4   2

The authorized representative in the EU for product safety and compliance is
Penguin Random House Ireland, Morrison Chambers, 32 Nassau Street,
Dublin D02 YH68, Ireland, https://eu-contact.penguin.ie.

For Saskia, who already understands more about human nature than I ever will

We All
Live Here

Chapter One

Lila

There is a framed photograph on Lila's bedside table that she hasn't yet had the energy, or perhaps the inclination, to get rid of. Four faces squished together in front of an enormous aquarium in some foreign holiday attraction—she forgets where now—a shoal of enormous iridescent stripy fish gazing blankly from behind them. Violet, pushing up her nose with one finger and pulling down the lower lids of her eyes so that she looks like a grotesque waxwork; Celie, in a Breton shirt, also pulling a face, although given she must have been thirteen by then, a little more self-consciously; Lila smiling vainly, as if hoping that this will be a lovely family shot despite all the evidence; and Dan, his smile not quite reaching his eyes, his expression enigmatic, his hand resting on Violet's T-shirted shoulder.

This last family photograph is the first thing she sees in the morning, and the last she sees at night, and although she knows she should keep it where it won't color her day, for some reason she hasn't quite fathomed she can't put it in the drawer. Sometimes, in her sleepless hours, she watches the strips of moonlight slide across her bedroom ceiling, glances at that photograph, and thinks wistfully about the family she could have had, all the pictures of holidays that will never exist—rainy weekends in Cornwall, exotic beaches with them all dressed in white—a joyful graduation in front of some red-brick university, perhaps Celie's wedding, proud parents at her side; all ghostly, ephemeral images of a life that have simply evaporated in front of her.

And sometimes she thinks about getting a big glob of Blu Tack and squidging it right over Dan's face.

LILA IS ATTEMPTING to clear a particularly stubborn blockage in the first-floor lavatory when Anoushka calls. When she and Dan had bought this house two and a half years ago—a large, "quirky" (estate-agent speak for "nobody else would buy it") doer-upper in a leafy part of north London—she had been enchanted by the decades-old bathroom suites in mint green and raspberry, thinking them and the floral wallpaper charming and quaint. She and Dan had walked around each room, building images between them of what the house would look like when it was done. Although, when she thought back properly, it was she who had walked around building images and Dan had said, "Mm, mm," in a noncommittal way and sneaked glances at his phone.

The day after they had picked up the keys the same charming and quaint plumbing had decided to reveal its true self in a malevolent series of blockages and overspills. In the pink bathroom, the one the girls used, a plunger and a twisted coat hanger now sit beside the cistern, ready for Lila (because it is always Lila's job, apparently) to attack whatever had decided to wedge itself stolidly in the depths of the bowl this time.

"Lila! Darling! How are you?"

Anoushka's voice muffles and Lila can just hear, *No, Gracie, I don't want carnations in it. They're such vulgar flowers. No, no absolutely no gerberas. She hates them.*

Lila leans over and uses her nose to touch the hands-free button on her phone. She gags silently as a slosh of water rides over the top of her rubber glove. "Great! Marvelous!" she says. "How are you?"

"Fighting the good fight for my wonderful authors, as ever. There's another royalty check on the way. It would have been with you last week but Gracie is pregnant and literally can't stop vomiting. Honestly, I've had to throw away three office wastepaper baskets. They were an actual health hazard."

Downstairs, Truant, the dog, is barking urgently. He barks at everything—squirrels in the garden, pigeons, bin men, casual visitors, air.

"Oh, how lovely," says Lila, closing her eyes as she pushes the coat hanger further in. "The pregnancy, I mean. Not the vomiting."

"Not really, darling. Terrible pain in the arse. Why these girls keep having babies is beyond me. I have a positive revolving door of assistants. I'm starting to wonder if there's something in the air-conditioning. Now, how are those lovely girls of yours?"

"Great. They're great," says Lila.

They're not great. Celie had burst into tears at the breakfast table after apparently seeing something on Instagram, and when Lila asked what had happened, Celie had told her she wouldn't bloody understand and stalked off to school. Violet had fixed her with a look of cold fury when Lila had said yes, she did have to go to Daddy's on Thursday—it was his night—then slid silently from the stool and not spoken to her for the entire school run.

"Good. Good," says Anoushka, in the distracted tone of someone who wouldn't have heard if you'd said they'd both been beheaded that morning. "Now, about this manuscript."

Lila pulls the coat hanger from the toilet bowl. The water level is still somewhere just under the seat. She peels the rubber gloves from her hands and leans back against the cabinet. She hears Truant still barking and wonders if she'll have to take the neighbors another bottle of wine. She has given away seven in the last three months, trying to stop them actively hating her.

"When are you going to have something to send me? You seemed very certain last month."

Lila blows out her cheeks. "I—I'm working on it."

There is a short silence.

"Now, darling, I don't want to sound stern," Anoushka says, sounding stern, "you did astonishingly well with *The Rebuild*. And you had that lovely little uplift in sales on the back of Dan's terrible deeds. I suppose we should be grateful to him for that at least. But we do not want to lose visibility, do we? We do not want to be so late delivering that I might as well be launching a debut."

"I—It'll be with you very soon."

"How soon?"

Lila gazes around the bathroom. "Six weeks?"

"Let's say three. Doesn't have to be perfect, darling. I just need an idea as to what you're doing. Is it still a guide to a Happy Single Life?"

"Uh . . . yes."

"Lots of tips on how to live well independently? Funny stories about dates? Some nice hot single-sex anecdotes?"

"Oh, yes. All of that."

"Can't wait. I'm already agog. I'll live vicariously through your adventures! *Oh, for goodness' sake, Gracie, not the new wastepaper basket.* I've got to go. I await your email! Much love to all!"

Lila ends the call and stares at the toilet bowl, willing the water to go down. As she sits, she hears Bill climbing the stairs. He pauses at the landing, and she can hear him steady himself as he makes to mount the next step. He and Mum lived in a 1950s bungalow ten minutes' walk away—sparsely furnished, full of light and clean lines—and he finds the many floors and clutter of this rickety house a daily challenge.

"Darling girl?"

"Yes?" Lila rearranges her face into something bright and cheery.

"I hate to be the bearer of bad news but the neighbors have been round complaining about the dog again. And something disgusting appears to be seeping through the kitchen ceiling."

THE EMERGENCY PLUMBER had sucked his teeth, pulled up four floorboards, and apparently discovered the leak in the soil pipe. He had drained the cistern, informed her that she would need a whole new system—"Mind you, I can't imagine you want to hang on to that bathroom suite too much longer. I've got grandparents younger than that is"—drunk two cups of sweet tea, and charged her three hundred and eighty pounds. She had started calling it the Mercedes tax. Any tradesman would see the overpriced vintage sports car lurking on the drive and immediately add twenty-five percent to whatever invoice they had prepared.

"So that's what was causing the blockage?" Lila had said, tapping out the pin number of her credit card and trying not to calculate the damage that would do to this month's budget.

"Nah. Must be something else," he had said. "You can't use it, though, obviously. And all the bathroom plumbing will have to be reinstalled. You might want to replace some of those floorboards while you're at it. I can push my thumb through them."

Bill had put a calloused hand on her shoulder as she closed the door behind the man. "It'll all work out," he said, and squeezed lightly. This was what, for Bill, passed as deep emotional support. "I can help, you know."

"You don't have to," she said, turning to him brightly. "I'm fine. All good." He had sighed gently, then turned and headed stiffly to his room.

Bill had lived with them for nine months now, having moved in shortly after her mother's death. Being Bill, it wasn't that he had been found sobbing hysterically or starving or letting the house go to ruin. He had just retreated quietly into himself, becoming a smaller and smaller version of the upright former furniture-maker she had known for three decades until he seemed like a shadow presence. "I just miss her," he would say, when she turned up for tea, bustling round, trying to inject some energy into the too-still rooms.

"I know, Bill," she would say. "I miss her too."

The fact was, Lila hadn't been coping well either. She had been in shock when Dan had announced he was leaving. When she finally found out about Marja, she realized Dan simply leaving had been a whisper of a blow, a thing that had barely touched her, compared to this. She had barely slept for the first six months, her mind a toxic whirlwind of finally drawing threads together, of recriminations, dread and cold fury, a million unspoken arguments in her head—arguments that Dan always managed somehow to evade: "Not in front of the children, Lila, eh?"

And then, just months later, even this had been dwarfed by the sudden death of Francesca. So when she suggested Bill move in for a bit they were both at pains to assure each other that this was really to help Lila with the girls, to provide a bit of practical help while she adjusted to single parenting. Bill kept the bungalow, heading off most days to work in his neat shed at the end of the garden, where he mended neighbors' chairs and sanded replacement stair spindles to stop Lila's children falling through the gaps in the banisters at Lila's house. Neither of them discussed when he was going to move home. It wasn't as though having him there got in the way of Lila's life (what life?), and Bill's gentle presence gave what remained of their little family a much-needed sense of stability and continuity. An anchor for their vainly bobbing little rowing-boat, which felt, most days, slightly leaky and unstable and as if they had abruptly and without warning found themselves adrift on the high seas.

LILA WALKS TO the school. It is the first week back after the long holidays and Bill had offered to go, but she needs to up her step count (she is haunted daily by Marja's endless legs, her still-defined waist). Besides, she has to leave the house to pick up Violet, which means she can stave off the guilt that comes with not having done any writing again.

They both know the reason Bill offers: Lila hates the afternoon school run. Mornings are fine: everyone is in a hurry, she can drop and run. But this is too painful: her acute toe-curling visibility as she gathers with the other mothers at the school gates. There had been a whole month of head tilt after it first happened—*You're kidding me. God, how awful, I'm so sorry*—or perhaps, behind her back, *You couldn't really blame him, though, could you?* And, of course, there had been the awful cosmic joke of the timing of it all: just two weeks after *The Rebuild* had been published, alongside a slew of her promotional interviews talking about how best to repair a marriage that had grown stale amid the demands of work and children.

Two days after he had left, she had walked grimly up to the playground and three of the other mothers, heads bowed together, had been reading a copy of the *Elle* article, helpfully titled *How I Made My Marriage Watertight*. Philippa Graham—that over-Botoxed witch—had hurriedly shoved it behind her when she saw Lila and blinked hard with pantomime innocence, and her two acolytes, whose names Lila could never remember, had actually corpsed with suppressed giggles. *I hope your husbands are right this minute contracting an antibiotic-resistant venereal disease from underage rent boys*, she had thought, and pasted on a smile ready for Violet to traipse out, schoolbag dragging behind her.

For weeks she had felt the murmur of appalled fascination follow her around the playground, the faint turning of heads and gossip exchanged from the corners of mouths. She had held up her head, skin prickling, jaw aching with the rigid faint smile she had plastered, like a kind of permafrost, across her face. Her mother had taken over play-date duty, explaining to the girls and their friends' mothers when she drove her little Citroën to pick them up that Lila was busy working and she would see them next time. But her mother wasn't here anymore.

Feeling the familiar clench of her stomach, Lila pulls her collar around her ears and positions herself at the far edge of the scattered groups of mothers, nannies, and the odd lone father, studying her phone intently, and pretends to be engrossed in a Really Important Email. It is her standard procedure, these days. That or bringing Truant, who barks hysterically if anyone comes within twenty yards.

Tomorrow, she thinks. *Tomorrow there will be no interruptions. I will sit down at my desk at 9:15 a.m. when I get back from dropping Violet, and I will not move until I have written two thousand words.* She decides not to think about the fact that she has made this exact promise to herself at least three times a week for the past six months.

"I knew it!"

There is a shriek of delight from a group of the mothers near the rainbow-painted bench by the swings. She sees Marja among them, leaning forward, Philippa squeezing her arm and beaming. Marja is wearing a long camel cashmere-type coat and trainers, her blonde hair pulled loosely and artfully into a huge tortoiseshell clip. "Well, you weren't drinking at Nina's, were you? I have a Spidey sense for these things!" Philippa laughs. She is just placing her hand on Marja's stomach when she glances over, sees Lila, and turns away theatrically. She mouths, "Oh, God. *Sorry.*"

Marja turns, following Philippa's gaze. She flushes.

Lila understands in her bones what has happened before her brain has a chance to register. She stares, unseeing, at the screen of her phone, her heart racing. *No. No. It can't be. Not after everything Dan had said. He couldn't do this to us.* But any doubt has been removed by the color flooding Marja's cheeks.

Lila feels sick. She feels dizzy. She cannot think what to do. She has an overwhelming urge to slump against the tree a few feet away but she doesn't want the other mothers to see her do that. She can feel the hot pressure of their gaze so presses her phone to her ear and hurriedly pretends to have a conversation. "Yes! Yes, it is! How lovely to hear from you! That's great. How are you?" She talks on, not knowing what is coming out of her mouth, turning so that she can no longer see anyone, her brain humming.

She jumps as Violet tugs at her hand.

"Darling!" She drops the phone from her ear, registers Mrs. Tugendhat standing beside her daughter. "Everything okay?" she says brightly, her voice too high, too loud.

"Why are you talking when there's nobody on your phone?" says Violet, frowning at the screen.

"They rang off," she says quickly. She thinks she may actually explode. A pressure is building inside her that feels too much for a body to contain.

Mrs. Tugendhat is wearing an emphatically hairy cardigan with batwing sleeves and a yellow cardboard hand-made badge on the lapel that says "Happy Birthday" in green Sharpie. "I was just talking to Violet about the end-of-year production. Did she tell you she's the narrator?"

"Great! Great!" Lila says, her face stretched into a tight smile.

"We don't like to do a nativity—we're multi-faith, these days. And I know it's a long way off . . . well, I suppose not that far off—four months—but you know how long these things take to pull together."

"I do!" says Lila.

"You're being weird," says Violet.

"And you *are* our resident Parent in Entertainment, since Frances left

Emmerdale. Not that she had a regular part anyway. So Violet thought you might do it."

"Do it?"

"Sort out wardrobe for the lead characters."

"Wardrobe," Lila repeats blankly.

"It's an adaptation of *Peter Pan.*"

Marja is walking away from the other mothers. She pulls the camel coat across her middle, and casts a quick, awkward glance in Lila's direction, Hugo, her young son, pulling at her hand as she passes the gates.

"Of course!" says Lila. A loud humming has started up somewhere at the back of her head. She can barely hear anything beyond it. She thinks tears may have sprung to her eyes because everything seems oddly glassy.

"You will? That's marvelous. Violet wasn't sure you would."

"She doesn't like coming to school," says Violet.

Lila tears her attention away and back to her daughter. "What? Don't be silly, Violet! I love coming here! Best part of my day!"

"You paid Celie four pounds to do pickup last week."

"No. No. I gave Celie four pounds. She needed four pounds. The school pickup was unrelated."

"That's not true. You said you'd rather chew off your own feet and Celie said she'd go if you gave her enough for one of those marshmallow coffees from Costa and you said, 'Fine, okay,' and—"

Mrs. Tugendhat's smile has become a little wobbly.

"That's enough, Violet. Totally, Mrs. Tugendhat. The thing. What you said. Of course I'll do it!" Something is happening to her right hand. She keeps flapping it in the air for emphasis. It feels entirely unrelated to the rest of her body.

Mrs. Tugendhat beams. "Well, we'll probably get started after the October half-term but that will give you time to get the costumes into shape, yes?"

"Yes!" Lila says. "Yes! We must go. Bit of a hurry. But we—we'll talk. We'll definitely talk. Happy . . . birthday!" She points at Mrs. Tugendhat's chest, then turns and starts walking down the road.

"Why are we going this way?" says Violet, jogging to keep up. "We always go down Frobisher Street."

Marja has headed down Frobisher Street. Lila thinks she may keel over and die if she has to look at that glossy tousled blonde head again. "Just . . . fancy a change," she says.

"You're being really weird," says Violet. She stops and pulls from her rucksack the packet of root-vegetable crisps that Bill must have put into her bag instead of Monster Munch. He's trying to improve their diet. Violet slows to eat them, so Lila is forced to slow too. "Mum?"

"Yes?"

"Did you know Felix has worms in his bottom? He put his finger up there at break to get one out and show us. You could actually see it wriggling around in his fingernail."

Lila stands still and digests this. Normally such information would have made her scream. Right now it feels like the least terrible thing she has heard today. She looks down at her daughter. "Did you touch it?"

"Ugh. No," says Violet, popping another crisp into her mouth. "I told him I was going to stay exactly ten miles away from him forever. And the other boys. They're all disgusting."

Lila pulls her palm down over her face slowly and lets out a long, shaky breath. "Never change, Violet," she says, when she can speak again. "You've already acquired so much more wisdom than I ever did."

Chapter Two

In the days since Dan leaving, and her mother dying, Lila has developed a series of strategies to get through each day. When she wakes, mostly between five and six a.m., she slugs down an anti-depressant citalopram with a glass of water, dresses before she has time to think, and walks Truant for an hour, striding up to the Heath where the early-morning dog-walkers cross muddy paths with the lone coffee-drinkers and grim-faced runners in earphones. She walks while listening to audiobooks or chatty, anodyne podcasts, anything to ensure she's not alone with her thoughts.

She returns and wakes the girls, bribing and cajoling them out of bed and onto the school run, trying not to take personally the harrumphing and cries of anguish about missing socks and phones. Since Bill moved in with them he has made breakfast, insisting that the girls eat porridge with berries and a variety of seeds instead of Lila's Pop Tarts and three-day-old bagels with jam. Bill is rigorous about diet and talks endlessly of fish oils and the scouring properties of lentils, ignoring the rolling of the girls' eyes, and their longing looks toward the box of Coco Pops. In the evenings he rustles up nutritional meals involving unfamiliar vegetables, and tries not to show his hurt when the girls grumble that actually they'd rather have a ham and cheese toastie.

When Lila returns from dropping the girls, she sits in what is laughingly called her study, a room near the top of the house still lined with the battered cardboard boxes of books they never unpacked, and attacks the most urgent admin of the day. This—and its accompanying financial calculations—exhausts her so she often has a little nap on the sofa-bed, or occasionally lies on the rug listening to a soothing meditation podcast, trying to ignore Truant's barking downstairs. She tries to eat regularly so that her blood sugar does not drop, and her mood with it. When she wakes up, she shakes off her grogginess with a mug of tea, and then goes to the shop for whatever they don't have. By then it's usually time to collect Violet, at which point she becomes *Mum* again, with no time for invasive thoughts, engaged instead in endless domestic warfare against mess, laundry, homework, the respective travails of her girls' days, until bedtime. Then she takes two antihistamine tablets (the doctor will no longer prescribe her preferred sleeping pills: apparently they are now considered a "dirty drug"), or sometimes, if in a pronounced insomniac phase, smokes half a joint out of the window. Finally, when she feels mildly confident that sleep is approaching tentatively, like a skittish horse, she switches on a sleepcast—in which soft-voiced actors read boring stories in monotones—and prays not to wake again within a couple of hours.

She does not want to think about her ex-husband and his effortlessly gorgeous new partner. She does not want to think about his and Marja's spotless home up the road, with its sparse selection of stylish objects and Noguchi coffee-table. She does not want to think about her absent mother, who had somehow made all of this mess so much more manageable.

Some days, Lila feels as if she's battling everything: the furious, slippery contents of her brain, her wavering, unreliable hormones, her weight, her ex-husband, her house's attempts to fall down around her ears, the world in general.

As the girls get up from the supper table that evening, leaving Bill gazing reproachfully at the unfinished bowls of venison and pearl barley stew ("It's a very good meal—high in protein and low in fat"), Lila realizes with an internal thud that a whole new battleground has just opened up: *Dan's new baby.* This child will be the half-sibling of her daughters, a constant presence in all their lives. It will have an equal right to whatever their father has—money, time, love. This child, more than anything else, makes it all real—Dan is never coming back, no matter how unlikely she had known that was. This child is going to be a new thing for Lila to deal with—possibly daily—for the next eighteen years. And the thought makes her want to ram her knuckles into her eye sockets.

HE CALLS AT EIGHT FIFTEEN. No doubt after Hugo, Marja's well-behaved six-year-old, has been in bed, bathed, compliant, in clean pajamas and with carefully brushed teeth, for at least an hour. Violet, meanwhile, is hanging by her legs from the banisters, singing the words to a rap song that has contained, at the last count, eleven different references to genitalia.

"Lila."

She feels the reflexive clench of her stomach at his voice. Takes a breath before she speaks. "I wondered when you'd call."

"Marja's really upset." He sighs. "Look, neither of us wanted you to find out like this."

"Marja's upset, is she? Oh." The words are out before she can help herself. "How distressing for her."

There is a short silence before he speaks. "Look, it's eighteen weeks. We thought it was best to get through the summer holidays and then . . ."

"But it's fine for the school mums to know."

"She didn't tell them. That bloody woman—what's her name?—she guessed. And Marja couldn't lie so—"

"No. God forbid there should be any lies involved around here. So when are you planning to tell the girls?"

Dan hesitates. She pictures him running his palm over the top of his head, his habitual gesture when faced with something he finds difficult. "Uh . . . well. We thought—I thought—it might be better coming from you."

"Ohhh, no." Lila stands up from the table and walks to the sink. "Oh, no, Dan. This one's yours. You want to tell the girls they're being replaced, that one's on you."

"What do you mean 'being replaced'?"

"Well, you've already moved out to play Daddy to someone else's kid. How else are they meant to see it?"

"You know it's not like that."

"Do I? You were their dad. Now you take someone else's kid to school in the mornings. Have dinner with him every night."

"I'm still their bloody dad. I'd have dinner with them every night if I could."

"Not if it involved living with us, though, right?"

"Lila, why are you doing this?"

"Me? I'm doing nothing. You're the one who ran off. You're the one who started sleeping with one of our actual neighbors. You're the one now raising someone else's kid while your own children see you two days a week." She hates herself for the sound of her voice, the words that are pouring out of her, but she cannot stop herself. "And *you're* the one who decided to impregnate a woman twelve years younger than you with another bloody baby. A baby which, if I remember rightly, you insisted to me you would never have, no matter how much I wanted it, because you could barely cope with the two we've got!"

It is at this point that something makes her look over her shoulder. Celie is standing by the fridge. She has an orange-juice carton in one hand and she is staring at her mother.

"Celie?"

Celie is ashen. She puts down the carton and bolts from the room.

"What?" Dan is saying. "What's happening?"

"Celie!" she shouts. And then, turning to the phone: "I'll call you back."

The door to Celie's room is bolted and loud music is playing. Lila tries the door, twice, then bangs on it, but gets only a muffled *Go away* in return. She stands for a moment, unsure what to do, then eventually slides down the door and sits, her back to the wood, listening to the relentless thump of the beat.

As she sits, a slew of messages begins to come through from Dan. She does not have the constitution to read them just now but catches sight of:

> you insist on making things more difficult
> than they
> like I said neither of us want to cause the
> girls any
> and they will learn to love the new b

She switches her phone to Do Not Disturb, and sits, trying to regulate her breathing.

Finally, the music lowers in volume. "I'm going to sit here until you talk to me, sweetie," she says, loud enough for Celie to hear. Her voice echoes into the silence. "I'm not going anywhere. And you know I can be really annoying like that."

Another long silence.

"I have a Thermos, a sleeping bag, and some mint cake. I could be here till Thursday if necessary."

Finally she hears footsteps crossing the floor. She hears Celie unlock the door and walk away again. Lila climbs heavily to her feet and opens it tentatively. Her teenage daughter is lying on her bed, her long black hair fanned dramatically around her head, her socked feet up the wall.

"I hate him."

"You don't hate him. He's your dad," she says, thinking: *I do, though.*

"He's so pathetic. You know she posted her test result on Instagram?"

"What?"

Celie holds up her phone. And there it is, a photograph of the white plastic wand with a little blue line, *OMG* in looping text underneath it.

"So much for not telling anyone." Lila hands back the phone, sits down on the bed, puts her hand on Celie's leg. "I'm sorry, darling. I'm so sorry you're having to deal with all this." She swallows. "And I'm sorry I . . . I don't always handle it very well."

Celie wipes a tear furiously from under her eye, wiping again when she sees the smudge of mascara on her finger. "Not your fault."

"Well, it certainly isn't yours."

Celie gives her a sideways look. "When did you know?"

Lila shakes her head. "I heard one of the mums talking to Marja about it at school today. That was why Dad called. I'm sorry you had to overhear it like that."

Celie shakes her head. "I already knew."

"What do you mean, you knew?"

"She has Pregnacare vitamins in their bathroom. She's had them for months. Why would you have those if you weren't having a baby?"

Lila feels another painful clench. So this was planned. She closes her eyes for a moment, grits her teeth, releases her jaw, then says: "Well, maybe you'll love it once it gets here. Maybe it will be a wonderful addition and you'll find that having an extended family is a really lovely thing. It's going to be fine, Celie. In fact I'll bet you love having another little brother or sister. Someone else to adore you. Just like we all do."

There is a short silence.

"Oh, God, Mum, you're such a rubbish actor."

Lila looks at her. "Really?"

"You have no poker face *at all.*"

They sit together for a moment. Lila sighs. "Well, all right, it may feel a bit odd for a bit. For all of us. But I know your dad really does love you. And these things tend to work out in the end."

Celie wriggles toward her, reaches out, and squeezes her hand. She slides it away again, but it's enough. "Are you okay, Mum?" she says, after a minute.

"I'm absolutely fine," says Lila, firmly. "I have you two, don't I? The only family I've ever wanted."

"And Bill."

"And Bill. What would we do without Bill?"

"Even if he does make us eat really gross food. Mum, can you have a word with him about all the lentils? They made me do a really loud fart in morning geography and I swear everyone knew it was me."

"I'll talk to him." Lila slips into her bedroom and takes a second citalopram before she heads back downstairs. The doctor was adamant that she should stick to the recommended dose. But the doctor's ex-husband wasn't busy impregnating half of north London. Lila grabs a second Citalopram.

"ALL OKAY?" BILL is washing up, classical music from Radio 3 seeping gently into the quiet of the kitchen. Even if she tells him she'll do it later, he'll start fidgeting while she watches television, then quietly absent himself from the living room, appearing half an hour later with a damp tea-towel and an expression of quiet relief. Bill likes order. And over the past few months she has come to understand that Bill needs to feel useful, even if she worries that a seventy-eight-year-old should rest more than he does. He turns to her, the tea-towel over his shoulder.

"Fine," she says. And then she adds blithely, "Dan is having a baby. With the Bendy Young Mistress."

Bill stands for a moment, digesting this. "I'm so sorry," he says, in his clipped, stately-home voice.

There is a short silence.

And then he says: "I don't really know what to say. Your mother would have known." He walks up to her and she thinks he'll give her a hug. But he hesitates, then puts a hand on her upper arm and squeezes it. "He's a fool, Lila," he says gently.

"I know." Lila swallows.

"And he'll be sorry when he's struggling with all those sleepless nights and nappies," Bill adds. "Teething. Toddler tantrums. All that dreadful mess and chaos."

I loved that chaos, she thinks sadly. *I loved being in the middle of it all, my grubby babies, my house of plastic toys and unemptied laundry baskets. I wanted five. A little tribe. And a house in the country filled with dogs and muddy boots and baskets of kindling we'd collected in the woods.* "Yeah," she says.

When she raises her head, Bill is watching her. He looks down at his highly polished shoes. Bill's shoes are always polished. She is not sure she has ever seen him without a neatly ironed shirt and shiny shoes. "Actually, she would probably have called him a wanker," he says suddenly.

Lila's eyes widen. She thinks for a moment, then says: "She probably would."

"A stupid fucking wanker. Probably."

Bill never swears, and these words coming out of his mouth sound so unlikely that they stare at each other and let out a short, shocked laugh. Another follows, like a hiccup. Lila's laugh becomes a half-sob. She has both hands over her face. "It never stops, Bill," she says, crying. "Bloody hell. It just never stops."

Bill squeezes her shoulder. "It will. That's it now. That's the three things."

She sniffs. "Since when did you become superstitious?"

"Since I didn't salute a solitary magpie and your mother got hit by a bus the next day."

"Seriously?"

"Well, I have to blame something." He waits until she's stopped crying. "You'll be okay, dear girl," he says softly.

"We'll be okay," she repeats, and pushes her hair from her eyes. She sniffs, wipes away her tears. "Do I look okay?"

"You look fine."

She studies his expression and screws up her face. "Jesus, Bill, you have a worse poker face than I do."

Chapter Three

Here are the things I have learned in my fifteen years of marriage: it's okay if you don't feel filled with adoration every day. We are all going to get grumpy over the discarded socks, the missed annual car inspection, the fact that you haven't had sex for six weeks. As the great Esther Perel says, love is a process. It is a verb. All marriages have peaks and troughs, and over those years you gain a greater perspective and realize that it is just part of the ebb and flow of your own, special, unique romantic life. Marriage can contain multitudes of emotions in one single day. You can wake up to the man snoring beside you and think you want to put a pillow over his head, and by eleven o'clock that same morning, you're wishing the cleaner would leave early so that you could grab him and lose a delicious hour in bed together. You can feel fondness, irritation, lust, gratitude all in the same half-hour. The trick is to understand this process, this ebb and flow, and not be panicked by your own emotions. Because as long as you're both in this together, a team, you know deep in your bones that this is just part of the glorious business of being human. Dan is my team, and we're in this together, and there isn't a day that I'm not grateful for that certainty.

Sometimes Lila remembers this extract, serialized helpfully in a national newspaper a whole fourteen days before Dan left her, and wants to curl up in a tiny hard ball, like a woodlouse trapped in a washbasin.

She had been so certain when she wrote it. She remembers sitting in the house, constructing that final sentence, feeling overwhelmed with love for her husband, her life. (She had often felt overwhelmed when writing about fictional Dan: he was so much less complicated than actual Dan.) Dan used to shake his head fondly when she talked about her father, had banned her from using her well-worn mantra: *Everyone leaves in the end.*

The first time she had said it to him, panicky in the face of his alarmingly consistent advances, unwilling to commit in the early months of their relationship, he had reached for her hand, folded it in both of his, and said: "You need to rewrite that story. Just because your dad behaved like an arsehole, it doesn't mean all men will." It had felt like a revelation, and then it had felt like a touchstone.

She thinks now that they were probably mostly happy for the first ten years, give or take the childcare juggling, the tiredness competitions when the babies were small. She definitely remembers a family holiday while she was writing her book when she had sat on the beach watching her daughters in the water playing with her mother (Francesca was very enthusiastic about the sea) and thought, hugging her sandy knees, how incredibly lucky she was. It had felt like being nestled in the very heart of something good and strong and solid: her mother splashing, Bill calling encouragement from under his sun hat, her beautiful laughing girls, her husband. Financial security, a new house, the sun, and the twinkling waves. It had felt like she had everything to look forward to.

And then—plot twist!—Dan had gone. And less than a year later, her mother too.

She has been mulling this for twenty minutes, her noise-blocking earphones on, staring out of the window, when she notices a man standing at the end of the front garden, gazing up. She watches him, frowning for a while, waiting for him to leave. But he doesn't. Just takes two paces to the right, puts his hand on the trunk of the tree, and stands there, apparently thinking. He is wearing a puffy jacket, a pair of slightly grubby jeans, and a beanie hat. She cannot see his face. She feels a vague stab of anxiety: two weeks ago her neighbor's car had been stolen from the front drive. She wills him to take a phone call, to move on, to do any one of a number of things that will tell her he is not a thief, not someone planning something sinister. But still he stands, looking up speculatively. She sits at her desk for a moment longer, then pulls the earphones from her head and races downstairs, four, five flights, clips a lead on Truant so that she is not alone, and opens the front door. The man looks round at her.

"This is a private driveway," she says, loud enough for him to hear.

He doesn't say anything, just regards her steadily as Truant sets up an urgent, deafening stream of barking. She remembers suddenly that she is still in her dressing-gown and pajamas at eleven o'clock in the morning. She had told herself that she was not allowed to get dressed until she had written a thousand words in an attempt to force herself to stay at her desk. Suddenly this feels like a categorical error.

"What?" he yells.

"This is a private driveway! Go away!"

He frowns a little. "I'm just looking at your tree."

It is a ridiculous excuse.

"Well, don't."

"Don't look at your tree?"

"No." Truant is pulling at the lead, growling and snapping. She loves him for this show of aggression.

The man seems untroubled. He raises his eyebrows. "Can I look at your tree if I stand on the pavement?"

He takes two steps back, clearly slightly amused. It makes her feel furious and powerless at the same time, this man's casual confidence, his apparent knowledge that she has no control over the situation.

"Just don't look at my tree! Don't look at my house! Go away!"

"That's friendly."

"I don't owe you friendly. Just because I'm a woman I don't have to be friendly. You're standing in my front garden and I haven't invited you to do that. So, no, I don't have to be friendly."

A shrill note has crept into her voice, and Truant's barking is deafening. From the corner of her eye she can see next door's curtains twitching in the bay window. No doubt this will be notched up on their list of neighborly misdemeanors. She lifts a hand by way of apology and the curtain closes.

"Nice car," he says, glancing at the Mercedes.

She had bought the sports car because it had felt like something her mother would do—impulsive and optimistic. She bought it from a specialist dealer because the first dealership she called failed to return her calls. And she bought the highest-specification, most expensive model her mother's inheritance allowed her—a 1985 Mercedes Benz 380SL—because the sharp-suited salesman in the dealership she'd ended up at clearly didn't believe she could afford it. ("Yup," said Eleanor, her oldest friend, drily. "You really showed him.")

"It's got a tracker," she yells.

"What?" He cannot hear her over the noise.

"It's got a tracker fitted! And an alarm system!"

He frowns. "You think I'm going to steal your car?"

"No. I don't think you're going to steal my car. Because then the police would track it and you would end up in jail. I'm just letting you know that that's not an option. And, by the way, there is no money in the house. Just in case you're wondering."

He frowns at his trainers for a minute, then looks up at her. "So you've come out here just to tell me I can't look at your tree and I can't steal your Mercedes or I'm going to jail and you have no money."

It sounds ridiculous the way he says it and this makes her even crosser. "That's about it. Maybe if you didn't just walk into people's front gardens, they wouldn't feel obliged to say anything at all."

"Actually I came into your front garden because I had an appointment with Bill."

"What?"

"I had an appointment with Bill. About doing the garden. But nobody answered the door so I'm guessing he's not in."

She deflates. "Oh," she says, and just then Truant, clearly maddened by this unending transgression, starts twisting against the lead, unsure whether he wants to fly at this man or flee. She wrestles with him, trying to calm him, but her tone has clearly sent him into a spiral of anxiety and he will not be settled.

"Bill's at his place." She has to shout this twice, as the first words are swallowed by the noise. "*His place.* Down the road. Look, I'm sorry. Come in and I'll call him. He's obviously forgotten."

But the man takes two steps back so that he is on the pavement. "You're all right. I'll call him myself." And he heads off along the street, pulling his phone from his pocket as he leaves.

"I'M NOT SURPRISED he ran away. You're quite . . . stabby since Dan left."

"Stabby?"

"Like most of the time you walk around looking like you could quite easily assassinate someone."

Lila eyes the fork she has been waving around as she told Eleanor the story of the Garden Interloper Who Wasn't and lowers it carefully. "I do not. Not like an actual knife stabby person."

Eleanor is between jobs, which means she is wearing carefully applied makeup. When she is on a job—she does hair and makeup for television—she says she cannot be arsed to do her own face too. Lila looks at her and wonders if Eleanor is aging a lot better than she is. She's . . . radiant.

"Well . . ."

"You're saying I look like a crazy person."

"Nope." Eleanor stabs a piece of sushi and forks it into her mouth with a single chopstick. "I'm saying, as your oldest friend, that you can be a little . . . quick to rise these days." Seeing Lila's crestfallen face, she says, "I mean, totally understandable given what you've been through and everything. But I'd save that for Dan. You just might want to be careful about the vibes you give out to randoms."

"Vibes?"

"Well, just maybe cut *this* a little." She narrows her eyes suddenly and stares at Lila, her face stony.

Lila pushes her plate away from her. "Is that meant to be me?"

"Well, not actual you. You do a jutting thing with your chin too. I don't think I can do that."

"Wow. Thanks."

"I say it with love, Lils. And there's a whole raft of people you should totally give that vibe to. Dan at the top of the list. But humble gardener just staring at a tree while he waits for your elderly stepfather? Maybe not so much. Try this." She slowly and exaggeratedly pulls her face into a smile.

"Funny."

"I'm not being funny. Try it."

"I know how to smile, El."

"Maybe. But you don't do it very much any more. I just don't want you to end up, you know, one of those tight-lipped divorcées. It's very hard to get lipstick to go on nicely once you get grooves." She purses her lips and points to the tiny lines that result. "How's Bill doing, anyway?"

Lila sighs, and takes a drink of water. "Hard to say. He could have his leg hanging off and still insist he was fine." She has a vision of him plodding silently around the house, plugged into his earphones so that he can listen to Radio 3. He seems to need a constant supply of classical music, his barrier against the rest of the world. "He's okay. I think. He makes the girls eat a lot of pulses."

"Which they love."

"You can imagine. I don't know. He and Mum had this kind of regimented thing going on. Schedules and healthy food and tidiness and . . . order. So it can be a little tricky living with him. Don't get me wrong, I'm glad he's there. I think it's good for us to have the . . . continuity. But I wish he could unbend a little." She sees Eleanor glance at her watch. "Are you going somewhere? You look really nice by the way."

"Do I?" says Eleanor, with the insouciance of someone who knows it to be true. She has a huge shock of wavy mid-brown hair with a white streak at the front that manages to be both natural and ridiculously cool. She is wearing a bright scarlet silk shirt and half a dozen silver bangles. "I'm seeing Jamie and Nicoletta this evening."

"Who?"

"The couple I was telling you about. We're going to a hotel in Notting Hill. I'm quite excited."

"Oh. The *throuple*." Lila pulls a face.

"We prefer *ménage à trois*. 'Throuple' is a very *Daily Mail* way of putting it."

In the three years that Eleanor has been single she has been on some kind of sexual odyssey, happily taking herself off weekly for what she calls her "adventures." It's a lot of fun, she tells Lila. No hang-ups about relationships or whether your body is perfect or whether you have a future together, all that stuff. It's just having a laugh and some lovely sex. She wishes she'd done it years ago instead of hanging on with Eddie.

Every time Lila sees her now it is as if her friend is morphing into someone unrecognizable. "Isn't it weird? I mean, do you have to work it all out beforehand? Who's going to put what where? Or take turns?" Lila feels icky at the thought. She can barely imagine showing someone her naked shin, these days, let alone bouncing happily into bed with a pair of strangers.

"Not really. I like them, they like me. We just . . . hang out, have some wine, some laughs, have a nice time."

"You make it sound like Book Club. But with genitalia."

"Not far off." Eleanor pops a piece of ginger into her mouth. "But less homework. You should try it."

"I would rather die," Lila responds. "Also, I can't really imagine being with anyone but Dan. I was happy with him."

"You used to tell me you didn't have sex for six months at a time."

"I hate your memory. Anyway. That was just at the end."

Eleanor raises her eyebrows and obviously decides to let this pass. "I think you need some joy in your life, Lils. You need to have a laugh, get laid, get the softness back around those shoulders. You're still pretty. You've got it going on."

"I am not going to a sex party with you, Eleanor."

"Go on the apps, then. Just meet someone. An experiment."

Lila shakes her head. "I don't think so. I will try to look less stabby, though. Oh, for crying out loud, how many times have we asked that waiter for the bill? Do I have to get up there and rip it out of his bloody hand myself?"

BILL HAS STEAMED fish for supper. The fuggy smell hits her as soon as she opens the front door, and she stands in the hallway and closes her eyes, reminding herself that he is doing a kind thing, cooking for them. That their house will smell like Billingsgate Fish Market for another forty-eight hours is just an unfortunate by-product.

Just don't let it be with lentils, she thinks, stooping to say hello to Truant who is greeting her as if she is the only safe person in the universe.

"Hello, darling. I've done fish and lentils for supper," he calls out, turning to her in her mother's apron. "I added some ginger and garlic. I know the girls say they don't like it but it's very good for their immune systems."

"Okay!" she says, wondering if there is any way she can order a takeaway without Bill knowing.

"How was your day, Lila?" He is mixing a dressing for a green salad, and Radio 3 is humming away in the background. His shoes are glowing like conkers and he's wearing a collar and tie, even though he has been retired for thirteen years.

"Oh. Fine. I met Eleanor for lunch, then had to go and see the accountant." She doesn't want to talk about the meeting with the accountant. Her mind had started up a low static hum as he had run through the columns of projected income and scheduled tax payments. "How was yours? Jesus—what is that?" She does a double-take at the picture resting against the worktop. It's a semi-abstract painting of a naked woman. A woman who has the same gray ringlets and tortoiseshell glasses as her mother. "Please tell me that's not . . ."

". . . your mother. I miss having her around. I thought it would be nice to have her in the living room."

"But, Bill, she's naked."

"Oh, that never bothered her. You know she was very relaxed about her body."

"I can tell you now that the girls are not going to be relaxed about having their naked grandmother above the television."

Bill stops and lifts his glasses from his nose briefly, as if this has only just occurred to him. "I don't know why you have to focus on the naked aspect. Really it's more about the character within."

"Bill, I can pretty much see everything within. Look, I know you miss Mum. Why don't you have it in your room? That way it can be the first thing you see when you wake up in the morning and the last thing you see at night?"

He gazes at the image. "I just thought it would be nice if she was part of the family. Looking over us."

"Maybe with pants on. A pants-on member of the family."

He sighs, and his gaze slides sideways. "If you like."

She feels suddenly guilty and puts her arms around him, as if in apology. He stiffens slightly, as though any physical contact is something of an assault. She thinks perhaps her mother was the only person Bill ever felt completely relaxed with.

"Maybe a nice photo. We could definitely do with some more pictures of Mum around the place," she says.

"It's like she never existed," he says quietly. "Sometimes I look around and I wonder if she ever existed at all."

She looks up at him then, at the grief etched on his face, the loss, and it feels like her own pales into insignificance. She has lost her mother, yes, but he has lost his soulmate.

"I have a box of pictures of her at the other house," he says, taking a breath. "Photographs and things. If you really don't want it there."

She notes—with a stab of something she can't quite identify—that he no longer calls his house "home." "Tell you what," she says. "Just leave it there for now. Given the amount of time the girls spend staring at their devices, they probably won't even notice."

Chapter Four

The call comes at ten fifteen, exactly eleven minutes after she typed the first paragraph she has managed in months, and nine minutes after she allowed herself the thought that maybe she can do this writing thing again after all. She picks up her phone, still staring absently at the screen, so that she doesn't see who the call is from.

"Is that Mrs. Brewer?"

"It's Kennedy. And—and it's Ms. now." Mzzz. She hates the word. How much nicer to be Mademoiselle or Lady Kennedy, something elegant and fancy. It's not like she doesn't feel abbreviated enough already.

"Uh . . . oh, yes. Sorry, we did amend our records. It's the school office. We just wondered if Celie had an appointment this morning we hadn't heard about."

"I'm sorry?"

"Celie. She was missing from first register. We wondered if maybe she had a dental appointment."

Her mind blanks briefly. Has she forgotten an appointment? She checks the calendar on her phone. Nothing. "I'm sorry—what do you mean, missing?"

"She's not at school."

"But I dropped her off this morning. Well, not dropped her off, but I watched her get on the bus."

There is a brief silence. The kind of well-worn silence that tells you as a parent that the person at the other end of the line knows you haven't a clue.

"Well, according to her classmates, she hasn't arrived. She's had so many dental appointments lately we wondered if she was having further treatment that we hadn't been told about."

"Dental appointments?"

Another silence.

"She's brought in notes excusing her from afternoon lessons . . . uh . . . three times this month."

"She—she hasn't had any dental treatment. I'll call her. I'll call. I'll—get back to you." There is a panicky feeling in Lila's chest. Her brain is suddenly flooded with headlines *Missing Girl Found Dead in Canal. Parents Say We Had No Idea.*

She calls Dan, her fingers jabbing at the buttons. "Lila, I'm in a meet—"

"Do you know where Celie is?"

"What?"

"She's not at school. They just called."

"But she was with you."

"I know, Dan. I just wondered if she'd said anything to you. Whether you had any kind of arrangement I didn't know about."

"No, Lila. I tell you everything."

Not everything, she wants to say, but now is not the time.

"Okay. I'll try her phone."

She calls Celie, and Celie does not pick up. After the fourth time she sends her a text:

> Celie, where are you? Please tell me
> you're okay.

It is four long minutes before Celie responds. Four minutes in which Lila's leg jiggles anxiously under the desk, four minutes in which every possible scenario has traveled through her body, sending her heart and nerve endings into overdrive:

> Just needed some me-time. I'm fine.

There is a nanosecond of relief as Lila blinks at the message. But then panic is abruptly replaced by blind fury. Me-time? *Me-time?* Since when did a teenager need me-time? She takes a breath before she types again:

> You should be at school. They called
> wanting to know where you are.

> Can't you tell them I'm at the dentist or
> something?

> Where are you? You need to come
> home. Now.

She watches the three little dots pulse on the screen, and disappear. She stares at her phone. NOW, Celie. She sees the dots pulse again and then there is nothing.

In Lila's whole childhood she had threatened to disappear only once. She had been eight or nine, and there had been some sort of altercation—she can't remember now what it was about. Her mother had never been the type to worry about messy rooms ("It's all creation! Even mess!") and she hadn't been rigorous with rules, so Lila's memory is a blank. But she does remember packing a child's rucksack and announcing rather grandly to her mother that she was leaving. Her mother had been gardening at the time, her knees on a little padded cushion thing that her own mother had embroidered. She had turned, one gloved hand above her brow, squinting into the sun. "You're leaving? As in for good?"

Lila, furious, had nodded.

Francesca had looked down at the soil, thinking. "Okay," she said. "You'll need some food, then." She peeled off her gloves and stood, then shepherded Lila through to the kitchen, where she started to rifle through cupboards. "You'll need some biscuits, I think . . . Maybe some fruit?"

Lila had held open her rucksack while her mother bustled around the kitchen.

"I think maybe a plate too. Because it's hard to eat if you don't have a plate. What about a couple of paper ones from that picnic we had? Then they won't be as heavy."

Lila remembered the vague sense of disorientation she had felt as this progressed, the way her fury had dissipated, her mother's practical enthusiasm, as if Lila had just suggested an entirely understandable adventure.

"I know!" Francesca announced, just as she was zipping up the rucksack, and Lila was starting to feel very unsure about what to do next. "Monster Munch! They weigh nothing, and you always love those. You don't want that rucksack to get too heavy."

Pickled onion Monster Munch were Lila's favorite food. She nodded, as Francesca searched the cupboards, opening and closing the doors. "Oh, bum. We don't seem to have any. Shall we go and get some from the corner shop?"

Lila can never remember what happened to the rest of her running-away plan. She does remember her mother walking to the shop with her, the heat bouncing off the pavement, then allowing her to choose several packets of Monster Munch, and announcing that actually she was going to have a packet too. They walked back slowly, eating the puffy crisps, talking about the fat tabby cat with one eye at number eighty-one, Francesca's favorite episode of *Doctor Who*, and whether they should paint the front door red. Lila realizes now that not only had her mother diverted her, but she had done it in a way that gave Lila an easy way to back out. *How did my mother always know exactly the right thing to do?* she wonders. And then: *Can you still buy pickled onion Monster Munch?*

She sees Celie before Celie sees her. She is in the pedestrian triangle of the shopping area, where empty takeaway cartons catch on the breeze and a few desultory plastic tables and chairs try to mimic some kind of café culture. Celie is sitting on the wall of a raised flowerbed and her head is dipped as she stares at her phone. There is not much Lila finds to thank Dan for any more, but his text message reminding her that they had Find My Phone on Lila's mobile elicited a heartfelt *Thank God.*

"Celie?" She sits beside her and touches her arm.

The girl jumps and flushes slightly at her arrival. There is a moment of vague confusion, then Lila sees Celie recall the Find My Phone and Lila wonders how long it will be before her daughter deletes it. "What's going on?" She is out of anger now. Just desperately worried.

"I don't want to talk."

Lila gazes at her daughter, at her long black hair, so unlike Lila's own. She wishes she smiled as much as she used to—those huge beams of light that once shone from her face. These days, Celie is a near-silent thing, holed up in her room or endlessly locked into her phone, somewhere unreachable by her now unreliable, inadequate parents. "Okay."

She sits a yard away from Celie on the wall, and tries to think how best to handle this. What would her mother have done? Several hours go by in her head until she fumbles for the only question she can think of. "Are you okay?"

Celie's voice emerges from somewhere near her chest, swallowed by the curtains of hair. "I'm fine."

"Do you want to tell me why you've been bunking off?"

Celie doesn't speak. After a pause, she shrugs. Examines something on her finger and gazes into the distance.

"You know the school called me about it."

She sees Celie sigh slightly, perhaps at the knowledge that the school will be monitoring her closely from now. She lowers her voice. "It's not a good time to be bunking off, my love. Not with exams coming."

She pretty much hears Celie's eyes rolling. They sit quietly. Celie has been biting her nails again—Lila sees that the cuticles are sore and ragged. Celie glances up at her, opens her mouth slightly. And then her phone rings.

"Lila, do you know where the silver polish is?"

"What?"

Bill's voice is muffled for a moment, and then he says, "Silver polish. I brought your mother's silver tea set so that we can have a proper tea. But it's become rather tarnished and I can't find any polish under your sink. Or in the back room."

"I don't think we have any. And I'm kind of in the midd—"

"No silver polish? But how do you polish your silver?"

"I don't think we have any silver. Bill, I really have to go."

Bill lets out a sigh of disappointment. "I suppose I could get some from that shop on the high street. Will they do it?"

Celie has turned away.

"I—I don't know, Bill. I'll have a look on the way back." She ends the call and then, tentatively, puts her hand on Celie's arm. "Is this about me and Dad?"

"Jesus, Mum. Not everything is about you and Dad."

There is something odd about her voice, as if it's just a fraction thicker, slower than it should be. She wonders briefly if Celie is struggling to hold back tears. And then she catches it, the faintest whiff, sweet and acrid. "Celie? Have you been *smoking weed*?"

Celie shoots her a furious sideways look, but it tells her everything she needs to know. "What in the—Celie, you can't smoke weed! You're sixteen years old!" She feels, rather than hears, Celie's muttered curse.

"What—Where did you get it? Is someone selling it at school?"

"Why? Do you want some?"

"What?"

"God, Mum, you're such a hypocrite. I know you smoke weed at night. You're acting like I'm some kind of freak but you do it."

"No, I don't."

"Oh, my God. Don't lie. I can smell it through my bedroom window."

"I—I—That's different. I just do it when I can't sleep."

"And I do it when I can't relax. What difference?"

"You're sixteen! And I'm forty-two!"

Her phone rings again. Bill. "Bill, I can't take this right now—"

"I know, darling. I'll keep it short. I just wondered if you're going past the hardware store, whether you could also get me some Bar Keepers Friend?"

"What?"

"It's a very useful polish. I couldn't help but notice a few places in the kitchen that are a little . . . grimy. I know you're very busy, so if you get me a pot of that I can get going and really—"

"Okay. Okay, Bill. I'll get it."

She puts the phone down, then on impulse reaches abruptly for Celie's bag.

Celie snatches it back. "What are you *doing*?"

"Where is it?"

"Let go!"

"The weed! Where is it?"

Lila tugs at Celie's bag, but she pulls it back, and for a brief, almost comical minute, they are seated on the wall, playing tug-of-war with the canvas satchel.

"Oh, my God! Stop!"

Celie manages to drag the bag back to her, and jumps off the wall, her face puce with anger.

"You can't smoke weed, Celie!"

"God, you're so embarrassing! Why can't you just leave me alone?"

"Because I'm your mother!"

She is still standing on the pavement yelling her daughter's name as Celie shoves her bag under her arm and half runs, half walks away, back toward the bus stop.

"It's my job!" Lila calls, and her voice is caught on the wind along with the empty takeaway cartons, and disappears.

It is at this point that Bill rings again. "You know, I was thinking I might bring some of my coasters from the other house. I noticed where the girls are leaving their drinks on the wooden tables there are some rather ugly ring marks. Could you get some furniture polish when you're in the shop—the beeswax, not the awful chemical kind? I'll make a start when you get back from the shop."

Chapter Five

Lila is not sure now how it started—probably her inability to combine the various remote controls and television options since Dan, or Tech Desk, as the girls used to call him, left—but for some months now Lila has been watching a Spanish soap opera, or telenovela. Most nights, if she can scrape an hour between shepherding the girls to bed and before she is too tired to see, she curls up on the sofa and watches a subtitled episode of *La Familia Esperanza*, an endlessly twisting narrative involving insanely glamorous Spanish-speaking women locked in intense warfare with each other and with the men they love. Everyone is dressed in vibrant colors, the weather is always warm, and the cast throw insults and pieces of furniture at each other with the joyful abandon of toddlers in a ball pit. Lila's favorite is Estella Esperanza, a tiny fierce wife the same age as Lila, who looks a little like Salma Hayek. She had been a downtrodden mouse in the first six episodes, but then discovered her husband, Rodrigo, had been cheating on her with his teenage secretary. After numerous episodes of wailing grief, the consolation of her sisters, and prayers in the local church, she has morphed into a vengeful angel, who tracks her husband and his paramour and thinks up endlessly inventive ways in which to hijack their new life together.

This week, having discovered that Rodrigo and Isabella are to go on a romantic trip to a seaside resort, she has somehow gained employment as a temporary maid at the luxury hotel, and filled the Nespresso coffee capsules in their room with laxatives. The episode prior to this, she had hired a male escort to flirt with Isabella at a bar, making sure that Rodrigo walked in on it. Estella, meanwhile, has been taking shooting lessons at a local gun range, helped, of course, by a hot but sympathetic tutor, and it is clearly only a matter of time before she pulls her stylish little pistol from her designer handbag and gives her husband what he deserves. But, for now, Rodrigo suspects nothing, because he believes his wife to be a downtrodden mouse. Sometimes Lila pictures herself in Estella's place, dressed in black, looking somehow stylish and wounded, striding through the playground scattering incriminating photographs of her former husband and yelling insults that sound so much better in Spanish or, on her worse days, pulling a gun from her designer handbag (she doesn't have a designer handbag) and just . . . well, scaring them all a little.

She doesn't talk about this little fantasy, not since she'd blurted it out to Eleanor one morning and Eleanor had stopped in her tracks and asked, *Are you okay?* But she keeps watching, willing Estella to do wilder and more terrible things, even as she sits in her tracksuit bottoms, with dog hair all over them, her hair pulled back in a scrunchie.

CELIE DOES NOT talk to Lila for the next three days. She arrives home from school almost by subterfuge, letting herself in silently so that sometimes Lila only realizes she's back when she hears Bill asking whether she'd like a drink and reminding her that she really should be drinking more water. Celie has avoided supper once, saying she was too busy with schoolwork, and on the other two evenings she sat at the table, eyes cast resolutely down, as if she wished she was anywhere but there. Lila has searched her room twice, found no sign of drugs and felt weirdly guilty the whole time she was doing it. Part of her is afraid to talk to Celie in case she gives anything away.

"You were just the same, darling," Bill says, when Celie briefly leaves the table for the bathroom.

"I was not."

"Oh, yes. You went silent for about two years. Drove your mother completely potty. And then you got to seventeen and started talking again. She'll come round. It's just very complicated being sixteen."

She doesn't tell Bill about the weed. He can barely cope with the idea of the girls drinking cola. Besides, he's preoccupied. He has decided, he announces over dinner, that he would like to tidy the garden. "I thought we could make it a memorial garden. Or at least a corner of it. It would be nice to have somewhere we can sit and commune with nature and remember your grandmother."

"Next door's cat poos in our garden," says Violet, who has been quietly burying pieces of carrot under her steamed chicken. "There's a LOT of nature in that corner."

"Well, I'll spray some citronella. That tends to put them off."

"There's still lots of poo in the ground, though. Loads of it. You could probably grow a whole poo baby out of the amount of poo in our garden. An enormous poo baby."

Bill is briefly flummoxed by this conversational turn, and Lila is grateful. Doing the garden is going to involve money, and she has reached the point at which she cannot think about finance without a huge anxiety knot landing, like a bowling ball, in her stomach. Emergency plumbers are costing hundreds every month just to keep the loos functioning. The sums she needs simply to exist reach dizzying amounts.

And she is still no nearer to creating an outline for her new book about the apparently relentless joy of being a single mother.

"What do you think about a memorial garden, Celie?" Bill says gently.

Celie has returned, and quietly moved her knife and fork to the center of the plate. "Sure."

"Wouldn't it be nice to have somewhere nice to sit and remember Grandma?"

"We could make a bench out of dried poo," says Violet, and starts cackling. "And we could sit on it."

"Vi, you're disgusting." Celie gets up and walks to the bin with her plate, shielding it so that nobody can see how much leftover food she is scraping away.

"I do have a rather nice wooden bench," Bill continues gamely. "I made it three months after Francesca died. It's a Lutyens bench. It's oak, so it's starting to weather nicely. I could bring it and put it in the corner by the lilac."

"We have a lilac?" says Lila.

"It would be nice to get the borders under control. It's a decent-sized garden. Maybe we could even do some raised beds at the end for vegetables."

"Not courgettes," says Violet, who is surreptitiously feeding bits of steamed chicken to Truant. "I hate courgettes."

"I had a nice chat with Jensen. He lives at the end of the road at the other house. We had a walk around the place while you were with your accountant, Lila. He has all sorts of ideas as to how we could tidy things up a bit."

"Jensen?"

"Landscape gardener. You met him last week. Apparently you didn't like him looking at the tree. Very amusing, he found it."

"I didn't know who he was."

"He's very much in demand but he was very fond of your mother so he says he'll squeeze us in as soon as possible."

"Kind of him," says Lila, who is wondering about cost per hour.

"And he's very ecologically minded—lots of bee-friendly plants, climate-friendly planting, no harmful pesticides, and recycled materials where possible."

"But *where* does he stand on poo benches?" asks Violet, her voice lifting.

Bill chooses not to hear. "Anyway. He's coming back on Friday to have a chat. Best to get the ball rolling, yes?"

Lila does not want to think where this particular ball is rolling to. Over the past few weeks she has noticed that Bill, while never fully discussing his intentions, appears to be making his stay permanent. Unfamiliar items keep appearing in her house, already clumped with piles of boxes from the move that she still hasn't had the energy to unpack, or things that the girls won't find a home for but cannot be got rid of so sit in corners, gathering dust. In her hallway a child's bike is propped against the wall. It's too small for Violet, but when she raised the possibility of taking it to the charity shop, both girls wailed that it was part of their childhood and she feels too guilty about the way their family has been fractured to go against their wishes.

And against this already cluttered backdrop she has noticed new items, a collection of piano music, a cedar-wood table bearing a carved map of South America, Bill's ancient stereo system and accompanying collection of 1970s classical LPs. When she poked her head around the spare-room door while Bill was out the previous week, she noticed that he had somehow moved in a whole mahogany wardrobe and its contents. It fills the alcove to the right of the fireplace, its frontage beautifully polished and glowing, reflecting light onto Bill's geometrically made bed. Inside it a row of perfectly ironed shirts hung an exact inch apart. Her bathroom cupboard now has a whole row of neatly lined bottles and packets containing Bill's medications, blood-thinners, anti-cholesterol, and heart pills, as well as an interminable array of vitamins and supplements.

Lila is not sure how she feels about this. She needs Bill here, she knows. The girls need an adult presence when she isn't there, and with his quiet cleaning and cooking he keeps some semblance of order when she seems incapable of it. But living with Bill is sometimes like living in the midst of a quiet domestic rebuke, especially when she comes home to find the breakfast dishes not in the sink where she left them but washed and stacked neatly on the drainer, or the window of the wood-burner gleaming when it had previously been obscured by soot. Bill's cooking, his tidying, his insistence on peace and order are a constant reminder that she is apparently unable to provide those things. And although she knows rationally that his activities are a help, some dark part of her feels them as a stinging reminder that she has failed.

She must have failed: otherwise Dan would have stayed.

"Anyway," says Bill, as he starts to stack the dishwasher with plates he has already rinsed, "he's coming along tomorrow to start planning his design. That'll be nice, won't it?"

CELIE HAS REFUSED to go to Dan's house this week, so when he calls, Lila is half expecting a tirade about how she has poisoned the girls against him. But his voice is oddly hesitant, almost conciliatory.

"I can't make her come, Dan," she begins, but he cuts her off.

"It's not actually that I wanted to talk about. Although obviously I would prefer it if she came. She is my daughter."

"They don't like not having their own rooms. Celie's at that age . . ."

"This house is pretty small, Lils."

Don't call me Lils, she wants to say, but bites it back.

"Well. It matters more to Celie. That kind of thing. I'm just saying." She wonders suddenly what will happen when the new baby arrives. Will there be any room for the girls at all? Seeing them off two nights a week is always bittersweet: yes, she wants them to have a relationship with their father, yes, it's sometimes a relief to have a break from Celie's mercurial moods and Violet's endless, endless demands, but they are her *babies* and there is not a day that she feels ready to start a morning without them.

"I know. And I'm trying to work out how I can make room enough for everybody." He doesn't mention the baby, she notices. It's always a vague reference. She wonders if he has misgivings about being a father again. She is dragged back to the conversation by his next sentence.

"So that's really why I was calling."

"What?"

Dan sighs heavily, as if even having to discuss this is causing him pain. "We will probably need to move at some point. Somewhere a little bigger. And things are not great at the magazine right now. There's talk of redundancies. I'm fairly confident I'll hold on to my job, but my monthly commitments are pretty horrendous."

Are we a "monthly commitment" now? she thinks.

"I mean that when the new baby comes I'm probably not going to be able to pay as much as I have been."

There is a brief silence.

"What?"

"I'm paying more than I'm legally required to as it is."

"Dan, they're your kids."

"I know. And I know you've taken a knock with the writing so that's why I've been trying to pay as much as I can. But I spoke to a lawyer and she says I have a legal obligation to make sure all the children are treated equally—"

"*All* the children?"

"Well, Marja and I are a couple now so I have to include Hugo. It's not like his dad exactly steps up. So that's four children to support, which is quite a lot. And Marja and I definitely need another bedroom.

This place only has three, as you know, and you're in a five-bedroom place—"

"Dan, I am not selling this house."

"I'm not asking you to sell the house."

"I paid for this with the book money. It's our children's *home.*"

"I know. I'm not saying anything about your house. Just that I'm not going to be able to pay quite as much in support."

She blinks. "How much less?"

"Probably five hundred a month."

She is silenced by this sum.

"I'll need to get another mortgage. And with rates what they are I'm not likely to get a great deal. I'm really sorry, Lils. But the money situation is what it is. You were always the bigger earner, and I was fine with leaving you and the girls in the house."

"My house. Our house. And I'm barely earning."

"Anyway, I just wanted to give you a heads-up. I'll look at what I'm legally required to pay, and hope I'll be able to give you a bit more than that."

She puts the phone down on him. She feels winded. She sees the expenses coming toward her that she could barely afford with Dan's input and now? *How is this fair?* She wants to yell. *How is it fair that you get to walk out and have a lovely new family and we all have to suffer?* She drops her head into her hands.

And then Bill's face appears around the door. "Sorry to interrupt, Lila darling, but Jensen is here."

She looks up and blinks.

"The landscape gardener."

A man's face appears around the corner, just behind Bill's. It's softer than she remembers, slightly dirt-sprinkled, with a thatch of sandy hair. "Hi—I just wondered if you had five minutes to pop outside so we could talk about what needs doing. By the way your tree out front is starting to lean. You'll need to do something about that."

"I know. I have to do something about everything." Her voice is a snap and she sees Bill's eyebrows shoot up.

Jensen seems not to notice. "I think it's possibly dying. Either way I'd suggest getting a tree surgeon to take a look. I know a guy whose rates aren't *too* astronomical."

SHE BARELY HEARS what Jensen is saying about her garden. It's an unseasonably balmy evening and the sun leaches gold through the gaps in the branches as he walks around, drawing images in the air of raised beds and shingle pathways. As he talks, her head is still humming with the ramifications of what Dan has told her. It's not just the financial anxiety but the injustice of it. She wants to scream, *How can you do this to us?* like an unending lament, through his letterbox.

"And I thought maybe you could have a water feature here. There's a salvage yard out in Kent, which has some really beautiful pieces that would look great. They're not as cheap as they used to be—everyone's worked out that salvage is the way to go—but it would provide a really lovely focal point."

"We could put the bench beside it," says Bill.

"The poo bench?" says Violet, hopefully. She has somehow found the diet cola, which Lila had hidden in the cupboard with the cleaning products, and is slurping noisily from the edge of a can.

"Poo bench?" says Jensen.

"Don't ask," says Bill. "Maybe we could have two water features. One each side of this lovely *Acer*. I bet if we cleared away some of these climbers there's a lovely shape under there."

Oh, God, thinks Lila. What if Dan decides he can no longer live nearby? Marja's son is young enough to transfer schools. If they want a bigger property and money is a problem maybe he'll move to one of the outer boroughs. Then Celie and Violet will have to get buses to their dad's house. They will not be down the road but in another postcode entirely. What if he moves out to the country? What if Marja ends up with the house Lila always wanted in the middle of nowhere with cow parsley and log fires and a brick kitchen floor?

"Lila?"

Bill's hand is on her upper arm. She looks up with a start and he is gazing at her, clearly awaiting a reply.

"Um . . . yes," she says, not entirely sure what she is being asked. "Yes" is usually the answer.

It is then, out of the corner of her eye, that she sees Celie walking across the kitchen. She is wearing her short bomber jacket and her eyes are outlined in a smoky black charcoal liner. "Actually, no."

"No?"

"Celie?" she yells across the garden. Celie glances toward her but turns away, clearly hoping to leave the house swiftly. "Celie! Where are you going?"

Celie stops.

"Out."

"Where 'out'?"

"Don't you like water features?" says Bill. "You always loved the fountain at the other house."

Lila starts to walk back toward the French windows.

"Celie! Don't you dare leave before we've spoken!"

Celie throws her chin upward in the manner of the perpetually thwarted. "Oh, my God, are you my actual jailer now?"

"I just want to know where you're going."

"Why?"

"It doesn't have to be a water feature," says Bill, his voice lifting. "I just thought a statue of your mother might be a bit much."

"Are you smoking weed again?"

"Weed?" says Bill.

Jensen takes a few steps toward Lila. "I can come back if this is not a good time."

"It's never a good time," says Lila. "There is not one single good time for anything right now. Not for my tree to fall down, not for my loos to block, not for my own book to make me a laughing stock every bloody day and certainly not for my husband to impregnate his much younger lover on top of her Noguchi bloody coffee-table."

"Okay," says Jensen.

Celie stomps up to Lila and faces off. "I'm going to get trashed in the park, okay? I'm going to get completely high on weed that you hypocritically say is bad for you, even though you're quite happy to use it yourself. I'm going to drink lots of alcohol, and smoke a ton of weed, then get felt up by strange men while I'm in a state of drug-induced inebriation. Is that okay? Or are you going to be extra about that too?"

"Sounds like a good night!" says a voice. And Lila spins round. She stares at the man who has just let himself in through the back gate. He is dragging a battered wheelie case and his broad smile reveals a row of impossibly white teeth. There is a brief silence.

Celie gazes at him, and then at Lila, who cannot speak and whose mouth is hanging very slightly open. "Mum?" she says, turning toward Lila uncertainly.

"*Gene?*" says Lila. And Truant comes streaking out of the French windows, like a large hairy bullet, and, without a moment's hesitation, sinks his teeth determinedly into the man's leg.

Chapter Six

Celie

Celie stands in the corner of the kitchen while the gardener dresses the old man's wound, kneeling at his feet like some kind of medieval serf. He has a bandage between his teeth and is liberally spraying the old man's leg with some kind of antiseptic spray. "Dog bites can be full of bacteria," he is saying. "I've flushed it with saline, but you're going to want to keep an eye on it and head straight for A and E if it doesn't look like it's healing."

The old man is leaning back in the kitchen chair looking weirdly cheerful. Celie guesses he's the kind of man who likes to be the center of attention, even if it comes at the expense of a dog bite. "Cats are worse," he's saying, with a broad American accent. "I worked with a guy in Tennessee once who got scratched by a feral on set between takes. His whole arm blew up and he was knocked out of the production for weeks. Director gave all his lines to an extra. Mind you, he was an asshole. If I'd known I would have filled his trailer with cats. Would have saved me a whole load of grief."

While the old man rattles on, Celie's mum is standing by the kettle, her face like stone. But it's a positive welcome mat compared to Bill's. Celie thinks she has never seen Bill like this. He is standing with his arms crossed firmly over his chest, his legs in power stance, like a second-rate politician. He has not taken his eyes off the American since he walked in, as if he's half expecting him to get up and run away with what's left of the family jewels.

Meena keeps texting, asking her when she's coming, but Celie ignores the buzzing in her jeans pocket. Meena is blowing hot and cold just now and she's not sure whether to trust her.

"I think that's it," says the gardener, getting to his feet. He's the only person smiling in the room, apart from the old man. Even Violet is unusually silent. "Like I said, you might want to head to A and E anyway. It went pretty deep for a puncture wound."

"That's quite the guard dog you have there, Lila," says the old man, examining the bandage.

"He's never bitten anyone before," says Violet, quickly.

"The dog has immaculate taste," mutters Bill, and Violet's head spins round. Bill never says anything mean about anyone.

"Good to see you, Bill," says the old man.

"Wish I could say the same, Gene," says Bill.

Gene seems not to hear that. He turns to the gardener man and holds out a broad, tanned hand. His veins pop out of his skin like worm casts. "I'm obliged to you, young man. Thank you for your attentions."

"No problem."

Celie glances at her mum, who is still stony-faced.

"Are you part of our family?" Celie says, finally.

"I am! And you must be Celia. The last time I saw you you were knee high to a—"

"A baby," interrupts Lila. "She was a baby when you last saw her. And it's Celie. Always has been."

Bill is the only old man left in Celie's family. She has another grandfather, her dad's dad, but Granny and Granddad Brewer live up in Derby in a small, terrifyingly neat house that they rarely visit because Granny Brewer doesn't like mess or chaos and their house is too small for guests, especially children, who mess up the net curtains and tread dirt into the carpet. The last time they went Violet was small and did a wee on the guest bed, which didn't have a mattress protector, and they were told that next time they would have to stay in a Premier Inn. Not like this big, vibrant man with a shock of dark hair and movie-star creases at the corners of his eyes and a . . . is that a Nirvana T-shirt?

"So you're little Violet! Bring it in, honey!" he says, holding his arms wide, and Violet, as if she's on autopilot, steps into them for a huge hug. "It's so great to finally meet you!"

Celie watches her mother's face remain completely immobile as this happens. Bill adjusts his position and lets out a small grunt, as if it's all he can do not to intervene.

"I'll—I'll be off then," says the gardener man, who is reaching for his jacket.

"No," says Bill. "Stay for a cup of tea, Jensen."

"You're all right, Bill. I'll just—"

"Stay," says Bill, really firmly. After a moment, Jensen glances behind him for a kitchen chair and sits down awkwardly. Bill turns and fills the kettle, his stiff old back radiating displeasure.

"Well, aren't you gorgeous?" Gene is saying to Violet. "You look just like your grandma. She had those big blue eyes when she was young." He turns toward Celie. "And you too! Aren't you just a long glass of cool water! Look at the pair of you!"

"What are you doing here, Gene?" says Mum, her voice cold.

"Sweetheart! I'm doing a short run at one of the London theaters so I thought I'd come and see the family! I can't believe how they've grown!"

"Yes," says Mum. "Sixteen years will do that to you."

"I mean I would have loved to come back before but things were kind of tricky with work and—"

"Barb?" says Mum.

"Barb?" He furrows his brow. "Oh, no. Me and Barb weren't much of a thing. She went back to Ohio in, what, 2007?"

"Brianna? Wasn't she the next one?"

"No. Brianna and I—Well, that ended badly."

"Don't tell me. She went back to the titty bar. Jane?"

"Jane I stay in touch with!" he says, almost with relief. "She's back over here, as you know. I think the west coast didn't agree with her."

"The west coast," Mum repeats.

"The lifestyle."

Mum nods to herself.

"*Titty bar!*" says Violet, delightedly, and repeats it twice, glancing round the adults as if hoping for a response.

"Anyway! Here I am! Just so happy to see you all again and hoping to get to know these two gorgeous girls a little while I'm here."

"While you're where?" says Bill, handing a mug to Jensen who takes it swiftly, apparently grateful to have something to focus on.

"Here," says Gene. "In the UK."

"Specifically where in the UK?" says Bill. He is being so weird.

"Well, London. Say, could I grab a coffee while you're up there?"

"I'll do it," says Mum, immediately, relieving Bill, who looks like he would rather be anywhere but there, but also seems oddly reluctant to leave. Then she adds: "You'll have to remind me how you take it."

"Oh, black, please, sweetheart. Gave up cream since the docs said I had to look after the old ticker. I don't suppose I could prevail upon you for some potato chips or something? I haven't eaten since I stepped off the plane."

Mum stiffens slightly, then reaches up to the cupboard for the biscuit tin. She puts it down on the table in front of him without opening it. "We don't have potato chips."

They sit in silence. Jensen the gardener is drinking his tea as quickly as he can, even though it is clearly boiling hot. Celie watches him sip, wince, and sip again. Upstairs Truant continues a furious, muffled barking, locked in Mum's room. She wonders briefly if the American man will demand that the dog is put down.

"Truant is a good dog," she finds herself saying. "He doesn't normally bite. It's probably because nobody ever comes in by the back gate."

"Oh, he meant no harm. I never hold a grudge against an old dog." He looks briefly up at Bill. "Well, mostly."

"It might be wise to get it checked out professionally, though," says Bill. "The risk of bacteria."

"Oh, don't worry. I'm sure Jensen here has done a great job." Gene pats his leg.

"I meant the dog," says Bill, and finally leaves the room.

CELIE TEXTS MEENA from the bathroom and tells her she can't come. Family emergency. It's not an emergency but there's a really weird atmosphere in the house and Celie is curious about it.

Mum never talks about the rest of her family. On the few occasions they have ever been brought up in conversation, her face does that closed-off thing that it now does when Dad turns up to collect them. As if a million thoughts are running through her head and she won't allow a single one to show through.

No, this is more than how Mum is with Dad, these days. This is like a cold, tired thing, like Mum is absently picking an old scab and not even noticing when it starts bleeding.

> You've got to come! Spence is here and he's brought the stuff!

Sorry, types Celie, and sends a bunch of shrugging-face emojis.

Besides, she's not sure she wants to smoke weed in the park today. She's not sure she wants to see the girls. She gets stomach-ache when she approaches them now, the silent glances, the compliments that don't sound like compliments, the sense that a dozen conversations are going on behind her back. There is no chat on their WhatsApp group anymore, and Celie has the horrible feeling that a new one has been set up without her. This is her daily dilemma: to go and sit with them, and feel the whole time like she's the butt of a joke that nobody will explain, or sit without them and know she will be anyway. Celie shoves her phone back into her pocket.

WHEN SHE COMES down again Bill is cooking with his back to everyone. He normally cooks on the old kitchen island, with its scarred wooden butcher-block top so he can chat to them, but today he has moved to the small space beside the draining board and is head down with his back to everyone, chopping determinedly, not even listening to his usual classical music. Mum is sitting in Bill's upright armchair. (Why do all old people want to be sitting up like statues in the evenings? Celie and Mum mostly lie on the two couches, either feet up on the battered old leather pouf, or spread along the length of them, a bowl of microwave popcorn between them.) Jensen appears to have snuck off. But Gene is taking up the sofa, his injured leg on the pouf, and keeping up a one-sided conversation about the house, how quaint it is, how much character, how she must love it here.

"It needs a lot of work," Mum says, when she clearly cannot get away with saying nothing any longer.

Gene looks up as Celie walks toward them. "Hey, sweetheart! Glad you can join us. Your mum has invited me to stay for dinner. Jensen thought it was best if I kept the leg elevated for a little longer, you know?"

Celie's gaze flickers toward Mum, who wears an expression that suggests Gene has invited himself.

"What's for supper?" Celie says to Bill.

"Pea and asparagus risotto," he says, and she lets out a brief sigh of relief. No fish or lentils. The evening suddenly looks a little brighter. "With a chicory and fennel salad."

Celie slumps.

"So how come you're cooking, Bill?" says Gene.

Bill doesn't turn around. *Chop chop chop.* "I cook every night," he says curtly. *Chop chop chop.*

"You come here every night?"

"No, I live here."

Celie glances at her mother. Nobody has actually said those words up till now, but her mother's face doesn't flicker.

"I'm just . . . helping with the girls. Lila has a lot on her plate right now."

Gene's genial expression seems to slip a little at this. "Well," he says. And then again. "Well. Cozy!"

"Have you two known each other for a long time?" Celie looks from one old man to the other.

"Long enough," says Bill, shortly.

"I'll say," says Gene, and the room falls silent again.

Truant is lying on the floor by Mum, his eyes trained on Gene, as if he is waiting for the slightest excuse to spring at him again. Celie goes and sits cross-legged beside the dog and strokes him near his collar, just in case he does. She does not want this man to cause their dog to be put down, no matter what he said earlier. Gene shifts in his chair and Truant lets out a quiet warning growl.

"Did you say you were an actor?" Celie says.

Gene's smile returns immediately. He bestows it on her like a shaft of sunshine. "I am! You ever seen *Star Squadron Zero*?"

Celie shakes her head, and sees a flicker of disappointment on his face.

"I spent years as Captain Troy Strang, leader of the Unified Star Forces. You should watch it on YouTube or whatever you kids watch, these days. It was a big thing, you know? 'Captain Strang, reporting for intergalactic duty'—that was my catchphrase. People still say it to me wherever I go." He raises his hand in brisk salute and Truant lets out a faint protesting whine.

"*Star Squadron Zero*?"

"It's why I had to stay in LA, Celia. I was lucky enough to hit a seam of gold. That doesn't happen very often in an actor's life. Doesn't happen at all to most. I played that damn captain for eight years. Got nominated for an Emmy once. We had Nielsen ratings that were off the charts."

Violet has come into the living room and sat down next to Gene. He puts his arm around her. "You want to see it, Violet?"

Violet nods. She clearly likes him.

"You got a cell phone?"

"Mum won't let me have one," she says.

"Because she's eight," says Celie, defensively.

"You got one, Celia?"

"It's Celie," says Mum, through gritted teeth.

"Of course it is."

Celie doesn't want to hand it over. She doesn't know what messages might come through while he's holding it. So she shakes her head and pushes her phone deeper into the front pocket of her hoodie.

There is a short silence. Mum sighs. "Violet, go and get the iPad."

When the extract is finally located, with a lot of squinting from Gene, who clearly can't see very well but doesn't have glasses, Celie moves to the sofa on the other side of Gene so that she can watch. She feels like a traitor, though she's not entirely sure why. Mum, who has clearly seen this before, gets up and goes to help Bill in the kitchen. She cannot hear what they're murmuring to each other, but at one point Bill reaches out a hand and rests it on the middle of Mum's back.

And then some tinny theme music is playing on the iPad and Gene is exclaiming with pleasure. "There it is! Twenty-four million Americans tuned in every week at its height. Isn't that a great theme tune? Da-dadadadada-da-DAAA . . . da-DAAA." He waves his right arm like a conductor.

And then there he is, his face thinner and unlined, his hair black and sleek against his head. He is wearing a blue nylon jacket with gold epaulets and a planet insignia on his chest. "I didn't think I'd see you again after the great Saturn disaster," he is saying, with his American accent, his voice low and tender.

A beautiful young African American woman with sprayed silver hair is gazing up at him through huge eyes. "They told me . . . you were killed in battle, Captain. Why would they do that?"

"Isn't she a doll? That was Marni Di Michaels. We were . . . very close for a while. She eventually married a football player. You know the Chicago Bulls? Or was it the Braves? What was his name . . . ?"

Celie stares at the woman, who is gazing at Young Gene like she could eat him. Oh, God, she probably had. She steals a sideways glance at Old Gene, who is mouthing the words of the script as it plays, lost again in his fictional world.

"The episodes where Captain Strang and Vuleva were together were the highest rated in the whole series. They killed her off in series three, and I told the director it was a mistake. And you know what? I was right, because—"

"Supper," says Bill, loudly, and starts moving the dishes with a clatter onto the table.

THEY ARE HALFWAY through a near-silent meal when Mum finally speaks. "So why weren't you in touch after Mum died?"

There is a brief pause, and then Gene sighs. "I'm so sorry, sweetheart. I had so much work and I couldn't get a flight so . . ."

"She was your wife."

"Not for a very long time."

"Wait, what?" says Celie, her fork halting halfway to her mouth.

"But she was. For ten years. I'm proof of that. It would have been a mark of respect to show up. For once in your life."

The girls are staring at Gene and then at each other.

"You're Mum's *dad*?" says Celie. She is about to say *we thought you were dead* but realizes it might not be the kindest thing. Instead she says: "But . . . how come you aren't in Mum and Dad's wedding pictures?"

Gene rubs at his ear. "Yeah. I had to be away filming. It was . . . tricky. The industry, you know? It's like a juggernaut. Nothing I could do."

Mum's face looks like it's sculpted from marble. Nothing moves on it. Violet closes her mouth as if she's just remembered she has one, then says slowly: "You don't look like a grandpa."

"Ahh, I never much liked that term. You can call me Gene."

"You never liked 'Dad' much either, as far as I can remember." Mum doesn't look up from her plate.

Celie is in shock. The only things she knows about her grandfather are these: that Mum doesn't ever drink because he drank; that he left when Mum was small; that he was unreliable, and Grandma had to cope all by herself, but we don't need to talk about it. That Bill is the exact opposite of him, and that was why he and Grandma were so happy. She's not sure now why she thought Gene was dead, but she has never even heard him mentioned by name until today.

Gene's smile is conciliatory, his voice soft. "C'mon, sweetheart. A lot of water has passed under the bridge. Can't I just enjoy dinner with my girls?"

Bill says, in a voice Celie has never heard him use before: "They're not your girls."

Gene's voice hardens slightly. "They're not yours either, buddy." The two old men stare at each other across the table, and Celie is overwhelmed by the weirdly exciting sensation that they are going to hit each other.

And then Mum reaches across the table between them for a bowl. "Who wants some more chicory salad?" And the moment passes.

Celie has never been at a supper like this. She has never seen that vein throbbing in Bill's jaw, or heard the weirdly clipped tone to her mother's voice. This is her grandfather! Her actual grandfather! She keeps sneaking glances at him, trying to see some kind of family resemblance, but with his unnaturally dark hair and his teeth and his tan he seems utterly unrelated to them. He keeps up a constant stream of chatter, his voice deep and rhythmic, talking about work he's been doing (just small parts, they probably wouldn't have seen them over here), reminding Mum of people called Hank and Betsy whom she doesn't remember, asking Celie and Violet about school, their friends, what it is they "get up to" around here. It is both fascinating and interminable.

Finally Mum gets up and clears the plates, and Celie, who never helps unless she's nagged, gets up and helps too: the atmosphere is so peculiar she feels the need to do something. She's not sure Mum even notices. Behind them Violet clearly grows bored and switches on the television, tuning into some children's channel that she's not usually allowed to watch.

Finally Mum finishes washing up, places the dishcloth neatly on the worktop, and walks back to the table. She pauses, then rests her hands on the surface, like she's letting everyone know that supper is over and she will not be sitting down again. "So. Gene. Where are you staying? We can get you an Uber if you don't fancy walking on that leg."

Gene's smile wavers. "Ah, yeah, that's the thing I wanted to talk to you about, sweetheart. Turns out my hotel was double-booked and I was wondering—"

"Oh, no," says Bill. "Oh, no."

"Well, hey, will you look at that!" Gene says suddenly, glancing up at the terrible picture of the naked old woman that Bill had hung on the wall. "Francesca as I live and breathe!"

THAT WAS THE POINT, Celie thought afterward, at which things had got really messy. Bill had leaped up, waved his hands violently backward and forward in front of the painting and forbidden Gene to look at it. Actually forbidden him.

"Are you kidding me?" Gene had said. "It's a painting!"

"Francesca would not want you looking at her naked!" Bill's voice was oddly hoarse. "Don't you dare look! You relinquished that right many years ago!"

"But it's okay to place her with her hoo-hah hanging out in a lounge where anyone else can see her? Jesus, Bill, get that stick out of your ass before it calcifies."

At some point Violet had come away from the television. She was staring up at the wall as if she hadn't noticed the picture until now. "That's *Grandma*?" she'd said, and she looked as though she didn't know whether to laugh or cry. "But—but you can see her *pocket book*!"

That was apparently it for Bill. He strode up to the painting, wrenched the frame violently from the wall, and walked with it out of the living room. They could hear him carrying it stiffly up the stairs, grunting

slightly at the effort. After a gap slightly longer than was entirely comfortable, they had heard his bedroom door slam.

Lila sits down heavily. "Jesus, Gene."

"What? What did I do? He hangs a nudie of your mom on the wall
and suddenly *I'm* the bad guy?"

"I think you should leave," Mum says, and closes her eyes for absolutely ages.

Gene takes a step toward her and dips, both his knees cracking like
pistols as he crouches so that he is looking directly into her face. "Honey.
Sweetheart. I just really need a bed for tonight. The hotel I was meant to
go to double-booked me and all the other central London places are a
little heavy on the old wallet. And it's kind of hard to walk around looking for a place now that my leg . . ."

"I don't have a room."

"I don't need a room. I can crash right here on the sofa."

Mum looks at him, and her face has this expression like when you're
going to do something you really don't want to. Suddenly he seems a little pathetic.

"Please," he says, perhaps sensing a momentary weakness. "I'm in a
lot of pain here. It would help me out so much. And I would . . . I would
really appreciate the chance to spend just a few hours more with the
girls."

Mum looks at Celie, and then at Violet.

"He *is* our grandpa," says Violet. Celie feels less certain, but shrugs. It
might be quite useful to have the heat taken off her for an evening.

"Fine," Mum says, throwing up her hands. "Fine. But you need to
leave first thing, before the girls get up for school. I don't want you and
Bill winding each other up again."

"Two nights?" he says hopefully.

"Don't push it," says Mum, and goes off to stand at the end of the
garden.

Chapter Seven

Lila

L ila Kennedy had been seven years old when Bill McKenzie came into her life. She had arrived back from a play-date with Jennifer Barratt one afternoon and her mother had been sitting on the sofa in the living room beside a strange man with a crew-cut and a tweedy wool pullover, a tray of empty coffee cups on the low table. When she had walked in the two of them had moved apart a couple of inches in a way that made Lila stop in the doorway.

"Hello, darling," Mum had said brightly. "Come and say hello to Bill. He's just put up the most gorgeous bookshelves in the study."

Lila could not imagine how something as boring as a bookshelf could possibly be described as "gorgeous," but her mum was always making dramatic exclamations about things so she assumed it was just part of the same pattern. Francesca Kennedy was, Bill had told her some time later, "one of life's enthusiasts." A sky was never blue, it was "the most perfect azure, like something one would see from a Greek island." The neighbor's cat was "just the most heavenly grump. I adore him." Lila would physically shrink into herself when her mother ate, especially soft cheese, because she would close her eyes and smile and say things like "Oh, God the *creaminess*! That is actually *orgasmic*," and let out little gasps of pleasure.

After several weeks of Bill's repeated appearances at the house, when he repaired cabinets, rehung doors, and fixed the tap in the loo that never stopped dripping, Francesca announced that Bill was "the kindest, loveliest man. I actually feel like the world tilts more correctly on its axis when he is here." Lila realized that the slightly stiff, well-spoken woodworker would probably be hanging around for a while.

She didn't really mind. By then Lila could barely remember her father, who had gone back to America to work when she was four years old and never come home. She could recall a few brief impossibly cheery phone calls, always interrupted by "Oh, honey, the first AD is calling me. Gotta go. Love you!" He burst back into her life on short visits every six months or so, bringing extravagant toys from America and marshmallows and Hershey's Kisses. Lila would sit with him in the front room while her mother stood in the doorway, watching them with a strange expression or "leaving them to it" while she went to the shops. But the visits grew further and further apart, the last one punctuated by a hissed and tearful argument in the downstairs hallway. By the time Bill appeared, her father had stopped coming altogether, only occasionally marking her birthday with a week-late card or an age-inappropriate toy.

Still, Lila was not sure at first how she felt about the tight little unit of her and Mum being interrupted by that man, with his starched collars and his classical music (she and Mum had previously liked to dance in the kitchen to the Beatles or Marianne Faithfull), and his exercise routines and morning runs, from which he would return drenched with sweat and quietly euphoric. He brought muesli, which looked like the bottom of the school parrot's cage, and foreign ingredients, like tahini and curry leaf, and was always making meals that made Mum pull that embarrassing face, and announce that he was "an actual culinary genius. You clever, clever man." Bill's ears would go pink with pleasure and he would look at her like he might actually melt. It was a little awkward to watch.

But even Lila had to admit that life was probably a bit better once Bill moved in. Things that went wrong in the house were put right straight away, and her mum never cried anymore, and he was careful with Lila: he asked her opinion on things and never interfered or tried to act like he was actually her dad. On her eighth birthday, when Lila's dad had yet again failed to send even a card (she had told herself she didn't care), she had come home from school to find Bill had made her a whole doll's house with working electric lights and windows on little sashes that slid up and down. It sat in the corner of her bedroom, like a portal into another world. Lila had been transfixed by it. She had dropped her schoolbag and knelt in front of it and started gently adjusting the furniture and folding back the tiny quilted bedcovers and seeing which bits actually moved like a real house. (A miniature mirrored bathroom cabinet with a little wooden tube of toothpaste! A tiny stepladder into an attic!) She had barely changed position for ten minutes, the rest of the world falling away. And when she finally turned back to look at the two people in her doorway, waiting for Mum to announce that it was "absolutely exquisite! Dreamy!" Bill had his arm around her, his face a question mark, and Mum was dabbing at her eyes a little sadly and saying, "I know, I know, I'm being stupid. It's just that this is what I always wanted for her."

It was a nice thing, what Mum was saying. But until that point, Lila realized afterward, she hadn't known anything was missing.

• • •

GENE DOESN'T END up sleeping on the sofa. Lila doesn't think she can bear the prospect of him snoring away in the heart of their household, while Bill huffs and puffs his way through the morning.

She pulls out the old sofa-bed in her study at the top of the house, shoving her desk, with effort, to one side so that it can extend fully, and locates the spare duvet in one of the removals boxes that hasn't yet been unpacked. She makes up the bed while Gene stands in the doorway, exclaiming that it is so great to be here, so kind of her to put him up, that he really is just so grateful. Even the sound of his voice irritates her. She thinks, as the low fizz of anger vibrates in the back of her head, drowning out conversation, that she could almost forgive him his absences, his failure to contact her after the births of her children, his complete inadequacy as a grandfather. His failure to turn up after Francesca's death had lodged like a radioactive bullet inside her, obliterating any sense of generosity or kindness. Francesca, who had never done him any wrong, who had brought up his child so that he could leave and lead whatever crappy hedonistic life he had chosen in Los Angeles. Francesca, who had struggled alone on her teaching assistant's salary for three long years until her parents died and left her enough money to buy a small house. Lila had stood at her grave, flanked by her girls, as her mother had been lowered gently into the earth, one solitary blushing peony on top of the wicker coffin. She had watched the broken figure of Bill opposite as he tried to stay upright under the weight of his grief, and she had known that whatever remaining feelings she had for her biological father had turned to ice.

"What time are you heading off tomorrow?" she says, trying to keep her voice from betraying any of this. He has sat down heavily on the sofa-bed, and is peeling his way out of his battered leather jacket.

"Oh, sometime in the morning."

"The girls get up at seven thirty. They may wake you as the only working bathroom is on this floor."

"Not me, sweetheart. You're all good. I'm dead to the world until eleven."

"Of course you are," she says shortly. After a pause she adds: "So are you in rehearsals?"

"Yeah, but they don't start till, like, midday or something. So you guys just pretend I'm not here and I'll take care of myself."

Lila hands him two towels, holding her hands outstretched as if she is unwilling to take a single step closer. "There's a spare toothbrush in the cabinet if you need it." She gazes at him as he takes them, noting the slack skin around his jaw, the network of crow's feet around his eyes, even if the Nirvana T-shirt suggests he doesn't want to admit to them.

He looks back at her, his eyes suddenly softening. "It really is good to see the girls."

"Yes," she says, folding her arms. "They're great."

"A credit to you. And I'm truly sorry about your marriage."

She swallows. "Yes," she says, her voice cool. "Me too."

His face is searching hers, as if he's hoping for some chink into which he can make it through her armor. But she's damned if he's earned it.

"I really appreciate this, Lila." He pauses. "I mean, I know I haven't exactly—"

She brushes her hands together. "I have to go to bed. Early start and all that."

"Oh. Sure."

She fights a vague reflexive guilt as she sees the old man's face, the awkwardness and faint melancholy flickering across it. It is only when she closes the door behind her that she realizes he has walked the whole way up four flights of stairs without once favoring his injured leg.

Chapter Eight

B ut isn't it even a bit nice? To see him again?"

"Nope." Lila steps to the side of the path to let a woman pass. Truant lets out a low growl at the woman's Labradoodle and Lila smiles apologetically as the woman hurries past, her expression nervous. It is a walk she and Eleanor do twice a week, Lila on the mornings that she doesn't have the girls, and Eleanor because she never sleeps past five after twenty years making up people for the film industry.

"He hasn't changed at all. Walked in like the last fifteen years hadn't even happened. Like our entire adult relationship hadn't been half a dozen birthday cards, most of which arrived on the wrong day. Honestly, El, I kept looking at him over the dinner table, and all I saw was the space I'd left for him at Mum's funeral. I actually hate him." Lila had watched two episodes of *La Familia Esperanza* when she went to bed. It's possible that Estella slept with the hunky gun instructor, but Lila cannot remember a thing that happened.

"What did the girls think?"

"Oh, he charmed them. The usual. Pulled up his old YouTube videos—'Captain Strang, reporting for intergalactic duty.'" She mimics Gene's accent. "Violet loved it. But then Violet likes anyone if she thinks they might be corruptible. Celie was less sure but he's probably working on her as we speak. He can't bear not to be loved. It's pathological. If he senses an ounce of resistance he just keeps on and on until he's found their weak spot."

"Well, it's only for a couple of days."

They have reached an empty part of the woods. Lila lets Truant off the lead and watches him trot off under the leaves that are just starting to brown, glancing backward periodically to check that she's still there, ever vigilant. "Yup. And then I won't see him for another decade. Possibly till I get an invitation to his funeral. Which I don't think I'll bother going to."

"God, remind me never to fall out with you." Eleanor finishes her coffee and tucks the empty cup into her rucksack.

Lila takes a last swig of hers. Eleanor holds out her hand to take the cup from her and tucks it into Lila's.

"No chance," says Lila. "I'm going to glom on to you forever. Like fox poo. I'll be hanging around indefinitely."

"You make it sound like such a delightful prospect."

Lila hooks an arm around her friend's neck and pulls her in for a hug. "I have to have you in my life forever, El. I think I would actually die if I had all this crap coming at me and you weren't there to stop me going mad."

"I'm not sure my superpowers stretch that far."

"It's a lot, isn't it? Bloody hell."

"We're at that age. It's always a lot," Eleanor says, with a cheerful smile. "That's why you need to go and have some fun. To balance it all out."

"Oh, God. Please don't tell me to have a threesome. I don't think I can cope with more of your sexual escapades."

"It was *so* much fun. We went to a fetish party. I didn't love the rubber gear, as it was just so hot, and I had to use industrial amounts of talc just to get it on in the first place, but such a nice bunch of people. We all went for a Vietnamese afterward. The guys would have preferred curry but we said we were worried about getting in and out of our rubber wear. I mean biryanis make me blow up like a balloon."

"Everything you're describing sounds like a very unpleasant fever dream. I do not want to consider curry and rubber suits in the same sentence." Lila has started to hate these discussions. She can't work out if they make her feel that her friend is growing away from her, or that life is passing her by. Possibly both. "Does it really not make you feel even a bit weird, El? I mean, is this really you?"

"Is it really me?" Eleanor stops and considers this. "I don't know. I'm not sure I know who I am these days. I thought I had everything all planned out for the rest of my life, me and Eddie, a couple of kids, nice house with a picket fence. Or at least a really nice apartment in the Congestion Zone. And look what happened. Now I just try to live every day with an open heart and an open mind and see what happens."

"Even if that involves curries and strangers in rubber suits."

"I know it's not to your taste, Lils, but you'll never move on unless you start looking forward. Seriously. Dan has done a bunch of horrible things, but if you let yourself be mired in it forever you'll have an utterly miserable time. I say that with love."

"So I should forget everything he and my dad have done and just be delightful to them, no matter what they throw at me."

"It's worth thinking about."

"Oh, God. I figure it's about six months till you start up a self-help podcast."

Eleanor flashes her another smile. "Ooh. That's an idea. How to liberate yourself through tantric orgasms."

"How to treat thigh chafing injuries when you can't get out of your latex bodysuit."

Eleanor fixes her with a beady eye and continues: "Why opening yourself up to new experiences will bring you happiness."

"Why opening yourself up to shady insurance salesmen named Sean will bring you pelvic inflammatory disease."

"You're just a ray of sunshine, Lils," says Eleanor, and stomps ahead on the path.

"That's why you love me," says Lila, and trots a little to keep up with her.

SOMETIMES, IF SHE'S in a particularly self-punishing mood, Lila thinks of how her husband's relationship with Marja must have formed at a point when he was supposedly being his most helpful. He had taken a three-month sabbatical from work—*Get Ripped!* magazine gave this to all employees of more than ten years' standing and his had coincided with the deadline for her book. So, for what she had thought of as three precious months, every weekday afternoon, instead of having to leave her screen and race to the school gate, she had been able to sit at home and write—an unheard-of freedom—while her husband hung around with the school mums, waiting for their fractious children to trail out of the red door. Sometimes he had even taken them to the park after school—"To give you more writing time," he had said, and she had felt almost giddy with gratitude and love. Until, of course, it had become clear that Marja must have hung out at the park on all those occasions too. And that during that three months something more than the usual staving-off of parental tedium, of the normal park-bench companionship with its shared paper handkerchiefs and cartons of juice, its childish complaints and scraped knees, had taken place. Perhaps Marja had made extra efforts to look nice, arriving in her yoga gear to show off her lithe silhouette, spritzing herself with expensive perfume before heading out to pick up Hugo. Perhaps Dan had made extra efforts too—she hadn't noticed much at the time, except her daily word count, her panic at getting it all done.

There must have been a day on which, seated on a park bench, or watching Violet on the swings, Dan had confided in Marja that he felt unhappy, or ignored, or that he had simply fallen out of love. Perhaps they had discussed sex, or the lack of it. Marja would have turned her limpid gaze on him, placed a beautifully manicured hand of sympathy on his arm. Perhaps she portrayed herself as brave, the single mother whose partner had moved back to the Netherlands and now did almost nothing to help her. She would have smiled. Leaned into him. How admirable she must have seemed, compared to the grumpy wife in sweatpants at home who moaned because he had yet again failed to buy the dishwasher tablets on the way home.

And then, one day, a whole new boundary would have been crossed. Lila still doesn't know exactly when that was, perhaps after his sabbatical had ended, during a "work" lunch or on one of the many evenings he had claimed to need to stay late at the office. She doesn't know when he and Marja had begun sleeping together, or when they first expressed their love for each other. She knows only the leftover bits: the date on which he told her, with almost comical formality, that their marriage was over. The date, sometime after that, when she understood after she'd glimpsed them sitting, foreheads touching, in a parked car on Garwood Street—why that was.

She occasionally wishes someone would acknowledge her fortitude in simply turning up to the school gates every day, at least without a flamethrower and a small army of mercenaries. She thinks she's done pretty well to stay standing. She thinks she might deserve a medal for making her legs walk to school every day, for standing and smiling and acting like it hasn't all half killed her. No, from the outside, she thinks it's possible that nobody would even notice any more.

Though she still hasn't managed to go back to the play park. Not once.

LILA ARRIVES AT the school at nineteen minutes past three, the very latest she can get there before they turn them out. Violet had begged her to get her a cinnamon bun from the nice Scandinavian bakery, and she's feeling mildly guilty that she'd been unable to resist buying one for herself as well and eating it outside the shop. Since Bill had arrived she and the girls eat sugary treats urgently and surreptitiously in the car, or outside shops, like junkies getting a fix.

Marja is standing with the other mums, clutching a Tupperware box of cupcakes for some bake sale for which Lila has no doubt missed the email, someone is discussing future play-dates, and Lila immediately moves to the other end of the waiting area and stares determinedly at her phone.

She has thought a lot about what Eleanor said, tried to reframe her life more positively. Every day I do this, she tells herself, I am moving one step closer to a better life. Every day I do this is one day closer to when Dan and Marja's and my little psychodrama is going to become yesterday's news. She has repeated this to herself over the several hours that she should have been writing. Except, she thinks suddenly, once the baby arrives, it will be coming here every day too. Marja will be pushing Dan's baby past her every day, with all those women cooing over it. Maybe Dan will come with her on the first day, like husbands often do, full of pride and protective of their amazing partner, *who was so brave, and so strong. Honestly, I'm in awe of her.*

"Excuse me."

A man is standing in front of her. He is tall and slim, with floppy, tawny hair, and sad eyes behind glasses. He has the kind of shambolic sexiness that was catnip to her before she met Dan. She blinks. She realizes he has said something that she couldn't make out. "Sorry?"

"I wondered where you got that." He is pointing at the bag with the cinnamon bun. "My daughter loves those things. We're new here so I don't really know where the good places are."

"Oh." She peers down at the bag. When she looks up she guesses, uncomfortably, that she has probably gone a bit pink. He has a remarkably direct gaze. "It's Annika's."

"Is that your daughter?"

"No. No. The bakery. It's called Annika's. I don't think there's an actual Annika working there. They chose it because it's a Swedish name. Just so we all know it's Swedish. And does cinnamon buns. This one is just at the end of the high street. I'm pretty sure there's another in Finchley, also called Annika's . . ." She tails off. "So which class is your daughter in?"

He says something but it's not Violet's class and everything has turned into a kind of humming sound around him. She realizes almost straight away that she hasn't properly listened to him so she just smiles and nods. And then nods again, just in case.

"When did she start?"

"Last week. She's finding it all a little tricky so I just wanted to cheer her up."

"Oh, I'm sorry."

He shrugs. "It's—uh . . . She's had a lot of change in her life over the last eighteen months." He stares at his feet.

Lila can't think of what to say. So she thrusts the bun at him. "Take it."

"What?"

"For your daughter. I can get another on the way back." It's half a mile in the other direction.

"No . . . no. I can't do that." He smiles and is briefly elevated from shambolically attractive to devastatingly gorgeous. "That's incredibly sweet of you, though."

"I insist." She is now pushing the bun at him, forcing it into his hands. "Please. I shouldn't give this to Violet anyway. We—we normally just eat fish and lentils."

"We've lived off so much Deliveroo lately I probably have their equivalent of gold status."

Why is he living off takeaway? Does that mean there's no woman in the house? Lila curses herself for her internalized misogyny. This man looks too cool for internalized misogyny. She tries to think of something to say about Deliveroo but Violet is coming out through the doors. "Violet! Oh, God, don't let her see it. She'll never forgive me. I'd better—Bye. Nice to meet you . . ."

"Gabriel."

"Gabriel. I'm . . ." She struggles to recall her name. ". . . Lila! Hah! So much for fish as brain food. Forgot my own name!" She lets out a strange high-pitched laugh she has never heard before, turns and walks briskly toward Violet, cursing herself. *How can I be behaving like I'm fifteen when my neck is old enough to be growing an actual wattle?*

"Did you get me a cinnamon bun?" says Violet, thrusting her rucksack at her.

Lila can feel the school mums around Marja giving her surreptitious glances. *Yes, that's me, talking to the new hot guy,* she tells them silently. *Suck on that, bitches.* "I thought we could get one on the way home."

"Oh, my God, Mum, you're so annoying!" Violet throws her head back and lets out a wail of despair. "It is *miles* from our house. And I'm *so tired!*"

Lila flashes the mothers a smile. Marja has her back to her. She usually has her back to her, these days. "I tell you what," she says. "We'll stop at the mini-mart and get a jam doughnut."

• • •

IT IS PERHAPS testament to how little male attention Lila has received over the past eighteen months that for the entire walk to the mini-mart and home again, she is feeling little electric shocks of pleasure when she remembers the exchange with Gabriel. The direct nature of his gaze. The almost shy half-smile when she thrust at him the bag with the bun. She thinks about it in the moments when Violet's incessant chatter is briefly quelled by the doughnut, which she eats with forensic pleasure, sucking the sugar from her fingers as she walks. There was definitely a charge between them, wasn't there? Would he have approached Lila if he hadn't been remotely attracted to her? He could have gone to the other mums. He didn't need to smile so much, or confide anything in her. Then she catches herself, and feels ridiculous. She is a forty-two-year-old woman obsessing like a schoolgirl. After everything she's been through. He's just a man who wanted a sugary bun. She maintains this stance for twenty strides. And then she is remembering how his eyes crinkled behind his glasses, his lovely mop of hair, the unexpected anticipatory pleasure of the next school run.

The circuit of pleasure and abrupt self-tellings-off comes to a halt when she reaches the front door and remembers. Gene is here, Gene, with his endless need for attention and approval, crashing back into her life without even a hint of apology for every way in which he has failed at being a father.

She closes her eyes momentarily outside the front door, takes a deep breath, puts the key into the lock, and walks in.

"The emergency plumber is here," Bill announces, as she walks through to the kitchen. Violet passes them both and collapses in front of the television, sweeping up the remote control without looking at it, so that all further conversation takes place over the sound of overexcited American teenagers shouting at each other in school halls.

"What? Why?"

Bill is peeling a motley collection of mucky, no doubt organic swedes. She wonders, with faint trepidation, which feels ungenerous yet entirely justified, what he is preparing for supper.

"That man blocked the toilet with paper. Why he needed to use half a roll just for his morning ablutions I don't know. But I couldn't unblock it."

Bill's expression tells of the double insult involved in having to clear up Gene's actual mess as well as his metaphorical one.

"Jesus. How much is that going to cost?" Lila sits down heavily beside the oblivious Violet. "Where is he?"

"No idea. Halfway back to Los Angeles hopefully."

Her head shoots up.

"He said he'd be back after rehearsals." Bill says it with the same disgust as if Gene had gone to a public stoning. "I suppose I have to include him in tonight's dinner plans."

"It's just one more night, Bill," she says.

Bill's silence and faintly bristling back conveys what he thinks of that plan. Then he says, "I'd be grateful if you could have a word with him about the . . . plumbing business. I wouldn't want to have to organize another emergency plumber tomorrow."

LILA SAYS SHE'S going to work for a couple of hours before supper. But when she walks into her office she sees the sofa-bed, the spare duvet rumpled on its thin mattress, and realizes resentfully that, with Bill and Gene here, she has no space in the house to herself. She heads for her bedroom, and, ridiculously weary, bypasses her bed and lies down instead on the carpet, staring up at the ceiling, listening to Bill's murmured exchanges with the plumber on the top floor. *I would like a life where I was flirting with someone over an outdoor table right now. Per-*

haps with a cold bottle of rosé. Not listening to a cross, elderly man negoti-
ate with a plumber over a blocked toilet, and nothing to look forward
to but some permutation of swede. She sighs heavily. Marja probably
never lies on a floor feeling she doesn't want to see a single human being
ever again. Marja is probably right now lying on a sofa with Dan rubbing her feet. He was always good at pregnancy foot rubs. Or maybe
she's one of those women whose hormones go mad during the early
months and right now they're in bed having—

Lila closes her eyes and counts to ten. Then she picks up her phone.
She checks the school email chain—which she rarely does—and sees
the announcement of a new child in class five, Elena Mallory. She thinks
for a minute, then types "Gabriel Mallory" speculatively into a search
engine, and waits to see what comes up.

Architect Gabriel Mallory wins award for "revolution-
ary" halfway house. Judges praise his "humane and
socially forward thinking design."

She stares at the picture of him holding his award. Of course he's an
award-winning architect. Of course he is. She rolls onto her stomach
and idly googles *Gabriel Mallory Wife.* Nothing comes up, not under his
name anyway. There's a bunch of other Gabriel Mallorys—men with
wraparound Oakley sunglasses and surfboards, bearded IT developers,
small boys in the arms of proud blonde mothers. She types *Gabriel Mal-*
lory Divorce and then, when nothing comes up, *Gabriel Mallory Wife*
Tragic Death.

"What are you doing?"

Lila jumps.

Violet is standing in front of her, staring down at Lila's phone.

"Jesus, Violet. You can't sneak in on me like that."

"Your boobs look really squishy when you lie on your front."

"Thank you."

Lila wrestles her way to a seated position. She looks down at her breasts, wondering if they are notably more squishy than anyone else's.

"Oh. Also Bill says supper is ready and Gene has come back and Bill says he smells like a drunk. And I'm not eating supper because it's got turnips in it so can I order a pizza?"

FOR A FEW YEARS, when the children were small, Lila and her mother would go to the supermarket together once a week. Francesca would accompany her ostensibly to provide back-up, a spare pair of hands to calm a screaming child, or pick up items ejected by chubby little fists from the trolley. They would sometimes have a cup of coffee afterward, if the frozen goods would last that long.

The habit continued long after the children had started school, even though there was no logical reason for them to shop at the same time. Francesca was relentlessly cheerful, treating the weekly supermarket trip like an amazing opportunity to discover new and exotic things. Lila would be pushing her way resolutely along the breakfast cereals, wondering which the girls were less likely to fight over, weighing up the terrifying amounts of sugar against the likelihood of them actually eating any of it, and would hear Francesca exclaiming from twenty yards away: "Lils! Look at this! How do you think you pronounce *'nduja*? Oh, lychees! I haven't had a lychee since I was a girl! I must get a whole bowlful for Bill." Once, when Lila was feeling particularly sour after a sleepless night or a fight with Dan, Francesca had repeatedly urged her to cheer up, to look on the bright side, to look at the wealth of amazing things in front of her and consider how lucky they were, until Lila had snapped at her, asking her why she didn't just leave her alone. *I'm not like you, Mum. I don't feel bloody cheerful all the time.*

Francesca had gazed at her quizzically, her curly gray hair bouncing on her shoulders, and then said cheerfully: "Fine! I will!" And as Lila watched, she had taken a sudden run with her trolley, then lifted both feet onto the back of it, so that she was sailing on wheels toward the far end of the aisle as shoppers moved abruptly, and grumpily, out of her way. As she went, she had turned to Lila and theatrically lifted an arm. "I'm going! I'm leaving you alone!"

Lila had stood there, stunned, as her mother had sailed around the corner, not sure whether to be embarrassed by her or impressed that she genuinely didn't care what anyone else in the shop thought. She had turned back to the supermarket variety of Chocolate Weetos, and a few minutes later there was a whoop and Francesca was whizzing back toward her on the trolley. "Yum Yums!" she exclaimed, jumping off just as the trolley collided with the dried pasta. "It is biologically IMPOSSI-BLE to be grumpy after you've eaten a Yum Yum. Here."

Lila had stood eating the sugary, doughy finger, while her mother watched her with the intent anticipation of a scientist who knows they are about to be proven right. "See?" she had said, when Lila was left licking her fingers, a rueful smile on her lips. "See? Aren't they the most glorious bringers of joy? I *knew* resistance would be futile."

Lila stares at the two elderly men now sitting at each end of her table, studiously ignoring each other as they pick their way through a plate of spiced swede fritters, and wonders how a woman capable of squeezing such epic levels of happiness out of any situation could possibly have ended up with either of these two. Bill's mouth has compressed into a thin line of irritation, and he speaks only to offer the water jug, or ask Lila whether the fritters contain enough salt. He does not address Gene, as if by simply ignoring him Gene might spontaneously combust and disappear.

Gene is clearly a little drunk. His movements have a certain deliberateness to them, and periodically he nods, his eyebrows shooting up, as if he is engaged in some silent conversation with someone nobody else can see. Violet, who has been told she cannot have a pizza, pushes the swede around her plate with a sullen air, occasionally shooting furious glances at Lila, as if she is responsible for this culinary betrayal.

"So, how were rehearsals, Gene?" Lila says. She notices that her voice has a kind of cool breeziness when she speaks to him, a tone one would adopt with a neighbor one felt obliged to make conversation with when trapped on a train platform.

"Oh. Good. Great. Director's very happy."

"What is it you're rehearsing?"

Gene blinks, chewing meditatively for a minute. "Just . . . a Swedish director. Not sure it's anyone you would have heard of."

"Director? Or writer?"

"What?"

"You said it was a Swedish director."

"No. He's English."

Lila gazes at her food for a minute. "What's the play?"

"Say, do you have any ketchup? I could do with a little sauce over here."

Bill looks up from his plate.

"They're spicy fritters. There's a natural yogurt dressing. They don't need ketchup."

Gene blinks slowly at him. "Well, I like ketchup."

"They're not made to go with tomato. Certainly not processed tomato with a load of sugar."

"Maybe I like processed tomato with a load of sugar."

Lila gazes at the two of them. Nobody moves. Then, with a sigh, she gets up and walks to the larder. She locates the ketchup at the back of the cupboard, somewhere among the three-year-old tins of coconut milk, and brings it over, handing it to Gene. Bill looks at her as if she has committed an act of treachery. "If he wants ketchup he can have ketchup, Bill."

"Don't mind me. I'm just the fool who has spent an hour carefully combining ingredients to replicate a certain delicate balance of flavors. Why should I care if he wants to splatter industrial goop all over them?"

"Can I have some industrial goop?" says Violet, eagerly taking the bottle and squeezing ketchup all over hers.

Bill sits very still.

Lila leans forward. "They're delicious, Bill," she says. "Thank you."

The doorbell rings at a quarter past eight, just as Lila is clearing the dishes from the table, and Bill is already standing at the sink, his back a rigid reproach to the last hour. Gene gets up, as he is nearest to the hall, and she hears a murmured conversation, followed by a raised voice. Lila puts the plates on the side and walks out to see what is happening.

"I said I was going to come to *you*. Later."

A woman is hauling a suitcase up the front steps, followed by two cardboard boxes, which she dumps with satisfied emphasis on the tiled floor.

"Well, I had the car so I thought this way I could make sure it actually happened." She looks up as Lila stands in the doorway.

"Oh, hello, Lila. How are you?"

Lila squints, trying to work out why this woman is familiar. *"Jane?"* Her father's first English girlfriend—or the first Lila knew about—after her mother: Jane, a massage therapist with long wavy blonde hair, who had been with Gene on and off in the UK and US for maybe fifteen years, who had offered to treat Lila's bruised knees with arnica and whose whole house had smelt of patchouli. She had treated Gene's behavior as if it was entirely to be expected from a man of his talent, and wore a permanent serene smile. She was the most level person Lila had ever met. This woman's hair is long and gray but still thick, her hands strong and capable. She still wears no makeup and her arms are sinewy and strong. Her broad feet are encased in a pair of comfortable red sandals like those a child might wear.

She pushes a box toward Gene and straightens, flicking her long hair back and brushing her hands as if delighted to rid herself of the burden. "Can't tell you how long I've had those in my attic. I did check the suitcase before I came and amazingly nothing has gone moldy or been eaten by moths. I think it was the lavender I put in with them."

"What—what's going on?"

"Gene called and said he's living here now. So I thought it was a good time to persuade him to take the things he'd left at my house for . . . oh, twenty-three years? It'll be a miracle if you fit any of those clothes, Gene. Though I guess you could sell the Grateful Dead T-shirts at Camden Market if you get stuck."

"I'm sorry?" says Lila, who is struggling to understand. "Living where?"

"I didn't say living," says Gene, who seems to have sobered up.

"Yes, you did," says Jane. "You told me you were living with your daughter. You said it yesterday when you called. It was the first thing you said. Also, there may be a couple more boxes up there. I couldn't get to them this evening."

"No—no! Hang on," says Lila. "He's just staying here. One more night."

Jane looks steadily at Gene. Her eyes contain something that Lila is not entirely happy about. "I see," says Jane. "Staying."

Gene turns to Lila, his smile full wattage, and places a hand on her shoulder. "I was going to ask you, sweetheart, whether I could make it a few more days. There's been a problem with the hotel and I just—"

She hears the distant *oh, no* from the kitchen before Gene has even finished the question.

"Just while I'm in rehearsals," says Gene, still beaming.

Lila looks from one to the other, feeling somehow out-maneuvered.

It is Jane who breaks the silence. "This is something you two probably need to sort out by yourselves," she says cheerfully. "And I have a client at eight thirty, so I need to get off. Lila, it's absolutely lovely to see you again. I've often wondered how you were. Lovely house. Gene, it was . . . Well, good luck." She pats his arm, gives a little wave to Lila and leaves.

Lila and Gene stand in the hallway.

"I hit a little bit of bother," Gene begins, "in the finance department."

Lila rolls her eyes to the heavens.

"It's short term. Very short term. Just till I get paid. But it's kinda tricky to get a hotel right now as I lost my credit card and don't seem to have enough cash to put down a deposit on a place."

Lila's jaw seems to have locked. She can feel every one of her teeth.

"So sweetheart, if you could let me stay until I get paid I'd be really grateful. Just a short-term thing. So I can spend time with you and the girls."

When Lila doesn't respond, he continues: "I'd be out of your way. I can just sleep up there and work around you all. Maybe help look after Celia and—"

"Celie. It's Celie. As in *The Color Purple*. And Violet."

"We don't need any help," comes the voice from the kitchen.

Lila doesn't move.

"It's that or I'm sleeping on the streets," he says, throwing down his trump card with the confidence—or desperation—of someone who knows that to throw a seventy-something man onto the streets takes the kind of mental willpower or coldness that Lila is unlikely to possess.

"You can't stay with Jane?"

"Her partner doesn't like me."

"Surprise," says the voice from the kitchen.

"And you have no other friends?"

"I'd rather be with family."

"Oh, now they're family," comes the voice.

"Will you knock it off, Bill?" says Gene. "This is between me and my daughter."

"You relinquished the right to call her your daughter years ago."

"Well, you sure as hell don't have the right."

Lila hears footsteps. Bill appears in the kitchen doorway, a tea-towel over his shoulder. "You have no right to ask anything of Lila, no right at all."

"Hey, fella, butt out. If my daughter wants to give me a bed for the night that's no damn business of yours. You're only squatting here yourself, as far as I can see."

"Squatting here? I've been part of this family for thirty-five years. Certainly three times the amount you ever were."

"You know nothing about me!" Gene is jabbing Bill in the chest now, with a long, thick finger. Bill, shocked, takes a step backward.

"Oh, I know plenty about you!" Bill whips the tea-towel from his shoulder and flicks it hard at Gene. It connects with his chin with an audible snapping sound. Gene's mouth drops open and his hand goes to his face. In the kitchen Truant, clearly sensing some kind of conflict, zips through to the hall and sets up a furious barking, nipping at the men's heels.

"Did you just whip me in the mouth, fella? Oh, man. I'm gonna whup your stiff old ass."

The two old men are pushing at each other now, Bill flailing the tea-towel at Gene's face, as Lila tries to grab the dog to stop it biting someone.

"Whup my ass? You're too drunk to stand up for more than fifteen minutes at a time."

"Oh, now you're going to get it!"

Their fists are up, their bodies shifting from side to side. Lila, her head buzzing, throws herself between them and pushes them apart. "Will you two get a grip?" she yells. "For goodness' sake."

"He started it!"

Lila blocks an admittedly feeble punch from Gene, who bobs and weaves on the other side of her, like a boxer on the deck of a swaying boat.

"Yes, and as with the last thirty-five years, I'll be the one finishing it."

"Bill!" Lila shoves him backward.

"Mum!"

There is a brief silence. And then a voice says, "Mum?"

Violet is standing in the doorway to the living room, her face uncharacteristically uncertain. Lila gives them a final shove apart, glares at them, as if to ensure that they know she means business, then stoops, pulling Violet toward her, pasting a broad smile onto her face. Violet's gaze flickers from one man to the other.

"It's okay, lovey. They're just play-fighting."

Violet's voice is tremulous: "They don't look like they're play-fighting."

The silence lasts just a fraction longer than is useful.

Then Gene switches on his smile. "Sure we are, sweetheart! Me and Bill go back a long way, don't we, Bill? Always joking."

It takes Bill a moment longer to recover his composure. He straightens his tie, which has been pulled from his collar in the commotion. "Always joking," he says, with a smile that doesn't stretch quite as far as his eyes. "Nothing to worry about, Violet. It's just a little joke between Gene and me."

"Yeah. A joke," says Gene.

"Because Gene actually loves it when I do this." Bill flicks out the teatowel again. It catches Gene's nose. Lila watches as Gene's expression grows faintly glassy. And then he recovers his smile.

"Sure. We're just a bundle of laughs. And Bill loves it when I do this!" He reaches out and pulls Bill's tie from his pullover, waggling it so that Bill's head retreats into his collar and he blinks several times.

"Hah-hah-hah," says Bill.

"Hah-hah-hah," says Gene.

"Oh, he's a veritable riot," says Bill.

"And now they are definitely stopping their play-fight. We've all had quite enough fun for this evening," says Lila. "Wouldn't you two agree? Quite enough play-fighting?"

Gene is the first to speak. He smiles broadly, takes a step toward his granddaughter. "Sure. See, Violet? Everyone here is friends. Say, why don't the two of us watch an episode of *Star Squadron Zero*? You're gonna love the one with the Martian uprising."

Violet scans the three adults' faces and seems to relax a little. She looks up at Lila, as if checking that this is okay, and Lila smiles encouragingly, suddenly reminded that Violet, for all her bluster, is still a little girl, dealing with a lot of upheaval.

"Of course. You two sit on the sofa and watch *Star Squadron Zero*. I'll help Bill in the kitchen."

"One more night," she mouths at Gene, as she passes, and tries not to notice the look of bemused horror on his face.

"You should tell him he has to leave immediately," mutters Bill, when she has settled Violet and Gene with the iPad. She can hear the tinny theme tune of the show, Gene's humming beneath it.

"One more night," says Lila, and tries not to feel despondent when Bill folds his tea-towel slowly and meticulously on the draining board and heads pointedly up to his room.

Chapter Nine

Although they are allegedly different, there is a weird uniformity to all publishing and agenting reception areas: the pale wood floors, the shelf of the latest bestsellers and not-so-bestselling books, rearranged daily to flatter and reassure whichever author is due in that day. A brightly colored sofa, possibly Ikea. And in the case of Anoushka Mellors, film and literary agent, a never-ending merry-go-round of identi-kit receptionists: sweet-natured twenty-something girls with lovely hair and a ready smile, whose names Lila can never quite remember. She sits on the bright turquoise sofa, checking *The Rebuild* on the bestseller shelf, and declines the coffee offered to her. She has been awake since five, and had already had three coffees by the time she'd set off. One more may push her over the edge from "slightly agitated" to "full on nervo."

"She won't be a minute," says the sweet receptionist, for the third time. "She just had to take a call with a very important publisher."

"No problem," says Lila.

Bill had been absolutely furious the morning after the fight. He had shown it, as was Bill's wont, in slightly peevish silences and a porridge so dense that the girls had held their spoons upside down for minutes as an experiment to see if any would fall off. It didn't. Violet had quizzed her relentlessly about the play-fight when Bill left the kitchen, asking if it was definitely playing if someone flicked your nose really hard with a tea-towel (yes), whether Gene and Bill liked each other (of course they did), and what Grandma would have said if she had still been here (she couldn't answer that one).

And then she had walked past her study on her way to brush her teeth and stopped dead in the doorway. Gene and his bag were gone.

She had stood there, taking in the empty room, the bed—of course unmade—and wondering how it was possible to feel so relieved yet at the same time conflicted in some undefined way. Her father had disappeared again. True to form. Always vanishing before the complicated conversations, before he was required to take ownership of any difficult situation. She wondered whether he had found some cast member to crash with, or perhaps some weary divorcée for whom he is still sprinkled lightly with stardust. She had felt a sudden, almost overwhelming melancholy. And then the girls had started shouting at each other about ownership of a particular hairbrush and Gene's disappearance had fallen out of her head. She had, however, tripped over his cardboard boxes in the hall on her way out, which felt somehow fitting.

Gabriel Mallory has not been at the drop-off area for two days.

"I hope you don't mind me saying, but I really loved your book."

Lila's head shoots up. The girl is leaning forward over the desk, a shy smile playing around her beautifully outlined lips. "I hope it's not unprofessional of me to say so."

"Not at all. Thank you," says Lila. "That's very kind of you."

"Me and my boyfriend were having a bit of trouble at the time—we do tend to trigger each other a lot. He's an anxious attachment style and I'm an avoidant attachment style—and I read a lot of what you said about how you talk to your husband and it really helped us."

Lila's heart sinks a little. "That's lovely to hear," she says, and then looks at her phone.

"I hope we're like you when we've been together for twenty years." The girl smiles fully now, a conspiratorial smile. "That whole thing about counting to fifteen before you react to anything. I do it all the time now. It's made *such* a difference. And the thing about radical acceptance and not trying to change your partner. You're both so *wise*."

Lila opens her mouth and closes it again.

The girl is looking at her expectantly.

There is a short silence.

"Actually, we're not together any more," Lila says finally.

The girl's smile drops.

"What? Completely not together? Like you've actually split up?"

"No. I mean, yes."

"But why?"

Lila smiles. "He—he went off with someone else."

The girl's eyes widen. "You're kidding."

"No. She's pregnant and having his baby."

The girl stares at her, as if this is some awful joke and she's waiting for the punchline.

"Oh," she says eventually. "Oh."

"Sorry," says Lila. She is not entirely sure why she's saying sorry, but she feels somehow as if she's let the girl down.

"That's okay." The girl's bottom lip is actually trembling. "It's just so sad. Oh, my God—haven't you got kids?"

Lila swallows. "It's fine. Honestly. They're fine. We're all fine." When the girl doesn't look convinced, she adds: "I'm actually writing a new book. About how much fun it is being single. That's what I'm here to talk to Anoushka about."

There is a short silence. The girl stares at a piece of paper on her desk. "I hated being single. It made me really sad."

The phone rings. The girl snaps to attention, replacing her headset on her hair.

"Anoushka Mellors Literary Agency," she says, in a singsong voice. "Hold on, I'll put you through to Foreign Rights."

"DARLING, HOW ARE YOU? You look *fantastic*."

Lila does not look fantastic. After five hours' sleep she looks like the woman who drinks Tennent's Extra outside Camden Town tube station and wears plastic bags on her feet, but she smiles and nods as if it might be true.

"How are those gorgeous girls of yours?"

"Fine," says Lila, automatically. "I've had both my dads staying. So that's been fun."

"*Both* your dads?" Anoushka blinks at her, briefly distracted from her screen. She is wearing a bright turquoise blouse and matching earrings, the kind of woman for whom dressing is always a statement.

"My stepfather, Bill, whom you've met. And my biological dad, Gene, whom you haven't."

"Oh, my goodness! How very modern! Two grandpas! I bet the girls *love* it."

Lila smiles blandly, recalling the two old men shoving each other and flicking tea-towels in her narrow hallway. "It's been . . . interesting. Anyway, my 'real' dad went home. So it's just us and Bill again." Bill, whose whole demeanor has become immediately sunnier, who now whistles in the morning, who has attacked the so-called memorial garden with a new fervor.

"How lovely. Right. To business! I have wonderful news."

"You do?"

"Regent House are desperate to read your new manuscript. Apparently sexy menopause is all the rage at the moment."

"Menopause?" Lila peers over the desk. "But I—I'm not menopausal."

"Let's not look a gift horse, darling. By the time it's published you probably will be. And they are *agog* for tales of sexy cougars having fun now that they've shed their boring partners. I said yours was absolutely chock-full of romantic adventures, and after the success of *The Rebuild* they're considering putting in a pre-empt."

Lila shifts in her brightly colored chair. "Even though they haven't seen anything?"

"You're a *Sunday Times* bestseller, darling. They know you can write. And you're about to give them what they want. Now obviously they're going to want to see the first three chapters. How far have you got?"

Lila pulls a thoughtful face, as if she's done so much she's having trouble with exact recall. "Um . . . not quite three chapters."

"Well, I suggest you finish chapter three as fast as possible. It's a sizzling topic right now, and we want to strike while the iron's hot. So if you could get something to me by the end of the week that would be amazing. We could have a deal by halfway through October."

"How much are we talking?" says Lila.

"Oh, definitely six figures," says Anoushka.

"Six figures?"

Anoushka smiles warmly. "Like I said, it's what everyone's looking for. We might even be able to get you a US deal. Actually, if you could put a little bit in about how you fit your assignations around looking after elderly parents that would be the icing on the cake. There are so many women having to look after both ends of the family these days. And you'll be a shining example of having it all." She holds up a hand.

"*Stairlifts, School Runs, and Sexytimes: How I Became a Midlife Minx.* I can see it now. If we're lucky we'll get it serialized in the *Mail.* They pay terribly well for those pieces."

"I'm not quite a midlife—"

"You might have to wear one of those terrible cobalt blue dresses that they always make women wear, and some horrible wedgie sandals, but it's a small price to pay."

"Right," says Lila, who is thinking about the last emergency-plumber bill. "Six figures."

"Men like your very naughty Dan will be screaming that they ever let their wives go. You'll be doing a public service. Wonderful! Shall we say Friday?" Anoushka leans forward conspiratorially. "Now tell me honestly. Does my office smell a bit vomity? Gracie hoicked up her breakfast again this morning. Didn't even make the bin this time. I swear we'll have to move offices at this rate."

SIX FIGURES. SIX figures would get her out of trouble. It would make Dan's reduction in their money less catastrophic, pay to get the bathrooms redone, give her a financial cushion, even if it did come in installments. Six figures would mean she was still in the big-time. Lila thinks about six figures the whole way back to the house, and is so lost in allocating her imaginary cash that she almost walks into Jensen, who is standing in the passageway that runs from the front garden to the rear with a wheelbarrow full of shrub clippings, their tendrils waving gently over the metal edges like the arms of an octopus. He stops when he sees her, shielding his eyes from the sun. He has the messed-up sandy hair of a schoolboy and a fine crescent of soil is lodged beneath each of his nails.

"Bill has gone to his. He said I'd be fine starting work anyway. Hope that's okay."

"That's fine," she says. She tries to make it sound friendlier than she feels. She is still not sure how she feels about a memorial garden, or that Bill is now making decisions about her house.

"Oh, and we have a bit of a situation in your shed."

"What?"

He starts to pull a face, the kind of face tradesmen pull when they're about to cost you a large amount of money. The shed will need pulling down, and a more expensive one will be recommended. The concrete apron is cracked and dangerous and will need replacing. It is housing a large family of rats that will need an expensive exterminator. Lila makes a split-second decision. Not right now, not when the prospect of financial salvation has just been dangled in front of her. Not now.

"I don't want to know."

Jensen straightens a little. "You don't want to know?"

"No," she says briskly. She has had two calm days and a good meeting. She, more than anyone, knows that you have to protect the small wins when they come. "Thanks, though."

As Jensen stares at her, she lets herself into her house.

Oh, the absolute bliss of a silent house. Lila stands in the hallway for a minute, absorbing the complete stillness in the air, only disturbed by the gentle wag of Truant's tail as he snakes his way delightedly to meet her. She crouches, rubbing his ears, feeling suddenly, unexpectedly happy. There is nobody in her house, and she has four hours in which to write the chapters that will launch the next stage of her life. Everything is doable.

Fifteen minutes later she is sitting at her desk, mulling over her first chapter. Should she write about *The Rebuild*? Should she acknowledge everything that has happened to her? Lila knows too well that women's disastrous love lives are catnip to readers. Nobody wants to read about a woman having it all: it just makes them feel they didn't try hard enough. They want to read about how it's impossible, about heartbreak and romantic catastrophe, to goggle at it as they sail past en route to happier destinations. Success is annoying. A life of pratfalls and disasters is . . . relatable.

Two years ago, she begins, **I wrote a book about what I thought was my happy marriage. Two weeks after that book was published my husband left me.**

She stares at the words, her fingers pausing on the keys. If she does this, she thinks, Dan will be very angry. He will hate her for dragging his personal life into the public sphere. The girls may be angry too. It is so personal, so close to the bone. She cannot write about her marriage without making reference to the children. But what else do I have? She remembers a quote she had once read on the internet: *If you didn't want me to write shit about you, you should have been nicer to me.* She takes a breath.

> **There is not much that is more humiliating than inviting the world into your marriage to teach them the lessons you've learned about maintaining happiness, only to discover that everything you had put out there was a lie.**

Suddenly the words are flowing, surging into her head and out through her fingertips in a relentless stream, unstoppable, alive. She picks and discards metaphors, writes dry, humorous references to her own hubris. She disappears into a world occupied only by her screen and her keyboard, lost in time. *This* is what she needed to write: a catharsis. Words have always been how she processes the world and now she realizes she needs them to process this. She writes a thousand, two thousand, three thousand words. She stops briefly to make a mug of tea and lets it go cold on her desk, lost in her own meditations. By the time she stands up again she has written 3,758 words and has her first chapter.

She stares at the word count and feels something unfamiliar and triumphant. "I can do this," she says aloud. "I can bloody do this."

Lila feels a little guilty about how brusque she was with Jensen earlier so she makes him a mug of tea, and steps outside. He is at the far end of the garden, up a ladder, from which he is carefully pruning a lilac bush, wearing a faded T-shirt and a pair of camouflage shorts that come to his knees. He has a farmer's tan, cut off at the neck and sleeves, and the tanned bits are the deep caramel of someone who spends most of their life outside. She walks to the end of the garden, tailed by Truant, and waits at the bottom of the ladder for him to notice her.

He stops and makes his way down the rungs, accepting the mug gratefully.

"Looking good," she says brightly, although she genuinely has no idea if the bush looks good or not.

He gazes at it. "Yeah. I won't go hard on it, although they're proper thugs. I could probably take four feet from it and it would still look about the same size next year."

She nods, as though any of this makes any sense. "Sorry about earlier. I mean, it's rare that I get the house to myself, these days, so I just needed to get in and . . . Deadlines . . ."

He shakes his head, as if it's of no matter, and swigs at his tea. Lila experiences a moment of peace, the kind of peace she can't remember feeling before. It's like smelling a fragrance from childhood, a reminder that there was another version of Lila from way, way back, one she had almost forgotten.

"I read your book."

It takes her a moment to register what he's said. "You read my book?"

"I didn't read the whole thing. I'm not a very fast reader. But I read a lot of it. Like I skimmed it."

"Probably best you don't read all of it. Turns out it was pretty much fiction." She smiles. She can smile about it today. With the new words, *The Rebuild* is already receding into the far distance.

"Yeah. Bill told me. Sorry about that. Oh, look. A squirrel."

She waits for him to ask more questions, but he stares at the squirrel and appears to have forgotten the conversation. It is then she sees his wedding ring. She wonders if the rest of her life will involve checking which men are wearing one and which aren't. She still misses her own—it was the only bit of jewelry she never lost.

"How long have you been doing gardens?"

"About four years."

"Is that what you wanted to do?"

"No. I wanted to be a male model. But David Gandy had me run out of town. Didn't like the competition."

"I've heard that about him," Lila says. "Very insecure."

"Horribly. You know, the dadbod fills him with fear."

She starts to laugh.

"What—you don't think . . . ?" He looks down at his stomach. It's not big but he puffs it out a little, happy to go with the joke.

Lila tilts her head. "I'm also really sorry about the whole staring-at-the-tree thing. There's been burglaries around here and—"

"And I give off strong criminal vibes. I get it. But you're okay. You have Bill."

She looks at him sideways.

He takes a final swig of his tea. "I'm serious. He gives good teacher face. You wouldn't mess with him."

"He can be very stern."

"He gave me quite the talking-to before I started. About how you were going through a lot. And how we should all give you a lot of space."

"He said that?"

"He loves you." He says it so simply.

Lila realizes suddenly how rare it is for her to hear a man discuss love in open, simple terms. After the early days, Dan rarely told her he loved her. If she asked him he would look at her with an expression that was half bemusement tinged with faint irritation, as if to say, *Why are you asking me that?* She thinks sometimes that she always felt she was a little too much for him, too needy, too angry, too sad, too hysterical.

She feels a sudden flood of love for Bill, for his unassuming affection. "I'm lucky to have him," she says, when she can't think of anything else.

He hands her his empty mug. "Yup. I'm still going to steal your car, though."

She laughs. She has turned to walk back across the garden when he calls: "Hey, the thing I wanted to tell you—the shed . . ."

She feels it then, the sudden clench, the sense that she is never allowed just to have a few hours of uncomplicated joy. And it is out of her mouth before she even thinks about it.

"No," she says.

"No?"

She stops briefly and turns. "I don't want to talk about the shed. I don't want to do anything about the shed. It can wait." It comes out a little more sternly than she'd planned, but she feels it viscerally. She doesn't want to hear what else she's going to be on the hook for. She wants one smooth day. Is that really too much to ask? "Look, I get that this is your job. It's a project for you. And there are probably things you think I should be spending to make all this better or more functional or more beautiful, but I can't do it right now. Okay? I'm not even sure I can be doing this. I don't have the bandwidth and I certainly don't have the money."

"I wasn't—" he begins, but she cuts him off.

"The bloody shed has stood here for twenty odd years, by the look of it. Whatever is wrong with it can just . . . wait."

This time the warmth has gone from his expression. He lets his gaze rest on her face for a minute, studying her, and then he compresses his mouth, lifts his eyebrows, nods to himself, and walks back to his barrow, brushing his hands together as he goes.

"I've got to go and pick up Violet," she says, feeling somehow awkward. And then hating herself for it. It's her house. She is allowed to place boundaries around what she's willing to do.

"Thanks for the tea," he says, raising a hand. He does not look back.

IT IS, OF COURSE, a complete coincidence that Lila goes to pick up Violet wearing a full face of makeup, with blow-dried hair that has not yet been pulled into an old scrunchie. And maybe kept on the outfit she wore to visit Anoushka's offices rather than her usual jeans or tracksuit bottoms (the writer's uniform, as Dan used to call it). And it is also possibly not a coincidence that when she walks in and bears left toward the play equipment where Gabriel Mallory is standing alone, rather than right toward the school building where the other mothers congregate, he lifts his eyebrows slightly and says: "You look very nice."

"Do I?" she says, sounding surprised. She has forgotten the awkward exchange in her garden. Gabriel Mallory is wearing a soft blue shirt and expensive trainers, an eco brand she's read about in a magazine. He has neat wire-rimmed glasses, the kind she suspects makes a face look even more handsome, and architect-like.

"Oh, yes," she says blithely. "I had a meeting in town this morning. Couldn't be bothered to get changed afterward."

"You should have meetings every day," he says. "It suits you. *Luminosa*." And then holds out a bag. "Oh, yes. For you."

She looks down. It is a paper bag from Annika's. The weight suggests two cinnamon buns.

"Well," he says, with a lopsided smile, "for you and your daughter. Sorry, I've forgotten her name."

"Violet," she says, trying not to flush with pleasure.

"It was really kind. It gave Lennie a boost."

"Lennie?"

"Well, she's Elena. But she wants to be a boy at the moment so she demands to be known as Lennie."

"I'll make sure I remember." She fiddles with the paper bag, trying not to look at him. There is something about this man that is physically overwhelming, as if her whole body wants to propel itself against him, crush her mouth against his soft shirt. It is a very unsettling sensation. "How is she doing?" she says, trying to disguise this inner turbulence.

He tilts his head slightly, looks over at the door to the school. "She's . . . okay. She misses her mum."

Lila opens her mouth to ask, but he gives her an awkward sideways glance and says: "She—she's not with us any more."

"You mean . . ."

He nods, and Lila feels briefly winded. "Oh my goodness. I'm so sorry."

"It's fine." He lets out a humorless laugh. "Well, it's not. It's been pretty awful. But . . . it is what it is."

"If it makes you feel any better, my soon to be ex-husband's new girl-friend is over there. Pregnant with his baby."

He raises his eyebrows. "Right." There is a short silence. "I guess we both have a lot going on, then," he says.

"Oh, yes."

"Well, you're clearly handling it like a Don."

Lila opens her mouth to respond, flushing, but the door to the school opens then and the children begin to flood out, pushing their way past the teacher in a pint-sized scrummage of brightly colored backpacks and already tattered pictures from the day, immediately welding themselves to their corresponding parents, like penguins returning across the frozen wastes.

"Here's to cinnamon buns then," Gabriel Mallory says, and gives her a little salute, as he starts to walk toward the throng.

"Buns!" says Lila, in response, and her voice does something high-pitched and strange.

She repeats "buns" sporadically under her breath, sometimes furiously, sometimes despairingly, the whole walk home.

WHATEVER THERAPEUTIC WOODWORKING Bill has done at home over the past few days seems to have consolidated his more cheerful state of mind: he smiles readily when Lila and Violet return home, and only mentions for the third time that it would have been nice if Gene had bothered to strip, or even make, his bed before he'd left. Lila, who has guiltily wiped the last of the sugary bun from her lips as she walked up the steps of the front door, smiles back. It has been, she thinks, with unexpected pleasure, a pretty good day. Celie is in a reasonably good mood—at least, she deigns to speak at least twice during supper—there is a roast chicken and salad instead of fish and lentils, and Violet, still basking in the secret mischief of their contraband buns, manages to make only one scatological reference during the entire meal. Even Dan calling halfway through to ask to switch his days this week because Marja's mother is coming over from Holland does not dent her general well-being. The girls eat their food without fuss, Bill discusses a friend with one leg from his teacher-training days who has got in touch with him via Facebook, and Lila spends most of the meal slightly lost in the imaginary arms of a man with a lopsided grin and a pair of sticky buns.

She is so lost in this train of thought that it takes her a while to notice Truant is barking again. The back door is open and she observes that the dog has set up the agitated staccato bark he reserves for blameless postmen and delivery drivers. He has been bad again for the last couple of days—it's as if he's set to high alert, always warning them that the sky is about to fall in.

"You really need to get that dog some training, Lila," Bill murmurs.

"I know," she says, muttering, "I'll do it in the same free hours that I have pedicures, waxes, and meditate." She leaves the table when she can ignore the sound no longer and heads out to the garden, still basically a war zone of freshly dug earth and slabs of York stone from Jensen's earlier efforts. Truant is facing the door of the shed, his hackles up, and his teeth bared. *Oh, God*, she thinks. *It* is *rats.* Jensen had tried to tell her and she had just brushed him off. And now she is going to pay for it. She sees Violet's bright blue baseball bat in the grass, and picks it up, in case they're the kind that jump at your throat. She isn't sure that rats actually jump at throats, but it feels like the kind of thing a rat might do.

Truant's barking has grown ever more urgent now, and she tries to shush him, worried that if she opens the door he will be involved in some horrific animal-on-animal massacre. She pulls at his collar and, when that fails to stop him, walks a step closer to the door. She can hear Bill calling from the kitchen: "What's going on? Lila? What's he barking at?" And waves to him, as if to suggest everything's fine and he doesn't need to worry. She pushes the door open an inch with her foot and hears a loud clatter from inside. Her heart racing, she swings the door wide—and there is Gene, half collapsed into the outdoor sofa cushions on the floor, blinking as he registers Lila's presence.

"Gene?"

He is wearing a sweatshirt, a leather jacket and a pair of tired-looking underpants. He pushes himself upright. Unfortunately this change in position shifts the pile of outdoor sofa cushions and brings an empty paint tin clattering down from a shelf onto his shoulder.

"Ow. Hey . . . hey, sweetheart," he says, with a glassy smile, placing the tin carefully beside him.

"What on earth are you doing in here?"

He looks at her, as if considering this question carefully. Then appears to forget it. There is an empty crisps packet on his belly and he blinks at it, as if he's just noticed it, then attempts to empty the crumbs into his mouth. He misses.

"You know," he says, collapsing slowly backward into the cushions again, "the weed they sell in this country is way too strong. They should have a rule against it."

IF THE NEIGHBORS were disturbed by Truant's barking, that's nothing to the sight of a seventy-five-year-old man being led across the garden in his pants while singing "Go Tell It on the Mountain." The curtains at number forty-seven are twitching so furiously it's as if the entire house is having some kind of seizure. Lila finally manages to persuade him upstairs and into the study, where she remakes the sofa-bed she had stripped and folded up not two hours previously, and finally, with the promise of more potato chips, persuades him to take a nap. "Isn't it great that we're back together?" he says, his veiny old hands clasping hers like some kind of sandwich. "The old team together again." Lila assures him that it is indeed great and, yes, what a team, and now it's time for him definitely to take that nap, thank you very much.

Bill takes another bottle of wine round to the neighbors to apologize for the commotion and is gone for a dismayingly long time. While they wait for him to return, she and Celie sit in the front room and listen to Violet's disconcertingly good impression of Lila's father stumbling across a room and breaking off to sing emphatic and repeated lines of the song.

When she has calmed Bill, and assured him that, no, she had no idea and, yes, she will make sure Gene leaves when he's straightened out, she disappears up to her bedroom.

. . .

WAS GENE THE problem in the shed?

Jensen's response is swift. **Yeah. Sleeping like a baby. I did try to tell you.** There is a short pause, and then he types again. She watches the pulsing dots. **I think he's been there a couple of days.**

Lila stares at the message, then closes her eyes and lies down on the floor.

Chapter Ten

Penelope Stockbridge is wearing hairclips with little green and turquoise glass butterflies. They are the kind you might normally see on a small girl, but Penelope Stockbridge doesn't seem to follow the normal codes for sixty-plus dressing, and every time she brings a tuna-pasta bake—and this will be the thirteenth tuna-pasta bake she has brought this year—there is some slightly off-kilter element of her dress that Lila always finds oddly compelling. Two weeks ago it was floral wellingtons, once a mohair scarf in pink and purple that came down to her knees, and occasionally—to Violet's delight—she wears a small cross-body bag in the shape of a kitten's face.

"It's for Bill," she says, in her soft, precise voice, as she always does. "I wondered if he was eating properly. You know, without *Francesca* around." She always whispers Francesca's name, as if the mere sound of it might be too distressing.

"That's very kind of you, Penelope," Lila says, accepting the large white rectangular dish covered with a neat lid of foil. It is still warm at its base. "I'm sure he'll be thrilled. Shall I get him for you?"

"Oh, no. I wouldn't want to be any trouble," she says, then stands expectantly on the doorstep, her smile painfully hopeful.

Lila calls Bill, who has been hanging an alternative picture over the television where *Naked Francesca* was once situated. He walks down the hallway still clutching his hammer in his broad fist, and when she sees it, this apparent display of unfettered masculinity causes Penelope to go a little trembly. "Penelope," he says politely. "How lovely to see you."

Her head tilts to one side so that the butterflies catch the light. Lila picks up a faint spray of scent, something floral and sweet. "I just . . . It's nothing. Just thought I'd drop this round. In case you were hungry."

"That's terribly kind," he says. "I'm very honored. But, really, Lila looks after me very well here. I don't want to put you to any trouble." He smiles at Lila, as if she does anything domestic to take care of him at all.

"It's no bother. No bother at all. I see you're busy," she says, nodding at the hammer. "Making anything interesting?"

"Oh, this and that." Lila stands between them, wondering if she should exit. But Bill still finds casual conversation difficult, especially with neighbors bringing gifts, so she feels obliged to stay.

"And how are the pupils?" he says, when the silence grows too long.

Penelope Stockbridge is the local piano teacher. Lila had once tried to sign up Celie but the wails of daily protest had proven too much for her and she had given up the fight after six lessons.

"Oh, mostly thinking up reasons why they haven't done any practice. Sometimes I find their excuses rather entertaining. I had one last week who said she couldn't find time because her goldfish needed daily skin treatments. Can you imagine?"

"Skin treatments for goldfish," says Bill. "That's inventive."

Penelope's glance flickers between them and then to her feet, in the manner of someone who is permanently concerned about outstaying her welcome. She has a narrow, grave face with large, expressive eyes. She had been married once, she'd told Lila. He had died before they could have children. Leukemia. She still remembered the devastation of those early months of widowhood as if it were yesterday. She gives a brief, flickering smile. "Anyway. I don't want to hold you up. I just . . . you know. I hope it's useful. Do say if you'd rather I didn't."

"Of course not," says Bill, gently. "It's so very kind of you. And very gratifying to be thought of so generously."

That brings a pink flush to Penelope Stockbridge's ears.

"I'll drop the dish back when we've eaten," says Lila. "Thank you."

"No hurry for the dish," she says, waving a slender hand. "You can keep it till next time, if you like."

Next time. Sometimes Lila thinks of Penelope's hopeful expression at each doorstep drop, the tentative adoration implicit in these tuna-pasta bakes—which Bill doesn't really like—and her heart aches. Will this be her in twenty years? So desperate for contact, or affection, that she is reduced to leaving culinary gifts on near-strangers' doorsteps?

"Bye, then," Penelope says. She brings a finger to one of the hairclips, perhaps checking that it is still in place. Lila wonders suddenly whether these eccentricities are not just a woman who dresses as she likes but tiny bids for attention, and her heart aches even more.

"Lovely to see you," Bill says politely, and as soon as she heads back down the path, he turns and walks the pasta dish resignedly to the kitchen. He will feel obliged to serve it this evening. The girls will love it. It has saved them from fish and lentils for another day.

SHE IS WAITING for Gene when he emerges from the bathroom at eleven thirty. She has sat in her study, on the edge of the sofa-bed, whose rumpled sheets and crisps crumbs speak of a restless, post-weed-and-alcohol sleep, and he startles when he sees her. He is wearing a towel around his waist which is too small for the broad trunk of him, and she registers his tattooed, slightly sagging body, and the way he suddenly sucks in his stomach as if he cannot bear to be seen like that even by his daughter.

"So," she says.

He lets out a vague sigh, as if he is braced for a telling-off, and walks past her into the room. She sees him casting his eyes around for clean clothes and points wordlessly to the Grateful Dead T-shirt she has laundered, ironed, and hung on the back of the door.

"I've washed everything that was in your bag," she says. "The woodlice had got in. And there were a *lot* of crisps crumbs."

"Thanks," he mutters, and turns his back to her while he dresses.

"Look," he says, when he's finished. He sits down on the other side of the bed. "I—I know it was kinda stupid for me to crash in there, but like I said, I had some problems with the hotel and I can't find my credit card, so it just seemed like a good solution for a couple of days. It's just till I get paid by the production and you know how these things are. They always take forever to pay up—"

"What's the production?" she says.

"What?"

"The production. That you're starring in. I'd like to come and see it."

It is the swiftest of hesitations, but it tells her everything she needs to know. She places her hands on her knees and lets out a deep breath. "There is no production, is there, Gene?"

"Sure—sure there is—"

"Please don't. You've barely said a true thing since you arrived. I think the least you owe me is an explanation for what you're doing here."

Gene swallows. When he looks up, he attempts a smile. It falls slightly when he sees her expression. "It's not like there's no *actual production*. It's just—"

"Gene."

"Okay. Okay." He puts up his palms as if to stop her. "Things got a little tricky for me at home. Nadira threw me out—and I owed these guys some money and they started to get real pissy about it. I thought I'd be better off working over here for a while, you know, with the whole dual citizenship and everything, until it all cooled down, so I just needed—"

"How much money?"

"What?"

"How much money do you owe? And to whom?"

"It's not a big deal."

"How much?"

"About fifty K." He looks up at her. "But only dollars, not pounds. So it's not so bad."

"Fifty thousand dollars?"

"They're not great guys. They're from Florida. This crazy trip I went on to a casino back in May. I think they must have slipped a Mickey into my drink. And work-wise things have been kinda quiet. There's not been a lot of jobs around, and I had this part on a low-budget production but the director was kind of a dick and we fell out and the guy fired me. And because of that car wreck I had to pay up for this guy's hospital bills even though I swear there was nothing wrong with him, and I had forgotten to renew the car insurance, and even though it was just a stupid little ding, the guy was threatening to sue me and then Nadira needed money for her kid to go to school and—"

"Nadira. I haven't heard about this one. Don't tell me. Under thirty?"

"No!"

"Thirty-five."

He rocks his head from one side to the other. "Okay, so she was thirty-four. But she was an old soul! We were great together!"

Lila's head sinks into her hands. "What do you want, Gene?"

"Just somewhere to crash for a week. Maybe two weeks."

"I'm going to ask that question again."

"Okay. A month. Give me a month. That should land me some auditions, let me remind the casting guys over here what I'm made of, and then I can get another place and . . ."

Lila lets her head rest in her palms for some time, long enough for Gene to tail off. He adds, "I'll help with the kids. I won't be in your hair. I just need to cut a break."

She can feel his eyes on her. She lifts her head wearily. "You really think you can get work over here?"

"I know I can. I have a meeting with an agent on Friday. He says there are a lot of openings for a guy like me. And with my history on *Star Squadron Zero* . . ."

Every cell in her body is telling her to say no. Bill will be furious. It will not be a month. She is not sure he is telling the truth about his work opportunities. But he is a seventy-five-year-old man desperate enough to sleep in a shed. And he is her father. Dammit.

She takes a long, deep breath, and then lets it out. "You can stay for now," she says. "And we'll see how it works out."

"Really? Sweetheart, you are the greatest. You won't even know I'm here—"

She holds up a hand, cutting him off. "There is no drinking in my house, and no smoking weed. If I suspect you're doing either of those things, I will throw you out immediately, and I won't care where you end up, because I have two vulnerable daughters." It's at this point that she remembers she had to stop Violet merrily singing "Smack My Bitch Up" on the walk to school that morning, and squashes the thought. "You are to be immaculately behaved around them. And you are to be nice to Bill, who is still grieving."

"Hey, he's not the only one who—"

"Properly nice. They were happily married a long time and he is a good man. And you are to put the sofa back every day in here so I can still use my workspace, and you are to help around the house when you're not out looking for work. Those are my rules."

"I'll take 'em," he says, beaming, and goes to give her a big bear hug before she can sidestep. Lila accepts it stiffly. "Lila," he says, "you're a mensch."

I'm an idiot, she thinks, and heads downstairs with a heavy heart to tell Bill.

Chapter Eleven

Marriage, I've learned over fifteen years, is a never-ending series of constantly shifting compromises. Your partner is not always going to behave in the way you want. You probably don't behave in a way they want. The trick is to look at the big picture, and ask: how do we move this forward? To think in terms of "us." For as long as you see yourselves as a unit, you have the same goal: to be together, and to be happy together. That's essentially the most important thing. So does it really matter if you would rather be watching *Sleepless in Seattle* when he's watching the rugby? Does it matter that he wants to stack the dishwasher in a way that irritates you? Will it make a huge difference if one of his parents comes to stay for a week, and you have to bite your lip and accommodate someone when you don't really want to? It's easy to find yourself viewing these things as a slippery slope: if I give in now, will I end up giving in on everything? Provided you're in a relationship of mutual respect, the answer to that is no. The key, I've

found, to moving forward, is asking myself, during these moments: do I want to be right? Or do I want to be happy?

"You have got to be fucking kidding me," she says.

"I want to stay close to the girls. I want them to be able to walk to see
me after school, like they do now. And the only way we can afford a bigger house around here is with a bigger mortgage. Like I told you, the
lawyer said I'm currently paying more than I'm legally bound to."

"Big of you, Dan."

"So I'm sorry but that's what I have to do. Hopefully you'll get a new
book deal soon, which will make things easier for you. But in the meantime I also have to factor in that Marja is going to have to take time off
work once the baby arrives."

"Fine. Basically we'd better hope I can get more work because Marja
sure as hell doesn't want to."

"She's pregnant, Lila. Not sitting around on her arse. C'mon, you
know how hard it was when the girls were newborns."

"I worked, Dan! I carried on writing, in case you've forgotten. I carried on working when I was on two hours' sleep wearing a bra filled
with cabbage leaves. I maintained a freelance career so that I could do
both things. And now because your girlfriend doesn't want to work, I
am looking at a catastrophic drop in our income. That's more than you
said in the first place, and that was bad enough."

"I'm paying you what I can afford."

"We can't live if you reduce it by that much!"

"Well, then, you'll have to get a smaller house."

He says it. He actually says it. There is a short silence as they both absorb the fact that, yes, he went there.

Lila's voice, when it comes, is icy. "Right. Just so I'm clear. So you
want me and your daughters to sell their family home and buy a smaller
house, so that you can get a bigger house for your new family."

"Oh, come on! Don't twist my words—"

But she has already put the phone down.

LILA WRITES ANOTHER three thousand words that afternoon. They come remarkably easily.

IT IS FAIR to say that the first couple of weeks of Gene's stay are not an unqualified success.

He sleeps late and rises like a bear out of hibernation, crashing into furniture and leaving wet towels and coffee spills in his wake. He seems incapable of looking after himself, beyond basic hygiene, and that is variable. He lives off coffee and cigarettes, cookies and potato chips. She has explained the washing-machine to him three times and every time he says, "Yes, yes, sweetheart, got it," then boils his T-shirts into children's sizes, or somehow manages to miss the spin cycle completely. He assures her daily that he is looking for work but is easily distracted, an old jester in constant search of an audience, heading out to the garden to divert Jensen with tales of Old Hollywood, or eagerly awaiting the return of the girls, so that he can watch *Star Squadron Zero* with Violet snuggled under his arm. In the early evenings he is restless, heading out to the bottom of the garden to smoke cigarettes that Lila hopes are just tobacco or disappearing to the Crown and Duck on the corner of the high street where he soothes himself with a couple of beers. He returns, usually late, for dinner, now filled with a level of bonhomie and garrulousness that makes Bill's jaw, already taut with tension, look like it might be about to grind itself into dust.

Lila is irritated that he goes, irritated that somehow he has the money for beer when he has offered her nothing for food or lodging. But the relief of having him out of the house for a couple of hours is greater so she says nothing, other than explaining yet again that cans need to be recycled or asking him to fold up the bed so that she can get to her desk. She prays he gets himself sorted out soon.

Because even with the sofa-bed folded there is something about his presence in Lila's study—the scent of his aftershave and the scattered piles of clothes—that makes her feel deeply unsettled. It is like being revisited by a ghost from her past. She often works in one of the girls' rooms while they are out.

"How's Bill coping with him?" says Eleanor. It is raining heavily and they are sheltering in a copse, while Truant looks out resentfully.

"Um, not great." Lila thinks of Bill's mouth, pressed into an ever-present line of disapproval, the way he walks out of any room that Gene walks into. The way he will often address Lila as an intermediary, even if Gene is clearly within earshot. "Do you think he will be eating with us this evening? If his drinking schedule allows?"

"Bill had your mum to himself for more than thirty years. Why is he so pissed at Gene?"

"Neither of them can let it go. It's exhausting. Gene hates Bill because I think he always assumed he could pick up with Mum again, like he does with all his girlfriends. And Bill got in the way of that. Bill hates Gene for causing Mum so much pain in the first place, because I guess he actually did have to pick up the pieces. And Mum would have told him how awful Gene was again and again over the years. She really saw through him. So I guess he only sees Gene through that prism." Lila lifts her hood from her head and shakes off the excess water.

"Wow," says Eleanor. "It's going to be a long few weeks."

"Violet likes him. So that's . . . nice."

"He's probably teaching her how to roll a spliff. Hey, what happened with the hot architect? Any news?"

There has been frustratingly little news on the hot-architect front. Gabriel Mallory frequently employs a babysitter to collect his daughter, a young Mediterranean-looking girl in her late teens who seems to know Lennie well, from the way they immediately take each other's hands and head out, chatting. Sometimes it's a woman she assumes is his mother, brisk, gray-haired, formally dressed, with the capable, no-nonsense air of a senior nurse. On the couple of times he has been at school pickup he has said hi to Lila, but has arrived too close to turnout time to engage in any real conversation. Lila has started to feel a little foolish that she ever imagined a flicker of interest in her.

Daily pickup has become increasingly difficult anyway, with Marja's growing bump. There is only one topic of conversation among the mothers when someone is visibly pregnant, and from her position on the other side of the playground, Lila endures the daily touching of The Bump, hears the conversations about scans, and sees the handing over of outgrown baby clothes. Every time she notices, something in her feels dead and cold. For the last few days, she has asked Bill if he will take over the pickup and excused herself. Instead she holes up in whatever part of the house is least full of angry old men or emotionally volatile teenagers and writes and writes, slowly shaping the three chapters that will get her out of at least one of the many messes that now make up her life.

THE MESSAGE COMES at nine forty-five one evening, when Lila is lying in a bath, noise-canceling earphones in, trying to forget about dinner in which Bill and Gene argued over the fact that Bill had moved Gene's boxes from the hallway into the shed. According to Gene, there were priceless *Star Squadron Zero* costumes and other memorabilia in those boxes, and they shouldn't be left in some damp beetle-infested outhouse, for crying out loud. According to Bill, Gene's hands must apparently be drawn on: he couldn't see any other reason why the man couldn't just walk out to the garden, pick the damn things up himself and move them into his room.

According to Lila, this was all just frankly exhausting and she didn't understand why she had suddenly acquired two more children as well as the ones she already had. According to Celie, she was not a bloody child *actually* and the fact that she was constantly being treated like one was half the reason she hated being in this bloody house anyway. According to Violet, there was no Ben & Jerry's ice cream. But there was an empty carton and a spoon in Gene's bedroom. This might have been the first point at which Violet's warm feelings toward her new grandfather cooled a little.

> Hey—I hope you don't mind me taking
> your number from the school
> WhatsApp. Just hadn't seen you at
> school lately and hope you're doing okay.
> Gabriel

Lila stares at the message, then pushes herself upright in the bath, reading it again. She thinks for a moment, and then types: I'm okay, thanks. Usual chaos. Just had a lot of work on.

> It's a bit relentless this single-parent lark,
> isn't it? Nice to meet a fellow soldier in
> the trenches.

> Hah! I'm under constant artillery fire
> here. Hope you're doing better.

All the better for speaking to you, he responds, and Lila's hairline prickles with pleasure.

Well, likewise.

Hang on in there, comes the reply. Maybe see you tomorrow.

Lila writes two kisses in answer, then deletes them. For the rest of the evening, she wonders if she should have left them.

Chapter Twelve

Celie

C elie has been watching the back of Meena's head for forty-two minutes. It is tilted permanently to the left, her long brown hair just visible through the two sets of seats in front of her. She is apparently gazing at China's phone. Every few minutes they giggle conspiratorially and turn toward each other or explode into laughter. Every outburst makes Celie's stomach clench, filled with the knowledge that they are either laughing at some private joke or, worse, that she is that private joke. Sometimes Ella and Suraya will get out of their seats and come to see what they're laughing at, and join in with the laughter, until Mr. Hinchcliffe, his patience exhausted by a full-day school trip, yells at them to get back into their seats while the bus is moving. It has been the longest bus journey of Celie's life.

The chill had descended by degrees these last weeks, but since she stayed at home instead of coming to the park to smoke weed the night her grandpa arrived, the atmosphere has become positively arctic. There is no sign of life on what used to be their friendship WhatsApp group. The last comment was on March 3, a plaintive *Where are we meeting tho?* from Celie that was never answered.

The girls have formed an impenetrable group that neither acknowledges her presence nor that anything is even wrong. The others smile blandly at her, say hi, but their eyes are blank and cold. Celie has no idea what she has done, or why they are doing it. She wears the right clothes, listens to the right music. Two months ago, she had tried a couple of times to message Meena privately and ask if something was up, if everyone was still talking to her. The reply was a simple *All cool.* Now she doesn't dare, guessing that this, too, will be the subject of spiteful laughter. Celie has simply, in the eyes of the group she has been friends with for almost five years, ceased to exist.

She stares at her phone, pretending to look at something, but seeing nothing. Sometimes her eyes fill with tears but she is frightened that someone on the bus will see them so she blinks them back furiously, or surreptitiously wipes at them with her sleeve. She is the only person sitting alone on the bus. She has walked the whole way around the zoo alone, a few feet behind Meena and Ella and Suraya and the others, her collar zipped high over her mouth, not willing to be seen to be completely abandoned, yet conscious that her classmates will be able to see her shameful isolation. She wakes up feeling sick, and she goes to sleep feeling equally sick, knowing she has been cast out, and never sure what has caused the estrangement. A couple of times she has simply bunked school—it feels easier not to go—but since Mum found her smoking, the teachers have been more vigilant, so she has no choice but to turn up at each lesson, to sit alone at the back, afraid to answer any questions in case this makes her a swot, afraid to say nothing in case it is apparent that she has been shamed into silence.

"She is, though, isn't she?" Another burst of laughter from two seats ahead. She stares at her phone, scrolls blindly through Instagram, trying to focus on the words. She had eaten lunch alone at the zoo, in the loos for half of it to disguise the fact that she had nobody to sit with, until Miss Baker came to find her, asking her if there was a problem.

No, Miss. There's no problem.

What could she say, after all? The other girls aren't talking to me? Or they sort of are but it's different? What school is going to legislate for that? They've had the talks about online bullying at school, the warnings about how cruel, how horribly effective it is. But this isn't that, is it? Sometimes she wishes one of them would just hit her, so she would understand what this was, have something solid to push against.

She remembers Charlotte Gooding, a sweet, solid girl who used to be in their group until year seven: someone once noticed that Charlotte made an odd noise when she ate lunch, a kind of *mmm-mmm* that she didn't seem to hear herself. The noise was noted, and then it became the only thing everyone noticed about Charlotte. Every time she sat with them at lunch Celie remembered the silent glances passed between them like a baton, the barely suppressed mirth. The way that this one small noise meant that other terrible things were noticed about Charlotte: the way she always double-tied her shoelaces, the way she sometimes had sleep in her eyes (*didn't she even wash?*), the stupid color she painted her nails on Own Clothes Day. In the hothouse atmosphere of school, Charlotte's crimes against humanity were marked off, one by one, until there was no room for her at the lunch table. She was left hanging vainly on the outside of the group, so nobody who might have liked Charlotte actually said anything to her, terrified that they, too, might end up tarnished. Charlotte slowly became a ghost and eventually switched schools altogether. Celie remembers this and her toes curl with shame and fear. Because it's her turn now. There will have been some small thing, and nobody is going to tell her what it was. Her whole body radiates anxiety, every movement self-conscious, every mirror-check of her appearance a desperate scan to see what has marked her out. The only time she feels even a bit normal now is when she smokes weed, which relaxes her and makes her forget the truth of what is going on. But Mum makes constant excuses to come into her room and she has a pretty good idea she searches it for drugs when Celie is out so that isn't even an option just now.

There is no point in telling Mum what's going on. She'd just tell her to find other friends—*They can't be your real friends if they're being mean to you, lovey*—or get upset and ring up the other mums, telling them to get their daughters to be nice to Celie. Which was *really* going to help. Or, worse, she would blame herself and get even sadder about Dad and the divorce and the new baby and make it all about her.

There's no point in telling anyone. It just makes her sound like an idiot. There is no actual evidence of anything, after all. It's like battling fog. Just an absence, vague whispers, a never-ending sense that something is badly wrong. This is the wall she keeps butting up against. She is not the girl this happens to. So how can it be happening to her?

Celie realizes she has been staring at her phone for too long. She feels suddenly nauseous. She checks the time. There are still twenty-five minutes of the journey to go before the coach arrives back at school. She looks up, but everyone is on their phones or talking to each other. She is the only person beside an empty seat. A wave of nausea washes over her and she is filled with the clammy certainty that she is going to throw up. She never normally looks at her phone in a car: it always makes her ill. Her hairline prickles, and she feels sweat blooming across her skin. She screws her eyes shut, wishing desperately for the feeling to recede. *Please not here. Please not now.* The coach goes over a bump and she feels something foul and acidic rise into the back of her throat. *Oh, God, it's going to happen.* She opens her watering eyes and takes a moment to focus. In front of her is a printed paper bag. She stares at it, then looks up. It is being held out by Martin O'Malley, the pale, red-headed boy who got picked on in year five. She meets his eyes, which contain a kind of sympathetic shrug, a knowledge that he knows where she is and she has to get on with it. Another wave hits, this time unstoppable. It is all unstoppable.

She snatches the bag from him and vomits.

CELIE IS LYING on her bed when her grandfather enters. He doesn't knock. He never knocks before he walks into any room. He just booms her name—he is STILL calling her Celia—as if in warning, then walks right in, that big stupid grin on his face. Mum has probably sent him to check up on her.

"Hey, sweetheart! How you doing?"

"Fine."

She is not fine. She actually wants to die. Martin had shielded her from the group by turning in his seat to block everyone's view of her as best as he could, but you cannot hide the smell of vomit, and within a few minutes, even though he had folded over the top of the bag and handed her a packet of Handy Andies, a murmur had begun to spread through the coach—a whispered *Has someone vommed? Oh, my God, can you smell that? OH, MY GOD.* Kevin Fisher had made loud gagging noises, shouting at Mr. Hinchcliffe that the smell was going to make him puke, and the girls had started shrieking and hyperventilating and even though nobody said anything to her, she knows the story of how she puked and stank the bus out was going to be all over school by tomorrow morning. She had waited until everyone had got off before she disembarked, hunched, tearful and wishing she could just disappear. Martin had put the sick bag under his jacket and chucked it quietly in the public bin. She was grateful, but you know, it was *Martin.* He is so uncool that a bit of her is fearful that just having him sitting next to her has lowered her standing even further.

"I just wondered if you wanted to take a stroll with your old pal Gene." He never calls himself Grandpa. It's like he thinks wearing one of his faded old rocker T-shirts every day shields the fact that he is basically decrepit. "Maybe show me round the neighborhood. All the streets look the same to me. All those brownstones."

"No, thanks."

He doesn't leave. He just sits on the side of her bed, without being asked, and gazes around her room at her posters and photographs. She still has the pinboard of her and all the girls up beside her bed, even though looking at it makes her want to cry. It's like if she takes it down it will be admitting that she no longer has any friends.

"Cute room." He turns to her, as if that requires some kind of answer. She shrugs. "When I was your age . . ."

Why did all old people begin half their sentences with *when I was your age*? ". . . dinosaurs ate your room?"

He blinks, then laughs. "Pretty much. I guess I am a dinosaur to you kids. I was going to say that when I was your age my room was covered with pictures of my favorite actors. Marlon Brando, Jimmy Dean, Steve McQueen—all the rebels. I guess it's kinda nice to have your friends instead."

"They're not my friends." It's out before she can stop it.

He glances at her, then up at the picture. "They look pretty friendly."

"Well, they're not. Not anymore."

"You guys have a falling-out?"

"Oh, my God, why do you have to ask so many questions? You're just staying here because you haven't got anywhere else to go. You don't have to pretend to care. It's so obvious you're not interested in any of us anyway."

She is shocked by the savagery of her words. But he doesn't seem troubled at all. When she looks up he is still gazing at the pictures.

"Yeah," he says. "I guess I haven't really stepped up in that department. But, hey, never too late, right?"

"Maybe you should talk to Mum about that."

"Well, I'm talking to you."

"Maybe I don't want to talk to you."

"Prickly little pear, ain't you?" She glares at him but he seems amused. "That's okay, kid. I guess I wouldn't have wanted some old guy interrogating me about life at your age either. Hey, you want to grab a Coke? Old Bill downstairs seems to have just herbal tea and water, and I need me some sugar!"

She almost laughs then, the thought of him calling Bill "old," as if he himself was some kind of juvenile.

"C'mon, sweetheart. I could do with some live company. This old house is way too quiet and gloomy to spend all our time hanging around here." He adjusts his neck in his T-shirt. "And, besides, I need to load up on potato chips before we have to eat another darn salad."

Maybe it's because the thought of staying another evening in her room with the picture of how her life used to be is just too much right now. Maybe it's because he's the one person who hasn't tried to offer a bloody solution. Or maybe it's because, actually, she really does fancy a Coke. Celie slides off the bed—not smiling, she's not ready for that—and follows the old man out of her room and downstairs.

LOOKING BACK, CELIE sees that evening as a blur of images: the tube journey to Soho, the way Gene (she cannot yet bring herself to call him Grandpa) talked to people in the carriage like they were all his friends, the way an old woman stared at him and then said: "Excuse me, are you that man from *Star Squadron Zero*?"

And the way Gene immediately seemed to grow six inches, shooting back at her: "Captain Strang, reporting for intergalactic duty, ma'am!" with this cheesy salute, and the woman went bright pink, grabbed on to his arm and got her daughter to take pictures of them together. She didn't even care that everyone on the tube was looking at them.

And Soho, where she had been once years ago when she was a kid, a warren of grubby streets packed with early-evening drinkers, spilling out of pubs and clogging up the pavements so that Celie had to keep walking in the road, and Gene pulling her into this coffee house or that pub and going on about how it used to be around here and who he hung out with, actors' names she'd never heard of. And how he stood in front of the gay sex shop, with all the harnesses and studs, frowned, tilted his head sideways, and said: "You know, you'd think with your climate the way it is they'd build a sweater or something into that leather gear, huh?" And then dared her to go in with him.

"*Oh, my God! Why?*" she had said, crimson with embarrassment and laughter, this old man peering in through the smoked-glass door.

He had shrugged. "Why not? You got to be curious, right? Or what's the point in being here?" So she had taken his arm and walked in, and tried not to laugh at the bored, muscular guy with the Freddie Mercury mustache behind the counter who obviously knew as soon as they walked in that they were not real customers. He looked at them through half-lowered lids, and muttered, "Do you need any help?" with a deep sigh running underneath every single word.

And Gene had said, in his most drawly American accent: "I don't know, pal. Do you have anything that is a little more flattering for the mature guy?"

And the man with the mustache said: "What did you have in mind?"

And Gene had looked at her and said: "I don't know. I'll ask my granddaughter. What do you think would suit me, sweetheart?"

And she had actually thought she might wet herself, because he kept his face completely straight, and put his finger to his mouth like he was actually thinking about it, so she said, "I—I'm not sure. I guess we should ask Mum. She's better at that kind of thing."

And then they walked out into the autumn sunlight and she couldn't stop laughing and Gene was grinning at her like it was the best fun ever. And they had eaten *pastel de nata* with a revoltingly strong coffee at a tiny coffee shop that made her heart race, then walked through Chinatown and stopped outside a tattoo parlor where Gene told her he had got his third tattoo, which he insisted on showing her, under his T-shirt, which he said had been for Grandma, whom he used to call *Francie*, but the guy misheard and wrote *Fancy* instead. It was all blurred and dark blue on the pale upper arm skin under his sleeve and decidedly un-fancy. "I might have had a drink," Gene muttered, frowning at it, and then said, "Ah, well, it's all life, right?"

And they had eaten noodles from a Vietnamese place that had a serving hatch built into the wall, and Gene had shown her all the theaters he had worked in, and told her which stars had been assholes and which ones he had fallen in love with. "Never date an actor, sweetheart," he said. "We fall in love way too easy." He still had a piece of noodle on the side of his mouth. And then the tube home, where two people recognized him and Gene posed for pictures again, like some kind of celebrity, and then they had walked up to the house and Gene had put his fingers to his lips like *Don't tell* but she noticed that it was a quarter past eight and they had missed supper and Mum was freaking out and had yelled, "Where on earth have you both been? Celie, why didn't you answer your phone? I was about to call the police!" And Celie realized she hadn't even thought to look at her phone. Not once. And Gene had his palms up and was telling everyone to chill out, which is exactly the thing you say to people to make them go completely nuts. And Truant was growling and there was this bowl of cold lentils on the table and Celie was suddenly really, really happy about the noodles. And it was at that point that Mum had seen the tattoo running up the inside of Celie's arm.

"Please don't tell me . . ." she began, then tailed off. It was as if all the color had leached from her face. "Oh, no."

"I don't believe it. Of all the irresponsible things . . ." Bill began.

"Blame me," Gene had said, his voice all soft and calm, and Violet's eyes, staring at Celie's arm, had grown as wide as saucers.

"But she's not even eighteen!" Mum was yelling, her hands clutching her hair. "What the hell were you thinking taking my daughter to get a tattoo?"

"Did it hurt?" Violet is at her shoulder, tracing the marks with her finger.

"Come upstairs and I'll tell you," Celie says. And they had run off in their socks, leaving Gene with all the shouting and commotion below them. It is there, locked into Celie's bedroom, that she tells her little sister what she and Gene had agreed not to say downstairs. It is not a real tattoo: it is washable ink, drawn by the tattoo artist as a gift after he remembered Gene from thirty years previously. They had decided it would be funnier not to say. Violet squeals with happiness and turns two somersaults on Celie's bed. "I want one!" she yells, her feet drumming on the wall. "I want one!"

It is, Celie realizes, as the noises from downstairs finally settle into grumpy recriminations as Gene obviously tells the truth, and her sister disappears to her bedroom to no doubt draw all over herself in biro, the first time Celie has laughed in weeks.

Chapter Thirteen

Lila

From: AnoushkaMellors@amagency.co.uk

To: LilaKennedy@LilaKennedy.com

So how is it going darling? Regent House called again this morning, desperate for three chapters and a synopsis.

ML
Anoushka xx

From: LilaKennedy@LilaKennedy.com

To: AnoushkaMellors@amagency.co.uk

Great! Almost ready to send.

Lila x

Lila has finished the three chapters. They are the most honest, brave, and, in her opinion, best chapters she has ever written. She has poured her very guts into them—the shock, the hurt, the anger, the sense of shame and vulnerability she has carried since *The Rebuild*'s paperback publication, challenging herself at every turn to write more honestly, to peel back layer upon painful layer, to expose it all, even if it means her own public humiliation. It is brutal, possibly (she thinks in her more satisfied moments) even a little heartrending. It is the bald truth of what it is to be left for someone else, to watch the man you love build a new family without you but in full sight. Her daughters are disguised to the wider public, as before (she calls them simply Child A and Child B), but she has been nakedly honest about herself and Dan. Given his name was in several online gossip columns along with their story (she wishes the literary pages had been as interesting) she cannot see any point in suddenly trying to hide his identity. She has described Marja simply as the Mistress. Why not? It's what she is. That was her choice.

And, besides, what does she owe them? This is her chance to claw back her narrative, to speak for all the women who have been left, who are trying to keep their remaining family afloat amid a series of cata-strophic decisions and choices that were very much not theirs.

She has read her words again and again, editing, refining, printing them out and trying to read them as if she were someone else, looking carefully for too much self-pity, or anything that makes her sound bitter, anything that will enable people to write her off. *Other women will get this*, she thinks, as she finally puts the three chapters into an email and, with a shiver of trepidation, presses send. *Other women will understand and identify. They are who I am doing this for.* She tells herself this so often she almost believes it.

Adding to Lila's sense of giddy anticipation is that Gabriel Mallory has texted her multiple times in the past week. Sometimes they are just questions about school ephemera, other times more personal. Every time her phone pings she gets a little shot of adrenaline, a second when she sees his name appear.

> Lovely to see you today, and looking so incantevole.

According to Google, it means "lovely."

It had taken Lila two hours to get ready for the school run that day.

> Hey—Lennie wants to know if Violet would like to come over some time. Apparently they dug up some worms together at lunch break. Sounds like a solid basis for friendship.

(Violet had been annoyingly reluctant when she asked. "What? Why? But she's in the year below me!" and "Mum, it wasn't even a live worm!") Lila has bribed her with ten pounds to say yes. It will probably cost her another ten to ensure she doesn't just stomp off to another room and stare at the television if and when they actually go.

And best of all: Sorry you had a bad day. Your ex is clearly an idiot, if that isn't overstepping a line.

Dan had arrived unexpectedly for the school pickup with Marja, his hand resting proprietorially on the small of her back, his expression loving and concerned. They were back from a hospital appointment, according to the snatches of conversation that floated above the playground. It was an unseasonably warm autumnal day and Marja had been wearing a soft black jersey dress that showed off her full breasts and rounded belly. She is one of those women who seem to have an inexplicable all-year-round light golden tan and the dress had slipped off one shoulder to reveal smooth, sculpted skin. He had nodded awkwardly at Lila as she hurried, head down, to where Gabriel was standing.

"That him, huh?" Gabriel had said, watching, and Lila had been so overcome with rage, sadness, and humiliation at the sight of them that she had been unable to reply. She and Gabriel had stood beside each other in silence for the seven interminable minutes it took for the children to come out. He had touched her elbow in solidarity as he left.

It's not. And thank you x, she had replied. And felt suddenly a lot better.

Sometimes she thinks about asking him on a date. An actual date. Eleanor says it sounds like he's interested, so why not? "For God's sake, Lila, if there's one advantage to getting to this age it's being able to say the thing you're thinking. You like him, he clearly likes you, so just ask. What's the worst that could happen? C'mon—you're a big girl."

He could say no. He could look embarrassed and shocked, as if he had just been kind, and explain that, thanks, he was flattered, but a forty-something single mum with two cranky daughters wasn't really part of his game plan. She could make the school run even more excruciatingly uncomfortable for herself than it already is. At the moment she can look forward with a flicker of excitement to one minuscule part of her day, to dream in the bath about his floppy chestnut hair, the wounded expression in his eyes that she is sure she could change, those long, sensitive artist's hands. She can close her eyes and play out a million scenarios in which she and Gabriel Mallory end up together, him propelling her gently across the playground, his arm slung lightly around her shoulder as Philippa and Marja and all those other mean mothers look on. Possibly while he talks to her softly in Italian. No, she thinks, better to keep a little prospect of something lovely for herself than to test it and lose it altogether. So she says nothing.

"I THOUGHT I might bring my old Steinway," says Bill, who is helping her take out the rubbish.

"What?" says Lila, hauling the reeking black bin bag into the wheelie bin. She is still haunted by the sight of Marja in her fecund state, Dan's hand resting on her back. Bill has the recycling box, and has washed and dried all the items before tipping them in. "The actual piano?"

"I miss playing. It's very . . . comforting."

She stops and wipes her face with the back of her sleeve. She really wants to say, *Couldn't you just play it at your house?* But Bill asks for so little and gives so much, and tolerates Gene's presence with, if not grace, at least a sort of grim stoicism. "But where would it go?"

Bill has clearly thought about this for some time. "I thought I could move that bench in the hallway and put it there. That way it wouldn't be in your way in the living room. You could just shut the door if I played."

Lila's heart sinks. Two years ago she had wept when Dan removed his meager selection of clothes, books, and technology from the house. Even though he had barely taken any furniture, the gap where a photograph had been, or the empty sections in the bookshelves—even the absence in the garage of the four-thousand-pound carbon-framed bicycle she had always resented—had made her feel it was all impossibly empty. Now, perversely, this house feels as if it's filling up with people, with their stuff. There is no place in it that is not cluttered with either one or the other. And—she realizes with a stab of discomfort that she feels awful admitting to—this means Bill is here for good. Nobody moves a piano if they're not planning to stay forever. She is now going to be living with a slightly depressed old man for the rest of his life.

"That's fine, Bill," she says, and hopes her smile stretches as far as her eyes.

OVER THE NEXT couple of days, Lila's good mood is punctured again and again, like a series of soap bubbles popped on the spikes of a holly bush. The piano arrives, wheeled up the road on two dollies by Bill,

Jensen, and two Polish friends, who smoke roll-ups and shake their heads mournfully when they see the steps up to the hallway. The piano is in place after forty minutes of sweating and cursing, and when the dollies are removed it lands in the hall with a dissonant chord and a horrible air of finality.

That afternoon Jensen hits a concrete layer while trying to build the new vegetable beds, and from four thirty the air is filled with the sound of his pneumatic drill as he attempts to break it up. This prompts two angry calls from the neighbors and the swift delivery of the last of Lila's emergency-gift bottles of wine.

Celie arrives home from school in a filthy mood and sweeps through the house without talking to anyone, her face like thunder and shrouded by a cloud of hair, then slams her bedroom door and refuses to come out. Bill sits down to watch the six o'clock news in the front room, as is his preferred habit, but Violet and Gene have congregated in there, away from the noise in the garden, and keep interrupting him with their YouTube videos of *Star Squadron Zero*, Gene providing a running commentary of what it was like to play that part, the high jinks the crew got up to, the guest director who was—inevitably—a dick. At twenty past six Bill, apparently tired of competing with the iPad, retreats to the hall where he sets up a rousing rendition of "Strangers in the Night," the notes filling the whole house because of the tiled floor and lack of soft surfaces. This leads Gene to turn up the sound of the iPad even further.

It is against this backdrop of piano, ancient sci-fi, and pneumatic drill that Anoushka calls. Lila stands in the kitchen with her hand against her free ear, trying to make out what she says.

". . . love it but saying it's not quite as discussed . . ."

"What?" says Lila, as Truant, maddened by the noise levels, decides to add to it with a manic, staccato bark.

". . . sex! . . . want more adventures . . ."

"What? Sorry, Anoushka, I'm having trouble hearing you."

"... sexytimes ... example ..."

"Sexytimes?"

"You ... extra chapter ... just so they get full ..."

"Jeez, pal," comes Gene's booming voice, as Bill's piano reaches a crescendo. "We're trying to watch TV in here!"

"And *I'm* trying to play the piano!"

"Oh, is that what they're calling it now? I thought Truant was murdering a cat."

"Will someone in this bloody house just bloody shut up for one minute so I can take a bloody work call?" Lila bellows.

"I'm not even doing anything!" comes Celie's outraged muffled voice from upstairs.

"I know, darling. Sorry, Anoushka, can you repeat that?"

There is a brief silence, before Jensen, who is wearing ear protectors, starts up again. Lila watches him as his whole body vibrates along with the drill, his jaw set with the effort.

"They want to see a sexytimes chapter. There's none of the fun, all of the gloom at the moment. They just want an example of the naughty escapades you've been having. Have you started work on any of that bit?"

"Sure!"

"So when can you get it to me?"

Lila stares through the window at Jensen. "End of next week?" she says, without a clue as to why she says this.

"Marvelous. They love the rest of it by the way, but they say they just want to make sure it's not too one note. We also want uplifting and naughty! Like a kind of literary push-you-up bra!"

"Push-you-up bra," Lila repeats.

"Wonderful! *So* exciting. Can't wait to read! Adieu, darling!"

It is all of seven seconds before the noise begins again. The iPad starts, the fuzzy electronic theme tune of *Star Squadron Zero* filling the living room, followed by Bill's determined piano in the hall, now using pedals for extra emphasis. From upstairs Celie decides to add to this with a particularly gloomy Phoebe Bridgers song. Lila can just make out the words: "I'm not afraid to disappear" and "The billboard said the end is near" before Truant starts barking again. Her head hurts.

Jensen stops the pneumatic drill. Lila opens the kitchen door and steps outside.

She texts Gabriel while standing on the patio. She does it quickly, before she can think about it: **Do you fancy going for a drink some time?**

I am a mature woman capable of asking for what she wants, she tells herself, as she presses send, adrenaline shooting through her body. *It's just a drink, not a big deal whatsoever.* She lets out a short hiccup of anticipation, and waits, glancing at the screen. She peers up at the sky, then back at the phone, looking for the pulsing dots that tell her he has read the message, but nothing comes. She stands for a minute, two minutes, three, now unable to tear her eyes from her phone. Finally, a sinking feeling descending in her stomach, she shoves her phone into her pocket and walks to the end of the garden to sit on the bench.

"BILL SAYS YOUR ex really is having a baby. I'd thought you might be joking." Jensen has been putting his tools away. He sits heavily at the far end and takes a swig from a bottle of water, wiping his forehead with the back of his arm.

"Nope. Not joking. The level of public humiliation wasn't quite enough, apparently." She smiles breezily. *Why did I send that message? Why? What was I thinking?*

She wonders if she can just use Eleanor's experiences and not tell her. Eleanor will read the book eventually but maybe she can disguise them. It will be at least a year before Eleanor can see anything. She takes her phone out of her pocket and puts it face down beside her, feeling faintly nauseous.

"You okay?"

She stares at him. Nobody ever asks her that question. Nobody ever just says, *Are you okay?* Not Bill, not Gene, not her children, not even Eleanor. Everyone tells her what she should be doing, or that it's going to be all right, or that she needs to be less miserable, less moody, less angry, but nobody ever asks her that simple question.

"No," she says. "Mostly not, actually."

"You know, when I was having a breakdown . . ." he begins.

It takes her a moment to register what she has just heard.

"Yup. Five years ago."

"Oh, God," she says, her hand to her mouth. "I'm so sorry."

"I'm not. I mean, it wasn't exactly a fun day out. But it showed me how out of whack my life had got. Now I'm at the other side, I try to view it as useful." He studies his scuffed workmen's boots. "Anyway. So when I was having my breakdown a guy I used to work with sent me a quote from Rilke: 'Keep going. No feeling is final.' Something along those lines. And I always think of that, when things are a bit rough. No feeling is final. The shitty times don't last forever. Even if they feel like it."

She smiles wryly. "Boy, do they." She can feel his eyes on her.

"Tricky day?"

"Yup. And the really annoying thing is I didn't think it was going to be."

"Those are the worst."

They sit in silence for a while. Her garden, she thinks, resembles the Somme. What was once a vaguely pleasing wilderness of overgrown plants and uncut lawn is now a mess of trenches, piles of earth, and concrete.

"You look like you could do with a drink."

She pulls her attention back to him. "Yeah . . . Not really one of my vices."

He raises one eyebrow.

"Oh, no, I'm not AA or anything like that. It's just . . . my dad drank. Drinks. And Mum hated it for that reason. And he kind of messed up his life." From the house, they can hear Bill's determined piano. "And is still messing it up, apparently. So I guess I've just never seen the appeal."

"You've never been drunk?"

"A couple of times. But I don't . . . I don't really like feeling . . . you know, out of control." *And if I started drinking while I feel like this*, she says silently, *I think I'd never stop.*

"Fair enough. Tough never to get a holiday from your head, though."

"I smoke. To get to sleep. Sometimes," she says, in case she sounds too prim. "But I can't anymore because I caught my daughter doing it. Apparently I need to be a good example."

"That's a terrifying thought." He laughs.

She asks him if he has children and he says no.

"Did your wife not want them? Actually, forget I asked. That's horribly intrusive. The kind of thing you're not meant to say. Sorry."

"My wife?"

She glances at his finger. The wedding ring is gone. "I—I thought you wore a wedding ring."

He turns over his hand, as if looking for clues. "Oh! No. That's my dad's old ring. It's a little loose on my right hand so when I'm gardening I wedge it onto the left so I don't lose it."

"Ah."

The discovery that he is single, and that she has noted it, seems briefly to silence them. Lila sits on the bench that Bill made for her mother and runs her hand gently over the arm, feeling the carefully sanded wood, all the hours of work, the love that went into this piece of furniture. She cannot imagine anyone making a bench for her, and shakes her head, trying to get rid of the thought.

"I'd better go in," she says, trying to make herself sound brighter than she feels. "Back to work."

"I'll stop the drilling for now. We're nearly there anyway," he says.

As she picks her way back across the rubble-strewn garden he calls: "You know, it's going to be a nice thing."

She turns to face him, shielding her eyes against the sun.

"The garden. It's going to be a nice thing." When she doesn't say anything he grins and adds: "Sometimes things just turn out . . . nice."

I ASKED HIM out. And he hasn't replied.

Eleanor's response comes within seconds: How long ago did you send it?

Two hours.

That's nothing. Could be in a meeting.

Not if you like someone. You message straight back if you like someone.

Lila, you haven't dated in almost twenty years. This is not how the world works now.

Also I have to write about having had loads of wild sexytimes for my new book. Can I borrow your experiences and pretend I'm you?

Only on one condition.

What's that?

YOU get laid first.

I'm trying! I literally just told you I asked
Hot Architect out for a drink. So can I?

Good luck! Let me know how you
get on Xx

Eleanor can be *really* annoying sometimes.

El, I need to get this chapter written asap.
I'm hardly going to be able to start a
whole relationship by then, am I?

What century are you living in??? Who
said anything about a relationship?

ANOUSHKA HAS SENT a follow-up email, including bits of the original from Regent House.

We absolutely love this project and are passionate
about Lila's writing, but we all felt it was a little too
downbeat in the early chapters. There is a lot of hurt and
betrayal and it is a little gloomier than we had expected.
We would love for the book to open with, say, one of her
crazier escapades, just so the reader knows that this is
going to be a story of redemption, a sexy phoenix rising
from the ashes, before we go into how she got there.
Plus we are all desperate to hear how fun life can

be on the other side of divorce—and we know a
multitude of female readers will be too! We are very
much looking forward to reading—the wilder the
better!

Lila glances away from her screen and down at her phone. It is now
two hours and forty-six minutes since she sent the text and Gabriel Mallory has not responded. Perhaps he is even now wincing as he tries to
work out how to let her down gently. She has had no intimate contact in
almost three years beyond a routine smear test. She is suddenly overwhelmed by a feeling that this book idea is going to fail, that she has
promised something she has no possible chance of delivering. She is
going to have to tell Anoushka the truth. What on earth had she been
thinking?

No. She ponders Eleanor's words.

There is another way.

Chapter Fourteen

For all that having a piano in your front hall is a little irritating, Lila has to admit that the sound of two people playing "Someone to Watch Over Me" as a duet has a definite charm. She has been paused at her desk for twenty minutes now, just listening to the sound of the keys, Penelope Stockbridge's slightly breathless laughter—the way she apologizes every time she laughs, as if that much naked emotion is something to be embarrassed about. She can't hear Bill's response, but his tone is cheerful and reassuring. Lila had never even considered Bill having a relationship with another woman after her mother, but she observes distantly that if it turned out to be Penelope Stockbridge she probably wouldn't mind.

"Oh, I messed up the left hand. I'm so sorry."

"Please don't worry. Let's go again from bar twelve."

All sound echoes up the central staircase of this house. You can hear conversations from the top floor as the words float upward, so when the front door opens, even if Gene wasn't bellowing, *Hey, I'm back!* she would have known immediately it was him. He seems to make twice as much noise as a normal human being, his footsteps heavier, the door slam more emphatic. It is as if he is determined to imprint himself on any environment in which he finds himself. Her heart always sinks when he arrives back. *Hey! The piano! Shall I sing along? I once met Ella Fitzgerald, you know. Down in a little bar in Los Feliz . . .*

Gene insists he is going to auditions, but she suspects he is just sitting in the pub, as she never hears him rehearsing anything. When she asks him how the auditions are going he says his agent is sure something will come up soon, and invariably changes the subject.

And something about Gene being in the house always makes it impossible to work. It is as if his presence means she is permanently braced for some kind of explosion, or the sound of something breaking, or even Truant's incessant protest. She stares at her screen for fifteen minutes, then gets out of her chair with a sigh of resignation.

She is on the first-floor landing heading downstairs to make another mug of tea when the music stops abruptly. She hears Bill's voice. "Are those my socks?"

Gene's voice, innocent and surprised: "Uh . . . I dunno. Are they?"

"You're wearing my socks!"

"Oh. I guess they got mixed up in the laundry."

"You know they aren't yours. You wear those awful cheap white sports ones, and they all have holes. Those are my Falke one-hundred-percent wool ones."

"Okay, pal, keep your hair on."

Lila arrives in the hallway and pauses on the last step. Penelope is sitting on a chair beside Bill, her hand on the piano music—she must have been in the middle of turning a page. Gene is standing in a leather jacket and jeans, his shoulders back and his legs slightly apart, a stance he only ever seems to use with Bill. Bill gets up, pushing the piano stool back on the tiled floor so that the wheels squeak.

"This really is too much. You cannot just help yourself to a man's socks!"

Gene ignores him and switches his attention to Penelope. He bows theatrically, and holds out a huge hand. Penelope, unsure what to do, gives him her tiny slim one.

"Gene Kennedy, as Old Bill here is apparently too rude to introduce us. Delighted to meet you."

Penelope, as all women do faced with the full force of Gene's charm, blinks hard and smiles back, fluttering a little. Gene takes slightly too long to release her fingers and a slow pink flush stains her collarbone. "Penelope Stockbridge," she says.

"I'm Lila's father."

This news obviously throws her a little, and she lets out a little "Oh!" of surprise. It certainly throws Bill, who sits down heavily on the piano stool and says crossly, "Do you mind? We're in the middle of a piano lesson."

"You're the one who stopped it, pal. I'm just trying to be polite. Hey, Penelope, do you ever watch television? You may know me from—"

"Just stop helping yourself to my socks! And if you have any others hidden in that hovel you call a room, I'd be grateful if you'd bring them downstairs."

"They're just socks, Bill. Jeez. I've never heard anyone get their panties in a bunch about a pair of socks before. Here, I'll trade you one of my Grateful Dead T-shirts if it bothers you that much. Don't you think a T-shirt would loosen him up a little, Penelope? Lovely to meet you by the way. That's a very pretty dress. I sure hope you come by again soon."

Penelope flushes even more deeply, her fingers now unconsciously stroking the base of her throat. Bill sits very still on the piano stool, a tiny vein pulsing in his temple. Gene, having clearly decided he has won this particular battle, waits a moment, beaming, then saunters down to the kitchen. "Oh, hey, Lila! Had a good day, sweetheart?"

Every interaction between her two fathers, Lila has noticed, has lately morphed into a battle situation with a winner and a loser. Gene is the usual victor, a master manipulator at skewing any exchange to his advantage, his weapons natural charm and a visceral awareness of anyone's weakness. She is not even sure he knows he's doing it. Bill, who struggles with communication at the best of times, is often reduced to spluttering fury although he's usually in the right. But she has only limited sympathy because it's like living with two particularly recalcitrant toddlers. And if she challenges them, they will inevitably deny that there is a problem.

I didn't do anything. If Bill has an issue it's nothing to do with me.

Lila, I leave that man (Bill rarely calls him Gene) *to do as he wishes. I'm just trying to mind my own business.*

Both behave fractionally better in the presence of the girls: it is as if they're in unspoken competition for their affections, and therefore aware that they shouldn't be in open conflict in front of them. Gene has clearly won over Violet with their nightly *Star Squadron Zero* episodes, and has made some headway with Celie since the evening in Soho. But Celie is old enough to understand what Bill has been to them, and inoculated with sixteen years of love from Bill and her grandmother, so is likely to be found sitting with him in what remains of the garden, or playing with the dog near him (she doesn't talk much) while he chops vegetables for supper.

One unexpected outcome of her two house guests is that Celie tends to come down for supper most evenings instead of claiming she is not hungry and is staying in her room. It is as if their constant bickering is a form of distraction for her, taking her away from her thoughts—or perhaps it simply takes attention away from Celie: instead of relentlessly asking Celie what on earth is wrong, or trying to make sure she eats something, Lila is usually engaged in diplomatic discussions over whether chips can be counted as a vegetable, or whether Bill's bust of

Virginia Woolf makes her look like she just had her arse squeezed behind Walmart.

"You really do play awfully well," Penelope murmurs to Bill, leaning back in her chair so she can look at him as she speaks. "Your finger positioning is excellent."

This seems to restore Bill's good humor. "You're very kind," he says, his smile unexpected and sweet. "I have to say I'm rather enjoying the discipline of practicing every day."

"I wish all my pupils were like you," she says, and blushes again.

Lila watches them until they notice she's there, then mutters something about tea and disappears into the kitchen. *Everyone*, she thinks, *absolutely everyone is moving on apart from me.*

And then, *Something has to give.*

Chapter Fifteen

He was dark-haired, with a slight Spanish accent, and when I walked into the bar, I saw him sitting at the table and was so nervous I nearly turned and walked out again. And then I heard my best friend's voice in my ear. Come on, Lila, I told myself. You have to get out there again. Just treat it as an experiment.

Easy to say, but when you're forty-two and have been in a monogamous relationship (at least on your side) for most of your adult life this is easier said than done. I had spent two hours getting ready, shaving legs that were positively Yeti-like, blow-drying my hair, and carefully applying makeup. I tried on and discarded seven different outfits, afraid that I looked too prim, too brassy, like I was trying too hard, or wasn't trying hard enough. It was actual decades since I had been on a date. But it wasn't what was going on on the outside that was the real challenge, it was my internal self: frightened of being judged by a strange man and found wanting, after my confidence had taken such a bashing; anxious that the date would go badly, and the conversation would dry up. I was basically terrified he would make a pass at me, and equally terrified that he wouldn't.

Juan had been fun on the chats we had had online through the dating app. He was a lawyer. He had been divorced—amicably—for six years. He had had two relationships in that period, one serious, one not. He described himself as someone looking for "fun and companionship" and joked that this was his first time on an app and that he had put down the blandest thing possible because he genuinely didn't know what to write.

"Lila," he said, standing to greet me. His smile was so warm and his accent was so delicious that it made something in me give way. This, I told myself, was going to be okay.

We talked for two hours. I don't usually drink, but had a glass of wine to steady my nerves. And then another because I was actually enjoying myself. And maybe it was because I hadn't eaten, or perhaps it was his charm and his good conversation, but when he suggested we continue the evening at his place, I thought, *Why not?* He seemed like a nice person—he had shown me photographs on his phone of his children, his dog, his parents—he had given me his business card. He felt like someone I already knew. And as we left the bar, and he gently steered me to the taxi, his hand on the small of my back, something happened. I could feel the charge, the heat of his body against mine. I realized I wanted to be closer to this man.

From the moment we got into the taxi, everything changed. He started to kiss me—tenderly and then with increasing fervor. I might usually have been self-conscious in a taxi but I wanted it too. I let go of my anxiety, forgot everything that was around me, everything except his skin, his hands, his mouth. His kisses grew deep, punishing. I felt my body, pressed back against the seat, jolted by bolts of electricity

Lila stops, her hands on the keyboard. She stares at the blinking cursor. "Oh, for God's sake," she mutters. And presses delete.

> There was little about Michael that would suggest how the evening was going to play out. On the outside, he seemed conventional. He worked in IT. He was younger than me, quiet and easy-going. He was tall, with the kind of broad shoulders that speak of regular gym attendance and an unassuming manner. We met for a meal at an Italian restaurant near my house and I realized I was doing most of the talking, which would normally have put me off. But there was something about the way he watched me, absolutely intently, that made me curious. Not just curious, a little aroused. It was as we left the restaurant, that he leaned over and murmured into my ear: "How do you feel about BDSM?"

"Oh, God," says Lila out loud. "Now I'm repulsing myself." DELETE.

> I met Richard at a nightclub, where I had spent most of the night dancing, letting my cares disappear on the thumping beat. I had danced until sweat stuck my dress to my body, and my hair dripped with it. He grabbed my wrist as I was walking out to the Ladies and something about his burning eyes

> Jean-Claude was a poet from Paris

> Vince was a builder, his whole body covered with tattoos and his muscular torso

She has been trying to invent sexy escapades for three days now, and none of them sound like anything but the worst, cheesiest pornography. Sometimes she thinks it's because distant griping means it's impossible for her to get her head into a place that is sexy and real. Sometimes she blames Gabriel Mallory, who failed to respond to a simple request for a drink and whom she has avoided by asking Bill to do the school pickup this week.

Sometimes she thinks it's because it's so long since she had any kind of sexual contact that she cannot imagine what it involves anymore.

Lila puts her head onto her keyboard and lets it rest there.

Vince was a builder, his whole body covered with tattoos and his muscular torso sdffffffffffffhjjjkjkjkjkkkkkkkkkkkkkkkkkkkkkkkkllll llllllllllsdffffffffffffffhjhjkhkhjkhkjhjk

"SO HERE ARE the lists of the costumes we need."

Lila has finally braved the school pickup, and of course Gabriel Mallory is not there and of course Mrs. Tugendhat is. She is wearing a pair of maroon paisley dungarees and thrusts a sheet of paper into Lila's hands. She looks like a vaguely malevolent children's television presenter.

"Ideally we'd like them by the start of term, but I understand that's not always possible, given the numbers. If you can't do them all, just do the lead eight."

Lila gazes at the list, having completely blanked on what Mrs. Tugendhat is talking about. *Peter Pan and the Lost Boys*, it says. And suddenly she remembers, six weeks ago, the request for costumes. "Eight?" she echoes.

"There's plenty of time really," says Mrs. Tugendhat. "We say homemade is best, but . . ." she lowers her voice and gazes behind her ". . . if you look on eBay you can often find second-hand ones that are just as good. Lots of parents get rid of their old school-play costumes that way.

But you didn't hear it from me!" She taps her nose, and grins conspiratorially, before walking off to collar someone else on her list.

Lila is staring so intently at the list as she walks out—*green tunic and tights for Peter, large fake mustache, pirate jacket, hook for Captain Hook*—that she walks straight into one of the school mums.

Except it isn't a school mum.

"Hey!" Gabriel Mallory says, as she blinks in shock. "How are you doing? Long time no see."

"I'm fine," she says quickly, and goes to steer Violet around him.

"What's that?"

She doesn't want to talk to him, but it's too difficult to move with Violet standing resolutely in front of her, suddenly engaged in conversation with Lennie. She cannot turn left because that would involve walking straight into the group of mothers, and she can see Marja's glossy blonde hair out of the corner of her eye.

"Oh," she says, not looking at him, "just something for the school play."

"The school play. Yes, Lennie has a part. I can't remember what she said. Maybe a Lost Boy. She's excited, anyway."

"That's nice," she says, still not looking at him. She feels as if the entire expanse of her skin is prickling. It is too hard being near him, too humiliating. She keeps staring at his vegan trainers. "We'd better go, we're . . . late."

"For what?" says Violet, the traitor.

"Uh . . . Grandpa is going to take you out," she says, quickly.

"Grandpa Gene?"

"Yes."

"Where?"

His jacket is crumpled linen and looks expensive. She is too close to it, too close to him.

She can feel Marja's presence nearby, can smell the fruity scent she

sometimes wears, something melony and fresh. Lila is basically the un-
wanted filling in the worst sandwich in the world. "He didn't say, sweetheart," she mutters.

"Is he taking me to get a tattoo?"

"Hey . . ." She feels his hand on her arm and her head shoots up. He
is smiling at her. His face is kind, his gaze intent. "I owe you a text."

"Oh, don't worry," she says, with a smile that is not quite a smile. "No
problem. Got to go. See you!" She almost pushes Violet past him, ignoring her protests, her repeated demands to know where Grandpa Gene is
taking her. *You know he doesn't like me calling him Grandpa. He said we
should call him Gene. I told him it was a girl's name and he didn't even care.*

Lila burns, barely registering Violet's monologue for the entire length
of the walk home. His kind, untroubled face. The way he looked at her
with faint bemusement, as if he'd done nothing wrong in not respond-
ing. The way all their texts, their conversations in the playground, have
clearly meant nothing to him.

When she gets home Bill is in the garden talking to Jensen and gesturing toward the house crossly in a way that suggests Gene has done yet
another thing to offend him. Lila hands Violet two chocolate biscuits
from her secret stash in the hardware drawer and runs upstairs to her
room.

She has four new emails. One is from the dentist, reminding her that
Violet has a follow-up appointment next week, one from the emergency
plumber, reminding her that the last unblocking is still to be paid for,
one is from British Gas, a new bill, and the last is from Anoushka.

> Darling, when can I tell them they'll have the new
> chapter?

Lila glances behind her at the sofa-bed that Gene—despite his
promises—has failed to make up. Through the open window she can

hear Bill remarking loudly and repeatedly, "Cigarette smoke is wafting into the kitchen."

And then Gene's yelled response that he is "halfway down the garden, for Chrissake."

Lila cannot do another supper between these two old men.

She looks down at her phone again. She thinks for a minute.

You know you said I looked like I needed a drink, she types.

Chapter Sixteen

The pub is in Hampstead, halfway down one of the tiny pedestrian streets that lead off the main road, where antique books jostle for space with delicatessens selling exotic salads, made with aubergine, for fifteen pounds a pot. Lila has to edge past a huge, angry-looking man with two Pomeranian dogs to enter, but once inside the pub is reassuringly shabby, all dark scuffed walls and wonky wooden tables, the kind of place she used to frequent all the time before she had children, and has barely visited since. Jensen is already there, somehow cleaned up in a blue shirt and dark jeans, and she feels momentarily awkward that she has not bothered to make up her face or even brush her hair. But what's the point? She just needs to be out, in company. She needs to be away from her house. And her gardener was literally the only man who might be available.

Violet had looked mildly outraged when she said she was going out. *But where?* And then: *Why can't I come?*

Lila had glossed over her question, announced breezily that they would all be fine without her, and walked out of the door before anyone had a chance to protest. She had strode the twenty minutes up the hill with a kind of grim determination, not looking at her phone, as its intermittent buzzing told of the slew of questions and protests that inevitably followed her departure. No, she is an adult woman, and she is allowed to do as she likes. Occasionally.

Jensen turns and sees her, and motions to a table where his battered canvas jacket sits on the back of the chair. She slides in, gazing around her at the other drinkers, deep in animated conversations that have already been lubricated by several drinks, or staring in silence into their pints. She inhales the yeasty air, trying to slow her pulse.

"So what do you want?" Jensen appears at the table and puts his drink down on a square coaster.

"Oh. Diet Coke. Please." She is grateful that he doesn't question it. When she and Dan had first got together, he had told her she was admirable for not drinking. He even gave it up himself for a while, especially when the kids were small. He had been anxious about something happening to one of them, and not being able to drive them to a hospital. He had been a surprisingly overprotective parent when they were little. But for the last few years of their marriage Dan had started drinking again—only "clean" drinks like vodka and slimline tonic, as he spent increasing amounts of his free time in Lycra on his carbon-framed bicycle—and from then he seemed to see her failure to drink as a kind of rebuke, or maybe a symptom of her joylessness. He would offer her one in front of friends, even though he knew she would say no, and roll his eyes when she did as if showing them what a trial it was to be with her. She wonders absently whether he drinks with Marja, whether before she got pregnant they would ease into their evening with an expensive bottle of wine and . . .

Jensen hands her a Coke, smiling. "I was kind of surprised when you—"

"This isn't a date," she says quickly.

He blinks. "Okay."

"I mean—sorry—not that you aren't a very nice man. I just want to make sure we're straight from the off. I just—I just needed to get out of the house."

He contemplates this for a moment. "And I'm the only person you could think of?"

"No. I have friends. Lots of friends."

He looks confused.

"I mean I would normally meet my friend Eleanor. But she's going to a sex party in Richmond. No, Rickmansworth. Somewhere with an R. Actually maybe that's tomorrow." She takes a swig of her drink. "I mean I do have other friends. But—actually—it's got so awkward since Dan left that I find everyone exhausting. Everyone who knows us, I mean. I've sort of pulled in my horns. It's like I have to explain everything, and talk about what happened, and I'm still getting used to the idea of him impregnating the Bendy Young Mistress so I can't face explaining about that either. I'm so tired of the head tilt, that godawful look of sympathy. Or maybe it's just their relief that it's not them. And you already know. I just wanted to come out for a relaxing drink and not to have to . . . explain."

She stares at her Diet Coke. "I'm sorry," she says. "I've just realized I have no idea what I'm doing here."

Jensen appears to consider this. "Have you been on many non-dates?" he says. "Because you may want to work on your opening."

"Was the sex party too much?"

"No. That was great. Could have done with more detail but, hey, let's see how the Diet Coke goes down."

He looks completely unruffled. She lets out a long breath. "Sorry. I haven't been on a date—or a non-date—since 2004."

"When's your next?"

"Probably 2044."

"I can tell you about my last, if it makes you feel any better."

"Not really. Not if it involved a delicious frisson, an amazing meal, and then loads of perfect sex."

"It involved an overpriced pizza and my date bursting into tears and telling me all about her ex-boyfriend. Whom she is definitely, definitely, definitely not still in love with."

Lila pulls a face. "Ouch."

"First and last go on the apps. I should have been warned that we weren't suited when she listed her interests as 'makeup.' I don't know if I'm cut out for relationships. Not modern ones, anyway. I've kind of shut up shop on that front."

Lila starts to laugh. "Oh, God. It's just all so . . . awful. Eleanor made me download one of those apps last year but it was like peering into the use-by section in Tesco. Everyone my age looked like they were well past their expiry date, or so bashed around that nobody was going to pick them up unless they were absolutely desperate."

His laugh is an abrupt bellow that makes the people around them turn to look. "How old are you, anyway?" he says.

"Forty-two. You?"

"Thirty-nine."

"Oh, you'll be fine," she says, leaning back in her seat. "You'll be looking at the early thirties. You're considered in your prime." Like Dan. "Good-looking, young, a man, you'll be fixed up in no time, even if you're not looking. Someone young and gorgeous."

He eyes her quizzically. "Why would you do that?"

"Do what?"

"I'm literally three years younger than you. Possibly less. And you're talking to me like I'm your nephew."

"I don't know." She picks up the beer mat and fiddles with it. "Maybe I just . . . feel old."

"No, that's not it . . . You need distance."

"What?"

"You need to push someone away before they can get close. Or just make out like there's no possibility of anything between us, so that you can't feel vulnerable, especially if I don't make a pass at you."

She feels herself bristle. "What is that supposed to mean?"

"No judgment. I just see the dynamics. Years of therapy, I guess."

Lila pulls a face. "Don't therapize me."

"I'm not. I'm just observing."

"You can observe what you like. Doesn't make you right."

"No, it doesn't." He takes another sip of his drink. "But I am." He smiles.

"Wow. You can be quite annoying."

"So my sister tells me. But you did it when you met me, remember?"

She folds her arms. "No, I didn't. I was not *overly friendly* on that occasion because I thought you were going to steal my car."

"You charged outside in your PJs and pretty much told me to get lost just for looking at your tree. Which is sick, by the way. You need to have it taken down."

Lila closes her eyes. "Can we not? Can I just have one hour where there isn't something I have to sort out that's going to cost me money? Unless you're about to tell me that Gene's living in that too."

There is a slight atmosphere, and she cannot work out whether it is friendly or spiky. The one thing it is not is relaxing. It is possible he senses this, because he pauses for a moment, then leans forward in his chair and puts his beer down. "You look very nice by the way. I'm saying that in a non-date, friendly, asexual, age-appropriate manner."

Lila is not so embittered that she cannot recognize an olive branch when she sees one. "You're very kind. And also a terrible liar. I haven't washed my hair in two days and I haven't got any makeup on."

"Well, like I said, makeup isn't really one of my interests. Hey, c'mon. Sorry if I therapized you. I'm not very good at small-talk, in case you hadn't guessed. Though I can try if it helps." He sits up. "Nice . . . décor in here?"

She follows his gaze. "I actually like old pubs," she says. "The ones where everything is still stained with nicotine and the stale smell of spilled drinks. I like things where you can see the history."

He nods.

"I don't know if you've seen the two old bathrooms in our house, but I really like them too, even though everyone keeps telling me we need to rip them out and modernize. They're not fashionable, but they're quirky. I don't like this thing where we have to keep moving on and moving up all the time."

He's still watching her.

"Oh, God, you're not going to therapize that, are you?"

He shakes his head. "No. Although I hope you appreciate how hard I'm having to resist it. I don't like new stuff either. When I had my kitchen put in my flat, me and my sister spent an hour kicking the cupboards just so they wouldn't look new."

"Are you serious?"

"They were wooden doors but with this terrible immaculate laminate paint on them. I just needed them to look a bit scuffed and dented to feel at home."

"Yes! It used to drive Dan mad, all the scuffs and chaos of our house. I used to buy battered old chairs from charity shops, or weird old pictures with faces I liked, and he couldn't stand it. He now lives in a minimalist paradise with approximately two pieces of perfect furniture in every room."

"He'd get on well with my ex-fiancée. She needed everything to match. At one point we had two cream sofas, a cream marble coffee-table, and cream curtains. I used to feel like I had to shower before I dared walk into the living room."

"You were engaged?" She doesn't mean to sound as surprised as she does. He just doesn't seem like someone who would get engaged, let alone to someone with cream sofas.

"Briefly. She didn't appreciate the whole breakdown thing so much. And then I left the City and she realized I wasn't going to make money anymore so . . . two strikes and I was out." He takes another swig of his beer. "Oh, and there was the whole business of her shagging my work colleague."

"Oh. Jesus. I'm sorry."

"I'm not. We were totally ill-matched. It just didn't show till things got tough."

"I used to think Dan and I were pretty well-matched."

Neither of them says anything for a minute. Lila stares at her Diet Coke.

"You can love someone and still not be compatible," he says.

"Or maybe compatible but just . . . not love someone anymore?"

He thinks for a minute. "That too. It's dangerously close to therapy-speak. Want another Coke?"

They talk for another forty minutes before the call comes. She likes listening, realizes it's rare that she gets to hear someone else talk about their life. It's oddly restful to hear about someone else's complications and mistakes. He tells her how he used to work on the Foreign Exchange, about liquidity and volatility and hedging, and how he finally got engaged after he woke up to find his girlfriend had scrawled "Do it or forget it" in lipstick on his windscreen. "Maybe, with hindsight, not the healthiest way to go into a marriage." And then had come the breakdown, and a short stay in rehab. He relays all this with the calm, wry tone of someone discussing events that had happened to someone he has never met. She wonders whether to prod him a bit—she's a little bit captivated by the demanding girlfriend with the lipstick—when the phone rings. It's Violet.

"Mum, you need to come home."

She looks up at him, one hand pressed to her ear, and rolls her eyes. Of course they wouldn't let her have two hours to herself. Of course not. "Violet, I'm just having a drink with a friend. I'm allowed to have a—"

Violet's voice is urgent. "No. You need to come. Bill put a photo of him and Grandma's wedding day on the sideboard in the living room and then Gene put a picture of him and Grandma at *their* wedding next to it, and when Bill saw it he started shouting and Gene said, well, he thought Grandma looked happier in his one and then Bill chased him out in the garden with a chopping thing and Gene fell over the concrete bits and now he's lying on the ground saying he can't get up and Bill won't come out of his room."

Lila stares into the middle distance. She may have counted to ten, or ten thousand, she can't remember. She takes a deep breath. "Okay, sweetheart. I'll be right home."

It is as if she has been allowed a tiny window into a different life, then had it slammed abruptly in her face. Possibly by someone blowing a raspberry.

Jensen is watching her, his mouth pressed into a thin line of sympathy. "I think I caught the gist of that," he says. "C'mon. I'll drive you back."

Chapter Seventeen

The young doctor in Triage recognizes Gene immediately. "I know you!" he says, looking up from his paperwork in the small curtained-off cubicle. With one hand he holds a sandwich, from which he takes an oversized bite as he sits down. Lila tries not to look at the little blob of mayonnaise on his chin.

Gene's face lights up, as it always does, and he immediately pushes his way up so that he is a little taller in the metal hospital bed and salutes. "Captain Strang, reporting for intergalactic—"

"No . . ." The doctor takes another mouthful and chews. "Dog bite, wasn't it? A few weeks ago? How are you getting on?"

Because of his age, Gene is attended to relatively quickly. Or within three hours, which, Jensen observes, is pretty much record time for Accident and Emergency. It is not a break, apparently, even though Gene has to be helped in, supported by Jensen, while grimacing wildly and letting out periodic moans of pain. But it is a bad sprain and will need to be rested and iced for at least a week. When they are discharged, with what Gene clearly regards as disappointingly mild painkillers, he thanks the medical staff with the slightly too emphatic gratitude of someone who relishes being the focus of attention. For the twenty-minute drive home, he talks endlessly of their niceness and how great it is not to need insurance for everything.

Lila does not speak for any of it, leaving all conversation to Jensen and Gene, using her time to text the girls to make sure they have done their homework, to reassure them that everything is fine, and finally, as it grows late, to ask them to go to bed. Even when she is not texting, she remains silent, her brain humming with a quiet fury that drowns out the casual conversation around her.

Bill is cleaning the kitchen. He has cleaned it relentlessly since Gene's arrival, with the pointed determination of a dog spraying his scent. When she opens the door, he looks up with an expression that is half embarrassment and half resentment that Gene has somehow arrived back in the house again. The two old men look at each other, and then Bill turns pointedly away. "He's alive, then," he says, with mock surprise.

"You nearly broke my leg, you asshole."

"I did nothing. You wouldn't have tripped on the rubble if you hadn't spent half the afternoon at the public house."

"I wouldn't have tripped if you hadn't come after me with a carving knife."

"It was a metal spatula! If you ever did anything in this house other than cause chaos and steal people's socks you'd have been aware of that!"

"Shut *up!*"

Lila drops her bag loudly on the floor. There is a sudden silence. She looks at Bill, then at Gene, who is being eased into the chair by Jensen. "So when does it stop?"

All three men are staring at her.

"This is *insane*. This is all *insane*. You are both headed toward eighty. My mother is six feet underground. You haven't even seen each other for decades. *When does it stop?*"

"*I'm* not about to be eighty," Gene mutters.

She's shouting now, unable to stop herself. "I've had it. I've honestly had it. I cannot live with you two behaving like a pair of toddlers over something that happened—what?—thirty-five years ago? My life is in crisis, my children are struggling, and I cannot do one more day of trying to mediate between two ridiculous old men who refuse to let go of the past."

She takes a deep breath. "So this is what we are going to do. If you both want to stay here, in my house, you are going to work out how to live peacefully together, and if you can't, you can both leave, because it's not fair to force me—your daughter—to make the adult decision as to who should go. Do you understand?"

"But, Lila—" Bill begins.

"No. I'm not interested. You are both adults, even if you seem to have forgotten that. You sort it out between you, or you find somewhere else to live. Oh, and you can make yourselves useful and babysit while you start your negotiations, because I'm going for a drink. Or to *finish* the drink that was so rudely interrupted. Jensen?"

Jensen, who is clearly stunned, glances at his watch and raises his eyebrows. "Uh—okay."

Before anyone can say anything else, Lila picks up her bag, walks back out of the house, and heads toward Jensen's pickup truck.

"WE COULD TRY to go back to the pub but it's gone closing time." Jensen is driving along the road, one hand on the wheel, the other resting on the gear stick. "Great tirade, by the way. I'm not sure I've ever seen Bill actually look *cowed* before."

Lila barely hears him. Her ears are still ringing from her shouting, her brain still humming with the image of the two old men, silenced in front of her. But mostly she is thinking. She checks her reflection in the passenger mirror and rummages in her bag for an old mascara. She finds a dog treat, a pen from a hotel she had stayed in sometime in 2017, and a tampon that has escaped its wrapping and is lightly dusted with crumbs. She wipes under her eyes instead, hoping she doesn't look too awful. "Do you have alcohol?" she asks.

"Do I have alcohol?"

"At your flat."

"Probably a couple of beers. But you don't drin—"

"I do tonight," she says. "Stop at the nearest shop."

It is so long since Lila drank that she has no idea what she should buy. And she is not sure that there is anything in this twenty-four-hour convenience store much more sophisticated than lighter fuel. She peers at the shelves behind the counter, watched by the guy at the till, who bears the wary expression of someone who has long learned that even benign-looking forty-two-year-old women may yet hurl themselves onto the cash register, start singing a national anthem, or wet themselves beside the freezer cabinet. She gives him a reassuring smile to suggest she will do none of these things, which he doesn't return. She has never liked red wine, and beer might make her gassy, so she finally points at a bottle of vodka and grabs some tonic, then hands it to the man. "What do you want?" Jensen is behind her. He asks for a couple of no-alcohol beers. "I'm driving you back later," he says, as if she has forgotten.

It is raining heavily by the time they are driving down Westling Street, and as they pass Bill and Francesca's bungalow, she averts her gaze. It gets her, even now. She can picture her mother waving from the front porch, the way she would always brush her hands on her jeans as she walked toward Lila along the path, as if perennially caught in the middle of doing something. Lila had not understood the comfort she had drawn from walking into that house every week until her mother was gone. It is then that she notices Jensen patting his jacket. By the time he pulls up a short distance down the road, he has patted every pocket at least twice and seems preoccupied. He cuts the engine, thrusting his hands deep into his pockets as, without the wipers, the windscreen is slowly obscured by the rain. Then he reaches over to the glove box, opens it, rummages inside, and lets out a quiet curse. She looks at him.

"Flat keys," he says. "They're not in my pocket. I was in a hurry when you called and I have a horrible feeling . . . I might have left them on the side."

"Don't you have a spare?"

"Yes . . . In the flat."

He stares through the windscreen at the block, as if he could somehow will himself inside. "My sister has a set but she works nights so I won't be able to pick them up till tomorrow. I'm . . . really sorry."

The feeling that hits Lila is unexpectedly bleak. All her plans ruined. Again. She knows this is a childish way to look at the world, but right now, she feels it, a foot-stamping tear-inducing rage.

Jensen sits back, thinking, then suddenly leans forward, his hand shuffling around again in his glove compartment. He pulls out a key on a small leather fob. "We could go to Bill's?" She looks at his palm, at the little brass Chubb key. "His spare. He gave it to me after . . . I think he just likes to know that someone could get in if need be."

Lila looks back up the road to where she can just make out the bungalow, set back behind a neat privet hedge. Quiet and empty, its windows like empty eye sockets in a blank face. "I . . . can't. Not in there. I mean—it's where my mum lived. Since she died it always feels . . . I just can't. Sorry."

He nods, not pushing her. He glances up at where the rain is now hammering on the roof of the car as the engine ticks down. Both of them are briefly lost in their thoughts. Lila can feel the bottle of vodka, disproportionately heavy in her lap. She wonders whether to just wrench off the top and take a swig or if that will make her feel worse. A forty-something woman drinking from a bottle in a pickup truck.

"Could you just . . . drive me home?"

"Bill's studio," he says suddenly. "He keeps the key to the studio in the kitchen. That's just his space, right? Not your mum's? Would that still be weird?" And suddenly Lila is alive again.

IT TAKES JENSEN a couple of minutes to let himself in and unlock the side gate to the garden. Lila bolts from the truck, throws the door shut, and runs in, her jacket over her head, the bottles tucked under her arm, her feet slapping through the puddles. Jensen hits a switch, shaking the rainwater from his shoulders, and the neon strip light above them flickers into life, illuminating the racks of tools, the worktable, the clamps and jigsaws. Sheets of graded sandpaper are stacked in a rack on the wall, the floor littered with wood shavings and sawdust. A piece of graph paper with some measurements and a pencil drawing of a table lie on the edge of the table, beside a tape measure and a hand plane with a burnished wooden handle. For all Bill's rigid sense of order at home, his studio is a reassuring mess of creativity and clutter. There is a stool in front of his scarred wooden table, and a newly finished garden bench alongside the door, probably another project for a neighbor. Since he let go of his business Bill has regularly made pieces to order. She has always suspected he would do it even if it wasn't for the money: for Bill, wood-working is meditative, calming, and she cannot remember a day when he hasn't been engaged in making something. Even on the day of her mother's funeral he had carved a little bird which he had placed on Francesca's coffin.

Jensen motions her to the bench and pulls the little stool over so that he sits alongside it.

"I grabbed you a mug from the kitchen," he said. "I didn't know where he kept the glasses."

"Classy," she says, as he pours in some vodka, then tonic. The strip-lighting buzzes quietly overhead, making them both look pale and shadowy-eyed.

"Do I look as awful as you?" she says, glancing up at it.

"Significantly worse. I'm always camera-ready."

She glances around her. "Look." There are two dark green paraffin lamps in the corner. Of course there are. Bill is prepared for every eventuality: power cuts, food shortages, earthquakes, and atomic bombs. She lights the lamps, turns off the fluorescent bulb, and suddenly the little workshop is restful, and oddly intimate. *Right*, she thinks. And takes three emphatic glugs of her vodka and tonic, ignoring Jensen's look of surprise. *Right*, she thinks. *I'll show you, Eleanor.*

THE TASTE AND strength of the alcohol are so disguised by the tonic that it takes a second mugful before she realizes it is having any effect at all. It is actually quite pleasant to feel so swimmy, to have the sharp edges of the day so delightfully blunted. Jensen is nearby on the stool drinking his alcohol-free beer and the rain is drumming on the flat roof and she is in a wood-scented cocoon, away from all the stress and conflict of drama. *Why don't I drink more often?* She has another swig. She is not entirely sure she'll go through with this, but it's perfectly pleasant being here, in this space, beside a man she feels comfortable with, as he talks about a walled garden he restored in Winchester.

"So," she says, raising her glass, "tell me something interesting about you."

"Something interesting? Is my walled garden boring you to tears?"

"The breakdown. Tell me how it happened." He looks a little startled again, so she adds: "Only if you want to, of course. I mean I'm not being . . . nosy."

"You are, a bit."

"I'm making conversation."

"Really? 'Tell me about the most traumatic thing that happened in your whole life'?"

"Tell me something else, then. Tell me about . . . Lipstick Woman. Your ex-fiancée."

While he speaks, she is looking at the way his shoulders move under his T-shirt, his broad hands. What would it feel like to have those on her skin? What would it be like to have sex with someone who wasn't Dan? When they had first got together, she and Dan had spent whole days in bed, the duvet scattered with sections of Sunday newspapers, the sheets full of crumbs from Marmite toast. They had so much sex in the first month that she had got cystitis and spent two days doubled over glugging cranberry juice. Then she thinks about the last six months they had lived together, the loneliness of having someone in your bed who didn't even seem to see you, the racing thoughts, the endless arguments in your head, the cold back of doom facing you night after night.

"Am I boring you?"

Jensen is looking at her. He has a nice face. Maybe she just hadn't noticed it properly before. "No," she says. "No. I was just . . . thinking."

"Anyway, so it was basically a lot of booze, a lot of drugs, a lot of evenings that ended with me desperately trying to remember someone's name. And then I got into the relationship with Irina and it was really volatile, like, I never knew what she was going to go off about. But there was this bit of me that thought, 'Better that than the girls whose names I didn't remember,' so I stayed with it. But it was just stress all day and then stress all night—she was the kind who liked to keep a fight going till five a.m., you know? You just kind of get acclimatized to the drama."

He has nice hair, she thinks. She could run her fingers through that hair.

He sighs. "And after we got engaged, work got more frantic and my body just started to fall apart in bits. And then I found out she was sleeping with my mate at work, and my brain just . . . It was like a spin dryer, going round and round and round. I couldn't sleep, I started to get panic attacks, I felt like I was braced all the time. But I thought I could plow on through. Until I couldn't."

"What happened?" she says, dragging herself back.

"Someone found me catatonic in the men's loos. Couldn't get up. Couldn't speak. Went home and couldn't stop crying. Stayed in bed for three weeks. I don't even remember it, to be honest."

He glances at her and away again, like this bit makes him feel awkward. "My parents didn't really get it. But my sister intervened. After rehab, she got me into therapy, moved into my apartment for two months, and made like an attack dog to anyone who wanted me to party. And one of the things that came out in therapy was that I really hated my job. Hated it. Every time I thought about going back there I felt ill again. So . . ." He straightens up. ". . . so I trained and did this instead."

He waits for her to say something, but she doesn't know what to say. She is suddenly overwhelmed by the feeling that she really wants him to be closer.

"And it turns out just being in a garden all day is good for me. Obviously I don't make much money but I—"

"Do you want to sit on the bench?" she interrupts, moving over to make room.

He studies her for a minute. "You want me to sit next to you?"

"Don't you want to?"

He's still reading her face, like she's a puzzle he can't quite work out. He doesn't speak, but gets up wordlessly and moves onto the bench, keeping a couple of inches between them when he sits—a tiny gap of plausible deniability. She pours herself another drink and takes a long sip.

"I think we need music," she announces. She gets up and makes for Bill's transistor radio on the worktable. She may have been a little unsteady on her feet, but she hopes he hasn't noticed. She switches it on and it goes straight to Radio 3—gentle classical strings in a minor key. The room feels suddenly filled with intent.

"This feels . . ."

"Nice?" she says hopefully.

"'Nice' is an awful word. Supermarket cakes are nice. Your nan is nice."

"I'm not a cake. Or a nan."

"You're certainly not. I'm just not sure what—"

It is at this point that she lunges forward and kisses him. It is not that she is overcome by lust, more that she doesn't know what to say anymore, and is afraid of what might come out of her mouth. Plus she hasn't kissed anyone in three years and really, really wants to see if she still can.

It turns out she can. His lips are fuller, softer than Dan's. She observes as they touch hers that she and Dan hadn't kissed properly for years. Not like this. Somehow proper kissing is the first thing to go in a failing relationship, the first casualty of long-held resentments and a lack of casual affection. Jensen smells of soap and a shampoo she recognizes but can't name, and tastes faintly of beer and there is a tongue involved and it is a little shocking, and then it is revelatory, and then it is just . . . dreamy. She had forgotten, she had actually forgotten, how good this was. She is pulled in, her capacity for thought floating away in little pieces, even as a tiny voice in her head is yelling, like a twelve-year-old: *I'm kissing someone! I'm actually kissing someone again!* He pulls back after a few years and blinks, his eyes on hers.

"Okay. That . . . was unexpected."

"But . . . nice?"

"No."

She feels herself prickle with embarrassment, and he says quickly, "Nice is way too inadequate a word to describe that."

She deflates slightly with relief. "I haven't kissed anyone in three years."

"I'm here to tell you you've still got it."

She feels the smile light up her face, goofy and unstoppable. "Really?"

He frowns, considers this. "Actually, I might not be a hundred percent sure. I might need to try again, just to check."

This time he pulls her gently toward him and he kisses her. It is a kiss filled with certainty, shot through with actual desire. She had forgotten the utter deliciousness of being desired and it smoothes out whatever wrinkles of discomfort were left in her and she feels her body turn fluid, molten. They kiss and his hands are on her, in her hair, holding her face, intertwining with her fingers, then sliding down her thigh. She surrenders to all of it, long-dormant cells in her body sparking to life, his weight, pleasingly solid, pinning her as she eases herself backward onto the bench. I can do this, she thinks, as he kisses her neck, making her shiver pleasurably, her hands pulling him to her. There is a brief flicker of anxiety when she remembers her underwear choices that morning—she's pretty sure nothing more exotic than an old Marks & Spencer five-set cotton brief—but then she decides that Jensen is not a man who is likely to worry about the lack of expensive lingerie. He has gently undone the buttons on her shirt with one hand, his mouth not leaving hers, and when he touches her breast she finds herself arching toward his hand, in thrall to her own body, to his—

He abruptly lifts himself up on his elbows. "I need to ask. How drunk are you?"

She opens her eyes. "What? Not that drunk."

"I mean, I'm not entirely sure what's going on here. Because we started with you being very clear that this wasn't a date and—"

She puts her hand to the back of his neck, pulls him to her so that their faces are inches apart. She wants his lips back on hers. She says softly: "Do we have to have this conversation right now?"

"Well . . . yes?"

"It's not very sexy."

"Nor is waking up tomorrow feeling like you took advantage of someone. I like you, Lila. I know you've been through some stuff and I just . . . don't want to be . . . more stuff."

"You are absolutely not going to be stuff." When he doesn't look convinced, she reaches out with her right hand and fumbles in her bag for her phone. She finds voice memo and says, into the microphone, her eyes not leaving his: "This is Lila Kennedy, stating for the record that she is a grown woman of sound mind and slightly more infirm body, absolutely not being taken advantage of by Jensen . . ." She stops. "I don't know your surname."

"That's disgraceful," he says. "What kind of woman are you?"

"A woman who is trying to put your mind at rest, and have an excellent shag."

"Well, now you've introduced a whole new pressure element."

"Okay, a mediocre shag. Just a shag. Look, why are you making this so difficult?"

"Phillips. It's Phillips."

He is kissing her again and laughing at the same time, which is odd, but nice, and then he stops laughing and she relaxes, and then feels something quite, quite different from relaxation, and then, as he stops kissing her and starts moving his lips down her stomach, she drops her phone and stops thinking altogether.

Chapter Eighteen

Celie

T he weirdest thing ever happened before school this morning. It made Celie laugh, and then it made her sad because it was the kind of thing that before everything got messy between them she would have called Meena straight away and told her and they would have laughed their heads off.

She was in the bathroom trying to cover up a really annoying spot on her chin that just wouldn't go away—honestly, it might as well be one of those flashing lights you get above zebra crossings. She could actually feel it pulsing. She knew everyone was going to notice it, and that would probably end up being the thing they used to talk shit about her today— that she was growing an extra head or she had the plague. Celie had just put a second layer of concealer on it and sealed it with powder and was about to do her hair but Violet had nicked her good hairbrush—the one that gets out tangles without you actually screaming and wanting to die—and she was about to run into Violet's room to tell her she was going to kill her when she heard the front door shut. There was something weird about the silence that came after the sound—and Truant didn't even bark—so she went a few steps down the stairs to see what was going on and there was Mum, standing in the doorway, staring at something Celie couldn't see. Her hair was all messed up at the back and had dust in it—flour or sawdust or something—and she was pale and wearing the same clothes she'd worn yesterday when she went out in a hurry, but she was sort of rumpled, like she'd slept in them.

Celie stared at her for a minute because, to be honest, she had assumed Mum was in the other bathroom brushing her teeth or in the garden clearing up dog poo, or something. She hadn't actually seen Mum, but that didn't really count for anything first thing as she could be anywhere in the house, and yet as Celie stood there she realized Mum must have been somewhere else last night.

Then she took two more steps down and peered over the banister behind her to where Mum was looking at something, her face a bit stunned, like she couldn't believe what she was seeing. And there was Bill, dressed with his tie and his shiny shoes, like he always is, even at seven fifteen in the morning, holding a wooden spoon with porridge still on it. And standing beside him was Gene, in a Joni Mitchell T-shirt and a pair of really scrubby boxer shorts and clutching a packet of cigarettes. They were both facing her and staring back at her and then, just when she opened her mouth to speak, they looked at each other, then back at her, and said, at exactly the same time in this really disapproving voice, *"And where the hell do you think you've been?"*

Chapter Nineteen

Lila

That is absolutely hilarious. How old are you?"

Lila and Eleanor are in the gym changing room. They have just done a workout class—since she turned forty, Eleanor has been religious about staying in shape—and Lila has sweat in places she didn't know could sweat (she thinks it may actually be coming out of her eyelids) and her T-shirt is basically two panda-eyes of wetness.

"Sixteen, apparently." She is still finding it hard to breathe.

"And they actually told you *off*?"

Lila rubs at her face with a towel. "Gene gave me this lecture about how it wasn't smart just to disappear and there were all sorts of bad men out there and I had no idea because I hadn't been out there and didn't I even watch the news about what happened to women out there late at night on their own?"

"But they knew who you were with."

"But Bill insisted they hadn't known where I was because they had assumed Jensen had dropped me off as I wasn't romantically involved with him, and then I hadn't answered my phone. And then when I said I had been with Jensen, actually, Bill said sort of pompously that he valued his relationship with Jensen very much and he hoped I wouldn't mess it up for him. And then he sniffed—this *really* judgmental sniff— and added that perhaps it wasn't the best idea to sleep with someone with whom I had a working relationship."

Eleanor cackles. "Well, that's you told."

"And *then* Bill said it was perhaps not the best example to set the girls."

Lila had stared at him, her cheeks flaming. "I'm forty-two years old," she had said, standing a little more upright. "I haven't even been on a date in twenty years. I've been too busy picking up the pieces while the girls' father was busy impregnating a much younger woman. I spend most of my waking hours trying to keep a roof over their heads and food in their mouths. And yours too, for that matter. So back off with your judgments—both of you."

Or, at least, that was what she would have liked to say. What actually happened was that she had apparently reverted to being sixteen, found herself mute, then muttered, "Well, thanks for your opinion," and, face glowing, had stalked past the two old men and up the stairs to take a shower.

"So—the important question. How was it?" Eleanor peels off her gym clothes with the casual insouciance of someone who is now apparently used to being naked in front of strangers. She actually sashays toward the lockers, like someone on a catwalk.

Lila stares at her towel. "It was . . . fun. I mean, it wasn't like steamy *Fifty Shades* shenanigans, not like you get up to. But we laughed a lot. And the sex was kind of . . . a sidebar?"

She couldn't quite articulate to Eleanor what had happened. How Jensen, in the end, had declined to have sex, but had instead done that thing to her that Dan hadn't done in fifteen years (he once told her he didn't really like it, that it made him feel claustrophobic). And she had felt at first deeply awkward and exposed, and then a little panicky, and then he had been so good at it that she had stopped feeling awkward, at least for the time it took her to come, noisily. Embarrassingly noisily, although she couldn't seem to do anything about that at the time. And afterward she had been braced to feel awkward again but he had made her laugh and seemed so comfortable with bodies, and her sounds, and stray hairs, and told her he couldn't go "all the way" on the first night as (a) neither of them had condoms, and (b) he needed to keep something back in case she thought he was easy, which had made her laugh again.

It had been almost three by the time they'd stopped talking, too late for Lila to go back without waking everyone. They had slept on a couple of garden cushions, and he had covered her with his jacket. He had fallen asleep almost immediately, his arm heavy across her waist, only the odd muffled snore coming from his side. She had barely slept, her whole body humming with the unfamiliarity of having a near-naked man beside her. For the entire day after it happened, she kept seeing his sandy-colored head between her legs and getting a shivery little charge from it.

Eleanor pokes her head over the shower cubicle.

"And you felt okay about it? After all this time with Dan?"

That was the thing. She really did. It was weird to feel this okay about having sex with someone you weren't in love with. It had occurred to her afterward that in the last few years of their relationship, Dan had approached sex like he approached his carbon-framed bicycle. Once the preliminaries were out of the way, his head would drop into his shoulders, his whole body a knot of concentration, and it was basically a matter of pumping his way to the finish. "It was actually really . . . nice."

" 'Nice'?"

"Happy. Happy sex. I can't really describe it. I mean, he's not my type physically, and he's not interested in a relationship, and he's a slightly annoying broke gardener. But in terms of me getting back on the bike, it was pretty much perfect."

As he had dropped her off, he'd told her he had to go and see his parents in Yorkshire for a bit. "Convenient," she had scoffed, and he had rolled his eyes and said he genuinely had to—she should ask Bill if she didn't believe him because he had already talked to him about it. He was sorry to leave her with all the mess in the garden but, you know, parents. She did know. He had texted her the following day, telling her he had had a great night and would love to see her again "or at least when I'm not in a trench in your garden," but she was mindful of what Bill had said about mixing business and pleasure and hadn't been sure how to reply. And now it had been three days, which had turned her not answering immediately because she didn't know what to say into something more weighty and awkward.

"Well." Eleanor's grin has spread halfway across her face. "I'd say that was a pretty good first attempt."

"Does that mean I can use your thinly disguised sexual escapades in my book?"

Eleanor is washing her hair, her fingers knuckle-deep in the foam on her head. She stops for a minute and pulls a face. "Actually, Lils, would you mind not? I was thinking about it and it just seems a bit weird. Even if you're pretending it's you, I think people I've been having fun with might recognize things, or be weird around me, and then I won't be able to go out with them anymore. It just feels a bit . . . off?"

Lila looks at her with the kind of disappointment that happens when you've just been blocked from doing something for entirely understandable and sensible reasons.

"Okay," she says, after a minute, trying not to sound resentful.

"Sorry," says Eleanor.

"It's fine. I'll work something out."

"I mean you've got your own stuff to write about now, right?"

"I guess."

Lila reaches into her locker for her bag, then looks at her phone, checking that there's nothing from the girls, and suddenly stares at the little screen.

> Hey, so let me know when you fancy that drink. I'm sorry it took so long to reply— stuff just mounts up, you know? You looked raggiante at the school gates yesterday btw x.

SOMETHING STRANGE HAS happened since the night of the non-date with Jensen. It is not an *entente cordiale*, exactly, but Lila's two fathers are definitely not actively fighting. When she arrives home from the afternoon school run, Bill is at pains to be cheerful and pleasant, asking after Lila's and Violet's day, occasionally cooking less challenging meals, and showing Lila small changes he has made around the house— the pinning up of a notice board, so that the girls know what to take to school each day, or the purchase of a new lock for the first-floor bathroom so that nobody was likely to walk in on her anymore (for "her" read Bill, and for "nobody" read Gene). There is notably less peevish closing of doors and passive-aggressive piano playing.

Gene, meanwhile, rises at an almost normal hour (nine thirty), folds the sofa-bed neatly, is out for much of the day, then makes a point of performatively greeting Bill first when he returns. *Hey, Bill! How's your day been?*

Perfectly pleasant, thank you, Gene. Yours? Bill responds.

Lila is not entirely sure whether this exchange takes place on the occasions she is not within earshot. But one evening the two men washed the dishes together after supper, Bill not even commenting when Gene put the plates back in the wrong cupboard, and over dinner the following evening they had a short conversation about a leak in one of the bathrooms, which involved nobody else at the table. If there is a slight gritted-teeth element to their small-talk, it means at least that Lila does not go about her day feeling like a bomb-disposal expert waiting for the next explosion.

Which is just as well. Because Lila has spent three days holed up in what was once her office, revising her opening chapter, which is now late, and which she has promised, absolutely promised, to get to Anoushka by Friday.

> **Two years ago I was a mostly teetotal, married woman, with two children, who hadn't so much as looked at another man. I married for life, considered my family my world, and was probably a little judgmental of people who weren't like me. So how did I end up on the floor of a workshop at the end of my first date with a younger man, sawdust in my hair, giggly with vodka, and having the best sex of my life?**

She had called him J in the chapter, and not revealed his occupation, figuring that way he could be pretty much anyone. And she had avoided the whole taking-her-elderly-father-to-hospital episode beforehand, describing it simply as "a bad day at the office." But the rest of it she had poured out almost verbatim: the way they had told each other about their lives at the pub, his lost keys, her determination to "get back on the bike," the bit where she had realized she didn't even know his surname, her terror and excitement and the thrill of getting naked again with another human being. She quite enjoys the process of writing it: it allows her to relive the whole evening in detail, to remember things she had forgotten (his watch strap getting caught in her hair, the way he ran out into the rainy garden afterward to pee), and then to observe it at a distance—the story of a woman reclaiming her life and her sexuality. She had tweaked it a little, ramping up the emotions, changing his appearance to dark-haired, giving it a conclusive ending: *"Well," said my best friend. "That sounds like a perfect first attempt."* But she hadn't had to change anything about how she'd felt in the moment, the unexpected ease of it all, the laughter, the sawdust, the smell of the paraffin lamps, and the endless drumming of the rain on the roof, the way, she realizes now, she hadn't once worried about what she looked like or how she came across to him.

> **He was a great guy, and completely not my type, and he taught me that, unlike during my twenties when sex was always tied up with all sorts of sexual politics—what my then boyfriend might have said or done beforehand, whether we were "in" a relationship, how drunk I was, or how insecure I felt about myself—sex in my forties was quite different: me inhabiting my body fully, unafraid to ask for what I wanted, comfortable with the idea that just because I was having great sex with someone didn't mean I needed to spend the rest of my life with them. In fact, the exact opposite: that I could go into a sexual encounter knowing I didn't want to spend the rest of my life with him. It was my first moment of liberation, and worth every hour on those lumpy garden cushions, and the sawdust in my hair . . .**

Suck on that, Dan, she thinks. She prints it off to check it for spelling and grammatical errors—they are always somehow easier to see on a printed page—and then, when she's satisfied there are none, she puts the chapter into an email, types in Anoushka's address, and presses send.

Then she closes her laptop, feeling oddly satisfied. She is a grown-up, independent woman writing about her sexual escapades. She is moving forward, taking care of her family, and reclaiming her financial independence. She has not had to make anything up. Even the fact that Truant has weed on the stairs (because nobody except Lila ever walks him) cannot dent her good mood.

> Sounds good! When did you have in
> mind?

> Pretty flat out with work
> most of this week but how about
> Thursday eve? Lennie is going to my
> mum's.

> Thursday's great.

She and Gabriel have been texting again, backward and forward most evenings, little snippets about the school gate or things their children have been up to.

> How's the finest-looking woman in the
> playground?

He comments specifically on her appearance, saying her hair looked nice in that style, or that she looked amazing in those jeans, often using Italian words she looks up afterward. He pays attention to tiny details that Dan would never have noticed about her. He is kind, considerate, clearly conscious of the psychodrama she goes through every day faced with Marja's presence.

> I know it's not my business, but I can't get
> my head round Dan choosing that girl.
> She has nothing about her, not
> compared to you.

She likes the "that girl," as if Marja is someone insubstantial. The texts are unpredictable, and come at odd hours, sometimes two or three in an hour, and then no reply at all. She imagines the stress of his daily life as a widowed father and the difficulties of managing a job as a top architect while trying to meet the emotional needs of his daughter.

It can be lonely sometimes, can't it? she ventures, late one evening, while she is in the bath.

His answer comes twenty minutes later. Her water has started to grow cold.

It can. I know you get it. x

He seems to see her in a way that nobody else does. It's like having a secret ally, one who sees only the best of you. In person, they usually exchange only the slightest of conversation—of course nobody wants to be the focus of the school mums' forensic gaze—but his looks are meaningful, and every time she gets a text from him a small thrill goes through her, and she reads and rereads it several times, relishing the warmth of his digital gaze.

I saw a woman who looked just like you at work today. I slightly wished it had been—we could have gone for coffee.

It was me. I'm hiding in your office in a million disguises. That's how I roll.

You're very funny. One of your many charms. Anyway, she wasn't half as good-looking as you x

It is most days now, and definitely flirtatious. Lila feels a little giddy on the walk to school, their impending date a glowing pocket warmer she holds tightly, a secret source of heat and comfort. When Philippa gives her one of her vaguely pitying looks—the ones that manage to combine *We're all so sorry for you* with *But it's totally understandable why Dan would have wanted to trade you in for Marja*—she meets it with a bland smile and walks over casually to stand in what she has come to think of as Gabriel's corner, even on the days when he is not in it. Which is, annoyingly, most days. She's in such a good mood that when a driver beeps at her to hurry up as she walks over the zebra crossing she stops and does just three jumping jacks in front of him, when really she would have been within her rights to do a dozen.

"So where are you going?" says Eleanor, who has popped round for coffee and to show off her new tattoo. It is a phoenix, apparently, rising from the ashes of her hip bone.

Lila wants to ask if it's some kind of comment on osteoporosis but suspects this is not really the point. "Um . . . not sure yet."

"He has confirmed the date, though?"

That was the thing. Gabriel had been annoyingly quiet for the last thirty-six hours. The last time he had mentioned it he said something about work, but that he was sure he'd make it, and now she doesn't want to be chasing him for answers. She suspects the kind of people he surrounds himself with are far too cool to have to chase people for date details.

"I mean, pretty much, yes. He suggested Thursday."

"When was that?"

"Um . . . Sunday?"

Eleanor gives her a steady look.

"Don't look at me in that tone of voice. He's been texting, and it was him who suggested it in the first place."

"After it was you who initially asked him for a drink."

"Well, yes, but that was forgotten. He could have just ignored it. But he was the one who said let's go out."

Eleanor pulls the kind of face people pull when they don't want to say what they would actually like to say.

"I'm sure he'll be in touch before tomorrow," Lila says firmly.

The sound of distant, fragmented piano playing, which has formed the backdrop to their conversation, has stopped and now Lila hears the sound of the front door opening and closing, the muffled goodbyes of Penelope Stockbridge's departure. A moment later Bill walks into the kitchen. He greets Eleanor warmly, observes, when Eleanor shows him her hip tattoo that, goodness, it really is . . . quite something. And then, his offer of more tea gently refused, makes himself some Earl Grey and sits at the kitchen table. The newspaper is in front of him but he looks meditative.

"Everything all right, Bill?" says Lila, after she and Eleanor have exchanged looks.

"Fine!" he says. "All fine, thank you!"

"He's moping because he likes Piano Lady and he doesn't know what to do about it." Gene strolls in from the garden, slugging a can of Coke. It's an unseasonably warm day and he is in a faded T-shirt with a picture of Bob Marley on the front. Lila hadn't known he was even in.

"That's not it," says Bill.

"It is. He likes her but he feels bad because of your mom."

"I like Penelope as a friend."

"Well, you shouldn't. She's hot to trot for you, my friend. Hanging on your every word. Watching you play your instrument like she wishes you were playing her."

"Oh, for goodness' sake, Gene. Not everybody's mind is in the gutter."

Gene grins, pleased with himself.

"She does come round a lot," observes Lila.

Penelope comes two or three times a week. Always just to help Bill with his scales, apparently. He's a terribly good pupil. It's so rewarding for her. This week she has also brought a pasta bake, a tray of scones, and some flowers that were simply taking over her borders. They would only have gone to waste. It was really nothing. Lila has found it rather charming. Penelope is such a careful, anxious presence, so eager to please, that it's hard to resent her.

"I think it's nice, Bill," she says. "I don't think Mum would mind if you saw her as . . . more than a friend."

Bill is gazing at his newspaper with his brow furrowed, the closest he comes to expressing deep existential trauma. "She is a very sweet lady," he says, after a minute. "I feel she's been dealt rather a raw deal in life. And I do enjoy her company. But, honestly, I wouldn't know how to go about . . . I don't know."

"Pal! Don't make it heavy weather! You're overthinking this," says Gene, scratching an armpit. "Just invite her to stay on for supper one evening. She'll jump at the chance."

Bill's look suggests he's considering whether Gene would be involved in that dinner.

"If you did decide to invite her for supper, we could all steer clear, couldn't we, Gene?" says Lila. "Give Bill a little privacy?"

"Oh. Oh, sure! Wouldn't want to cramp your style." Gene gives him a vigorous nudge, which Bill endures politely.

"I don't know . . ." Bill says again.

"Fella. C'mon. Who knows how much time we have around here? You gotta live life while you can. Hey—what would Francie have done? She knew how to live, right? She sucked the marrow out of every moment."

They are all briefly silenced while they think of her.

"She certainly did," says Bill, and lets out a shaky little sigh.

"It's not a betrayal. It's what she would have wanted. We all have to move on! Doesn't mean we think about her any less."

Lila wonders quite how that squares with the fact that Gene couldn't even be bothered to mourn her mother's death, but he's being sweet to Bill so she decides to let it pass.

"You're right," says Bill, after he's thought about it. "Maybe I will ask her if she'd like to join me for dinner."

"Attaboy! Your old pal here will vamoose. Just say the word."

Afterward, Lila wonders if Gene's generosity of spirit is entirely altruistic. Should Bill move on with another woman, he is unlikely to want his room at Lila's in the future. But Eleanor would no doubt have labeled that as an incredibly cynical and bleak view of human nature, even for her, so Lila nods encouragement and lets that one pass too.

"By the way, honey," says Gene, "we fixed your john."

"I'm sorry?"

"The lavatory," says Bill. "The green bathroom. The one that kept blocking. We had a look on the outside wall this morning and we worked out that whoever installed it hadn't put the soil pipe leg at the right angle where it feeds into the bathroom. That was why it kept backing up."

"It was basically horizontal," said Gene.

"It absolutely was. So Gene and I went to the plumbing-supplies shop, got a new piece of pipe, and re-fixed it to the main pipe at a slightly altered angle. I trust you'll find that it solves the problem. I think we did rather a good job."

"You fixed the loo?" Lila cannot get her head around the idea of these two men at a plumbing-supplies shop together. Let alone having the practical skills to fix the problem.

"We certainly did," says Bill. "Flushes like a dream now."

Lila cannot speak. She looks at them, at their sweet, proud expressions, and is suddenly flooded by an unfamiliar feeling. It might be uncomplicated affection.

"Even after a big curry," adds Gene.

"Oh," says Lila. They stand there, all basking in the moment. And then Lila gives her head a shake. "So, hang on, that bloody plumber has been charging me three hundred quid every few weeks for what? Sticking a coat hanger down the bog? I'm going to kill him."

Chapter Twenty

Celie

Truant never gets onto the bed—it's one of his "things," along with never asking for a belly rub, only taking treats from Mum and Celie, and acting like everyone who comes to the door has come to murder them in their beds. But right now he is gazing at her from her duvet and Celie could not love him more. He understands. He is literally the only person in the world who does. The moment she walked into her room and finally let out the tears that had been swelling inside her head for the entire bus journey home, he had put his nose around the door, stood on the threshold for a minute, then nimbly leaped up and settled beside her. Not actually touching, his body is curled so that he is not suggesting he is definitely there in a support role, but she knows he is. Because Truant never gets onto the bed, and Celie has never felt sadder in her life.

The party is going to be a big one. China's parents are away, and she and Meena have sent out invites on Snapchat and she is literally the only person in year eleven who hasn't got one. The girls who were her best friends in the whole world for the whole of school have organized a party and she isn't invited. Even Martin O'Malley is going. Martin O'Malley and that weird girl Katya who only joined in year nine and everyone says smells of cheese. And the only reason she even knows about the party is because Martin O'Malley came up to her in the lunch queue and asked her if she was going. She had thought briefly that she might keel over from the shock—it was like being kicked in the stomach—and then she recovered and said no, maybe, not sure, she hadn't decided yet, but she was pretty sure she has no poker face because he had a horrible look of sympathy in his eyes when he walked away.

She reaches over and strokes Truant's soft black head. He looks a little wary, his eyes sliding toward her, but doesn't move, and then she puts her face into the pillow beside him and cries hot, silent tears.

She is not sure when Gene appeared, but it becomes obvious when Truant sets up a long, warning growl. She lifts her head and sees him standing there, his wrinkly old fingers on the door handle, his head cocked toward her. "Hey, what's going on, *chica*?"

She turns away from him. She does not want to have a Gene conversation right now. "Nothing."

"You got a headache? I have some Advil in my—"

"No."

A pause.

"You mad at your mom?"

"No, I am not mad at Mum."

She turns away from him and stares at the wall, willing him to disappear. And his voice comes from behind her. "Got your period?"

She pushes herself upright. "Oh, my God, just go *away*!"

He pulls a face. "Yeah, see, that's the thing. I can't just walk out and leave a lady crying. Doesn't feel right." He stands in the doorway, while she rubs furiously at her eyes, wishing he would just leave. But he takes another step toward her. Truant's growl grows louder. "You sure you don't have your period?"

"Please just go."

He goes, and she breathes a shaky sigh of relief, but he is back within minutes and this time opens the door without even knocking. She is about to yell at him but he throws something toward her, which lands on the bed. Truant jumps out of his skin and disappears behind the curtains, letting out brief warning barks, interspersed with growling.

She picks it up, trying to ignore the noise. Reese's Peanut Butter Cups. "What's this?"

"Try it."

He is clearly not going to leave until she does. She opens the wrapper and takes a small bite. She can taste peanut butter and overly sweet chocolate. It isn't bad, but she isn't really hungry. She takes another bite, letting it melt on her tongue. She will eat it and thank him, say something about how great he is, which is all Gene ever wants from anyone, and then he will go.

But instead of leaving, he sits on the bed beside her uninvited, and opens a second packet, popping a whole one of the chocolate discs into his mouth and letting out a little "mm" of pleasure. He speaks with his mouth full. "I keep a supply of them in my case. All this low-calorie stuff that Bill does—it's good for you, I guess, but a man needs to have a little sugar in his life, you know what I'm saying?"

Celie nods, and starts on the second. They eat in silence, listening to Truant's protests fade into sporadic grumbling growls, just to let Gene know he is still there, behind the curtain.

"I had a little cry this morning," Gene says, as he finishes chewing.

Celie twists to look at him.

"Didn't get a part. Kind of crazy, really, but I just knew I would be great in it. Just one of those medical dramas. It would have got me out of a hole. Would have got me back in the game over here. I got a call-back and then—after making me hold my breath for three days—goddammit if they didn't go with the other guy. He couldn't even act!"

He pops the other peanut butter cup into his mouth and chews. "And I *know* he wears a hairpiece."

Gene lets out a long sigh. And then he nudges her. "C'mon. Help me take your dumb dog out for a walk so it likes me and doesn't bite me again."

Celie sinks back onto her pillows. "I don't want to go out."

"Aww, c'mon, Celie. Help me out. I need to get this mutt on side. And you know the women are mad for me over here. The only way I can keep them off me is if I have an attractive young chick at my side."

"You can't call women chicks any more."

"Young ladies."

"Worse."

"Really? Okay. Let's settle on arm candy."

She rolls her eyes.

"I'm talking about me, not you. C'mon, finish your Reese's and let's get outta here."

THE HEATH IS BUSY at this time of day, its pathways covered with a carpet of ginger leaves, couples with takeaway coffees walking arm in arm, and children released from school jumping stray branches on the ground, brought down by the autumnal winds. Celie doesn't want to talk, really, but Gene never stops so she just lets him go on, about his failed audition, about how he misses the LA weather, about a woman who looks like a girl he once dated who cut the toes out of all his socks and he didn't even discover it till a week after she'd gone. She wonders whether that means he wore the same pair of socks all week, or whether he just walked around LA barefoot, but she can't be bothered to ask. She keeps thinking about how awful it'll be in school on Monday, the way the excitement about the party is going to ramp up toward the weekend, and how everyone will gradually find out that she's the only person not invited. It's like a disease, she thinks, being unpopular. People might not even know about it, but when they see you being isolated they'll be worried they might catch it and steer clear. She's already eaten lunch by herself four times in the last week.

"I think I might change schools," she says, when it's clearly impossible for her to say nothing. "There's a sixth-form college up the road I might go to."

"Okay. Sounds like a plan. Why'd you wanna change schools, though?"

Gene has hold of the lead and Truant is lagging behind them, as far as it's possible to get from Gene without actually pulling himself out of his harness.

She shrugs. "I might get better exam results."

He looks at her for a moment, then pulls a packet of cigarettes from his pocket and flips one into his mouth. He lights it and takes a long drag, blowing a thin plume of smoke into the air. "You don't like your school?"

"It's okay."

"Nobody leaves at your age unless they hate their school."

She kicks at a stone. Her voice when it emerges is choked, as if there is a giant pebble lodged in her mouth. "I used to like it."

He doesn't say anything. Just keeps walking but she can feel his gaze on her. And suddenly she's crying again. About Meena and the party and the anxiety knot she has in her stomach the whole time.

"Hey," he says. "Hey." He puts his arm around her and she doesn't even care if anyone sees. It's just all too much. "C'mon. Tell your old pal Gene. What's going on?"

"You won't talk to Mum?"

"Do I look like a tattle-tale?"

So she tells him. About how she might as well have leprosy because not a single person except the absolute rejects will talk to her, and how Meena was her best friend and knows all her secrets—including the fact that she wet the bed until she was eight and how she used to sleep with Mum for ages after Dad left because it felt like everything was falling apart and she was suddenly weirdly afraid of the dark and how she went with that boy from year thirteen in the park last November because she was stoned. Now it's like her whole life is in a box that Meena is just carrying round letting everyone peer in and laugh at her. And how she feels sick all the time and she can't talk to Mum because Mum is always stressed and miserable and distracted, and Dad doesn't think about anything but Marja and the new baby, and she doesn't know how she'll survive the next two years if she stays where she is because it feels like heading into a war zone every day.

And when she stops, Gene is standing beside her and he has his big old arm around her shoulders and he is pulling her into him and her face is against his T-shirt, which smells a bit of beer and cigarettes but not in a bad way. And he just squeezes her and kisses the top of her head and lets his face rest there for a minute. "Ah, sweetcheeks," he says. "That's rough."

"I don't know how to make it stop. Because I don't know what I did." She is wiping at her eyes, embarrassed, and he walks her over to a bench and sits her down until she can stop crying. It only takes about ten minutes. She can't look at him now, just sits with her shoulders hunched, her elbows resting on her knees, hiccuping gently.

"You know, I don't know much about much. But the one thing I do know about is acting."

Oh, God, she thinks. *Not another Gene On Stage story.* But he continues.

"Now, I don't know what you did. Or if you even did anything. But I do know that these girls—mean girls—they're going to be reading you all the time. Girls are super good at that. Boys, you know, we're just going to throw a few punches at each other and sort it out and it's all pretty much forgotten. But girls, they're complex. And right now, you're walking around just like—"

He gets up and stands in front of her, hunching his shoulders and dropping his chin. He looks sorrowful, defeated.

"I don't walk like that."

"Yeah, you kind of do. Body language is my special skill, sweetheart. That's what I do. And what you're projecting right now is defeat."

She stares at him, horrified. She pushes herself a little more upright.

Gene is talking directly to her now, his face uncharacteristically serious. "Now I'm not saying how you stand is going to make a whole bunch of difference, but it will make *a* difference. And right now these girls know you care about what they're doing to you. They know you're hurting and it makes them feel powerful. It makes them forget what's going on with their own lives. Because, honestly, they will all be having a crappy time individually."

"How would you know that?"

"Because it's only hurt people who hurt people."

She stares at him.

"Celie, baby, you look around at people who are happy in themselves in their lives—they're just busy living, having a good time. They don't set out to be mean to other people. Their energy is going into other things. It doesn't even occur to them to hurt someone else, or to try to make them feel small. In fact, they're more likely to be building other people up. So you know what you're going to do?"

Celie shakes her head.

"You're gonna feel sorry for them. These stupid, sad, mean girls who can only get their kicks from trying to make other people feel bad. Yup." He holds up a hand as she starts to protest. "But, also, you're not going to give them anything to make them feel better."

She frowns.

"You're going to change the way you show up. So instead of this"—he walks, shoulders hunched, looking sad, glancing sideways as if he was apologetic for even being there—"you're going to go in there on Monday looking like you don't give two shits."

She blinks.

Gene corrects himself. "Sorry—you're going to look like you couldn't care less what these girls think or do. You're going to walk in, own your space, hold your chin up, and change the energy around you. Like this."

He lifts his chest a little, walks determinedly to the patch of grass in front of her, and has a small smile on his face, like everything is faintly amusing.

"I can't do that." She pushes a curtain of hair from her face.

"Sure you can. You just have to practice. Go on. Do it."

She shrinks into herself, glancing around at the people who are walking their dogs nearby. This is too much.

But Gene keeps standing in front of her. "C'mon. Do it. I'm not going anywhere until you've done it. Stand up."

She sighs. He really isn't going anywhere. She gets up reluctantly from the bench.

"Straighter. C'mon. You're still bent double."

She straightens up a few more degrees, lifts her chin.

"That's it! More! You got it! Now walk to that tree."

She starts to walk, lengthens her stride, keeps her chest up. She feels a little self-conscious, but she doesn't want him yelling at her in public so she tries her hardest to stay really upright. It is actually a little shocking to feel how different this is from how she has been walking.

"Breathe! C'mon! A lot of this is in your breath. Breathe deep from in here! You're strong! Powerful! You're in a bubble that they can't penetrate. Now walk back past me and give me some attitude!"

He really isn't giving up. She turns, lifts her chin and walks back toward him.

He's animated now, gesturing toward her. "I'm one of those girls, okay? Look at me, being all mean and pouty." He flicks at his hair and purses his lips. "You know what I'm up to but you don't care. I'm basically beneath you, Celie. I'm pitiable! You put it on, baby, your body is going to start feeling it! And then you're going to feel it! C'mon!"

He is yelling now, pouting his lips together, and it makes her half embarrassed, half want to laugh. She slows her walk as she passes him, lifts her head and gives him a faint, dismissive smile.

"Yes! That's what I'm talking about! Sassy Celie! Give me Sassy Celie!"

She laughs. He is so ridiculous.

"C'mon. Back again! Give it to me worse now. Hands on hips! You can't even be bothered to engage with me! I'm barely worth your attention! I'm dirt under your shoe!"

She pivots, walks past him the other way, and she gives it to him. A sly flick of her gaze, up and down and up again, the smallest of sneers in her smile. She tells him silently he is nothing. Her chin is up, her shoulders locked, and she pivots again.

"Oh, *yes*! C'mon, baby. Now you've got it! Oh, man. More of that look! I'm dying here. I'm shrinking. I'm shrinking. Look, I'm nothing!"

Gene is crumbling, falling to his knees and then onto the ground. "I'm dead!" he says, flopping backward onto the grass. "I'm actually dead. You killed me."

She stops, laughing, feeling suddenly lighter. Weirdly, it works. She doesn't know how well she'll pull it off on Monday, but it does work. Or, at least, it's something, a tiny piece of armor to take to the war zone. She thinks of walking past Meena and China and their shock as they see she doesn't care what they say. She visualizes the bubble protecting her. She will move through her day like this, letting their unfriendly stares bounce off her, their whispered words unable to get through her invisible shield. Then she relaxes her position and grins, waiting for him to get up. He rolls over onto his side and pushes himself up to a sitting position in the grass, staring at his legs.

She waits. Finally he raises his head and looks at her, and lifts a gnarled old hand, puffing slightly. "Yeah, you're gonna have to give me a hand up, pumpkin. The old knees aren't what they were."

Chapter Twenty-one

Lila

Lila breaks first. She texts him on Thursday morning, after deliberating for an hour. It is the thought of Eleanor's exasperated *Well, why don't you just ask?* that finally propels her to the little keyboard on her phone.

> Hey—are we still on for this evening?

He doesn't reply for a couple of hours—probably stuck in meetings—and then just after midday her phone pings.

> Sure. Early drink? You okay to come to near my work? Can't be back late because of Lennie.

Early drink is a little disappointing, carrying as it does the implication that it will finish fairly quickly, but everyone's lives are complicated at Lila's age, and she knows this better than anyone. And, besides, Lila is determined not to let this date be too big a deal. She works until two, if you can really call scrolling distractedly through the internet work and, yes, she goes to get a blow-dry but she's wanted to try out the new salon on the high street for ages. And while she's there it seems daft not to get a manicure, because manicures always make you feel better about life generally—she read that in a magazine. She wears her good lingerie because it's important for women to feel good, even if nobody is going to see it. And if she takes a long time to get ready, it's because the weather is really changeable at the moment and she isn't sure what kind of venue they'll be meeting in (googling the bar really doesn't help—what if they're seated outside?) so the fact that she takes most of the day to get ready is really just a coincidence. As is the fact that she gets there twenty minutes early and has to hover at a street corner in Clerkenwell two blocks away so that she doesn't look too eager. You can never tell with public transport, these days.

He arrives ten minutes late, walking into the bar in a bluster of apologies. A meeting overran, he's so sorry, he hopes she hasn't been waiting long. The bar—a pub that has clearly been stripped back to wood and white, its tables marble and its chairs mismatched and antique—is swiftly filling with office workers, people jostling for tables and shedding bags and formal jackets, the detritus of the working day. She stands to accept a kiss on the cheek, and feels herself color at the contact. "No! No, it's fine. I just got here."

She had bought herself a still water, and he buys a beer after he checks that she doesn't want anything else. He's in a soft, midnight blue shirt and light brushed-cotton jeans, and she suspects his wardrobe is full of such clothes: unshowy in a way that tells people in the know that they cost a fortune. She's in a black V-necked sweater and black jeans, an outfit so neutral that she could fit in anywhere. He smiles as he arrives back at the table, and sits down, and for one terrifying moment she wonders if she'll be able to speak, if they'll have anything to talk about.

"So you escaped today's school run, then?" he says, his eyes crinkling.

"My stepfather does it half the week." He has slim, slightly tanned fingers, and there is a callus on his middle finger, probably from all the architectural drawing. "Also, that way I get an occasional break from seeing the Bendy Young Mistress." She blushes as she realizes she shouldn't refer to Marja that way. "That's what my stepdad calls her," she adds quickly, glancing up at him, but he's smiling. He is actually beautiful when he smiles.

"Hah. He's quite right. Nice to have someone at home to help, though. Half the time I feel like I'm running on the outer limits of what's possible. Lennie seems to have so many appointments and after-school things. Half of them her mother put in place before she went, and I haven't the heart to tell her she can't do them any more."

Lila really wants to ask about his wife, but feels it may be too early in the date, so she says: "What does Lennie like to do?"

"Ballet, modern dance—although between us, she's like a baby elephant clumping around the room. Zero natural ability, bless her. She does a needlework class nearby on Saturdays and horse-riding on Sundays. We gave up Mandarin Chinese. That was the one thing I felt was a little overboard. I mean, she's barely seven."

They talk aimlessly about children and schedules and the impossibility of work-life balance for a bit, and Lila tries to focus on what he says, but the physical reality of being near him seems to send her nervous system into a kind of rapid spiral. When she looks up from her drink he is gazing at her, his expression soft.

"It's nice knowing you're going to be at the school gates. It always makes me feel better."

"Really?" She can't keep the surprised pleasure from her voice.

"Yeah. This past year has been . . . a struggle. I feel obliged to pick Lennie up as much as possible, just so she knows I'm there for her, but I find that whole school-mums thing pretty bizarre. I wouldn't know what to say to half of them. And being a guy on your own in the playground makes you an object of—I don't know—attention? Curiosity?"

Lust, she thinks. Lust. And then puts her fingers against her mouth to stop her saying it aloud. "I know what you mean," she says carefully.

"Of course you do. You've been there too."

"I can't bear them," she blurts out. "It's like being judged every day by the worst people. I mean, before, I thought it was just because I worked. And a lot of them don't. They've made their children their career. And that's fine! Each to their own and all that. But there was always this unspoken disapproval because I hadn't managed to make cakes for the bake sale, or get the right uniform ready, or prepare a Harry Potter outfit for World Book Day. And now that Dan has gone off with Marja, well, it's a different kind of attention altogether."

Oh, God, but his eyes are so beautiful. Blue-green, suddenly made darker and more distinct by the color of his shirt. He has a way of focusing on her intently, as if everything she said contains an impossible worth.

"That must have been really tough."

She can only nod.

"You know he's going to regret it one day, right? You must know that."

She finds it hard to believe Dan is actually going to regret finding the woman of his dreams, with her smooth caramel skin, exotic accent, and subscription to *Interiors* magazine. But she nods, as if she's surprised by and resigned to this sad twist of Fate.

"Are you okay, though?" he says. "If it's not too personal, I mean, are you over him?"

This is probably a loaded question. Like she could suddenly become the woman on Jensen's date who cried and rambled on about her ex-boyfriend. So she smiles broadly, and says emphatically: "Oh, yes.

With hindsight I can see we weren't right for each other." She fiddles with an earring. "I'm fine. I mean, it was horrible at the time, but in the long run it's probably for the best."

"And are you seeing anyone?"

This is most definitely a loaded question.

"Not right now, no," she says, after considering for a moment, as if there has been a queue of suitors she has reluctantly decided to wave off for now. "I've been trying to focus on the kids."

He nods understandingly.

"You?"

He looks down. "Like you, just focused on Lennie, really. What I really want to do is bury myself in work and not think about anything, but she's a great kid and I need to make sure she gets through this period unscathed. Or as unscathed as she's going to be." He keeps looking down. "I guess I'll find out in ten years when she's in therapy."

"I'm sure she's doing okay," she says. "You're clearly a great dad."

He raises an eyebrow and shakes his head. His hair flops briefly over one eye and he pushes it back. "I'm not sure she'd agree with you. I'm pretty sure she'd say there's way too much homework and bath-time and violin practice and not enough television watching and McDonald's."

"You're clearly very cruel." She smiles so he knows she's joking.

"The worst. But she only has to sleep in the cupboard under the stairs when she's really bad."

She is not one hundred percent certain, but she thinks his knee might be touching hers under the table. At first she had thought it was the table, but there is a definite warmth emanating from it, and when he laughs, it moves slightly. When she establishes that, yes, it definitely is a knee and not the table leg, she is almost paralyzed by what it might suggest. She barely hears the next few things he says. Her knee has become radioactive, sending heat through the rest of her body. It's almost unbearable.

"Lila?"

"Mm?" She drags her attention back to the table.

"Did you want another drink? A real one this time?"

A brief dilemma. She doesn't want to seem like a killjoy—haunted as she is by the way Dan would roll his eyes at this point—but at the same time she feels as if she needs all her wits about her. She needs to be the best version of herself she can possibly be. But if he's suggesting they both have a drink, does that mean . . .

"Uh—vodka tonic? Hell, let's make it a double." She grins, as if this is just how she rolls. "What are you having?"

He stands, reaches into his pocket. "I won't have one. I have to drive Lennie back from my mum's later."

Afterward, she thinks she has never felt so intensely aware of her body in her life: her smile, the angles from which he will see her, the way her hands move on the table. She tries to drink deceptively slowly—the vodka tonic is very strong—and to be light, entertaining company. She asks him a few serious questions—how long he was married (twelve years), how they met (through a friend), whether he had always wanted to be an architect, but it is only with the last question that he speaks freely. He answers any questions about his wife with the shortest possible responses and looks away when he speaks. She thinks losing his wife must have been deeply traumatic, and not just for their daughter. He seems a lot more comfortable asking questions of her, wanting to know about the girls, how it is dealing with a teenager. ("Oh, God," he says drily. "I'm going to have to lock her in that cupboard for six years, aren't I?")

"Do you miss her?" Lila says, before she can stop herself.

"Who? Oh—my wife."

"Yes." Lila feels suddenly prurient, as if she has overstepped. But he holds her gaze long enough for her to color slightly, his head dipping while he thinks.

"I do miss her. But . . ." He winces. ". . . we had just separated before she died. So it's complicated."

Lila does not know what to say.

"She was an amazing woman. Everything was very passionate, very high octane. But it could be a little exhausting."

"I know someone else who had a relationship like that," Lila says, suddenly thinking of Jensen. "He said he sort of became acclimatized to the drama."

"You do. But people like that also leave a huge hole. She was very vibrant. And a fantastic mother."

"I'm so sorry."

"Don't be. My taste in women has changed now. I value something a little calmer." He looks directly at her as he says this.

His knee is still pressed against hers so she feels emboldened. "Can I ask why you split up?"

He looks briefly uncomfortable. "She . . . was surprisingly insecure. I think she saw things that weren't there, if you know what I mean. I just eventually . . . ran out of reassurances."

"Oh, that's tough." She wants to say something about how jealous Dan had been but in truth there had been whole weeks when she was not even sure he knew she was still in the house.

"By the way, people don't know much about all this at school. I'd appreciate it if you—"

She is just shaking her head reassuringly, in a way that suggests there is nothing she cannot keep secret, when his mobile phone rings. He looks down at the number and his face falls. He glances up at Lila. "Excuse me," he says, "I have to take this."

He stands as he answers it. "Hi. No, she's not with me. I'm out." He turns and starts weaving his way through the packed tables, turning briefly to give Lila the universal sign for *I'll only be a minute.*

She sits, watching him walk out onto the pavement, where she can see him in animated discussion. He does not look happy as he walks backward and forward. At one point he takes a deep breath, as if he is trying to control himself. Finally he ends the call, takes a moment, then turns and walks back in. When he arrives at the table she is gazing at her phone, as if she is reading emails, oblivious, and she looks up, her face blank. "Everything okay?"

"I'm really sorry. I'm going to have to leave," he says, and Lila struggles to stop herself looking crestfallen. He does not sit down again. He doesn't elaborate further.

It takes her a beat, and then she gets up, reaching for her bag. "Oh! No problem! I should probably head home myself."

He walks her to the tube station, suddenly distracted and quiet. The streets are still thick with people walking home from work, the road heavy with slow-moving traffic and she realizes that this is it, the end of the date. A busy tube entrance at a quarter to eight in the evening rather than a late night inching-together of bodies on a sofa. He is not going to see her special lingerie, and now she has hand-washing that she could have avoided. She feels heavy with disappointment. She stops beside the tube entrance, stepping against the wall so that the steady deluge of people feeds past them. "Well, that was nice," she says, because she cannot think of anything else to say. She isn't sure he's even listening anymore.

Gabriel looks at her, suddenly intent, as if he's just spotted her there. "Lila, it was lovely. Really lovely. You don't know what a special person you are. I—I would have had a very different kind of day without you. I love that we got to spend some time together. You're the one person I feel I can really talk to. You really . . . seem to understand what I'm dealing with."

He takes her hand then and, as she watches, lifts her palm to his lips and, placing it over his mouth, kisses it, his eyes locked on hers. The intimacy, the blatant sexuality of the gesture knocks her breath clean from her chest. She is about to speak, but then, with a nod, he turns and is striding down the road. She is pulled into the crowd and heading into the station, her entire body ringing like the vibrations of a giant bell.

"DARLING, THEY LOVE it. They're putting together an offer and I'll call as soon as I have it. But, my goodness, I loved it too. How absolutely thrilling. How liberated! What an utter inspiration you are!"

Lila is just walking back from the tube station when Anoushka calls. She is so locked into her memories of the last couple of hours that it takes her a moment to grasp what her agent is even talking about. "Oh!" she says, and stops on the pavement. "They really liked it?"

"Just the right amount of sexiness and naughtiness. I was *totally* in your shoes for the whole chapter. And what a dreamboat! Please tell me you're seeing the mysterious J again."

Lila doesn't want to think about Jensen. She wants to think about Gabriel, the way his wrists emerge from his shirtsleeves, the floppy lock of hair that falls just in front of his glasses. She wants to think about the hot, soft pressure of his lips on her palm. She can still feel their imprint on her skin.

"Oh. No. I don't think so. I'm—I'm sort of seeing someone else now."

Anoushka's voice is shrill: "Another man! Already! Oh, Lila, you really are living the dream. Is he as nice?"

"Better." Lila can hear the smile in her voice. "He's basically everything I want in a man."

"You must be giving off pheromones! You're every middle-aged woman's fantasy!" Anoushka always speaks in exclamation marks, but today they're extra emphatic. "You must tell me your secrets! Rupert has been the most dreadful bore this year. It's like all he wants to do is sit on the sofa and watch *The Repair Shop* every night. I need to be rolling around in a workshop being filthy with some gorgeous stranger! You need to include a how-to guide in your manuscript!"

"So," Lila drags her attention back to the call, "what do you think they'll offer?"

"I've told them if they want a pre-empt it's got to be a good six figures. And she didn't balk. So let's wait and see. But I have high hopes. High hopes!"

Anoushka rings off and Lila walks home in a daze. It takes her two streets to realize that the unfamiliar feeling she is flooded with is hope.

THAT NIGHT, AFTER the girls have gone to bed (or after Violet has gone to bed: she has no idea how late Celie stays up in her room), she watches an episode of *La Familia Esperanza*. Estella Esperanza is being pursued by a younger man, the gorgeous doctor who treated her bullet wound from two episodes previously. His expressions of love are ardent, and he seems to understand the deep conflict within her. But she doesn't take him seriously, locked as she is onto the memory of her husband, her obsession with separating him from his younger lover. Lila, who is eating a packet of shortbread biscuits in lieu of dinner, takes a short breath as the doctor lifts Estella's hand to his mouth, flooded again with the feel of Gabriel's lips on her palm, the strange, erotic certainty of the gesture. Estella pulls away her hand, furious and vulnerable, and says something in rapid-fire Spanish that is subtitled: *You make too many assumptions! Don't touch me!*

Lila stares at the screen, then looks down at her phone. She types: **Really loved seeing you today. Let's do it again soon x**

It makes her blush even to type it. She waits a few minutes, but he doesn't answer. There are no pulsing dots suggesting a carefully crafted reply, nothing. Her message disappears into cyberspace and hangs somewhere in the ether. Don't overthink it, she tells herself, as she feels her post-date high start to plummet. He's a busy man. And he was clearly having a bad evening. She wonders, briefly, if she should be a more high-drama kind of woman. Whether that would make men respond to her, make her absence an unforgettable hole in their lives.

And then her phone buzzes.

Me too, Bellissima. See you very soon x

Chapter Twenty-two

Gene has won two roles. The first is a straightforward toothpaste advert: a day's filming in which he mostly just has to show off his impressive dental work. Apparently the selection of older English actors he was up against had teeth like yellowed fence posts. He is also to be an elderly businessman visiting from New York in a well-funded period drama and has so far spent a week "in character," harrumphing gently at the dinner table and pontificating about the dreadful charlatans of Wall Street. His two lines have required endless rehearsal, and from any point in the house one might at any given moment hear the carefully projected words "But, Mr. Arbuthnot, if one owns a shipping line then one is guaranteed a lifetime of security. Can you really say that about Dow's list of stocks?" spoken in an infinite variety of ways, with the emphasis placed variously on *guaranteed*, *lifetime*, and *stocks*. Violet can now repeat the lines verbatim, and has taken to muttering them under her breath while watching television or brushing her teeth. Truant has been triggered by an over-emphatic shouted recitation of the second line and now grumbles audibly whenever Gene starts speaking. It is one day's filming, at a stately home in Oxfordshire, and Gene has rarely been more cheerful.

"They pay well, honey," he says to Lila. "I'm going to be able to give you some rent! And, you never know, if I make an impression in this drama it could be a recurring part."

She should be pleased for him. But while she accepts his hugs, and smiles at the latest infinitesimally different performance, she sometimes wonders whether she will ever feel about Gene as one is meant to feel about a father. She can never just see him as he is, because she sees simultaneously the shadow version of him at the same time: the gap in the little gathering of mourners around her mother's grave, the missing paternal arm around her shoulders when she needed it most.

He has been taking Truant for a walk in the afternoons "so you can focus on your work." Bill says, with some surprise, that it's a nice gesture, but all Lila can think is that it's pure Gene: he cannot bear it if there is one person who does not love him, and if this person happens to be a dog, he will simply charm that dog into submission too.

Eleanor says she should give him a break, he is at least trying, and you cannot hang on to anger forever (apparently at this age it's terrible for your naso-labial folds) but she still finds herself niggling at him—*So when's the next audition, Gene? Any news on that other job you went for?*—all underpinned by what she actually wants to say, which is *When are you going to leave again?*

She stands at the sink, watching as Gene takes advantage of Jensen's arrival back at work to recite lines at him in the garden. He is now wearing a tweed jacket of Bill's (he has asked to borrow it) and a cravat, and Jensen is standing in front of him, his hands resting on a metal gardening fork as Gene walks up and down declaiming in what might well have been a statesmanlike manner, had he not been wearing a pair of faded Stars and Stripes Y-fronts underneath the tweed jacket.

"But, Mr. Arbuthnot, if one owns a shipping line then one is guaranteed a lifetime of security . . ."

Jensen's eyebrows are raised and he is nodding in an encouraging manner. He seems to have an infinite amount of patience for these old men and their foibles. But, then, he doesn't have to live with them.

Lila looks back at the washing-up, then at her phone, checking for text messages she may have missed. Gabriel has not suggested another date. When Eleanor had asked about follow-up she had simply said, "Oh, yes, he texted," with the kind of secretive smile that suggested content that cannot be shared in public. Eleanor had been a bit non-plussed by the whole palm-kissing thing, but as their tastes are clearly very different in the sexual arena just now, Lila isn't going to worry about that.

Bill, meanwhile, is preparing for his dinner with Penelope Stock-bridge. He has changed his mind about the menu three times, eventually settling on sea bass with a fennel and lime salad followed by a lemon parfait pudding. This has required three separate trips to the supermarket as Bill, normally possessed of an ordered mind, has clearly found the idea of a dinner date so discombobulating that he has forgotten vital ingredients, mislaid roasting pans, and lost confidence in his dish choices twice.

"Pal, you could order in two hamburgers for all she's going to care. She just wants a big ol' slice of Bill pie, you know what I'm saying?" Gene says laconically, dipping his finger into the parfait and jumping when Bill swats him with a tea-towel.

"I don't know whether it's too informal to eat in the kitchen. Is it too informal? Does it suggest a certain lack of finesse?"

"Serve it on a tray in the bedroom," says Gene, with a lascivious wink, and at that point Lila has to ask him to take Truant for another walk.

He is just leaving, having been reminded twice to put on some trousers, when Jensen appears at the back door. "Hey."

"Hey!" she says. She is wearing rubber gloves covered with soap bubbles and has to lift her arms to push her hair off her face.

"Just . . . wanted to say a proper hello. You're not . . . the most talkative on text."

Lila winces internally. He had sent a further two texts in the ten days he had been away and she had been so consumed with thoughts of Gabriel that she had failed to respond to the second and sent a simple cheery *Hope you're having a nice time with your folks* to the third.

"Yeah," she says awkwardly. "Sorry. I'm not really a big texting person."

He doesn't seem to mind. He stands on the threshold of the garden door, his boots covered with dirt, his sandy hair awry on one side, like that of a toddler who has just been roused from sleep. "No problem. I just wondered . . . if maybe you'd like to go out again sometime."

When she falters a response he adds quickly: "Not a big deal. I just enjoyed our chat. We could go for another Diet Coke."

"Sure!" she says, too brightly. "But I—uh—can't do this week. Absolutely flat out with work. And, you know, these two . . ."

He studies her face, then looks away, back down the garden. "Bill's pretty worked up about this date, huh?"

"He really is."

Eleanor would no doubt say she should date them both, keep her options open. But what she feels for Gabriel is so consuming that it feels wrong to string Jensen along.

"So what are you doing while the dinner is happening? I hear you've all been banished from the premises."

"Oh, we're just going to get a pizza." The way he stands there makes her wonder if he's half hoping to be invited along, and there is a brief, weighty silence. Finally he looks at his feet. "Well. Better get on with it." He looks up, as if struck by a thought. "Hey—don't forget that tree. I don't want to load you up with problems but you need to do something about it. I think it's listing a little more than when I left."

"Sure," she says, waiting for him to go. She wishes this didn't feel so awkward. She smiles, and it feels horrible. Not a real smile at all.

Another elongated pause, and then—after a beat—he nods and heads back into the garden.

SOMETIMES LILA MISSES her mother so badly she feels she could become one of those people who sit by gravestones and talk to the dead. If it wasn't so damp out and if she could be bothered to drive all the way to Golders Green, this would be exactly the kind of day when she would sit among the faded plastic flowers and the engraved marble urns and talk to Francesca. How do I tell someone nice that I'm not really interested without hurting his feelings? How do I know if the man I am interested in is interested in me? How am I meant to cope with all this *stuff*, all of the time? Francesca had had a way of looking at you, her gaze intent and direct behind her tortoiseshell-framed glasses, as if she was really absorbing the question, and taking your feelings into account, even if they were probably not the feelings you should be having. And her answers were always wise, filled with compassion and not too prescriptive: *Oh, darling, that's very tough. I know you can find a way through this but if you wanted some advice, I'd suggest . . .* or *What is your gut telling you, Lila? You're a terribly smart person. I think you probably know the answer to that one already.*

Lila had been able to talk to her about anything. As a teenager, hers was the mother who never judged but who talked to her as if she were an adult, treating the most minor problem as if it was of utmost importance. She would take Lila on drives so that she didn't face her directly (she told her long afterward she had read that you should discuss things with teenagers while not looking them directly in the eye—"you know, like dogs") and while she never condemned Gene in front of her, she was always scrupulously honest in how she described her own feelings, admitting to anger or sadness or a sense of abandonment in a way that somehow managed to tread the tricky tightrope between truthfulness and overwhelming Lila with adult emotions she could not yet handle.

There was a period—Lila was fifteen or sixteen—when even Lila's friends would ask Francesca for advice, sitting in the kitchen with her while she made them tea or handed out homemade muffins, and told them what she would do, and the many ways in which they were all doing wonderfully and were going to be absolutely fine. For a while, Lila had been slightly annoyed by how much her friends wanted to hang out with her mother. But in the trickier years of her marriage she could talk to Francesca about Dan without fearing that, like some mothers-in-law, his failings would be totted up and stored away as evidence to be used against him at a later time when Lila inevitably felt more benevolent toward him. She would always preface her responses with *Well, you know I adore Dan and always will*, followed by careful statements like *but in this case I think he may be being a little unreasonable. I'm sure he's not doing it deliberately. Why don't you ask him gently how he would feel if the positions were reversed?* She was also, enjoyably, not averse to the occasional *They can absolutely fuck right off* if the situation merited it. With hindsight, she had just seemed better at being human than anyone Lila had ever met. She had been not just an ally but someone whose advice always seemed so firmly rooted in what was right, or appropriate, that Lila had felt she had a permanent hotline to good sense. Until, thanks to a number 38 bus and an unseasonably rainy day, she didn't.

Some days, it feels impossible, just impossible, that she isn't here anymore.

But Bill has a date with someone else, and she needs to sort out her own problems. Lila peels off her rubber gloves and heads upstairs to get ready.

• • •

THERE ARE PIZZAS, Gene is saying, and then there are pizzas. Sure, these are fine, but for *real* pizza the girls need to try Antonio Gatti's place in downtown LA. "I mean, the guy comes from a long line of pizza-makers from Sicily. His father made pizzas, his grandfather made pizzas . . . They have a whole bunch of black-and-white photographs on the wall of the men of the family. The interior is nothing—you'd walk straight past it out on the sidewalk. It's no fancy-pants kind of joint. But he does something to the base so it's as light as a feather, you know what I'm saying? And the mozzarella . . . my God . . ."

Gene has been talking about the superiority of American pizzas for almost twenty minutes, and Lila is watching the girls and marveling at how patient they are. No phones or electronic devices are allowed at dinner time—a rule that extends to restaurants—but right now he has been going on for so long that she almost wants to offer them her own as an escape route.

Gene folds a slice and feeds it into his mouth. "I gotta say, though, I'm liking this spicy salami with the chili. Got a kick to it, doesn't it? What you got there, Violet?"

"Ham," Violet says, her mouth full.

"What kind of ham?"

"Ham ham."

Lila watches Celie quietly and industriously demolishing a vegetarian pizza, pausing occasionally to push her hair behind her ears. It's good to see her with an appetite.

"How'd it go today, honey?" Gene is talking to her.

Celie's eyes flash toward Lila and then back at Gene.

"How did what go today?" Lila says.

"It went fine," Celie says, cutting a piece of pizza with a knife and fork.

"Did you kill, though? Did you actually . . . *destroy*?"

She allows herself a small smile. "I destroyed," she says, and Gene explodes at the table.

"I knew it! I knew you could do it! Give me a high-five!" He swings his meaty palm across the table and, to Lila's surprise, Celie's hand rises to meet it with a resounding clap. "There's no stopping you now, sweetheart. You got to listen to your old pal Gene. I got it all in here." He taps the side of his head, leaving a smudge of tomato sauce on his temple.

"Do what?" Lila is struggling to keep up. "Hang on, what—what did you destroy?"

Celie looks down at her plate. "Nothing," she says primly.

Lila is about to protest when her phone rings.

"How come you're allowed your phone—" Violet begins, but Lila holds up a hand.

"Anoushka?"

"Are you sitting down?"

"Yes?"

"A hundred and seventy thousand."

Lila blinks, takes a moment to register what she has just heard. "Are you serious?"

"For two. I think I can push them to one eight five but—"

"No! No! That's fantastic! Oh, my goodness, Anoushka, that's amazing news!"

"We retain world rights so there should be further sales available through translation. They've sent me a very compelling marketing plan, and they say this will be one of their tent-pole publications for next year. So I think it's good news, darling."

Anoushka talks on about the minutiae of the deal, giving her a breakdown of the negotiations and where there may still be "wiggle room," but Lila is barely listening. She feels almost weak with relief. She says, "Yes," when it seems appropriate, but her brain has basically become a giant humming thing. Her financial woes are solved. Her house will remain her house. When she finally ends the call, the rest of the table is looking at her expectantly. "I've got a good deal for my new book." She is beaming. "I wrote four chapters and my agent sent it to a publisher and they've offered me a good deal."

"How about that! Two pieces of good news!" Gene reaches across to hug her. She accepts it a little stiffly. "We should have a glass of champagne!"

"They don't do champagne here," says Lila, who has noted that Gene is two beers in.

"Is it a fiction book?" says Violet, lining up her crusts in a row at the side of her plate. Lila picks up her knife and fork again. "Um, no. It's—it's non-fiction."

"What does that mean?"

"It's more about . . . real-life stuff."

"What real-life stuff?" says Celie.

"Uh—it's about—uh . . ." Lila is flummoxed. She hadn't expected the girls to be remotely interested. They had been barely aware of the last book she published, thankfully. "It's sort of about life at my age."

"What about life at your age?" Violet pushes her plate toward the middle of the table.

"Just about—well, about how we have to juggle lots of things and try to find happiness in different ways from when we were younger."

"Is it about us?" says Celie. Her huge, pale eyes are locked on Lila's face now. Her gaze is unwavering.

"Not really. I don't mention you by name."

"Then what are you writing about?" says Violet. "You always say me and Celie are your life."

Lila seems to have developed a stutter. She takes a swig of her water. "It's—it's more just adult stuff. Just, you know, all the things I—I deal with in a day."

"Am I in it, sweetheart?" says Gene, cheerfully. Evidently he cannot conceive of the possibility that he would not be included in the most positive light.

"Uh—possibly? I haven't got that far yet."

"You need to make it clear that I've done a lot of stuff. I mean if this thing does well it could open doors for me. You can check my IMDb page if you need the details. Can you make sure you include *Star Squadron Zero*? It's good for everybody to be reminded of that one."

"So what have you written about?" Celie is still staring at her. "You said you'd written four chapters."

"Shall we get the bill?" Lila looks at her watch. "Surely Bill and Penelope will have finished their main course by now."

"You said we could have ice cream." Violet crosses her arms.

"Honey, it's only half past eight. Give the guy a chance." Gene puts a hand on her arm. "You know Bill—it will have taken him this long to warm up! Let him have a couple of glasses of wine with her at least."

Lila smiles awkwardly. "How do we think he's getting on, then?" she says brightly, trying to change the conversation. "Do we think Penelope will be wearing something extraordinary?"

"Butterfly shoes!" says Violet, delightedly. "And a hat made of zebras!"

Lila lets out a small breath, and waves for the pudding menu. But when she looks over again Celie is still watching her.

THEY WALK BACK to the house at a sedate pace, Gene off to the side, taking advantage of the walk to smoke a cigarette. Normally, Lila would be slightly frazzled by the girls bickering animatedly behind her, but tonight she registers the snappy conversation and muttered insults with only half an ear. She had never considered the possibility that Celie might be interested in the contents of the book. What would happen if she actually read it? Would Lila need to have a conversation with her to prepare her for it?

She tries to imagine how her mother would have handled it. Francesca had Scandinavian levels of nonchalance when it came to sex and nudity. She would walk around the house with nothing on while searching for things to wear, and because she had done it since Lila was small, Lila had thought nothing of it. When Lila, as a teenager, had protested about the noise emanating from her mother's bedroom one night, Francesca had looked bemused. "But, darling, sex is lovely! You can't be inhibited just because someone might hear you. It's only happy sounds after all."

Lila is not convinced Celie would be entirely overjoyed to hear about Lila's happy sounds. For a start, Lila has never been a walking-round-the-house-naked kind of person. It was fine when Celie was a baby (although she could probably have done without Toddler Celie telling her she had a "funny floppy belly") but Dan had never been hugely comfortable with random nudity and she had slowly absorbed that vague discomfort for herself. They got up; they showered; they were always dressed downstairs. They only had sex when they could be sure both girls were fast asleep, and often checked on them twice beforehand just to be sure. Is Celie likely to take after Francesca, relaxed about sexuality, comfortable with the idea of her mother having an erotic life? Or will she be appalled?

As they approach the front door, she is pulled from her thoughts by the tinkling of Penelope's laughter. The sound of a jazz piano recording drifts toward them. She checks her watch: 9:40 p.m. Gene mutters, "Attaboy," and grins at her, and they let themselves in.

Penelope Stockbridge and Bill are bent over an old photograph album, their heads almost touching. The lights are low and two candles burn gently in the middle of the table, the detritus of the meal pushed to one side. The dirty plates, unusually for Bill, are piled up on the work surface, for washing later. The air is filled with the smell of good food and wine. Penelope looks up abruptly as Lila walks into the kitchen, as if she has been lost in her own little world.

She glances down at her slim watch, then back at Lila, her neck flushing. She is wearing a 1940s-style tea dress in dark red silk, and an ornate comb made of something like ivory pins her hair into an elaborate dark brown twist.

"Hi," says Lila.

Penelope looks instantly awkward. "Oh, is that the time? Goodness. I had no idea."

Gene's voice booms from behind them. "Hey, kids, don't break up the party on my account! I'm headed into the garden for a smoke anyhow."

Lila sets her handbag on the side and gives Penelope what she hopes is a reassuring smile. "I'll be putting the girls to bed. Please don't get up."

"I don't need putting to bed," says Celie. "I'm sixteen."

"Yes, you do," says Violet, gazing at Penelope. "Or you'll be playing gooseberry." She says *gooseberry* with salacious relish.

Penelope blushes. "Oh I really wouldn't want to outstay my welcome . . ." She glances at Bill, uncertainly.

"We were just looking at pictures of me in my army days," Bill says. His voice is cheerful and he looks open and relaxed, a little like he did years ago. Lila feels a weird pang, unsure if the fleeting feeling is because of her mother, who should have been sitting across the table, or because she, Lila, is not having evenings like these, basking in the adoration of someone who wants nothing more than to be with her.

"Bill was terribly handsome in uniform, wasn't he? Still is," Penelope adds, then blushes again.

Truant, furious at having been left behind, has bolted to Lila and is now weaving himself through her legs, his eyes slightly manic and his tongue lolling, so that she has to grab the work surface to stop him knocking her over. In doing so she manages to unbalance a delivery box, which falls to the floor, along with an open cookery book. The noise and sudden chaos of the kitchen seem to unsettle Penelope. Or perhaps it is just that the atmosphere has shifted, a fragile little bubble broken. She stands, and smoothes her skirt.

"I should go. It's late and you've all got things to do."

"Oh, really. You don't have to," Bill begins, but she is already reaching for her coat, holding it in front of her with thin, pale fingers. "Then let me walk you back to your house."

"Goodness! It's only four doors down."

"I absolutely insist," Bill says, helping her into her coat.

Penelope is glowing. She smiles at them all. "It's been so very lovely. Bill, the food was exquisite. What a wonderful cook you are. Thank you so much. I really have had the loveliest time."

"The feeling is entirely mutual," says Bill. "You are wonderful company." And with a last burst of breathless thank-yous from Penelope they head to the front door.

"Are they going to snog?" says Violet, fascinated, as it closes behind them.

"Oh, God," says Celie. "Yuk." She trudges upstairs to her room, clearly exhausted by having to spend so much unscheduled time with her family.

"Does Bill have false teeth? Will he have to take them out first?" Violet presses her nose against the window as they pass. "Will they put their tongues in each other's mouths?"

"No, Bill does not have false teeth, and I have no idea how or even whether he is going to kiss Penelope. That's their private business," Lila says, peeling her away and pushing her toward the hallway. "Now upstairs and brush your teeth. And don't tell Bill you drank two glasses of cola. He'll never forgive me."

Gene reappears from the garden just as Bill walks back in, all of two minutes later. Truant is at Gene's heels, looking expectant. She suspects he's been feeding him cheese-flavored crisps again.

"Pal! What are you doing?"

Bill closes the front door. "What do you mean what am I doing?"

"You said you were walking her home!"

"That's exactly what I just did."

Gene throws up his hands in horror. "No no no no no! You don't literally just walk the lady to her front door and walk away again. That's the best bit of the evening! That's the bit she's been waiting for! What did you do?"

Bill seems a little discomfited. He glances at Lila then back at Gene. "I—I walked her to her front door, told her I'd had a lovely time, and made sure she was in safely."

Gene smacks his hand against his head. "Bill! Get back there! With luck she's not even sat down yet."

"You really think I disappointed her?" He looks crestfallen. "I mean, I didn't want to make any assumptions."

"Bill, that little lady likes you. She really likes you. She's brought you a hundred and sixty-nine tuna-pasta bakes. She wears little glittery clips in her hair hoping you're going to notice. She listens to you play the same damn piano piece day after damn day. Her whole face lights up at your every word. Get back there, knock on the door, tell her you forgot something, sweep her into your arms and kiss her properly. C'mon. Don't let the side down here."

"You really think—"

"Stop talking, man! Go get her!"

Bill looks briefly uncertain, but Gene is already propelling him toward the door, and opening it. "Don't come back in less than twenty minutes!" he yells, shoving him out onto the step.

With a slightly anguished look, Bill disappears from view.

"What if she doesn't want to be kissed?" Lila says, as Gene closes the door again.

He grins at her, his smile wide and his unnaturally white teeth glowing. "Lila. I may be a fuck-up on many things, but on women I am an expert. You watch, in twenty minutes, old Bill there is going to walk back in here looking probably a little dazed, standing two inches taller, and insanely pleased with himself. I could set a kitchen timer to it."

Annoyingly, he turns out to be absolutely correct.

Chapter Twenty-three

Dan calls when she is three-quarters of the way through chapter five. The writing has come remarkably easily since she got the deal. She is back into what Instagram calls her "healing" journey. She has been looking online at the experiences of other newly divorced women for inspiration and her literary vocabulary is thick with words and phrases like "boundaries," "red flags," and "emotional self-awareness." With luck, by the time she gets to the end of this more feelings-based chapter, she will have some other bedroom escapade to write about. Or, as the Instagrammers put it, she will be embracing her full womanhood and owning her sexuality.

Gabriel has been texting again, usually in the evenings. He is affectionate in tone, complimentary, a little vague on actual plans, but right now she will settle for him just showing up on her phone. He calls her "Bella" as if it is a nickname. At first she had sent him question marks, wondering if he had actually meant to text someone else. He had lived in Italy in his twenties. Of course he had. "Hi, Bella," "Night, Bellissima."

She finds herself glancing surreptitiously into mirrors as she passes, wondering what he can see.

Dan, on the other hand, always greets her as if he is putting down a marker. "Lila."

"I'm in the middle of writing," she says coolly, dredging up the research she has done on boundaries. "I'd appreciate if we could talk afterward."

"It won't take a minute. I wanted to see if we could switch weekends. My parents would really like to see the kids and they can't do my weekend. Can I take them this week?"

"Why can't they do your weekend? They'll have had enough notice." Their calendar is a constant rebuke, a shared digital document that makes Lila's skin prickle every time she has to consult it.

The sound of rustling in the background. Dan's voice is distracted, as if he is doing fifteen things and she is the least important. It used to irritate her when they were married, his inability to make her feel she was the sole focus of his attention. "Dad has a golf thing and Mum wants to get her hair done."

"So you want me to change all my plans because your mum may or may not get her hair done?" Lila does not have any plans but that is not the point.

"Marja can only do this weekend. Next weekend Hugo has some kind of trip planned with her ex. He's coming over from Holland."

"Oh. So this is about Marja. I see." Dan is taking the whole family up north to see his parents. A lovely blended family trip. How perfectly cozy. Lila feels her calm resolve start to leach away.

"It's not just about Marja, Lils."

"Don't call me Lils."

"Why? Why are you being like this?"

"Because 'Lils' implies an intimacy we no longer have."

He sighs. He has this way of engaging with her as if he's at the end of his tether, dealing with an irrational madwoman. "Okay. Lila. Please can I take the kids this weekend. You can have them next weekend and the weekend after."

She takes a moment to consider how helpful she wants to be. "Fine by me. But you'll have to ask Celie. She has her own plans these days."

"Well, anything she wants to do she can just do from mine?"

"I'm not saying she can't. I'm saying it might be wise to ask her. She's practically an adult."

"Fine. I'll ask her." There is a short pause, and Lila prepares to put the phone down.

"Oh, and I was wondering if I could pop round this week to pick up some of the baby stuff from the garage."

"What?"

"The old cot and baby seat for the car. I think there's some other stuff in those boxes too. I'm going to need them soon."

Lila is poleaxed by the casual sense of entitlement. "But—they're not yours."

"They're as much mine as they are yours."

"Dan, they were our family things. They were our children's. You don't just get to come and pick them up for your new family. That's just—that's just—No."

"Lila, you're being ridiculous. What do you need them for?"

She opens her mouth to speak but the cruelty in his comment has briefly winded her. "No," she says finally. "You can't have them."

"Lila, this is nuts. I'm having a baby in a few months' time. I have no money. You are never going to use those items again. Or, if you do," he says with exaggerated equanimity, "it's not likely to be for at least another year. So I'd like to come and pick up *our* baby things."

"They're gone," she says quickly.

"What?"

"I threw them away. When I was having a clear-out."

"I don't believe you."

"I don't care."

"Lila, you're being irrational and selfish. They are not your things to dispose of."

"We had an agreement, Dan. You took everything you wanted when you left. You literally said it to me, that you were taking everything you needed, like you were telling me we were the unwanted part of that equation. You don't get to swing by whenever you fancy it and help yourself to more."

"I'm not 'helping myself.' I'm asking for the baby seat and cot that I helped pay for—items you don't need—to look after my new baby."

Lila's jaw has clenched. "Sorry," she says. "I took them to the dump ages ago."

There is a long, loaded silence. A silence that tells her he knows she is lying, and that she knows he knows it.

Finally Dan says: "You are fucking impossible." And puts down the phone.

LILA IS LOADING the baby seat and cot into the Mercedes when Jensen arrives. She has been rooting through the garage, which still contains a teetering mass of boxes from when she and Dan moved in—she can't remember what most of them contain—and is pulling out an overstuffed crate of large plastic baby toys. She dumps it on the back seat when she sees him standing by the gate. She's had to lower the roof of the convertible to get everything in, and now the plastic arc of dangling ducks, an enormous rubber giraffe, and the wooden bars of the cot stick out of it, like some kind of clown vehicle.

"Having a clear-out?" he says.

"Something like that."

He watches as she adds a plastic baby bath. "I've caught you at a bad time. I'll come back."

"No, no, it's fine. What is it?" She is aware that she's radiating ill-humor. The call with Dan has left her in a filthy mood. She hates that they've been separated this long yet he can set her off, like a hair trigger, reducing her to tears of rage and impotent fury. But he is not having her precious baby things for the new child. The idea of Marja carrying Lila's car seat into the playground—the car seat that should have housed her third baby—makes her feel as if her head is exploding.

"Are you sure you're okay?"

She lets out a long breath and brushes the dust from her jeans. "I'm fine. Sorry."

"I just came to drop an invoice off to Bill."

"What invoice?"

"The latest installment of the garden."

She frowns. "Bill's been paying for that?"

Jensen looks briefly uncomfortable, as if he has just revealed something he shouldn't. "Uh . . . yes?"

"No," she says. "I'll pay it. It's my house."

"But he—"

"Just give me the invoice."

He hands it over reluctantly. She unfolds the piece of paper, reading it and wincing reflexively before she reminds herself that this is fine. She will get her first payment for the book within weeks. "I'll sort it out when I've done this," she says, mustering a smile that isn't really a smile at all.

His hands are thrust deep into his pockets. He seems troubled, which makes her feel bad, but right now she has to head to the dump. Some small part of her is afraid that Dan will even now be on his way here, convinced she is lying, and she wants to be able to throw open the garage door and reveal that she is not "fucking impossible" actually, because the items really have gone. *So take that, Dan!*

They stand there for an awkward moment. Then Jensen takes a step backward and lifts a hand. She sees his pickup truck parked across the street and experiences a residual prickly glow, thinking of the two of them in it in the dark, the weight of the vodka bottle on her lap.

"That's it, really. I guess . . . I'll see you Monday." Jensen gives her a little wave, then turns and walks back toward the van.

Lila gets into her car, checks she has her purse and her phone, and turns on the ignition. A click. Then nothing.

She wiggles the gear stick to make sure it's in neutral, and unlocks the steering wheel, then tries again. The engine resolutely refuses to turn over. "Bloody hell."

She tries to calculate how long it has been since she started the Mercedes, whether she has left lights on, draining the battery. It is clearly not going anywhere. She tries one more time, even though she knows what will happen even before she does it. Then she bangs the steering wheel with a fist and lets her head come slowly down to rest on it. Why the hell had she bought a stupid unreliable vintage car instead of the sensible modern runaround she could have got for a tenth of the price? She had heard her mother's voice in her head when she had seen it: *Lila! Darling! You should do the thing that will make you happy! Always use your finest, most favorite things for everyday!*

"Flat battery?"

She isn't sure how many minutes she's been there, her eyes screwed shut, but when she opens them, Jensen is standing a few feet away on the drive.

She nods, oddly embarrassed. He must have witnessed the whole thing.

"Want me to go home and fetch my jump leads? I could start you up."

She makes a few mental calculations and pulls a face at him. "I don't think I have time." She sighs. "Jensen, could I ask you a massive favor?"

He waits.

"Could you drive me to the dump?"

"HAVE I DONE something to offend you?"

They're unloading the pickup truck at the dump, having finally reached the head of a long, bad-tempered queue, the cars packed full of attic detritus and garden waste, and are moving swiftly between PLASTICS and RECYCLABLES. The contents of the boxes she has grabbed seem to be divided into multiple categories, and Lila can feel the impatience of the drivers behind her while she rummages through them, trying to work out what goes in which.

She hurls the enormous rubber giraffe into NON RECYCLABLES, feeling a brief stab of discomfort as its cheerful, innocent face disappears. *Sorry,* she tells it silently.

"I thought we got on well the other week. We had some nice chats but since I've been back you've been kind of . . . avoiding me." He pauses while he removes the pieces of the cot from the back of his truck. "Are you really skipping this? Should we not put it by UNWANTED ITEMS? Someone might have a use for it."

"Oh. Maybe."

He pauses while he walks the cot pieces up to a different section, then returns. "I mean I wasn't expecting us to have some big relationship on the back of . . . what happened, but it would be nice to feel we were at least friends . . ."

"Of course we're friends."

His expression is so genuine, and his sense of hurt so palpable, that she deflates. She stands there, the baby car seat in her hand. The feel of it is so oddly familiar: it brings back a thousand small journeys, the curled, shrimpy weight of her sleeping baby locked over her aching arm. "I'm sorry," she says. "You are—It was a really great night. And I haven't deliberately avoided you. Things have just . . . got a bit complicated and I just can't—I can't—"

Jensen interrupts her, pointing: "That should definitely go in UN-WANTED ITEMS."

She pulls a face. "It's really grubby. I can't imagine anyone wanting to put a baby in there." She can see the food stains on the padded cushioning, and all over the blue vinyl belt. At least, she hopes they're just food stains.

"They can wash the cover, surely?" He is about to take it from her when a man in a high-vis jacket approaches. "We don't take car seats," he says. "They might have been in an accident."

"But it hasn't," says Lila.

"So you say," the man says, tapping his nose, and walking off. Lila stares at him for a moment, then sighs and throws it into NON RECY-CLABLES. She can practically feel the drivers bristling behind them.

"Hey." Jensen holds up a hand. "It's fine. I had zero expectations. I know you're coping with a lot right now. I just—I guess I just wanted to make sure we were okay."

"We're fine," she says, throwing a box of broken plastic toys into the skip with a loud clatter. She's not entirely sure which of those things she feels more guilty about.

HE ASKS AGAIN when they pull up outside her house twenty minutes later. "We're definitely cool, then? I mean, I'm going to tell you—when you didn't respond to my texts I was a little worried that I went too far that night. I felt—well, actually, I really worried about it."

She shakes her head firmly. "You absolutely didn't. I promise. Remember? I even did a phone recording to absolve you of any responsibility."

"You were kind of drunk, though."

"I was good drunk. Not paralytic-incapable-of-saying-no drunk."

He moves his head from side to side as if weighing this up. "You absolutely sure? You don't feel weird about it?"

She can smile at him then. She does not want him to feel anxious. "Jensen. I'm really fine. Not weird in the slightest. I just—I just have a lot going on right now. And we kind of agreed that this wasn't a thing."

The flicker of surprise that passes across his face makes her wonder if he had thought it was a thing.

"Okay," he says, as if gathering himself. "No. Sure."

They sit there for a moment. Then she reaches for the door.

"If you wanted more of a thing, I'd be happy to give it my full consideration," he says.

"I'll bear that in mind."

"I can't guarantee I would think about it immediately. I'm a very busy man. But I absolutely would put it on my very long list of things to consider. Maybe even higher than two-thirds of the way down."

"Thank you," she says. "I'm immensely flattered."

And then, just like that, things are fine between them. She thanks him again for the trip, and climbs out.

"I'll charge your car battery Monday when I come," he calls through the window, one arm lifted in salute. And then he drives away.

Hey Bella. Hope your day is going well x

Not bad thanks! Usual chaos. How are you? X

So-so. Lennie struggling a bit this week. Missing her mum and can't remember her lines for the school play so that's my job in the evenings. But we're basically doing okay x

Glad to hear it. Do you fancy another
drink some time? X

Love to, Bellissima. Missed you at the
school gates x

She cannot work out whether Gabriel Mallory is chaotic, a bit vague, or just still grieving his late wife to a debilitating degree. He is charming and attentive, but frustratingly hard to pin down to actual dates. When they had finally agreed on one, he canceled at the last minute due to a work meeting. On the flip side he calls her every other evening or so, and they usually talk for a delicious half-hour, or until Lennie summons him from upstairs and he has to go. The conversations are lovely, full of tales of his work, his difficult clients, what he is watching on television, and sometimes how he is feeling. He is always careful to ask after her, how she is, what is happening in her world. He is drily funny, his voice soft and intimate, tells her that nobody makes him laugh as much as she does. He is the absolute opposite of Dan: when he's talking to her he makes her feel that nobody in the world is more important. She confides in him when she's feeling sad, when she's frustrated by the girls, her fury at her dealings with her ex-husband, and he always knows the right thing to say to make her feel better (usually something along the lines of Dan is an idiot, he'll regret what he did, she's better off without him, she's doing amazingly). She comes off the phone glowing, his compliments ringing in her ears.

Sometimes she thinks about his dead wife, how awful it would have been to lose a partner. If you had been wounded that badly you wouldn't want to jump straight into a different relationship, would you? You'd be cautious, a little wary. Lila tries to be accommodating of this state of mind and doesn't push for clarification. Things will pan out as they pan out, she tells herself. And tries not to check her phone twenty-nine times an hour.

One afternoon, the previous week, he had called her, flustered, and said his mother was stuck on the other side of London and his babysitter couldn't pick Lennie up: could she possibly help him out? She had collected Lennie with quiet pleasure, noting how the gaggle of school mums registered with pointed glances the extra child in her care, and whom she belonged to. She's pretty sure Lennie has never been to any of *their* houses. When they had arrived home, and once the girls were settled in front of the television, she had raced upstairs to check her makeup and tried to work out whether there was enough food to invite him to stay for supper. She had gone twice around the living room and kitchen, trying to make it look a little more stylish, a little less of an insane mismatch between two determinedly different old men and two young girls. She had shut Truant into her bedroom, so that Gabriel wouldn't be put off by a swivel-eyed barking dog. She had squirted room spray in every corner, hoping to make her house feel pleasant and welcoming. But he had arrived at the door at a quarter past six, told her, distractedly, that he had to race off for a Zoom meeting, and after effusive thanks— *You're a lifesaver. Thank you so, so much*—had kissed her cheek and left her standing on the doorstep as he and his daughter jogged down the road with barely a backward wave.

GENE IS ANXIOUS about filming tomorrow, his anxiety manifesting itself in an almost manic need to recite his lines repeatedly, talk, tell jokes, or just be in front of an audience. Even Truant has slunk off to bed, exhausted by the attention. So Lila takes Gene on the school run. Her motivation is not entirely altruistic: since her last conversation with Dan she has felt slightly nervous about the possibility of him turning up, or whether Marja will have reported what happened between them to the other mothers. The school playground can feel gladiatorial at the best of times and it helps to go in armed with another person. Plus Gene loves a potential audience: she feels him straighten up slightly as soon as he spots the clusters of women, his eyes already scanning their faces to see who might have recognized him.

"So this is where you come every day, huh?"

"Yup." Lila briefly catches Marja's eye as they pass her, and both women look away.

A small part of her knows she might have been a little childish and mean to throw away the baby things, but another part of her is still yelling silently that it's utterly unfair to have to give the items you bought for your precious family to your husband's mistress for his new baby. This is what she keeps telling herself in the moments when she feels uncomfortable about it.

Gene, she notes, as they settle into Gabriel's corner, has already been spotted. She had been spared this experience for most of her life having grown up on a different continent from her father, but since he has been living with her she has become aware of the little frisson that passes through a certain age demographic when he passes—a sort of double-take, followed by a frown, or a smile, a muttered *Is that the guy from* . . . Eyebrows furrow, little flickers of recognition . . . Gene, for whom this is his lifeblood, loves it. He seems to feel that any day in which he is not recognized is a day wasted.

It takes all of three minutes before one of them sidles up, a mousy-haired woman whose name Lila can never remember. She is always accompanied by a buggy with a mute, bottle-sucking child inside, almost obscured by the hood of a padded anorak. "Hi, Lila," she says, looking straight past Lila. "Um . . . I'm sorry to interrupt but I have to ask, were you the actor in . . ." The woman is gazing at Gene, her smile half hopeful. "I mean you just look so like—"

Gene steps forward, cutting her off. "*Star Squadron Zero.* Yes, ma'am. Captain Troy Strang, reporting for intergalactic duty." He salutes, then holds out a hand for her to shake.

As she takes it, her face lights up. "Oh, my goodness! It is you! I loved watching your show when I was little. My mum had such a crush on you!"

Gene beams. "How about that! Please give her my best."

"Oh, could you sign something for her? It would make her day." She starts rummaging in the back of the buggy and eventually pulls out an envelope. "Honestly, we even had one of your calendars up in our kitchen. She used to say she had a different Captain Strang for every month!" Gene, it turns out, despite his chaotic habits, is never without an autographing pen. He scribbles a message, checking the spelling of the woman's name, asking polite questions about her, her health, how she's doing. As they pose for a selfie together—"Oh, my goodness, she is not going to believe this! Captain Troy Strang in our playground!"—a few other mothers, emboldened, trickle over, bearing phones or bits of paper. Lila notes with mild irritation that Marja is among them. She is walking with the gait of a heavily pregnant woman now, her pelvis rocking slightly as she moves, one hand unconsciously supporting herself as she approaches.

"It's Troy Strang! Captain Troy!" the woman is saying, and suddenly Gene is in the midst of a hubbub, Lila pushed gradually to its edge, watching as her father signs and poses, his manner garrulous and charismatic, his smile as wide as a mile. "No," he is saying. "No plans to bring it back just now. But we're working on it!" and "Yes, Lila's my daughter. You didn't know? Well, I had to spend a lot of time away filming . . . We're just loving hanging out again." It's all Lila can do not to roll her eyes.

"And who are you?" he says, readying his pen as Philippa Graham rummages through her handbag. "Oh, I can't find any paper. Do Marja first," Philippa says, her head down as she searches. Marja steps forward, cautiously, holding out a tiny notebook.

"Marja?" says Gene, becoming suddenly still. He glances at Lila, searching her out above the other heads. "*The* Marja?"

There is a sudden hush. A few mothers exchange glances.

There is nothing for it. Lila nods.

Gene looks her up and down. "So you're Marja. Huh. I guess you guys have worked your stuff out, if you have to see each other here every day." His smile has vanished, and he keeps his eyes on Marja as if assessing her.

Lila and Marja exchange quick, embarrassed glances. "Um. Not really," says Lila, after a beat.

"What do you mean, not really?"

A couple of mothers drift away awkwardly. "We—we haven't actually spoken. Since Dan . . ." Lila feels herself color, unsure why this is making her so uncomfortable. She stares at the school door, willing the children to be let out. Willing this to end.

Gene frowns at her. "You both come here every day and nobody says anything?"

"Gene, we really don't need—"

"Since he left you?" He turns to Marja. "Hang on, you're telling me you've never even said sorry?"

"Sorry?" Marja's voice is halting.

"For breaking up a family? For sleeping with my daughter's husband? You literally come here every day and don't say a word to my daughter? Jesus! How English can you all get?"

"Actually," says Philippa, stepping forward, "she's Dutch. And she doesn't owe anyone an apology. Things happen. It's just life."

Gene swivels round and looks at her incredulously. "And who the fuck are you?"

Philippa lifts her chin, coloring. "I'm Philippa Graham."

"And what business is this of yours, Philippa Graham? Or are you just here because you enjoy the drama?"

Philippa's eyes widen. "That's a horrible thing to say. I'm just . . . looking out for my friend." She looks down at Marja's belly. "And her unborn child."

"Ohhh," says Gene, his face softening. "That's nice. You're looking out for the unborn child. Right. Looking out for the children."

With this affirmation of her benevolence, Philippa's equanimity is restored. She nods primly. Gene smiles. Lila lets out a small breath. He starts to write on the paper she has proffered. "So, Philippa Graham," he says, still looking down at the paper as he writes, "have you been looking out for the *actual* children involved here as well as the unborn? Dan and Lila's children? The ones whose lives were upended? The ones who are still struggling with what happened to their family? How much have you been looking out for those children, huh?"

Philippa's jaw drops.

"Got it. I thought so." He thrusts the paper at her. "Why don't you skedaddle off over there, lady, and leave us to it, given this is clearly a *family* matter?"

There is a brief silence. Philippa glances at Lila and then at Marja. Everyone else has now drifted away, clustered into little murmuring groups across the playground, pretending not to be watching what is going on.

"Are you okay, Marja?" Philippa says pointedly, touching Marja's elbow.

"I'm fine," Marja says quietly.

Philippa waits another beat before she leaves, as if showing that she is not intimidated by this man, intergalactic battle captain or no. They wait until Philippa has moved ten, twenty feet away, looking repeatedly over her shoulder as she goes. And then Gene stands between the two women. "So you guys don't speak. Never have. How's that working out for you both, huh?"

"Gene," says Lila. "Please don't do this. I really don't need you to get invo—"

"I'm sorry, Lila."

Marja's heavily accented voice cuts across them. Lila turns and stares at her. Marja's mouth is compressed into a thin line, and she is clearly uncomfortable. "I'm sorry. I really am." For the first time Lila notices how tired she looks, how pale. Lila wants to say something in reply but nothing will come out. She just stares at the woman who's suddenly utterly unlike the glowing, calculating nemesis who has existed in her head for so long. Marja looks at her feet. "And I'm very sorry about your children."

Lila cannot speak. Their eyes lock, and Lila thinks, *My God, she actually does look sorry.*

Then Gene claps his hands together. "There—that wasn't so hard, was it? Oh, look! There's my girl! Violet baby! Vi! Look who came to meet you! It's your old pal Gene!"

At this point Lila has to take a step out of the school playground. It is too much: the stares of the other mothers, the odd discomfort she feels at Gene having made Marja apologize, the hideous, hideous visibility of it all. She is dimly aware of the other mothers filing past her onto the pavement, the snatches of conversation about *Star Squadron Zero*, and she cannot identify what she feels: sadness? Anger? Grief? Relief?

She is interrupted by Violet, tugging at her sleeve. "Mum! You still haven't done the costumes! Mrs. Tugendhat needs to talk to you."

"Oh, Violet, not now, lovey."

"No, now! She said you were meant to bring them this week!"

She looks across the playground. Gene is standing talking to Mrs. Tugendhat, who, she can tell even from here, was a *Star Squadron Zero* fan. Her plump hand is pressed to her chest and she sports the kind of animated expression some people wear when overwhelmed by actual conversation with an actual famous person. Gene is smiling, his shoulders thrown back, his battered leather jacket standing out among the puffy coats and brightly colored Boden jackets.

"Mum." Violet's voice is urgent. "They're starting dress rehearsals in two weeks. We have to know that everything fits."

"I know, love. I know. I promise I'll sort it."

Violet is still tugging at her sleeve, but as she looks up, Gene is posing for a picture with Mrs. Tugendhat, taken by one of the mothers, and then, with a courtly kiss to her hand, letting her go. The teacher is walking back toward the school, her neck flushed purple with pleasure, the costumes apparently forgotten. Gene walks over to where Lila and Violet are waiting, nodding at a few stray mothers, who smile and blush as he passes. "You okay, sweetie?" Outside the gates, he pulls a cigarette from a packet and lights up.

"I'm fine," says Lila. She actually wants to go and lie down.

"Nice lady! She's going to bring me some memorabilia she has in her attic. Apparently her husband has an original *Star Squadron Zero* bubble-bath bottle! You know they did them in the shape of four of us back in 1980? It was me, Vuleva, Vardoth the Destroyer, and Lieutenant McKinnon. Mine sold out in a week if I remember right."

"That's lovely," says Lila.

"Say, I should take a look on one of those auction sites. I have loads of that stuff tucked away here and there. I think Jane may have another box somewhere in her house. I bet it would fetch a fortune if I sold it."

They walk halfway to the house before anyone speaks again.

Then Gene nudges her. "Hey—you want to know what I wrote on the piece of paper for that Philippa lady?"

Lila shrugs distractedly. "Your autograph?"

"I wrote: *Dear Philippa, I've atom-blasted radioactive space demons who were nicer than you. Signed, your old pal Gene.*" He is still chuckling to himself by the time they reach their street.

Chapter Twenty-four

Gene had told Bill the story of his altercation with Philippa Graham over supper twice, and although Lila knew Bill probably wanted to disapprove—he couldn't imagine anything worse than getting involved in other people's emotional dramas—he couldn't help but laugh. "Well, she sounds perfectly dreadful," he said. "Well done, you."

"I know, right? I wish I could have seen her face when she read what I wrote." The two old men had dissolved into giggles again.

Bill has been laughing a lot more lately. He whistles when he's preparing breakfast, and sometimes, from her desk upstairs, she can hear his soft baritone singing along to the choral classics. He is no longer a shadow of a person. It's as if he took a brief leave of absence from himself and has now returned. Perhaps he's one of those men who's just better with a woman around. Perhaps at that age most men are.

Penelope Stockbridge is there most days now, either popping in to play the piano, or staying to join them for supper. According to Violet, who tracks these things assiduously, Penelope's wardrobe choices have included: a pair of pink satin ballroom-dancing shoes, a dark green sequined beret, a jumper with a knitted cat on the front, and a pair of earrings in the shape of tiny pink glass elephants, which have been promised to Violet when she's finally allowed to have her ears pierced ("finally" is given extra weight). A previous version of Lila might have resented her house becoming home to yet another quirky person of pensionable age, but she doesn't really mind. Penelope takes nothing for granted, is eager to help, and hyper-sensitive to any possibility that she has outstayed her welcome.

Sometimes she brings Lila flowers from her garden, handing them over with exaggerated casualness. "Oh, they're nothing. I just thought they might be cheering. I always find real flowers such a tonic for the spirit, don't you?"

She has given Violet two free piano lessons, her manner grave and serious, but full of effusive praise when Violet gets something right. "Oh, I think you have a natural talent, Violet. You let me know if you'd like to do more, won't you? I think you'd be marvelous at it."

Lila wonders if this is Penelope's way of trying to create yet another reason to pop in, but in truth Bill is probably all the reason she needs. They take regular walks around the Heath together (not with Truant, whose energy is too chaotic for them), stop in coffee shops, discuss the news, admire Jensen's work in the garden. Over a period of weeks Penelope has become a fixture in their unconventional, extended family. Lila tries not to miss the tuna-pasta bakes.

Two days ago Bill, watching Jensen planting a couple of shrubs in the garden, had turned to Lila and said: "Are you sure your mother wouldn't mind? Me seeing so much of Penelope, I mean." And Lila had threaded her arm through his and said, no, absolutely not. That her mother of all people understood the importance of living as well and happily as one could.

"And you, dear girl? You're okay with it? I mean, it must be a little strange for you. But—you know—I want to make it clear that I would never have looked at another woman had she not . . . Francesca was everything, everything to me . . ." His voice had tailed off. She had been able to reassure him that, yes, she knew. And, no, Lila cannot find it in herself to mind. Because a strange harmony has settled over her ramshackle, mismatched house, and after the past few years she more than anyone knows just to accept and enjoy these moments when they come.

Lila avoids the school gates as much as possible during this time. Gabriel is on a big project, and working long hours at his practice, and between there being almost no possibility of seeing him there, and her faint residual terror of Philippa Graham, she has handed over pickup duties willingly to Gene. He seems to enjoy having a daily role, and Violet likes having a celebrity grandpa, now that the story of who he is has filtered down from parents to her classmates, and Lila suspects there may be sugar-based diversions involved on the way home. It allows her more time to sit in her study and write uninterrupted.

"I STOLE YOUR keys." Jensen appears in the doorway of the study, knocking twice to announce his arrival. Lila, who has been deep in thought about whether hair removal is indeed a political act if you only do it before you go on holiday, turns in her seat, startled.

"What?"

"I stole your car keys. You were right about me all along." He grins, and holds them up in his palm. "I charged your battery off my truck. Now you need to take it for a spin."

"Oh! Um, I'm kind of in the middle of—"

"Bill says you've been writing all afternoon. You need breaks. C'mon, twenty minutes."

Lila is suddenly conscious of the chaos in the little study: the still-packed cardboard boxes stacked against the wall, Gene's crumpled bedding, the printer with two empty mugs on it, that she is probably wearing her pajama top under her sweatshirt. Jensen is not, for once, in gardening clothes but wearing a dark blue sweater with a lighter blue shirt underneath—which means he must have made the trip just to help her. "That's . . . really nice of you."

"I'm a very nice man."

He hands her the keys as they stand on the driveway. She unlocks the Mercedes and notes that he is climbing into the passenger side. "Just to make sure it's all working," he says, when he sees her look at him. She settles into the seat, checks the mirror, and fires the engine, which, obligingly, starts first time. But Jensen's voice cuts in: "What are you *doing*?"

"What do you mean what am I doing? I'm starting the car."

"No—no—no!"

"I know how to start my own car, Jensen," Lila snaps at him. "You're not going to tell me how to drive, are you?"

"No. What are you doing leaving the roof up?"

Lila follows his gaze upward.

"C'mon! You have to put the roof down! It's pretty much the law if you have a convertible."

It's a cold day, but dry, and the sky is the kind of crisp azure that tells of frosty nights ahead. They button their jackets to their collars, and she shakes her head at the madness of it as he turns the heater to full blast. And then she pulls out onto the road, feeling the engine purr obligingly in front of her, trying not to feel like an idiot, first for snapping at him, and then for being the kind of show-off numpty who drives around in the cold with the roof down.

"I never see you take this car out," Jensen observes, as they head toward the high street. He runs his hand over the walnut dashboard. "It's a pity."

Lila, who has deflated slightly, has to shout over the sound of the V8 engine. "I bought it for my mum. As a sort of tribute, I mean. It was the kind of thing she would have done, buying a completely unsuitable car for everyday use." She indicates and pulls onto the main road. "Besides, I'm not sure I'm really a top-down kind of person."

When he doesn't say anything she adds: "It's just . . . impractical, right? It's a gorgeous thing, but it's not very reliable and English weather means it's only usable for a couple of months a year."

"But that's not the point of a car like this. You put the top down and turn the heater right up and you scrape every bit of joy out of the day with it."

"And freeze your head while your toes boil. I don't think so."

"Lila, you're looking at this car in totally the wrong way. This Mercedes is not just a car. It's an injection of serotonin. You need to climb in, open her up, and just enjoy yourself. Even if it's just a few times a week. Roof off, music up, and you'll feel like you've had a mini holiday."

Lila glances at him. "You're very fond of telling me what to do, aren't you?"

"Only when you need it." His fingers reach for the music console. "C'mon. Let's do it—let's have the full mood-enhancing experience."

She feels a little self-conscious with the 1980s disco beat pumping at the traffic lights—she's sure people are looking at them. But Jensen doesn't seem to care, nodding in time to the music, smiling with pleasure, tapping the side of the car with his broad hand, and turning it up louder when his favorite songs come on. After a few miles, when it becomes clear that he isn't going to stop, she decides just not to think about the possible judgment of strangers, but to do what he's doing, and enjoy the—admittedly quite pleasurable—assault on her senses.

"Why did you say that?"

She's slowing to let someone out when he turns the volume down.

"Say what?"

"That you're not a top-down kind of person. What did you mean?"

She stops at a zebra crossing. A small boy casts an unembarrassed, lingering look at the Mercedes bonnet as he dawdles across in front of them, tugged gently along by his mother, who is on her phone.

She shrugs, suddenly not wanting to look at him. "Well, my life isn't really a top-down kind of life, is it? It's . . . I don't know . . . school runs and moody teens, grumpy elderly men and dodgy bathrooms, and we've run out of dog-poo bags." She taps the steering wheel. "This car is for the kind of person who takes impulsive trips to Paris, and has white linen trousers and a selection of handbags without crumbs in the bottom." This sudden realization makes her feel oddly melancholy. "I think I bought this for my fantasy life, rather than the one I actually live in."

His silence is unusually long. For Jensen, anyway. "You are absolutely a top-down kind of person," he observes eventually. "You're just at a pinch point so you can't see it right now." He turns to her, at the exact moment she is brave enough to look at him, and his expression is almost unbearably kind. "You'll have your top-down life before you know it, Lila. You're getting there."

Mortifyingly, and for no obvious reason, her eyes prickle. She tries to laugh it off.

"Don't be nice to me, for God's sake." She wipes them furiously. "Ugh. I think I preferred you telling me how to drive."

"Well, I wouldn't have been nice if I'd known there were *crumbs* in your handbag," he responds. "In fact, I wouldn't have agreed to come if I'd known." He gives her a sideways look. "C'mon, we're out of the twenty mph zone here. Put your foot down a bit. Honestly, what kind of driver are you?"

They take off on the winding roads around the Heath, and she feels the car growling underneath her, the insistent pull of the torque, the steering wheel warm in her hands, and Jensen turns up the music, singing "I'm Every Woman" unselfconsciously and off-key, and Lila finding herself singing too, starts to get a whisper of what he means. There's something about the cold blasting onto her cheeks, the exposure to the world around them, the music in her ears, her hair whipping around her face, that clears her head, scatters her endless looping thoughts. And then she is singing along, not caring who sees, laughing at Jensen's made-up lyrics, the beauty of this ridiculous, unsuitable car.

The feeling of joyousness lasts a good hour after they return home and put the car to bed, their cheeks and ears glowing, and for some time after he has dismissed her thanks as unnecessary and headed off to his next job. It's another hour before she wonders whether that feeling was something to do with Jensen.

GENE'S ADVERT IS due to air on the Thursday evening. He professes to be nonchalant about it—"Hey, it's just an ad, not exactly Arthur Miller"—but Lila suspects that no one in the local postcode is unaware that Gene will be selling Strong Yet Sensitive whitening toothpaste at a quarter past eight this evening. When she had popped into the corner shop that morning for orange juice the young Turkish man behind the counter, who has never once acknowledged her presence even though she's used the shop at least four times a week since she moved in, handed over her change and said: "It's Gene's advert tonight, isn't it? My mum says she's going to watch."

Gene has invited them all to join him for pizza before it airs—"I'm paying"—but Bill has sweetly offered to cook instead. He is making American fried chicken with corn fritters and a tomato salsa in tribute. Penelope is coming, and Eleanor, and Jensen has apparently been invited too. There is a carefully worked-out schedule in which food happens beforehand and, according to Bill, they will all have finished the washing-up and be seated around the television "with homemade chocolate and pistachio cookies," ready for Gene's appearance.

Lila takes it all in with only half an ear. Gabriel has asked her to come

for dinner the following evening, and her brain is a hot jumble of anticipation and nerves. Because dinner is not a casual drink after work. Dinner is serious. It is an invitation into his home. It is a word laden with
possibility. Dinner means they are Moving Forward.

ONE OF THE things Lila most enjoys about her new life is the scent of
cooking that greets her when she comes into her house. In the early
months after Dan left she could barely rouse herself to cook: she had
been so hollowed out with grief and shock that normal household tasks,
like cooking and cleaning, had felt completely beyond her. They had
lived on toast, or takeaways, or if Lila was feeling reasonably pulled together, pasta with a jar of pesto sauce, perhaps with the addition of a
handful of frozen peas if she was worried about the girls getting rickets.
Bill's arrival had brought order and home-cooked meals to their house,
but the smell of steamed fish or salad had not been exactly *welcoming*.
Since the advent of Penelope—and perhaps even his *entente cordiale*
with Gene—Bill's cooking seems to have relaxed a little into something
less rigidly nutritional, and more comforting. It frequently contains car-
bohydrates or crispy chicken skin or even a cheesy topping, so that Lila's
kitchen is often the source of delicious aromas that prompt immediate
Pavlovian hunger pangs. The girls ask, "What's for dinner?" with genuine anticipation rather than faint dread.

Everyone is excited about the fried chicken.

Along with that, and her upcoming date with Gabriel, the other thing
adding to Lila's general sense of satisfaction is that the garden is almost
completed. The area that has seemed, for months, to be a continuing
eyesore of clay soil, paving slabs, and piles of dead vegetation has very
gradually, then quite suddenly morphed into something elegant and
beautiful. When they had moved in, the end of her garden had been a
wilderness of shrubs and apparently random pieces of half-buried con-

crete, the fences covered with sprawling dark ivy, its focal point a shed missing a good portion of its bitumen roof and colonized by bristly-legged spiders so enormous that Lila had occasionally thought about charging rent.

Now the centerpiece is Bill's carved oak bench, sheltered by a small willow tree on one side, a Japanese acer on the other, and a new, small square pond beside it. Lilac and lavender bushes for bees punctuate each side, and two small raised beds house a variety of herbs, a winding reclaimed York stone patio charting the space between them. A red-brick wall, its surface softened by centuries of weather, has been re-vealed by Jensen's endless pruning and hacking, and water trickles from a wall-mounted fountain in a never-ending tinkling stream. It isn't fin-ished, but already it's ridiculously peaceful. It's the first thing that draws the eye as Lila glances out of the window, and every time she does, she feels as if she has somehow been granted the kind of garden that only other people have.

"I've put giant purple alliums in those raised beds," says Jensen, ap-pearing beside her as she looks back at the house. His fingernails are black with soil and he shoves his hands into his pockets. "They'll come up in May, June, and be a bit of a riot. Stop it looking too tidy. I thought it sounded like your mum—some fun and chaos amid the order."

Lila, unexpectedly, feels a lump rise in her throat. "That's lovely," she says. "She would have liked that."

"And just a truckload of spring bulbs, cyclamen, daffodils, that kind of thing. She was always cheerful, wasn't she? And you can't have enough cheery stuff by the end of winter." He surveys his work with quiet satis-faction, and they stand for a moment, watching the hubbub of activity just visible through the French windows.

"You said it would be beautiful," she says, turning to him.

He rubs a hand over his head. "Well, I'm always right. I did tell you that."

"Yeah, now you've ruined it."

He laughs. "I tell you what, I'm going to be ready for that fried chicken. I'm starving."

They start to walk up toward the house.

"You're doing okay, though?" Jensen says. "Gene tells me you have a new book deal."

She smiles. "Yeah. Yeah. Not quite a top-down life yet but things seem to be . . . settling. How about you?"

"Good. Quiet, just as I like it."

"Quiet is good," she says emphatically. "I'm a big fan of quiet. 'No alarms and no surprises.' Isn't that what Radiohead said?"

"I think that song was about suicide. But I get your general point."

She stops walking, is about to speak, then changes her mind.

"You were about to say I'm quite annoying, weren't you?" Jensen says.

"Yes," Lila says. "Yes, I was."

THE FRIED CHICKEN is sensational. Gene says so, at least four times, twice while he is actually chewing a mouthful, but the sentiment is so genuinely expressed that Bill seems not to mind the morsels of food spluttered in his general direction. Instead of dishing it onto individual plates, he has filled a platter with it and placed it in the center of the kitchen table. Hands frequently reach out for another piece, making the atmosphere somehow more relaxed than usual over dinner. The corn fritters are also a success, especially with Violet, who eats them with her fingers, her lips covered with grease and tomato salsa, and even the green salad that Bill has placed to the side (old habits die hard apparently) is swiftly demolished. Bottled beer and fizzy drinks scatter the table and some kind of upbeat jazz music plays gently in the background. Lila gazes at the visitors to her once-silent kitchen table: Bill and Penelope beside each other at the far end, talking animatedly about a piece of music they have decided to attempt, Gene telling Violet about the events on set at the stately home, the foibles of the actors, how the director was a dick, sorry, not a very nice person, and Violet sometimes even listening, Eleanor and Jensen, who seem to have hit it off, chatting about an exceptionally grotty bar they had both frequented in Camden Town. Celie, who has been more upbeat lately, is surreptitiously feeding Truant pieces of chicken under the table, occasionally breaking in to contradict something Violet says. It is a scene of life and warmth and color, and Lila feels oddly emotional at the sight of it, as if it is only now she can allow herself to acknowledge how far they have all come.

"It's not a traditional family," Eleanor had said, earlier that evening, when Lila had commented on how much easier she was finding it, "but that doesn't mean it's not a family."

"How long do you think before you're completely finished, Jensen?" says Bill, across the table.

"I'm waiting on the outdoor lights. Just a couple each side of the bench," Jensen says. "And a couple more plants to go in. And then that's pretty much it."

"You've done a wonderful job," Bill says. "Wonderful."

"It looks very beautiful," Penelope says, and then, in case that's too presumptive, "I mean, as an outsider, it all looks very beautiful to me."

"Penelope is a wonderful gardener," says Bill. "You must take a look at her house, Jensen, when you have a minute. She has astonishingly green fingers."

Penelope demurs, coloring. She is wearing a chain with a tiny toothpaste tube pendant "in honor of the occasion." She had apparently crafted it from modeling clay and paint the previous day, just for fun, and has promised to show Violet how she did it. Lila is a little worried about what Violet will choose to make, but she guesses that Penelope will have to get used to her family one way or another, poo benches, X-rated rap lyrics and all.

They are settled in front of the television ten minutes before the allotted time for the advertisement broadcast. A plate of warm cookies is passed backward and forward along the two sofas, drinks refilled, a happy hum of conversation breaking across the television commentary. Violet is on the floor, as there is barely enough room for everyone, and Truant, who is not happy about the numbers currently in the house, eyes them all suspiciously from behind the curtain. Lila has found herself seated on the sofa beside Jensen, which makes her feel oddly self-conscious, but Eleanor, who has had several glasses of wine, is drumming up excitement, calling: "*We want Gene! We want Gene!*" sporadically, which draws everyone's attention, including Jensen's, so she mostly hangs on to her feelings of equanimity.

And then, breaking into a nature documentary about reptiles in Australia, there he is on the screen: her father, dressed in an unfamiliarly formal white shirt, his hair tamed and trimmed, gazing, concerned, at his teeth in a mirror.

It's never too late to look a little brighter, says the female voiceover, and on-screen Gene, having brushed, suddenly smiles, his great shit-eating grin, and the whole room erupts. "Yay, Gene!" Eleanor, who is positively giddy, reaches over and high-fives him, the kids jump up, Bill says, "Very good, very good, Gene," Truant starts barking, and as they all applaud, Lila absorbs what Eleanor said and thinks, *Yes, maybe this is a family.* With all its mad history and chaos, heartbreaks, stupid jokes, ridiculous triumphs, and distinct lack of Noguchi coffee-tables, maybe this is my family.

Chapter Twenty-five

The dinner date is to take place on Friday evening. Every time Lila thinks about it she experiences a shiver of nervous anticipation. In the last two days, she has been to the local salon where she had everything waxed, and her nails manicured. Her hair has been blow-dried so that it falls in glossy brown waves, and she has treated herself to new underwear, having decided that almost everything in her drawer was either too old, or gaped in unhelpful places (thank you, divorce diet). She is wearing a black silk dress, high in the collar but with a small slit up the skirt, which always draws compliments, and which she hopes makes her look sophisticated yet casual in a Parisian sort of way. She reads affirmations on Instagram, reminding herself that she is strong, desirable, a survivor, that her experiences have shaped her into someone unstoppable. She spends only forty minutes or so feeling bad about the skin on her neck.

He has been specific about timings so she ensures that she is ready for seven. His address is not far away, and she will walk there as long as it isn't raining. She is better moving if she is nervous.

She texts him at six forty-five.

Just heading off x

He responds immediately. Slight snafu at work. Could you come a bit later? Say 9-ish? Want to get Lennie to bed before you arrive.

She had been under the impression Lennie was staying at his mother's.

I'm totally fine with Lennie. She knows me.

Yes, but she'll get overexcited and then not want to go to bed. Better if she's asleep x

It is written in the inarguable tone of a parent who knows their child best. Lila rereads the message twice, then sighs and heads downstairs, where Bill is in the middle of serving dinner. It's just him, Gene, and the girls this evening and they are having spaghetti bolognese, which makes Lila a little wistful. She loves spaghetti bolognese and she has barely eaten today.

"You look pretty, sweetheart," says Gene, who is taking his place at the table. "Going out?"

"Yes. Just drinks with a friend."

"What friend?" says Violet.

Lila is about to tell her the truth, but something stops her. "Just some-one from school," she says.

"Girls' night out, huh?" says Gene.

"I thought you might go out with Jensen again at some point," says Bill, a little pointedly.

"Jensen and I are just friends," she says firmly.

Celie snorts into her pasta.

"What?"

"Friends who like *sleepovers*," she mutters.

"Did you have a sleepover with Jensen?" says Violet, her eyes boggling. "Jensen the gardener Jensen?"

"It was ages ago and, yes, we had a . . . sleepover."

"Was it a pajama party?"

"Something like that."

Celie snorts again.

"Well, if you and your 'friend' are likely to be out late," Bill says, with a raised eyebrow, "it would be good if you could let us know. Just so we don't worry. Again."

"I'll text you," Lila says.

"You wouldn't let me do that," says Celie.

"I'm twenty-six years older than you," says Lila. "And I am ruler of this kingdom."

"You want to eat first?" Gene gestures toward the bowl of pasta. "Bill's made a banquet here."

God, but it smells delicious.

"I think we have plans to eat. But thanks."

She walks to the pub, because she cannot think what else to do with the hour and a half still to wait and she is too on edge to stay at home. She sits in the corner, at a small table, and nurses a Diet Coke while staring at nothing on her phone. Her pulse is a thin drumbeat of nervousness. When she finishes the Coke she orders a gin and tonic. She needs to settle her nerves a little. *It's just dinner*, she keeps telling herself. *You don't need to get yourself in a panic about it.*

While she is drinking the gin, a man approaches her, forty-something with a dark, tightly cut business suit. She glances up, and he is looking directly at her, his expression a faint question. *Why is it impossible for a woman ever to sit and exist by herself?* It's the dress, she thinks. It looks like she's trying to attract sexual attention.

"I'm very happy by myself, thanks," she finds herself saying, as he comes to a halt in front of her, a little more snappily than she'd intended.

"Actually, I just wanted to ask if you were using that chair."

She has another gin and tonic to dispel the vague humiliation of the chair incident, and the fact that the businessman and his friends are now gathered in a large, noisy group around the next table, making hers look solitary and ridiculous. And then at ten to nine, as the decibel level in the pub is getting higher, and the band comes on at the far end, lifting everyone's voices a further notch, she gathers her bag and, a little unsteadily, heads for Gabriel's house.

HE ANSWERS THE door on the second ring, a little flustered. "Really sorry," he says, holding up a finger. "I'm just on the phone. I'll be two minutes." He disappears back up the stairs at a jog and she is left standing in the hallway, unsure where he wants her to wait.

She stands frozen, hearing a door close upstairs. *What would Mum do?* she wonders. After a moment, fortified by Francesca's imagined ease in such a situation, she sheds her coat, and walks through to the kitchen.

It is, almost comically, the kitchen of an architect: the back of the house is a glass cube, in the center of which sits an oval marble table that she has seen in various magazines, and whose designer's name she cannot recall. She cannot see anything cooking yet, but thinks it's possible that something's in the fridge waiting until she arrived. She's so hungry she thinks she might pass out.

She gazes around the room, which is immaculate, ordered, and tasteful, the walls the color of unpainted plaster, the kitchen units a bold cobalt blue. A huge modernist chandelier hangs in the center of the ceiling, and there is nothing on the pale granite work surfaces except an over-sized ceramic jug, none of the clutter and detritus of normal kitchen life. The side of the upper kitchen unit, hidden from view as she walks in, is the only area where minimalism takes a back seat—full of Lennie's drawings and various letters from school, as well as a cork notice board. She scans the photographs on it—not the messy, gurning ones she has at home but a few beautifully shot, atmospheric pictures of Lennie, and a few that show big groups of people, clearly on holiday somewhere hot and beautiful. There are no pictures of his late wife. A large abstract painting hangs on the wall, and the chairs are leather and chrome, vaguely Eastern European and brutalist. She feels suddenly glad that she wore the black silk dress: most of her wardrobe would have felt too chaotic for this room.

He walks in rubbing his face, as if he's rubbing away the phone call, just as she's thinking about stepping into the garden. "So sorry," he says, greeting her with a kiss on the cheek. "Just a nightmare week at work. And Len gets upset if I'm back late so I knew she was going to take longer to go to bed. So sorry. Let me get you a drink."

He opens a cupboard to reveal a hidden wine store, from which he pulls out a bottle of expensive-looking red. "Red okay?"

"Fine," she says, without thinking. Even slightly disheveled, he's gorgeous, his eyes an intense and vivid turquoise, his shirt soft gray with a tiny Japanese logo on the cuff. He carries a vague scent of aftershave, something aniseedy and expensive.

"Sit, please," he says, gesturing toward the table. "You look very lovely. I'm afraid I haven't had time to cook so I thought we could order in."

She makes a swift calculation. At this time on a Friday night they will be lucky to get anything before a quarter to ten. But what can she do? She smiles, hoping he might put out some crisps, and he pours two glasses of wine before tapping into an app on his phone. "Done!" he says, and she takes a big swig of her wine, because she suddenly doesn't know what to say.

"Beautiful kitchen," she says, when she's recovered.

He glances around, as if this might never have occurred to him. "Yes, it's not bad, is it? It's the one thing I had done before we moved in. I would have liked something more ambitious." He takes a swig of his wine, closes his eyes for a moment, as if savoring it, then says: "But most of life is a compromise, isn't it? So how are you? How's the writing coming?"

"Okay," she says. "It's actually okay."

"What are you writing about?"

"It's . . ." she says, haltingly. "It's a follow-up to another book I wrote about rebuilding a marriage gone stale."

"Ah." He looks awkward.

"Yup. I know."

"Well, I think that's very brave. It doesn't surprise me at all—you are, of course, fearless. But I don't think I could write about personal stuff."

"Oh, you don't include your real self," she says quickly. "Not the important stuff. What I write is very much a curated version of my life. You have to—uh—ramp things up just to keep the publishers happy."

"I'm sure. Not really my world. My dad had a book published once. But it was about Ancient Greek architecture. Quite different. Pretty dull, if I'm honest, though obviously the entire family had to buy a copy."

"I make my children buy copies of mine with their pocket money."

He laughs, and she starts to relax.

"Did you always want to write books?"

"I never intended to actually, unlike half the population. I wrote a jokey online article about my marriage while I was working in marketing and an agent approached me to expand it into a book. And then there was this bidding war and it went on to sell a few hundred thousand copies and sat in the Top Ten for a couple of months." She tries to say this casually, as though she is not trying to impress him. As though she is clearly equal to his architectural prizes and designer chandelier.

"That's incredibly impressive," he says, obligingly. And she tries not to preen a little.

"So what's the rest of your family like? Do you have brothers and sisters?"

"Two brothers. We're all horribly competitive." He grins at her. "My elder brother is a lawyer and the younger one is a doctor. We're basically a middle-class cliché of a family."

"And some mother's absolute dream."

"Oh, I wouldn't go that far. You?"

"Just me. One mother, two fathers. I think I'd love a couple of siblings to share that particular burden."

"Well, it's nice for your girls. To have their grandparents around, I mean."

"Do you still see your wife's parents?"

His face closes. "It's tricky. They took Victoria's side when we split, and relations are a little strained. They do see Lennie, though. She does a couple of weeks with them in the summer."

"I'm so sorry you've had to deal with that as well."

"You're very kind. It's been . . . less than ideal." He gets up and pours more wine, as if to change the conversation.

She would like to ask him more about this. She would like to ask him how Victoria died. Whether he has been out with anyone since. She wants to ask him approximately eight thousand other questions. But Lila has realized that she really is quite drunk. She gazes at her second glass, which seems, inexplicably, to be empty, and suspects Gabriel is some way behind her. She has to keep reminding herself to stop talking. She thinks she might be too emphatic when he says things. And some-times she catches herself grinning goofily at him. She tells herself to relax. She is on a dinner date with Gabriel Mallory. Why shouldn't she let go and enjoy herself a little?

She is not entirely sure what time the food comes. She is aware of him pulling out plates and cutlery and they sit at the marble table, which is uncomfortably cold against her bare arms. At some point he has put on some kind of Cuban folk music and dimmed the lights. They eat something with charred corn and meat skewers and she thinks she is so hungry by now that she could eat the cardboard containers it comes in. She listens to him talk, and the way the light bounces off his hair, and the soft, almost hesitant nature of his smile, and even though she has eaten and drunk, she cannot relax, because a question is thumping like a muffled drum beat at the back of her head. Her brain, though, skewed by the drink, keeps veering off in unexpected directions.

"Tulip!" she says abruptly.

He looks startled.

"Your table. It's a Tulip table."

"Yes," he says, nodding. "Eero Saarinen. From a 1955 design."

"I knew it!" She slaps the table slightly too enthusiastically and his hand shoots out to save one of the glasses.

Finally he clears away the food. *He is like Bill*, she thinks. *He cannot leave stuff on the side.* She may have said this aloud. She sits and watches, just holding the glass, letting the music and ambience wash over her. She feels, in this beautiful kitchen in her black silk dress, with this man, like a woman in a film. She feels like the best possible version of herself . . .

"So, shall we sit in the other room?" he says, when he has finished, offering her his hand. It is warm and strong and his fingers close around hers like they were meant to be there. "It's a little more comfortable."

THE LIVING ROOM is smaller than she expected: it contains a large curved sofa made of a dark turquoise tweed and an enormous television screen. There are no toys or clutter. Just a sideboard that appears to have no doors, a dome-shaped chair, and a long, low coffee-table made of some kind of concrete. Two swooping lights illuminate small spots around the room and a beautiful antique Persian rug covers a pale herringbone oak floor. A navy blanket that looks like cashmere is folded over one end of the sofa. The Cuban music has somehow manifested itself in this room too. She takes a seat on the sofa and he sits beside her.

"It doesn't look like you even have a child," she says, gazing around her. She makes sure she smiles admiringly when she says it, so that it doesn't come across as a criticism.

"Ah. Yes. It's my weak spot. I need to know there's one space in the house that I can come to in the evenings and just relax. She has a playroom across the hall—if it makes you feel better, it looks like the aftermath of a particularly manic jumble sale in there."

"I might have to look in later," she says. "Just to make sure you're not perfect."

"Perfect," he repeats, raising one eyebrow. He has turned his body toward hers, one knee crooked in the cushions, one arm along the back of the sofa. His hand is touching her shoulder.

"Well, in the domestic sphere anyway."

"There's only room for one person to be perfect around here," he says softly. "And that role is clearly already taken."

She blinks slowly at him.

"You're just wonderful, Lila," he says. He takes her hand in his, turns it over and runs his thumb over her palm in a way that causes her breath to stop in her chest. "I thought it the moment I saw you in the playground. You just cope with everything life throws at you with such grace and calm—you have this special air about you."

"Special?"

He shrugs, as if it's obvious. "You're so caring and kind. And obviously very beautiful. And you're always there to talk to, whenever I'm feeling low. I don't deserve you, really. I mean I'm just—I don't know—all over the place half the time. I hope you don't mind me telling you this."

"Not at all. But you're being way too complimentary."

He looks at her, his smile almost gone. His eyes are gazing into hers, brimming with seriousness. "I'm really not. It's been a tough couple of years, and I told you that knowing I can check in with you, or see you—well, it's really lightened something for me. I struggle to open up to people. But even if I don't get to see you enough, I know you're there. I can feel our connection. You make me think I can get through this. You . . . you're something else."

As she gazes at him, he gently takes the wine glass from her hand and places it on the coffee-table. He is still holding her hand, which he lifts to his lips and kisses. She feels the reverberations of that kiss at a cellular level, like an internal meteor shower in her body. And then he leans forward and, gazing intently into her eyes, waiting for just an exquisite fraction of a second before he finally does it, he kisses her.

AFTERWARD, SHE WISHES she hadn't drunk quite so much because things had taken on a dreamlike quality. She was aware of his kisses, their increasingly frantic nature, the distant snatches of the music, the feel of the tweed sofa under her bare skin. She remembers him unbuttoning her dress, telling her she was beautiful again and again as each inch of her was exposed, and then she remembers something more urgent and animal steadily taking over, their fingers clutching at each other, the kisses deep and punishing, the point at which his reason disappeared and instinct took over. He needed her. He had actually needed to be inside her. The strength of his desire was like being given something.

She is not sure how long they lie on the sofa afterward. She feels calm, satisfied, like a storm has passed over and now she can relax. Her arm is slung over his back, his skin faintly tacky with sweat, and he is still on top of her, his torso wedged between her legs, his soft hair draped on her collarbone. She feels his skin against hers, can smell a vague scent of something spicy and woody in his shampoo, like the kind of thing you would smell in an Hermès bottle. He is surprisingly slim, his muscles clearly defined under his skin. She wants never to move again. She could stay like this forever, with his hands on her, his weight pinning her. She thinks she will wind herself around him all night, so that every inch of her body is in contact with his. She is already anticipating doing this again—she is not sure she'll be able to leave him alone.

Gabriel's head shifts and he tilts his head to see her. "You okay?"

She smiles, a slow, easy smile. "I'm more than okay."

"Sorry if that was . . . a bit rushed. I got overexcited."

"Really. It was lovely."

"You're lovely."

They lie there for a moment longer and then he starts to shift, taking his weight on his left elbow so that he is no longer on top of her. He seems faintly dazed and, without his glasses, somehow more vulnerable, his eyes having the slightly unfocused look of the habitual glasses-wearer.

"Are you warm enough?"

"If you stay on top of me, yes," she says, grinning.

He looks at his watch. "Jesus. It's a quarter to one."

She's about to say something about time flying but thinks it will be corny. So she just pulls at the wool blanket at the far end of the sofa to cover them up. "So," she says, "we should probably get some sleep?"

His expression changes a little. He gazes off at the edge of the room, then turns to her, a little apologetically. "Actually, Lila, would you be okay if we didn't sleep?"

"You want to do that *again*?"

"What I mean is, I don't think it would be good for Lennie to wake up to find you here. I mean we don't know each other that well, and I don't want her getting the wrong end of the stick. I just think at this stage it would be better . . ." His voice tails off.

"You—you want me to go home?" It takes her a moment to grasp that, yes, this is actually what he is saying.

"If you wouldn't mind. Just for now. She's been through such a lot and I don't want her getting confused at this stage. It's been a lot for her, you know?" He puts his hand on her shoulder. "I'm really sorry to ask."

Lila lies there for a minute, then sits up and reaches for her dress. She realizes it's inside out, and starts pulling at the fabric, trying to get it the right way round. "No, no," she says. "It's fine."

"At any other time there's nothing I'd like more than us to be together all night."

"It's fine. I get it."

He waits while she pulls on her clothes, digging her knickers out of a gap in the sofa cushions, feeling suddenly self-conscious as she wriggles into her bra. It takes her a couple of attempts to get everything together, and she wishes he wasn't standing there, watching.

He walks her to the front door. Perhaps he notices the expression on her face, because he pauses in the hallway and takes her in his arms. "You're lovely," he says. "So lovely. We'll do this again." He gently tilts her face to his and kisses her, his eyes soft and serious. "Hey," he says, when he senses a faint reluctance in her response. "Hey."

She doesn't know how to feel. This is not how she expected the evening to end. He kisses her properly then, pulling her in to him, not letting her go until she softens and kisses him back.

"You're okay?"

"I'm okay," she says, and smiles reluctantly at him.

He helps her into her coat, then pulls the two sides of her collar together, gazing into her eyes. "Text me when you're home. I want to know you're safe."

She has walked a few steps down the path when he says, in a loud whisper: "Hey, Lila?"

"Yes?"

"Probably best not to say anything at school just yet. You know what those people are like."

She of all people knows what they're like. "Just between me and you," she says.

"Just me and you," he says, blows her a kiss, and waits at the door as she walks back down the street.

Chapter Twenty-six

Celie

Gene has a meeting with his agent, and gets the same bus as Celie so they're seated together on the top deck. Celie will get off first, to walk the rest of the way to school, and Gene will stay on all the way into the West End. He is clearly not used to being up so early and keeps yawning and rubbing his eyes, but talks as much as ever, his loud American voice carrying across the seats so that Celie has to keep shushing him. British people like their public transport quiet in the mornings, aside from the psychopaths who play music without earphones or have conversations on FaceTime.

"So what did you choose?"

"I went for Animation."

"Good call. This country is way too cold for nine months of the year to do Track."

"I think I'm the only one in my class who's signed up."

Gene has been telling her she has to find the thing that she enjoys doing. "Life is going to batter you, honey. She's a cruel mistress. So you have to find the place in your head where you can get lost in a good way. Otherwise it's just drink and drugs and bad women."

Celie is pretty sure she isn't going to end up losing herself in bad women, but she gets his general point.

"Honestly, if I'd put more love and work into the acting I could have got an Academy Award," Gene is saying. "I had all the studios lining up at my door. I should have carried on going to acting class, worked on my craft, not got distracted. The fame thing kind of went to my head for a bit. I guess it knocked me off course." He rubs at his head. "In all kinds of ways."

"You mean leaving Mum and Grandma?"

For the first time his voice drops a few decibels. Gene looks briefly uncomfortable. "I guess. Your mom finds it hard to forgive me for that."

"Have you said sorry?"

He looks at her as if this is a radical concept. "Not in so many words."

"Mum says you told Marja to say sorry."

"Sure, but that's . . . that's different."

"You told Marja if she broke up a family and she had to see Mum every day then she should say sorry. How is that different?"

Gene pulls out a cigarette from his packet, remembers he is not allowed to smoke on the bus, and puts it away again. He shifts in his seat. "It's complicated."

"Not really. You're the one who fucked up. You should say sorry."

"Celie! Don't curse in front of your grandpa!"

There is a brief silence.

"'Grandpa,' huh?" says Celie, speculatively.

"Your old pal Gene." He sighs. "Maybe you're right. Kind of hard to open up that can of worms, though. Your mom can be a little . . ."

"Scary."

"Yeah."

"You should try it, though. She's not as tough as she looks." Celie considers her mum. "I think she's sort of expecting you to leave again. I think she thinks everyone is going to leave her." She studies him. "Are you going to leave again?"

He shakes his head. "I kind of like hanging with my family. And, hey, who's going to sort out your problems if your old pal Gene isn't here? Who's going to get you fake tattoos and make you stand up straight? Who's going to make sure little Violet gets her share of doughnuts? Who's going to make sure Bill steps up for that little piano lady of his?" He lifts his head and gazes around the bus. "Who's going to give the women of northwest London something to talk about?"

A few women glance over, then look away. He pulls her to him and kisses the top of her head. He smells of toothpaste and old leather.

"You're ridiculous," she says. But she doesn't push him away.

CELIE'S STOMACH DOESN'T hurt before school any more. The pain disappeared almost immediately on the first day she was able to walk past the girls using her Invisible Gene Shield, as he put it. They had all been gathered by the school gates, smoking, even though, strictly speaking, they were on the wrong side of the gates to do it. When Meena's gaze had slid toward her, instead of shrinking she had met it, lifted her chin with the faintest of smiles, and carried on walking. She had felt them all staring at her the whole way to biology, but instead of like before, when she would have felt crushed by the weight of it, her head buzzing with the thoughts of what they might be saying, she had pulled her invisible shield around her and murmured, *Oh, you're all pathetic,* and pictured Gene rolling on the grass yelling: "I'm dead! You killed me!" Every time she'd done it after that it had become a little easier, so that now, three weeks on, she barely even notices them. Yes, she is still a bit lonely, but she's started eating with the girls from Music, who are a bit geeky, but always seem pleased to see her, and move their chairs up if they're on a packed table so that she can join them.

They don't talk about other girls. At all. It makes her realize that 90 percent of what Meena and the others talked about was who was doing what, who was stupid, or dressed badly, or had made an idiot of themselves. It was like other people were their currency. Harriet and Soraya talk about music, or films they've seen, or what they want to write next (they are both grade-eight musicians and Soraya composes her own pieces). Soraya had once played them a song she had recorded on her phone, while they were eating in the canteen, and Celie had plugged in her earphones to listen at the same time as Harriet and although it wasn't brilliant—Soraya's voice is a little thin and the song is about cats—the thing that had struck her was that Soraya was completely trusting: that Celie wouldn't laugh at her, that she would listen carefully. Soraya took for granted that what she was doing was worth trying, and would be received in the same spirit. If she had shown that to Meena, Meena would have corpsed with laughter and told everyone who would listen that it was pathetic.

Celie realizes she quite likes talking about things, rather than people. She is pretty sure that when she leaves the table Soraya and Harriet won't say anything mean about her. Although she still glances behind her twice as she leaves the canteen, just to make sure.

ANIMATION CLUB IS held at four p.m. in the art department, which is actually two Portakabins joined together. Celie makes sure she gets there at the last possible minute, as she feels weird about queuing up outside not knowing anyone there, and when she walks in she finds a table at the back in the corner where she can see everyone without anyone necessarily being able to see her. She scans the room, checking for anyone she might recognize—mostly boys from the two years above, but not the kind who dick around in class and steal each other's bags to dump them in the bins. These are the shadow kids, the boys who are quieter, who hang around at the edges of things. There are two other girls, one of whom is in the year above and nods at Celie—the most outward greeting you were ever going to get from a year thirteen—and then, one row ahead, she spots Martin, his red hair glowing. He glances behind and gives her the kind of brief wave someone gives when they expect not to be acknowledged but feel they should do it anyway. She gives him a small smile—it feels unkind not to—and tries not to think of what it means that she is now doing extra-curricular classes with someone like Martin.

"Now, we're going to start with storyboards. Don't worry if your drawing skills aren't up to much at this stage—we're really looking at how to construct your story. Depending on whether you want to do two-D or three-D animation, we can use software to help you create the images later."

Mr. Pugh is the kind of teacher who tells you to call him Kev, and sits on the corners of desks in jeans and trainers. She suspects he tells people he's the kind of teacher the kids think of as a friend. There is one of these in every school.

"Martin. You did storyboards last time round, right? Do you happen to have one in your folder?"

Celie cringes for him. To be the first person called up to show your stuff is mortifying. Especially in front of the older kids. But Martin doesn't seem troubled. He reaches down into his folder and pulls out a large sheet of A3 paper. Mr. Pugh strolls up to his desk and holds it up so that everyone can see.

It takes her a couple of seconds to register that this is Martin's work and that it's really good. There are maybe twelve squares of drawings, some of which have been heavily shaded. She can't see clearly from where she is but it looks like someone experiencing a nightmare, then emerging into daylight. There are monsters that stretch across the frame, an anguished face, a giant teddy bear, and finally the face of a concerned woman, who might be a mum. Mr. Pugh is explaining how Martin has divided his story up into key scenes and that each one has an image.

"We're going to stick to fairly simple animations at this stage so you can get the hang of it, but that means the stories you create should be quite short. Martin's Nightmare, as you see here, fits the brief perfectly."

Someone asks something about software, and the difference between two-D and three-D, but Celie isn't paying attention. She is looking at the contents of Martin's folder, which seems to contain lots of storyboards. She can see semi-hidden images, some in color, others in black-and-white. He is sorting them, placing them back in the folder carefully, and when he realizes she's watching he turns his head and gives her a brief, neutral grin. Not the kind of grin you give if you feel a bit embarrassed about something, just the kind you give if you feel okay about what you're doing and don't see the need to defend it to anyone.

Working out your story is trickier than it sounds. Celie isn't sure what kind of story she wants to tell. Everything in her life this last couple of years has been depressing. She can't exactly animate her parents' divorce, or Grandma getting hit by a bus, or Marja getting pregnant, or Meena and the others blanking her, or what it was like getting stoned on the Heath. She thinks about superheroes and cartoon animals—the normal stuff—but it just doesn't seem very interesting. Everyone else seems to have come with a story already: she can see them sketching out their squares, cursing quietly as they get their drawings wrong. She leans over her board, trying to look as if she knows what she's doing, but she starts to feel uncomfortable and exposed, like maybe she shouldn't be here.

"You okay?" Martin has walked past her and stopped at her board. He can see that there is nothing in her squares.

She pulls a face and tries to look casual. "Just struggling for ideas really."

He looks at the doodles she has done along the edges.

"I'm not really into superheroes and I don't know what else to draw."

Martin nods, as if this is completely to be expected. He has a strange air of authority in this club—he's like a different person.

"How—how do you come up with your ideas?"

"Uhh." He looks away from her when he talks, and she wonders if he's shyer than he lets on. "Honestly? The first year I came I did an animation about bullying. It was pretty crap, but Mr. Pugh said the animation was good. And last year I did more kind of surreal stuff, dreams, nightmares, inanimate objects coming to life, that kind of thing. I don't really know what I want to do half the time so I just have a small idea and try to make it bigger." He blushes a little. "If that makes sense."

"I don't have any ideas, though." She doesn't want to do an animation about bullies.

"I'm trying to remember the prompts he gave us last year." He stares at his feet for a minute. "Oh. Okay. What's the last thing that made you laugh?"

She thinks about Gene on television with the toothpaste, the way he mimicked the many different ways the director had made him smile at himself during filming—*Now give me Satisfied Smile! Now give me Sexy Smile! Unsure Smile! Confident Smile! Make Love to the Camera Smile!* Then she thinks about him being mischievous in the gay sex shop. Him and Bill having a stupid old-man fight in the hall with tea-towels, as if she and Violet were meant to think they were joking.

"My two grandpas," she says, "who hate each other. Or hated each other."

Martin smiles. "Yeah. Two old men fighting. That's funny."

Her face falls. "Except I can't draw old men."

"Hold on." Martin walks back through the tables and squats by a low bookcase. He comes back with a well-thumbed oversized paperback book titled: *How to Draw Characters*.

"Copy some of those," he says, flicking through the pages. "Even if they're not exactly what you want, they'll give you some ideas. It's quite good—it does step-by-step guides." There are instructions on how to draw an egg and turn it into a face, how to draw emotions, how to age a character. He hands her the book, hesitates, then heads back to his table.

"Thanks," she says, probably a moment too late. She isn't sure if he hears her.

"How was Animation, honey?" says Gene, when she gets home. He's in the living room lying across the entire length of the sofa, watching the news on the television and eating crisps from the packet, which means that Bill is out. Truant is sitting staring at him, every fiber of his being fixated on the possibility of stray crumbs.

"Good," she says. She has a folder under her arm full of pictures of old men fighting. One has bright white teeth and a toupee, his opponent has a stick, a suit and tie, and she has created a storyboard in which they are arguing over who gets to climb aboard a bus first. As they fight they gradually knock over all the old ladies at the bus stop, then all the passengers on the bus, including mothers with prams, and finally the driver. Last, they pull out their bus passes and complain about their frailty.

Martin had burst out laughing when she showed him and she doesn't even think he was doing it kindly.

"So what did you draw?" he says. "Anything you can show your old pal Gene?"

"Not yet, Grandpa," she says, and smiles as she trots up the stairs.

Chapter Twenty-seven

Lila

A h! Ms. Kennedy! I had been hoping to speak to you." Mrs. Tugendhat is making her way across the playground. She is wearing a long draped tunic, and her stately manner gives the impression of a boat in full turquoise sail navigating calm seas, even as the wind blows her hair around her head in an unruly cloud.

"Hello, Mrs. Tugendhat," says Lila, trying not to grimace. She had come early because she had been hoping to catch Gabriel.

"It's the costumes. We were hoping we might see something by now. The dress rehearsal is creeping up!" She raises both eyebrows as she says this, as though they are sharing some great joke.

The bloody costumes. Lila knows she should have spent an evening on eBay sorting them but somehow it disappears from her brain every evening.

"Are they coming together?"

"Yes. Yes," Lila says reassuringly.

"I sent you the measurements. You got the email, yes? Goodness, these children are so large now! When I started teaching they were all pint-sized. Pint-sized!" She thrusts a plump hand downward to indicate the height of a child who would have been, at best, a toddler. "Can you let me know when we can expect them?"

It feels like the constant chorus to Lila's life sometimes: *When can we expect more chapters? When can we expect the costumes? When can we expect the noise to stop in your garden?*

"I'll be in touch," says Lila, guessing, uncomfortably, that the thought will probably have disappeared from her head by the time she reaches her front door. Because Lila's head, for the last week, has been 98 percent full of Gabriel. He had sent her a slew of messages the following day—That was a lovely evening. I couldn't sleep afterward. You are so beautiful, Bella—but he has made frustratingly little effort to see her. She had more or less assumed that this was it now, that they were a *thing*. That they had laid the building blocks of something lovely, and this was the next step to a stage that might involve more dinners, or sleepovers, or even introducing their families.

Two days ago she had broken and texted him from the bath.

> Are we okay? You're v quiet x

The answer had come back an hour later.

> Course we are, Bella. Sorry, just a mad
> week at work x

She had been briefly reassured, and again when he had texted her the following morning: Morning, Bellissima. Woke up thinking about you and the other night x

Since then, nothing.

Lila knows she should just call him, or even text saying she feels a little weird about his lack of communication. But something in her worries that that could come across as a bit *extra*, as the girls put it. She doesn't want to seem clingy just because they slept together. She is a forty-two-year-old woman after all. Her thoughts spin and whirl in her head, vacillating between one course of action and another. She hasn't dated for almost twenty years. She feels like an astronaut on a moon landing, navigating a completely different landscape. How does this whole thing work now, anyway? Normally she would discuss it with Eleanor, but she has an uncomfortable feeling that she knows what Eleanor will say, and it is not positive. She will tell Lila to put her cards on the table, to be direct, to say what she wants. Or she will tell Lila that he is a dickhead so walk away and stop thinking about him. But Eleanor doesn't understand Gabriel fully; doesn't understand what he has been through. She wasn't there for that delicious intimate evening, has never seen how sweet he is to her, or experienced the level of their connection. So she has begun actively avoiding Eleanor's calls, or texting her back saying, *Sorry! All nuts here! Xxx*, and feeling uncomfortable about that too.

Gabriel's mother has just appeared, hurrying across the playground with her car keys in her hand. Lila gazes at her, briefly wondering if Gabriel has said anything about Lila to her. They must be close, mustn't they? Is that where he gets his advice? The woman briefly meets Lila's eye as she hurries past, holding Lennie's hand. Lila smiles and the woman smiles back, but it's in that vague way you smile when you don't really know someone and feel obliged to return a gesture. Lila sighs, holds out her hand as Violet, who is in a crabby mood, thrusts her rucksack into it, then braces herself for another long and unsettled evening.

• • •

ESTELLA ESPERANZA HAS slept with the handsome young doctor. But she is allowed only half an episode of pleasure, before it emerges that the doctor has actually been employed by Rodrigo to seduce her, so that he can divorce her for infidelity and keep the majority of his fortune (Lila is not entirely sure how divorce settlements work in this part of South America but it seems a little unfair). This time, Estella is not broken by a man's betrayal. She has been through too much, these last two series, for that. Any woman who has survived marital betrayal, a near drowning (she fell out of a speedboat while following Rodrigo), the near-loss of one of her children, and an assassination attempt by a man dressed as a giant centipede is not likely to be shaken by the discovery that a man barely young enough to cultivate bum-fluff on his chin had ulterior motives. When she discovers from a sisterly nurse that he is not a doctor, but merely posing as one, she waits for him to meet her in the treatment cubicle, tells him sweetly that she has a problem with her ankle, waits for him to bend over to examine it, then kicks him, hard, in the face, while wearing a pair of vertiginous black and gold Yves Saint Laurent stilettos. While he is groaning on the floor, clutching his face, she slides nimbly off the treatment gurney, steps delicately over his prone body, and hissing at him, *Next time*, pendejo, *be careful who you try to fool*, walks elegantly past the curtain and out through the hospital lobby.

Lila stares at the credits until they fade, and then, a little wearily, she turns off her light and goes to sleep.

THE FOLLOWING MORNING Eleanor appears on the doorstep, two minutes after Bill leaves for his workshop. Lila, who was on the way upstairs to her study with a mug of tea, startles as she opens the door.

"Why are you avoiding me?" Eleanor walks straight past her into the kitchen, shaking off her mackintosh.

"I'm not avoiding you."

"You've missed four dog walks and you're not taking my calls. You're avoiding me."

Lila trails after her into the kitchen and switches the kettle on. She puts her hands to her face. "Ugh. I did something stupid and I know you're going to say it's stupid, which makes me feel even more stupid than I did when I did the stupid thing."

"What?"

"I can't cope with you telling me off right now, El."

"I didn't come here to tell you off! I needed to talk to you."

"Oh." Lila's hands drop from her face. "Why? What's the matter?" She's been so wrapped up in her own life that it hasn't even occurred to her that her friend might need help. By unspoken agreement the conversation is halted until the second mug of tea is made, the door closed, and both are seated at the kitchen table with the tin of biscuits between them.

"I don't know what I'm doing with my life."

Lila waits. This could, after all, cover any number of potential categories.

Eleanor pulls a face. "The sex-party thing. I was at this event and I just didn't feel as giddy as I do normally. It was about eleven at night and I was in this crowded room watching two people go at it and there was something about the whole vibe of it that made me feel really depressed."

"And?"

"And I really wanted to be home having a mug of tea and chatting to someone about what was on the telly."

"Really?"

"I don't regret doing it. For the first few months it felt like an adventure, like I was making up for lost time. But it was this BDSM party in west London and there was polythene taped to the walls and the music was awful and it was like all the fun disappeared and I just had . . . the ick. I looked at all these glazed eyes and hairy buttocks and I just felt a bit . . . urgh. It was like someone turning the overhead lights on at the end of the party and all these crazy cool people you've been dancing with all night are just sweaty idiots with their mascara halfway down their faces."

Lila resists the urge to say that every party Eleanor has described made her picture exactly this vibe. "What did you do?"

"Made a French exit and got an Uber. Jamie and Nicoletta have called a couple of times since but I just . . . don't fancy it anymore. It's literally like a switch has been flicked. Don't pull that face, Lila. Do you think I need HRT?"

"No. I think you need a mug of tea and a nice man to watch the telly with."

Eleanor exhales. "Oh, thank God. I thought now you were having all your own sexy adventures you'd be telling me I'd lost the plot and just needed extra hormones or something."

"Two. I've had two. And I'm not sure I'm made for sexy adventures either."

They sigh and take a sip of tea.

"I slept with the hot architect."

"But that's great!"

"And I think he's cooled on me."

"What do you mean?"

Lila tells her about the lack of texts, the vague promises that aren't met. She tells her her darkest secret: that somehow she fears she had forgotten how to do sex properly, or hasn't kept up to date with the latest moves, or had done something boring or repulsive to make Gabriel go off her. She had spent almost half an hour examining her jawline in a magnifying mirror looking for stray chin hairs.

"Don't be daft. It's nothing you've done. He's one of those men. He's bread crumbing you."

"He's what?"

"I've read about it on the internet. It's a thing. They give you just enough to keep you on the hook, but not enough to suggest a real relationship."

Lila shakes her head. "That's not it. He's not that kind of man."

Eleanor pulls out her phone and types something. Then she starts to read: "*Blows hot and cold.*"

"Okay. Maybe."

"*Uses a generic nickname.*"

"Mm. He calls me Bella. That's not quite generic."

Eleanor pulls a face. "*Implies he wants a relationship, and says things like 'you're just my type' or 'you're too good for me' but with no real follow-up.*"

Lila is getting a sinking feeling.

"*Avoids too many dates. Something always feels off.*"

Lila feels a bit sick now. "He's a bit hard to pin down. You really think that's what it is?"

"*Gives you a sob story so you invest in him emotionally.*"

Lila puts down her mug. "His wife actually died, though. Is that a sob story?"

They agree that that one could go either way.

"*Asks for photos.*"

"Sexy photos? No. He doesn't do that." She feels briefly flooded with relief.

"It says here they may not even be aware that they're doing it. And he could be genuine. But if you can tick a few of those it's probably worth thinking about."

Lila thinks of the many conversations she and Gabriel have had. The long, almost nightly chats. The fact that she is the only parent at school who has taken Lennie home. The way he looks at her. The way he understands what it's like for her. "I don't know. He's maybe some of that, but he's definitely more than that too. I mean, I don't want to write him off just because he's had a busy week at work."

"Then don't. But don't drive yourself nuts about it either. C'mon, Lila. Just have a straightforward conversation with him. You're forty-two years old."

"I knew that was coming."

"That's why you love me."

They sit for a moment, taking turns to reach into the biscuit tin.

"Bloody hell, El. Do you remember when we were sixteen and we thought we'd have all this stuff worked out by now? I thought I'd know it all by thirty." Lila takes a bite out of a slightly soggy chocolate-chip cookie.

"I've got a horrible feeling we're going to be having a variation of this conversation when we're eighty-five."

"He left his dentures on the side of my bed. Do you think that means he likes me?"

"He keeps smiling at another woman in the nursing home."

"I'm sure I saw his mobility scooter parked outside the local pole-dancing club."

"He can only get it up with fourteen Viagra tablets and a hoist. Does that mean I'm not attractive enough?"

They begin to cackle, and then, unaccountably, get an attack of the giggles. It is the best Lila has felt all week.

JENSEN ARRIVES AT lunchtime, just as she is taking a break from editing the first three chapters. She does this when she writes, going back over her previous work and honing, polishing, substituting words if she can think of better ones. It's the part of writing she enjoys most. He appears at the French windows with a wave just as she is downstairs making tea, and it seems a little off not to offer him some. They sit outside in the garden to drink it. He is dressed in non-gardening clothes, surprisingly smart in a pale gray cashmere jumper and dark jeans, headed to a potential job on the outskirts of London. "It's a lot of work. I'll probably have to take someone else on to get it all done. But it's a beautiful old house and they want to restore the garden to its Georgian origins, so it's been pretty nice just doing research and trying to work out what I should suggest to them." He has a folder of drawings with him and shows her a couple: beautiful, precise diagrams of hedging, and geometric paths.

Her own garden is finished, the last of the plants dug in and watered, and for the last week she has sat out here every evening, Truant at her feet, just enjoying the space and the peace. It is as if she has been given a whole extra room in her house, a place where she can feel quite different, a place without a complicated history. Weirdly, Jensen and Bill had been right: when she sits on the bench that Bill made she does think about her mother. But it is a good feeling, more of a warm remembrance than a gaping maw of absence. Her mother would have loved this space. She would have used words like "heavenly" and "divine," and murmured, *Just look at how the light moves through those plants, Lila! Can't you just wallow in all that birdsong?*

"You really did a lovely job," she says, breaking the silence. And he pulls a quick face, like people do when they're not good at receiving compliments.

"I'm glad you think so," he says, then scuffs at the path with the toe of his shoe. "This one was personal." He gives her a quick sideways smile, and it is a little awkward but his eyes are kind.

Lila feels a faint pang in his presence. His broad, open face holds no secrets.

"Well," she says. "You don't have to be a stranger, just because you've finished working."

"Yeah? What shall I do—just knock on your window at odd hours, demanding tea?"

"Absolutely. Maybe with a special free-form dance around the pond if you require biscuits."

"I'll start working on my choreography."

She remembers how openly she was able to talk to him about the night they had spent together. How it had been funny, and straightforward—on his side, anyway—instead of making her feel anxious and unsure of herself. This realization—with its parallels—makes her feel faintly ill at ease, and when Truant suddenly streaks across the lawn toward the kitchen and starts baying at the door, she is almost glad of the interruption. "I'd better see what he's barking at," she says, standing.

"Sure. Oh! I actually popped by because I wondered if I could get a copy of that invoice I gave you a couple of weeks ago. My accounts software has apparently gone nuts and I need to see the last one so I can calculate what's left to settle."

Truant is inside the house now, apparently hurling himself at the front door.

"Sure," she says, distracted. "I think it's upstairs on my desk by the printer. Just give me a moment." She has to shout now to be heard as she jogs toward the house.

"Don't worry," he says, from behind her. "I remember where the printer is. I'll get it."

It's a delivery. For next door. Lila resists the urge to point mutely at the number on her door, clearly two digits out from the address on the packet, and has to endure a short speech from the man in the uniform about how hard the delivery company works him and his colleagues, how they are given no time between drop-offs, which is why things go to the wrong houses, all while Truant snarls and writhes at her heels, trying to get through the narrow gap in the door. Then the driver decides he might actually have something for her and walks back across the road to his van, returning at a frankly leisurely pace with a parcel for Bill. She suspects it will be more sheet music: Bill has been ordering tranches of piano music so that he has new things to practice with Penelope.

When she finally shuts the door, shooing the dog away, and places the package on the hall table, her ears are ringing. Which may be why she doesn't register the silence for a few minutes. She walks to the kitchen and looks out, but Jensen has gone. She thinks he must have let himself out through the garden while she was engaged at the front door, and walks over to pick up the empty tea mugs. He has left his folder of drawings on the bench. She picks it up and brings it inside, deciding she should probably call him to let him know. It won't be good if he turns up at this new job without them.

She's just about to dial his number when she hears footsteps on the stairs. She looks up, and Jensen is standing at the bottom, in the hallway. His face is ashen, and he's holding some sheets of paper. He stares at her.

"*My sexytimes with J—or how, after twenty years, I got back on the bike.* What—what the hell is this?"

She realizes, with a sick feeling, what he is holding.

There is a brief silence.

"Jensen, I can explain. It's not actually what—"

"*He had joked earlier about his 'dadbod.' True, he wasn't sculpted like a Greek god, but there was a friendly homeliness to his shape.* 'Friendly homeliness,' huh? Nice."

"It's not actually you," she stutters.

"*He told me he got engaged after his girlfriend scrawled 'Do it or forget it' on his windscreen.*" He looks up at her. "No? Who is it, then? *We rolled around on the floor of the workshop until we were covered with sawdust and wood shavings . . .*"

She feels as if her entire body has turned to ice.

"So you were just using me for . . . material?"

She shakes her head dumbly.

"But this *is* for your book, right? The one about rebuilding your life? This is a chapter of your book."

She doesn't speak. She cannot move. It is as if all the muscles in her body have liquefied. He is tapping his finger on the typewritten pages. "I told you everything. Everything I'd been through. And you have taken the night we spent together and just—just vomited it out into something you're going to sell?"

"I—I can change the details. I—"

"Who the hell *are* you, Lila?"

He looks at her with an expression she hasn't seen before. It is, she realizes, something like revulsion.

"You told me you didn't want a relationship because you were dealing with a load of stuff. I thought you just needed time. I got that. I thought I'd sit back and wait for the clouds to clear and see how it went. I actually thought you were a really nice person. Just a nice, honest person who was coping with a lot."

He puts the pile of papers on the hall table and gives a bewildered shake of his head.

"Turns out I'm still a really shit judge of character." He walks to the front door and stops on the threshold. He turns, takes a breath, like someone struggling to control himself. "You know what? Irina was a terrible, terrible girlfriend. But at least she never pretended to be anything else." He gives her one last scathing look, and walks out of the front door.

Chapter Twenty-eight

Lila has been unprepared for how shaken she would be by Jensen's reaction, this new version of him who finds her abhorrent, someone he no longer recognizes. She hadn't realized how much she'd enjoyed having his benign presence around until it was gone. She finds it impossible to work on the book. Even the garden feels tainted—an immaculate green rebuke. Every time she sits down she hears his voice: *Who* are *you, Lila?*

It has become impossibly clear to her. How on earth had she thought she could write about her life in this way, without considering the impact on the people around her? She remembers Celie's pointed questions at the pizza restaurant, her niggle of anxiety about how the girls would react to her stories. She hadn't even considered Jensen's feelings.

Eleanor, on their dog walk, pulls the kind of face that suggests his reaction is no surprise, which doesn't make her feel any better. "You're going to have to talk to your publishers," she says, when Lila recounts the awful day.

"Without all the sexy stuff they'll cancel the contract. And then I'll have no money."

"But you're going to have to lose that chapter whatever you do. You can't possibly go ahead with it. Not after this."

Lila's head drops into her hands. "Bloody hell, El. Do you think I'm a shitty person?"

"No. You're a person who was in a mess and maybe lost sight of something." Eleanor stops and puts a hand on her arm. "Though I had been wondering, Lils, how you'd feel when some of that stuff was published. It's quite exposing, writing about your sex life. And I'm not sure you're in the right place—or even that you're the right person—to deal with that. Do you really want to be that person anyway? Selling your intimate life for money? It was one thing when you were writing about how to rescue a marriage—I can see that has value. But writing about your sex life—isn't that just encouraging a kind of voyeurism? Opening yourself up to all sorts of judgment?"

"Says the woman who has spent the last eighteen months—"

"I know. I know. But me going to those parties didn't affect anyone except me. And nobody knew who I was. It's not something that'll follow me around forever."

Lila cannot talk anymore. So Eleanor talks, in the way that old friends do when they understand the particular depth of the pit you're in. Eleanor has taken up salsa dancing. She goes to a place in Waterloo full of exotically dressed old men who want nothing more than to sling her around a dance floor. She has also started going for weekly massages, so that she can, as she puts it, stay connected to her body. "Only middle-aged women masseurs. Really strong ones who aren't afraid to get their elbows in. Honestly, I feel great afterward and it costs a lot less than the sex parties once you factor in the sex gear and talcum powder. You should try it."

"I can't afford it," Lila says.

• • •

ONE OF FRANCESCA'S golden rules was that if you were sunk in despondency you should move your body. *Do something, darling.* Go for a walk or empty a wardrobe or dig something in the garden. Whatever gets you out of your head and into your body. Lila has now stared at her screen for an hour and forty minutes and all she has achieved is to sink further and further into melancholy. When she is not melancholy, she is jittery, her brain refusing to be still long enough for her to focus on her work. Every time she reads what she has written she is flooded with shame, the angry voices of future readers.

Who are *you, Lila?*

It has turned cold, as if winter has arrived overnight, and the garden has felt chill and unwelcoming even without the drop in temperature so she decides to organize the house. Gene has brought back three large cardboard boxes from Jane's house and, being Gene, has simply left them in the hall "because there's no space for them in my room." That there is definitely no space for them in the hall either is unacknowledged. As is the fact that he is now referring to "my room." Between Gene's extra stuff, and the never-ending exodus of things from Bill's bungalow, Lila feels like her house has started to resemble one of those eccentric junk shops where a moose's head sits on a chamber pot and the shelves are full of books that nobody will ever read.

She will clear some things from the attic. Gene's boxes can go up there. If nothing else she can create some space in the hallway, and at least then she can feel as if she has achieved something. She is coming downstairs when she passes Bill on his way up. He has had a new haircut and looks oddly vulnerable and shorn. He is carrying a newspaper under his arm and in his right hand holds a tray with two cups of tea. Penelope is behind him. Lila wonders briefly if they are going to drink tea in bed.

"Oh, Lila, I saw Jensen yesterday."

Lila's stomach drops at the mention of his name.

"He was in a very odd mood. He was actually rather curt, if I'm honest."

"Perhaps you caught him at a bad moment," says Penelope. "He's normally such a friendly chap."

"Yes. Perhaps a bad moment." Bill ponders this. "Oh, he did say I should remind you about that tree at the front."

Lila feels sick at the thought of Jensen being unfriendly. It's like nature going wrong—waterfalls running upward or cats barking like dogs. She has done that to him. "I'm going to sort out some things in the attic," she says, in an effort to change the subject.

"Oh, good idea. I'll come and help you when we've had our tea." He turns to Penelope. "You're heading off soon anyway, aren't you, darling?"

Darling. Something in Lila contracts at the casual use of the word and she is not sure whether it is grief for her absent mother or just evidence of love that she seems incapable of grasping for herself.

"I am. Cameron Williams has a grade-four exam tomorrow and we need to practice his sight reading. But I can help for a little while if you think I might be useful."

"You're terribly sweet. But, no, I think Cameron's needs are probably greater just now."

They are still murmuring companionably about minor scales and arpeggios as Lila pulls down the loft ladder and disappears into the attic.

LILA SITS ON the dusty floor and gazes around her in the too-still air, watching the dust motes settle in the dim light, and wonders if this was actually a really stupid idea. There is something about an attic, after all, that induces a kind of melancholy. Perhaps it is the sight of long-neglected items gathering dust unseen and unloved. Perhaps it is the evidence of a family life that has long passed. Lila looks around at the many boxes, Dan's old CD collection that he had failed to take with him, the small coffee-table he had brought from his parents' house when they had first moved in together, the bags of the girls' outgrown clothes that remind her of when they were small, needy, and affectionate. There are other boxes here too: three labeled "Francesca" that Bill brought round after her mother died, things, he said, that he couldn't bear to have in the house but neither of them could throw away.

Then she thinks of Gene's extra boxes in the hall, and remembers she needs to do something to make her feel she has a grip on life. Dan's stuff will be the easiest to deal with. She hauls over the boxes of CDs, starts going through them, and then, overwhelmed by the sight of music they had enjoyed when they were first together, starts carrying the boxes downstairs without looking at them. She will text him when she has finished to ask if he still wants them, and if not, she will take them all to the charity shop. And that will be two boxes gone already. And Marja will be welcome to the best of U2, and the Smiths album she always had to pretend to enjoy.

She has been up there for almost an hour when Bill arrives. His gray head appears through the loft hatch and he holds up a mug of tea that she takes gratefully. "Goodness," he says, peering around. "What a lot of stuff." As if he hasn't filled her house with his own, she thinks, but she thanks him for the tea and carries on going through the Christmas decorations. In this box there are baubles Francesca bought, clumsily painted modeling clay decorations that Celie and Violet had made at school and she had never been able to discard. Lila has to steel herself not to think too hard about the kind of Christmas she will never have again. She thins them out, removing everything too broken to be useful, and drops a bin bag with the threadbare tinsel and smashed glass balls onto the landing, feeling a vague sense of satisfaction at another small space cleared.

Bill works alongside her in near silence, going through a box of old photographs. He says her name occasionally, drawing attention to a picture of her when she was small or the three of them on holiday in Scotland when Lila was a child, Francesca beaming—always beaming, morphing steadily from blonde to gray. He chuckles sometimes, pointing out some of Lila's more challenging teenage hairstyles, sighs softly at a picture of him and Francesca on honeymoon in Italy. "I think I should frame this one," he says occasionally.

They break for lunch and Bill helps her carry some of the boxes to the car. They can only fit two boxes and three bin bags in the boot, but she decides to carry on with the attic clearing. She cannot contemplate sitting in front of the laptop, with its implicit impossible decisions. The girls are at Dan's tonight, which means that in theory she can do as she likes, but some part of her wishes they were with her, their conversation and myriad needs providing her with distraction from what is going on in her head.

They clear almost one whole side of the attic: battered Lloyd Loom chairs that she accepts she will never repaint, stained rugs that she had thought might come in useful one day, defunct electronic equipment, impulse purchases (mostly Dan's), and boxes of plastic toys she had forgotten they even owned. She stares at the toys, wondering whether she should take them to the dump to avoid Dan having them, but the whole thing seems too complicated to contemplate right now, just another mess she is somehow enmeshed in, and she shoves them to the low part of the eaves, not wanting to deal with it. It is moving these boxes that reveals the doll's house. She and Bill let out a low *aah* as it is revealed, glancing at each other in a brief moment of nostalgia.

"I'd forgotten it was even up here," says Lila, softly, hauling it forward so she can see it better.

Bill sits on a plastic Ikea footstool. "I did enjoy making that," he says, leaning forward to run his hand over the dusty roof. "You were so delighted when we gave it to you."

"I really was." Lila opens the front, revealing the five rooms inside. There are the tiny stairs, onto which he had glued dark red stair carpet, the bathroom with its claw-footed bath. The furniture and fittings have been stacked into Tupperware boxes, which they open and exclaim at the perfection of everything, the exquisite details, the smallness of it all.

"Your mother sent off to Germany for lots of these things," Bill said, examining a set of plates. "She was determined to get the best. She had such fun setting it all up for you."

"I think it's the best present I ever received." They exchange a brief, awkward hug, and Lila rests her head on his shoulder, feeling grateful that one man in her orbit thinks she is an acceptable human.

Lila is just pulling on a light switch, exclaiming delightedly as it comes on, when Gene's head appears through the hatch. "Hey, hey! Is this a party?"

He is beaming. He has been to an audition this morning and Lila suspects it has gone well. When it hasn't he usually retreats to his room for a few hours to watch old videos of himself and prop up his battered ego.

"We're just clearing some space," Lila says. "And we found my doll's house."

"Well, isn't that a beauty!" Gene exclaims.

"Bill made it," Lila says. "For my eighth birthday."

It takes her a moment to register the change in atmosphere. She is still exclaiming over the lights, testing each room to see which works, when she realizes Gene is gazing at the house with something less than admiration. "Good job," he says, his face expressionless. And there is a short silence.

"Did Violet not want it in her room?" says Bill, who seems oblivious.

Lila pulls a face. "She's never really been a doll person." The dolls Violet had inherited from Celie had tended to end up with punk haircuts and amputations. When Violet had seemed half-hearted at the prospect of having the doll's house, Lila had not pushed her. She did not want the intricate little home ending up as Barbie's Crack Den.

"Well, it's just a doll's house, right? I mean not everyone likes them," Gene murmurs. He is peering into one of his boxes. "Not everyone wants to play house."

"Lots of children love playing house," Bill says, moving a stack of family albums. "Lila loved it when she was a little girl."

"Sure. But she liked other things as well. It's fine for kids to do something a little wilder and more adventurous."

"But not everyone wants to be wild. Lila very much relished her little house when she was growing up."

"How about we leave it up here and start on some other boxes?" says Lila, briskly.

She stands, a little stooped to accommodate the roof beams, and makes her way carefully toward some boxes near the water tank. She pulls one toward her and prizes open the lid. Immediately something gives inside her. It is one of Francesca's boxes. She stares at the familiar handwriting on the letters, at her mother's jewelry box, and has to let out a small breath. "It's Mum's stuff," she says, to nobody in particular.

There is a short silence. Bill straightens behind her.

"Do we want to do this now?" she says, turning to him.

Bill puts his hand gently on her arm. "I think we should. It's been long enough."

"I'll just take a look at these boxes Jane brought over," says Gene from the other end of the attic. "I've got a load of memorabilia and my agent says there's a fan convention coming up that's contemplating including *Star Squadron Zero*." Lila is not sure whether this is said from a position of diplomacy, or whether he is actually only interested in his old *Star Squadron Zero* junk, but either way she's grateful.

She and Bill spend a quiet twenty minutes sorting through the first box. There are certificates and school reports Francesca had kept from her own childhood and from Lila's. There are old passports and defunct bank books, costume jewelry and unfashionable scarves. She tries to be ruthless, telling herself she should keep only the things she would be happy to have on show. She tries to think of how Francesca would handle it. *Lila darling, it's just stuff. Keep a few beautiful things and try to focus on the future.*

They pause when they get to the letters. There is one from Lila, on a school trip, telling her mother in childish, rounded handwriting how much she misses her, which makes her well up. There is a batch of love letters from Bill, wrapped in a dark velvet ribbon, which Bill holds to his chest briefly, then puts safely to one side. And then they are down to the detritus of the box, letters Francesca had sent to her own parents, or long-forgotten pen friends, a couple of old boyfriends from her teenage years declaring love from long distances.

Lila finds a letter from Francesca's oldest friend, Dorothy, and starts reading about Francesca's trip to Dublin. "People don't write letters any more, but they should. These are so lovely. It's like hearing Mum's voice," she says, scanning the text. "Oh, sweet, she talks about Mum buying Celie a dress while she was there. I think I still have that dress somewhere. It was white with blue checks. Violet would never wear it."

Bill shifts to see what she is reading. He frowns. "Are you sure she said Dublin? She told me she'd only been to Ireland once, as a child. She can't have gone again." He takes the letter from Lila's hand, examining it. "What date is the letter?"

Lila sees the date before he does. And blinks.

"Why would she be writing about Francesca going to Dublin? We never went there."

"This is dated 2006?"

"I'm sure it was lovely to be in Dublin. Of course Gene met you at the Temple Bar—of course he did. I can imagine the riotous atmosphere once he got everyone going . . ."

Lila makes to snatch the letter from Bill, but he has seen it too. He stares at Dorothy's writing, then looks up at Gene. "Francesca was in Dublin . . . with you?"

"Uhh . . . she—she—Say, can I have that?" Gene has come over, and is holding out his hand.

The atmosphere in the attic has stilled. It is as if a monstrous vacuum has swept in and sucked out all the air. Gene's glance flickers between them. "I was filming over there. She just . . . came to hang out for a few days."

When nobody speaks, Gene rubs at the back of his head. "It was just a short trip. Look, pal . . . we go back a long way."

Bill stares at Gene, taking in what is implicit in Gene's few words, his unusually awkward manner. Gene looks at Bill and then at Lila. "It didn't mean anything," he says.

"To you! It didn't mean anything to you! It meant everything to me!"

"It was only that one time . . ."

"Oh. Well, that's all right, then."

"It was . . ." Gene clears his throat. "We were both feeling a bit down. I was with Jane at the time and it was a little tricky. The whole menopause thing. She was really emotional about everything. And your mother she . . . well, she—"

"She what?"

"Oh, you don't need to go into the details."

Bill is completely rigid. "I absolutely do need the details."

Gene pulls a face. He sighs. "I think she said she was . . . just a bit . . . bored."

"Bored?"

"Hey, I'm sorry. It was just that old . . . connection, you know? We couldn't help ourselves. We go back a long way, like I said. These things are hard to resist."

Bill is breathing hard. He sits very still, staring at the floor. He looks like someone who has been punched, hard, in the stomach and is working out which of his internal organs is no longer operative. Then he swallows, and makes his way quietly and abruptly toward the loft hatch. As Gene and Lila protest, he climbs through the hatch and starts making his way down the metal steps.

"Bill!" Lila tries to go after him but he holds up a hand. "Bill, where are you going?"

"I need some space," Bill says, his voice quiet and choked. She can just see the top of his head now that he has made it to the landing. "I'm going home."

Lila watches as he walks carefully down the stairs, one hand on the banister. A few moments later she hears the front door close.

The house is silent. Lila's head is spinning. She looks up at Gene. He holds his hands up. "Well, I didn't know she was going to write a damn letter about it."

"Of all the people in all the world you could have slept with you had to sleep with Mum? You had to wreck the one thing Bill had left of her?" Her voice is shaking. Suddenly Lila erupts. It is as if thirty-five years of pain and frustration and loss have burst through. She wants to throw the box of letters at him. She wants to push him out of the loft hatch. "You wreck everything! My God! You just crash through people's lives with no thought for how it impacts on them!"

"Sweetie, I—"

"You could have left her alone! Hadn't you caused us all enough damage already? She loved Bill! And you couldn't bear it, could you? The one chance you got and you wrecked that too. You're a monster!"

"Lila honey—"

"Get out!" she yells. "I should have known you'd destroy this too. It's all you do, isn't it? Come blundering in, seduce, get bored, and destroy everyone's happiness. You're like—you're like some terrible disease. Just go. Go! I never want to see you again." Lila scrambles down the stairs, and runs, sobbing, into her bathroom.

Chapter Twenty-nine

For the next few days, Lila cannot clear her mind of the image of Bill's ashen face, the way he seemed suddenly hollowed out, as if the one foundational thing that had been holding him up had collapsed, taking him with it. She feels his grief and shock as if it is her own. And it is her own because she keeps circling to the image of her mother, blithely flying off secretly to have sex with the one man she had sworn she would never see again. Francesca, who had seemingly held the world's wisdom in her cheerful gray-ringleted head, had made the worst decision Lila could possibly imagine and she feels as if her own moral compass has disappeared with Bill's.

Gene left. She had heard some movement in the house, heavy feet on stairs, a murmuring to the dog, but she had been crying too hard to pay much attention. She had emerged after an hour to find her study space cleared, the bed folded back into a sofa, a pile of sheets and pillows neatly folded at its side. She had gazed at the space where her father had been and felt absolutely nothing, except perhaps a nagging regret that she had ever been stupid enough to let him in again. When she had spied the Post-it note with *I'm sorry* on it, she had screwed it up in her fist and dropped it into the wastepaper basket.

BILL HAD DECLINED to pick up her calls, sending a short text after the fourth: Darling girl, I know you mean well but I really just need to be alone right now.

But the following day—after a night of fitful, intermittent sleep—she had driven round there. The curtains of the bungalow were drawn and it had taken Bill ten minutes to answer the door. When he opened it, Lila had been shocked at his appearance: he had looked worse than he had when Francesca had died, grayer and more frail. The bungalow had held a chill atmosphere of emptiness, as if his presence were not enough to make it feel like a home again.

"Please come home," she had said, placing her hand on his as they drank tea. "He's gone now."

"I can't, darling. I need to sit and digest this by myself for a bit. I'll come and get my things when I'm ready."

Instead Penelope had come the following day for his medications. She had been glassy-eyed with sadness, as if it were she whose memories had been destroyed. "He's so sad," she said simply, clutching the bag of pills from his medicine cabinet. "I feel . . . helpless." She had clutched Lila's wrist with her thin hand, gazing at her mutely before she left.

Two days later he had arrived with an empty suitcase, and removed some of his clothes and personal items. He had rung on the doorbell, as if he were a visitor, and was scrupulously polite. Lila had thought he felt she was also to blame, even as she assured him that Gene was gone, that Bill's place was here, that they needed him. "Mum really loved you, you know," she had told him, as she sat on the bed while he packed carefully, folding each shirt with military precision. "Whatever stupid decision she made, you must know that."

Bill had let out a long sigh and sat on the bed beside her. "That's what makes it all so incomprehensible. She knew he was ridiculous. She knew he had been repeatedly unfaithful when they were together. The number of times we talked about him, how unreliable he was, how angry he made her . . . It just makes no sense to me that she would be sucked in by him again."

He had grown silent. Then, "I had a feeling something was off. I've been remembering it, once I checked the dates. There was a period when she was a little distant. I couldn't put my finger on it. I thought if I left her alone it would just . . . die down. She said she was going to stay with Dorothy in Nottingham for a few days. I didn't think for a minute . . ." He tails off.

"So you just left her alone."

"I—I'm not very good with emotional situations. I thought it was something she just needed to get out of her system. I didn't realize it was . . . *him*." His voice strains as he refers to Gene. He cannot say his name.

"I'm so sorry, Bill. But we still love you. We would love you to come home."

"I think my home is back there," he says quietly. And the words go through her like a knife.

About an hour after he left, she noticed that he had left behind the portrait of Francesca.

ON FRIDAY, SHE heads again to Bill's. She decides to pop into the supermarket at the end of the road to get him some flowers, a kind of peace-offering, even if peace isn't hers to offer. She strolls the aisles, then picks the nicest ones she can find that aren't lilies—they have always been too funereal since her mother died: some stocks in a deep raspberry red. She scans the buckets, trying to find the best possible bunch, and then, on impulse, picks up a second, as if she can show him through sheer horticultural mass how much he means to her. When she looks up a woman is standing beside her, gazing at the tub of flowers as if she is working out which ones to take. Just as Lila registers this, she sees, beside the woman, Jensen, dressed in his work gear. Lila straightens and flushes, as if she has been caught doing something wrong.

"Hi," she says, her mouth powdery and dry.

"Hello, Lila," he says. He doesn't smile.

"Oh, *you're* Lila." She sees the woman reassess her, as if through a new prism. She has pale red hair, cut in a sleek bob, and is wearing a black polo-neck and white jeans. She has the air of someone who knows exactly who she is, and is unafraid of what anyone else may think that might be.

Lila glances at Jensen, who is carrying a small basket of shopping: she takes in red wine, salad, and a chicken, the kind of thing one might buy if one was preparing a nice dinner for two.

"How are you?" she says tentatively, trying to ignore the woman's stare.

"Fine," he says. His face is expressionless.

She cannot help herself. "I'm so sorry, Jensen," she blurts out.

"Yes," the woman says calmly, before Jensen can answer. "You should be. C'mon. We should head to the checkout." As Lila watches, the woman takes Jensen's elbow and they turn away from her to walk down the aisle.

THE GIRLS HAVE been particularly fractious over dinner, arguing over a teddy bear, which, until Lila brought it down from the attic, neither had even remembered they owned. They are unimpressed by her attempt at supper (a chicken tray-bake she had retrieved twenty minutes too late from the oven) and furious when Lila tells them that Dan wants them to switch overnight days to Thursday this week (he has a work event and Marja is apparently not up to managing three children alone). She has told them that Bill is having a few days at the bungalow and that Gene is away for work. It is too much to explain the truth.

When Celie disappears upstairs to her room—complete with obligatory teenage door slam—and Violet settles herself in front of the iPad, Lila doesn't have the energy to persuade them to stay. She cleans the kitchen, trying to keep her attention on a listless radio panel show, and walks Truant around the block. Finally, when Violet is in bed, she runs herself a bath and sinks into it gratefully. Then when she can bear the silence no longer, she calls Gabriel.

"Hey, Bella," he says, picking up immediately. He sounds upbeat, as if he is glad to hear from her. "What's going on?"

She wants to match his cheerfulness but, right now, it's beyond her.

"I'm . . . I'm having a tricky time actually. Just thought it would be nice to hear a friendly voice."

"What's up?"

She tells him about the attic and the discovery of the letter. He listens carefully, then lets out a long sigh. "Oh, that's tough."

"I don't know what to do about it."

"I'm not sure there's much you can do. You might just have to let your stepdad simmer down a bit. I'm sure he'll come back when he's ready."

"You think?" She isn't so sure. Bill hasn't so much as dropped in since he picked up the suitcase of belongings.

"It's pride. He's suffered a blow to his ego. No matter how old he is that's going to hurt, especially when that blow has come from your biological dad."

Lila is not convinced that's right. Bill's pain seems so much more bone-deep than that. It isn't just ego: she watched the very backbone of his life crumble in front of her. But it's so nice to talk to Gabriel that she doesn't challenge him. "So how are you?"

He tells her how busy he is at work—two huge new projects have come in—a respite center, and a house for a multi-millionaire who changes his mind daily on major decisions. He's working at home this evening from his office at the end of the garden. His voice is cheerful, a little detached. It is, she thinks uncomfortably, a conversation he could be having with a work colleague.

"How's Lennie?" she says.

"Fine. Very excited about this *Peter Pan* production. Though she's pretty exhausted when she gets back from the rehearsals."

They talk of school a little, and school plays they have starred in (he was a tree in *Robin Hood*; she was a teapot in a compendium of nursery rhymes) and of television they have watched, and the water starts to go cold so she leans forward and turns on the hot tap.

"What are you doing?" he says.

"Oh. Just running the tap. The water's gone a bit cold. I'm in the bath."

"You're in the bath."

There is something contemplative in his voice, as if he's considering this. It makes her laugh. "It's my safe space."

"I'm not sure I'd call it a safe space. Not if I was there, anyway."

A flicker of something travels through her. "Oh, you're dangerous in bathrooms, are you?" she says lightly.

"I'm dangerous in places where you're naked."

"That's for sure." She has a sudden memory of the two of them in his front room, the tangle of limbs, the urgency.

"You said we were going to do that again." She keeps it light, flirtatious. His tone has made her a little reckless.

"We will. But in the meantime you should tell me more about what you're doing in the bath."

She is about to make a joke, but something in his voice stops her. "Uh . . . talking to you, clearly. And . . ." She swallows. ". . . thinking about you."

"And what do you do when you think about me?"

His voice has lowered. It makes her feel faintly light-headed.

"You really want to know?"

"Yes."

"You want to have *that* conversation?"

"I absolutely want to have that conversation."

Lila has never had *that* conversation. The one time she had tried with Dan he had been at first disconcerted, and said she hadn't sounded like her, and then when she had tried again, he'd joked that she sounded like a cheap porn movie. She had been so cross with him that she had never tried again.

"This is new," she says carefully.

"I like new."

So Lila has that conversation. She tells him in a low voice what she is doing. Or at least what her pretend self is doing, given that what she is actually doing is sitting in cooling bathwater and hoping desperately that neither of her girls is lurking outside the bathroom door. She is emboldened by the sound of his rapt attention, his lowered voice, his increasingly short answers, and lets her imagination run riot. When he tells her what he is doing she feels faintly giddy with power. It turns out it's easier than she'd thought to do this. You simply have to forget everything else, to shed your self-consciousness, word by word, to close your eyes and inhabit this imaginary self, so much wilder and less inhibited than she actually is. It turns out the conversation is swift, and effective, and has a gratifying, audible end.

Lila lies in the bath, completely still, listening to the sound of his breathing.

"Are you okay?" she says, after a minute.

"I . . . am definitely okay," he says. "That was . . . unexpected. But amazing. Thank you."

"Thank you" is an odd response, but Lila decides that manners are always a good thing. She still feels giddy, unable to believe she was able to produce a response like that from saying a few words down a phone. She is shocked by the intimacy of it, the trust implicit in it. *We just did that*, a voice in her head keeps saying. *We just did that thing.*

"Did you get there?" he says.

"I did," she lies. And he lets out a little *hm*, which might be satisfaction, or might just be him considering it.

"So when are we going to see each other?" she says, after a pause.

"Soon. Let me just get this nightmare week out of the way and we'll find something nice to do."

"Sounds good," she says. "I could do with something to look forward to."

And then Violet has opened the bathroom door and is standing there in her turquoise pajamas, her face clouded with crossness. "Mum, I really need a poo and Celie is in the other bathroom putting a stupid facemask on and she won't come out."

"I'd better go," she says hurriedly, and tries to turn her flushed, slightly dreamy expression into something resembling maternal concern.

Chapter Thirty

The unexpected telephone interlude with Gabriel makes the next few days bearable. Frankly, something needs to, because she still feels Bill's absence in the house like an open wound. And the girls are starting to ask difficult questions about Gene's absence. Lila wrestles her way through each day, finding reasons not to sit at her desk: tidying or accompanying Eleanor on dog walks or attending exercise classes.

Eleanor is cheerful, the previous months apparently wiped from her own mental slate. She has signed up to a dating app for minor celebrities—apparently her work as a makeup artist seems to have got her through the vetting process—and every time she sees Lila she is brimming with entertaining stories about former soap stars who have messaged her privately, or long-forgotten nineties pop stars whom she hadn't recognized. "I mean half of them are apparently influencers or DJs from Ibiza I've never heard of, but it's nice to have the interest."

Lila tells her about the bath episode and she is delighted. "That's great! As long as you aren't intending to write about it."

"I am absolutely not writing about it," Lila says.

She cannot work out what to say to Anoushka. Any day now the contract will arrive and she will have to tell her that she cannot write the book as planned. She has considered hundreds of alternatives to suggest to the publishers, but even she is unexcited by half of them.

Moving Forward From Divorce—An Emotional Journey.

How to Find Inner Happiness Through Re-organizing Your Under-stairs Cupboard.

What I Discuss With My Dog in the Mornings When My Kids Have Gone Out Without Saying a Word to Me.

She calls Bill every day, but he no longer wants to discuss anything related to her mother, and she finds the conversation grows sticky after they have covered what the girls have done and what she is cooking for dinner. At night she has imaginary arguments with Francesca: *How could you hurt Bill like you did? How could you choose* Gene? The mother of her memories seems to have evaporated, replaced by someone Lila doesn't know, and she is grieving her loss all over again.

Lila goes to school pickup wearing earphones. She seems to need a constant supply of words in her ears, drowning out her thoughts, like she did in the early days after Dan left. It doesn't seem to matter what she listens to as long as it drowns out the competing voices in her head.

The playground is oddly empty when she arrives. It takes her a couple of minutes to register it. There is another mother she vaguely recognizes walking away from the school office door. As she passes Lila she raises a small smile.

"You too, huh?"

Lila frowns and removes her earphones. "I'm sorry?"

"You forgot the rehearsal this evening? Like I did?"

The rehearsal. With all the domestic shenanigans Lila has failed to open a single school email this week. But she has a vague memory that there was a run-through at some point. "It's today?"

"There's another hour to go."

"Oh, for God's sake." Lila looks at her watch. It will take her twenty minutes to walk home and another twenty to walk back. This is the maternal time-vacuum, the endless hours lost to waiting, the slots of time that are never enough to do anything useful. She sighs.

"Yeah. Me too. Curse of the working mums. I can never keep up with the emails."

The woman has blonde hair cut in a shaggy bob, and the kind of wardrobe that speaks of a professional life, even if part time.

"I'm going to grab a coffee up the road. No point going home just to come back again," she says. And then she glances at Lila. "You're welcome to join me if you like."

It is a tentative offer, but apparently genuinely meant. Lila has always been wary of the other mothers, but she is pretty sure this one is not part of the school cabal. She has seen her on her own, lurking a short distance away just as Lila does. And she has a nice, friendly face. "Sure," she says, suddenly grateful not to be alone with her thoughts. "That would be lovely."

THE CAFÉ IS nearly empty at this time. It closes at five, and there are only a couple of people at laptops in the far corners, pretending not to notice the staff busily sweeping around their chairs. The woman's name is Jessie and her son is in year six; she runs a shop selling art supplies a couple of miles away. She is a single parent and bought her own flat two years ago. When they sit down with their cups and a compensatory slice of lemon cake, she looks at Lila and says: "I've got to get this out of the way. I don't really talk to people in the playground, but I heard what happened to you and I just wanted to say . . . I'm really sorry. It must be very tough having to deal with that situation every day."

There is not a flicker of guile in the way she says it. No subtle fishing for information, no sly judgment. Her gaze is clear and honest, and full of empathy.

Lila tries to meet it with equal openness. "Yeah, it's not been the most fun."

"My ex disappeared when Hal was a baby. Wasn't cut out for fatherhood, apparently." She rolls her eyes. "He does help with the money, though, so that's something."

They talk for a while about the exhaustion of doing it all single-handed, the fear that they are getting things wrong, that their children will grow up harmed by the lack of a full-time father in the house, the parallel pleasure in not having to consult anyone about your decisions, the lack of abandoned pants on the bathroom floor. Lila sees so few women apart from Eleanor that she has forgotten the casual joy of this kind of conversation: the trading of comic failures and frustrations, the sisterly commiserations.

Leaning forward, as if to shield herself from exposure to the rest of the room, Jessie tells Lila that she occasionally invents business meetings in far-flung places so she can persuade her parents to take her son and get a night off.

"Really? What do you do with it?" says Lila, charmed by the frank admission, the sheepish grin on Jessie's face.

"Most of the time I just flop. I have all these good intentions—I'm going to have a big night out, or treat myself to an evening of self-care. But honestly, more often than not I lie face down on my sofa and fall asleep at nine o'clock."

"No . . . men friends? Sorry, that's such a weird phrase."

Jessie laughs wryly. "Well, there is someone, but it's complicated. Or it's complicated for me. I can never work out which. You?"

"There is someone, but it's early days. We're just sort of taking it step by step."

When she says it like this, she can almost believe that it's somehow a plan of hers, the slow, uneven pace, as if she has orchestrated it. She thinks suddenly that she might like Jessie, feels a vague relief at the thought that future trips to the playground may include a friendly face. She is enjoying this unexpected foray into normal life, just a cheerful exchange of human frailty with another like-minded person.

"God, but I'm so bored of step by step, though. Aren't you? Do you think there are any men out there who just say, 'Hey, I really like you. Let's do this'? I remember when I was younger I genuinely thought that's how it was going to be. You liked someone, they liked you, and ta-dah! You started seeing each other and that was it. It's like that kind of man has just disappeared off the face of the earth."

"My ex was that man," Lila says, stirring her tea. "Until he ran off with someone else, obviously." She refuses to think about Jensen.

"Men are so bloody difficult, aren't they? I mean, this guy I'm seeing . . ." She looks up, suddenly awkward. "Sorry—is this too much?"

"Not at all," says Lila. Hearing about someone else's complicated love life is making her feel a little better about her own.

"I've been seeing him for a while. But I'm starting to think he's a commitment-phobe."

"Why?"

"I don't know if it's—what do they call it now?—a 'situationship.' I mean we go out occasionally, he's lovely, we have great sex. But it doesn't feel like there's any real progress. He's just not very reliable, is evasive when I talk about getting the kids together, or maybe seeing each other more regularly."

Lila feels an uncomfortable stab of recognition. "How often do you see him?"

"We speak a lot. But I only really see him about once a week. I mean in a serious, you know, date-sort-of-way."

"He's bread crumbing you," says Lila, firmly. She feels a weird satisfaction at being able to name it.

Jessie frowns.

"My friend told me about it," Lila continues. "There's a kind of man who keeps you dangling with little crumbs of a relationship—texts, calls, the odd date—but they never make you a priority. Is it that?"

"'Bread crumbing.'" Jessie pulls a face. "I don't know. He's nicer than that."

"My friend Eleanor read me out a whole list. It's definitely a thing." Lila is briefly flooded with sisterly solidarity. "Honestly, all these dating concepts now that weren't around when we were younger. I need a manual just to know what I should be worried about."

Jessie eats a chunk of her cake. She has the kind of prettiness that doesn't require makeup—freckled, even skin, long pale brown lashes. Lila suspects she's in her mid-thirties at most.

"Ugh. I don't want to think he's got some kind of playbook. I really like him. That's the annoying bit." She pushes away the rest of the cake. "Sorry. I shouldn't be boring you about it."

"No," says Lila, suddenly filled with zeal. "It's really important we talk about this stuff. Women need to support each other, right? And you seem really nice. And you're gorgeous, obviously. I'm sure there are loads of guys out there who are more straightforward. Don't let him waste your time."

Jessie shakes her head. "No. He's nice. I don't think he is . . . intentionally doing that thing. He's just . . . he's . . ." She sighs. "You might have seen him."

"What?"

"He's got a child at our school."

Something ice cold and weighty drops into Lila's stomach. It's as if her body knows what Jessie is going to say before she says it.

"He's the father of Lennie in year five. Slim guy, glasses. He's an architect. Gabriel."

Lila is not sure what her face does from that point. She is vaguely aware of nodding, of a kind of benign interest in her voice. "Gabriel," she repeats.

Jessie's words are rushing out of her now, like a kind of confessional. "We started talking in a coffee shop last year. His wife died, you know. I'm not sure how many people know that. And earlier this year he moved his daughter to our school for a fresh start. And he's lovely, honestly. When we're together it's great. That's why it's so confusing."

There is a typhoon inside Lila's body. Everything feels like it's spinning in a great vortex, Jessie's voice growing louder and then quieter as if she is only half there, drowned out by a rushing sound. She hears, *Sex is so great, you know?* And *We have this amazing connection* and *I don't want to push him. He's been through so much* and *He doesn't really want people to gossip about us* and it's not even that she doesn't know what to say—it's that her mouth feels as if it's suddenly glued together, as if words are an abstract concept she is no longer capable of forming.

"Are you okay?"

She focuses. Jessie is looking at her carefully. "Uh . . . headache. Sudden headache. I get them occasionally." She rubs a hand across her forehead.

"You've gone really pale. Do you want a pill? Let me get you some water." Jessie is rummaging in her bag.

Lila tries to calculate how quickly she can leave. Every fiber of her being wants to hurl her body out of the door. "I need some fresh air. I—I'm going to head back to school."

"Don't go by yourself. You need someone with you if you're ill." Jessie starts to gather her things.

"No. No. I'm fine. Finish your tea." Lila waves a hand. "You're really kind. I—I just—I'm so sorry. It's been . . . really lovely talking to you."

Before Jessie can get up, she has grabbed her bag and is weaving through the empty tables and out into the bright light of the afternoon street beyond. She can just make out Jessie's *"Maybe see you tomorrow!"* as the door closes behind her.

Chapter Thirty-one

Celie

❧

Something is going on at Dad's. Marja lies on the sofa a lot, or hides in her bedroom when Celie and Violet are there. She used to make special meals on the nights they were staying: big dishes of Asian food or enormous bowls of pasta and salad, all laid out on their little kitchen table, with posh ice cream to follow, like she was trying to use dinner time to make them all feel like a family, but now she just asks them to pick something from the takeaway menu, her face pale and apologetic, and retreats. When she is in the living room, she and Dad are always speaking in low voices. Celie wondered for a while whether it was down to her: she has spent the last eighteen months letting Marja know, in a million subtle ways, that she might have to be there, but it doesn't mean she's ever going to consider her and Hugo *family*. Marja wants them all to forget what she did, stealing Dad from Mum, and act like they're some kind of blended Instagram family. She uses this fake-friendly voice to talk to Celie, and offers her spare skincare samples and things that she's bought at the shops and apparently can't use. But Celie does her best never to talk to her beyond one-word answers, and makes sure the moment Dad lets her leave the table she heads to her and Violet's room to sit on her phone. It's annoying because Hugo always wants her or Violet to play with him, and Dad is always saying: *C'mon, girls, just give him half an hour.* But who wants to play with a six-year-old boy? If Marja wanted a babysitter she should have hired one.

She has watched Marja turn from this yoga woman, with her stupid defined shoulders and her Lululemon leggings into a big fat whale, and sometimes she wonders whether Dad feels bad he left Mum for her now that she's changed, whether it will make him go off her, but Dad still seems bewitched, always hovering round her, checking she's okay, squeezing her hand when they think Celie's not looking. It's revolting, the way they're all lovey-dovey in front of her, like she's just meant to pretend it isn't happening. But now Marja is nearly always upstairs, and Celie is wondering whether her determination not to let Marja have an ounce of affection has finally had an effect. She feels a little weird about it, admittedly, given that there's going to be a baby, and she isn't sure whether Mum would even want Dad back after all this time. Mostly she just doesn't want to have to deal with more stuff.

Because things are also weird at home—Bill is still staying at the bungalow and Gene is away working so the house is really quiet. And Mum is preoccupied, taking extra-long baths or always out, earphones in, with Truant. Her mouth is doing that turned-down thing when she doesn't even realize she's making her lips look thin, and you have to ask her twice for anything because she's not really listening. Celie had looked through her phone once—Mum is hopeless at passwords: they're always either Celie1 or Violet1 or something like that—but there's not much in her messages, except for a bunch of times she asks Bill to come home. At first Celie thought they must have had a row, but she keeps telling him she loves him and he keeps saying he just needs some space. Celie asked Violet if she had done something to annoy Bill—she was remembering the time Violet used his personalized note cards to draw space aliens—but Violet swears she hasn't. So basically they spend their lives shuttling from one weird atmosphere to another.

She talked to Martin about it when they walked to the bus stop after Animation the previous week. He had done a whole storyboard about having a new baby brother and how he had imagined it turning into a ginormous monster that ate his parents before the last frame showed it as a tiny little wormy newborn. He had told the group it was based on his feelings when his mum got pregnant by his stepdad.

"Do you like your brother?" she had asked him. "Your stepbrother, I mean."

"Half-brother," he said. "Yeah. He's okay. He's a little dude." He had glanced at her. "I wasn't sure I was going to like him because at first I thought my stepdad was a bit of an idiot. But it's weird. Like when I first went to the hospital to see him, he was just—I don't know. Just this tiny kid. And I'd never had a brother, so I suppose it felt . . . nice? He can be quite annoying and stuff and he goes in my room when he shouldn't. But yeah. I like him being around."

"I think I'm going to hate my dad's baby," Celie says, as they sit on the bus-stop seats that are set at a slant, so you always feel like you're about to slide off. "It just feels like it's all his fault."

"How?"

"Well, if the baby hadn't come along Dad might have gone back to Mum eventually. And now . . . that's it."

Martin considers this. "I don't know. My aunt went back to her husband even though she had a baby with someone else. Sometimes if people love each other that much they can find a way around it."

Celie wonders whether her mum and dad love each other that much.

She doesn't really remember them hugging in the last years they were a family, or even smiling at each other. Mum was always working and Dad was always out, and they were a bit snappy with each other apart from when they were on holiday.

"I think I'm just still mad at Dad and Marja. So I guess I'm going to be angry with this kid too."

"You should talk to your dad."

Except Celie doesn't have the kind of dad you can talk to. The one time she told him she hated going to his house he just told her she wouldn't always feel that way, and when she said she would, he got frustrated and told her she was being "deliberately difficult." And that when she was older she would learn that life was complicated and things didn't always work out how you wanted and you had to adapt. She didn't bother saying anything to him after that. Marja tried to talk to her once, before she got pregnant. She sat down while Celie was eating breakfast and said she understood Celie probably had some complicated feelings about the new set-up and she wasn't going to try to take her mother's place. Celie had almost laughed. *You couldn't begin to take Mum's place*, she wanted to say, but instead she just slid silently off the tall breakfast stool and took her bowl of cereal upstairs.

She doesn't talk to the girls at school about her parents. Soraya's and Harriet's families are still together, and she gets the feeling they wouldn't really understand. She would have talked to Gene about it but he doesn't bother texting now he's away working. She doesn't even know what country he's working in. Bill sends the odd text saying politely that he hopes she's well and that she's doing her homework and he will see her very soon, but it's like getting a message from a teacher—weirdly formal—and she never knows how to respond beyond just sending him a couple of kisses. He doesn't even understand emojis.

Celie walks to her dad's house, dragging her feet and staring at her phone. Her mum will have dropped Violet there straight after school—

she tends to pull up in the street and just wait in the car until she sees
that Violet has been let in. Celie, being older, has been given a key to the
house but always rings the doorbell anyway, just so they know she
doesn't think it's home. She stands in the porch, wondering whether
Mum remembered to pack her overnight bag and drop it with Violet's.
She forgot the previous weekend and Dad had to drive back to theirs so
that Celie could pick it up and he was really grumpy about it, even
though he didn't even have to get out of the car. Apparently he doesn't
like leaving Marja alone, even though she has, like, actual months before
the baby is due.

Nobody answers the door. Celie rings again, leaving her finger on the
bell for a count of five, even though she knows this will irritate Dad.
There is still no answer. Finally, she digs around in her bag for the key
that he gave her and lets herself in.

Marja's house is always immaculately tidy, but today the living room
is strewn with Hugo's toys, a plate with crumbs, an open book, a cushion on the floor. Celie stands in the doorway and gazes around. She
walks through to the kitchen—the radio is still on, and there is a note
scribbled on the kitchen table.

> Had to take Marja to hospital. Get Mum to pick you up.
>
> Dad x

Not even a "sorry." Just *Get Mum to pick you up.* Celie stares at the
note, feeling a simultaneous swell of irritation at her father's lack of caring, combined with the vague relief that she will be able to go home tonight. She puts the note on the table, and sits for a moment at the kitchen
island. Then she stands and opens the kitchen cupboard with the treats
in and helps herself to an expensive nut and dark chocolate bar, the kind
that costs two pounds in the corner shop. She leaves the wrapper on the
side, and goes upstairs. You are meant to take your shoes off at the door

in Marja's house—she has pale wood floors and cream carpets—but Celie keeps hers on, deliberately scraping her feet on each step, just in case there is any dirt left behind.

Marja's bedroom has zero clutter: all the clothes are folded neatly or hung behind the doors of the fitted wardrobes that don't even have handles. You have to press them in one place to get them to open. The bed is made neatly, with two color-coded cushions on each pillow and one of those blankets that isn't a blanket covering the end of the bed. Celie opens the wardrobe and gazes at Marja's clothes, which are nearly all cream or black or white. It is basically the most boring wardrobe she has ever seen. She opens the drawers, ready to be repulsed by sexy underwear, but all Marja's knickers are plain gray or black, with only one bra-and-knickers set that is made of silk with some lace stuff. Marja doesn't have a lot of stuff, not like Mum, but she does have really expensive skincare and perfumes.

There is a whole tray of makeup, laid out carefully with a magnifying mirror, on the dressing-table in front of the window. Celie sits down and picks up the different tubes and wands, opening them to try the different colors. She outlines her eyes with Marja's Chantecaille eyeliner, then uses the Chanel eyeshadow palette. Marja's skin is darker than hers, so the foundation doesn't work, but she uses a little cream blusher and highlighter, then examines her face closely in the magnifying mirror, searching for pimples and open pores.

When she has finished doing her face, she sniffs the perfumes. There are eight different bottles, and she tries each on her wrist until the scents have all blended and she can't tell which is which. She tries the hand cream on the back of her hand, rubbing it in with her index finger until it is absorbed. Then she picks up the really expensive moisturizer and sniffs it. It has a subtle, flowery smell. She gazes at it for a while, then gets up and walks to the en-suite bathroom. She squeezes the tube so that a manic white worm of cream wriggles its way into the plughole, and then does the same thing twice more, so that the tube is nearly empty. She puts the lid on and goes back to the perfumes, unscrewing the lids that will come off and pouring most of the precious gold-colored liquid into the washbasin. She tops up the bottles with water. She does the same with Marja's luxe-looking cleanser and then her serum. Then she rinses away the residue, and replaces the bottles carefully on Marja's dressing-table.

She looks around at the bedroom again, then heads downstairs and calls her mother.

"WHY YOUR FATHER can't schedule her appointments around the times you're with me, I don't know." Lila is shaking her head as she drives Celie home. "He only texted me about Violet ten minutes before school pickup."

"I don't mind," Celie says.

Lila shoots her a glance and her face softens. "Sorry. I shouldn't moan about Dad in front of you. And I don't mind either," she says. She reaches out a hand. "I get you for an extra night, after all. Hey, how about we order takeaway tonight? How about a really big unhealthy pizza with extra cheese and whatever toppings you fancy?"

Mum's cooking has been so terrible since Bill left that Celie's *Yes* probably came out more enthusiastically than she meant. But Mum doesn't seem to notice. She hasn't worn makeup for over a week now. Her hair is scraped back in a ponytail, she has big shadows under her eyes, and she is wearing the same sweater she has worn for three days this week. For a while Mum had looked like herself again, but now she's mostly like someone who's got out of her sickbed to answer the door.

"When is Gene coming back?" Celie says.

Mum keeps her eyes on the road. "I'm not sure," she says. "He . . . he . . . I think his job may keep him away for a bit."

Celie stares at her knees. She can smell the perfume on her hands and it's making her feel a bit sick. She thinks she could have talked to Gene about what she's done. There isn't really anyone else she could tell without them freaking out. "Is he definitely coming back?"

Mum makes the face she does when she knows something she's not saying. "I—I don't know, lovey. I'll talk to him at some point and we'll work it out."

THE FOLLOWING DAY Mum asks Celie to pick up Violet. She has an important work meeting, apparently, and even though Celie moans at her that Violet's school is in the wrong direction, and she'll have to wait ages because of the stupid play rehearsal, Mum is adamant that she cannot go herself. She is being really odd. She didn't eat more than a slice of the pizza at supper, and she could tell she was on the phone with Eleanor all night because she could hear her murmuring, *I know. I know. I just don't know what to say to him,* when she went past her closed bedroom door.

"Celie, I very rarely ask you for anything. But I do need you to do school pickup for me just now. Bill will do it tomorrow, but he can't today, and your school finishes in time for you to meet her."

Parents are so selfish.

Celie gets to the playground at a quarter to five, fifteen minutes before Violet is due to finish, and eats a packet of salt and vinegar crisps that she bought on the way over. She should really have bought some for Violet too so she needs to eat them quickly and throw the packet into the bin so that Violet won't find out and go on all evening about how mean she is.

Celie has felt weird all day about the perfumes. She's not sure what came over her the previous afternoon and part of her has been waiting for Dad to call and ask her what the hell she thought she was doing, to tell her she's a horrible, horrible person. But he hasn't said anything. She has carried the knowledge of what she did like an increasing pressure all day, pushing at the inside of her head, like something uncontainable. She texts Martin while she waits, her fingers pinking at the ends from the cold.

I did a weird thing at my dad's.

She tells him about the perfumes, and the creams. There is a short pause, the dots pulsing, and she thinks he's about to tell her she's a freak, or that he doesn't really want to talk to her any more. Maybe he'll join Meena and the other girls in ignoring her. The dots go on long enough for her to regret even telling him. And then he says: **When my mum got together with my stepdad I went through her drawer and threw all her birth-control pills out of the window into next door's garden. I think I thought it would stop them doing anything. All it did was get me a baby brother, haha.**

PS though no baby foxes this year so who knows what happened

It makes her laugh, and feel a bit less weird, but a few moments later the anxiety returns, a big knot in her stomach, like she's waiting for something terrible to happen all over again.

It's almost five when the doors to the primary school open, and the kids start to file out, dragging rucksacks or clutching creased pages of their play script. There are loads of other parents in the playground by then, and she keeps her head down, her hood up, focusing on her phone so she doesn't have to talk to anyone about how they remember when she was at school there, how much she's grown, all the stupid things adults say. It takes her a moment to notice that Violet, when she walks over, is not on her own. At her side, holding her hand, a big grin on his face, is Gene, chatting briefly to Mrs. Tugendhat, who has her hand pressed to her chest, like she's literally trying to contain her heart. They talk for a moment and he nods vigorously, then puts his hand on Mrs. Tugendhat's arm. When the teacher finally walks off she touches the place where his hand had been, like she doesn't even know she's doing it.

"Hey, kiddo," he says, pulling Celie in for a hug. He always does this, like he doesn't even notice whether you actually want one or not.

"I thought you were away working."

He pulls a weird face. And then his grin returns. "Well, I am! But I had an early finish and I missed you guys, so I thought I'd just stop by and walk you home. I can't stay long—gotta get back to work—but I just wanted to see your smushy little faces."

And even though he's really irritating, and he's wearing his stupid Grateful Dead T-shirt, which makes him look like an old hippie, Celie feels something inside her collapse with relief.

Chapter Thirty-two

Lila

❦

"S o what are you going to say to him?"

Eleanor and Lila are at the launch of a new makeup brand. Eleanor gets sent enough free makeup to open a small branch of Boots the Chemist, and Lila is always happy to accept free stuff, especially as she has no clue what she should be wearing anymore. They are standing in a Georgian room with floor-to-ceiling windows while young people, who are clearly off-duty models, hand round champagne and tiny canapés of mostly unrecognizable food. Around the edges of the room people stand in front of illuminated mirrors, trying out the free testers to a soundtrack of ambient music. Eleanor is currently blending three different shades of foundation on Lila's cheeks, pausing and frowning while Lila looks longingly as tiny portions of fish and chips in paper cones pass by, just out of reach.

She has spent a week trying to work out what she will say when she sees Gabriel Mallory. She has ignored his texts, the last two of which have suggested they go out for dinner—in one he calls her *dolcezza*—and she has invented a work deadline to avoid doing the school pickup. She had felt wretched for two days, then woken up clear-headed, with just a slow-burning anger, at him for his duplicity and at herself for not picking up on it.

"I don't know. I've thought about it a bit"—it has actually consumed her every waking moment—"and I just want to ask him what he thought he was doing. I mean, how the hell did he think Jessie and I wouldn't ever meet?"

"And she's only the one you know about."

This thought has not escaped Lila. She keeps thinking of the way he had described his late wife as "seeing things that weren't there," the way Victoria's parents no longer want to speak to him. She waits as Eleanor gets a cotton bud and runs it carefully under her eye.

"I thought I might write a letter. Just telling him how awful he's made me feel, and how I'd assumed we were all too old for this kind of rubbish."

"Spoken like someone who has never been on a dating app."

"Is that what they're like?" Lila blinks at Eleanor in horror.

"It's pretty much a jungle out there. If the jungle was full of duplicitous, preening, toxic chancers, that is. The actual jungle might be preferable. Oh, no, not this shade. You look like someone off *Love Island*."

"Do you think a letter is a bad idea?"

Eleanor picks up a lipstick and unscrews the lid, testing it on the back of her hand. "The problem is, you're treating him like someone who (a) will bother to read it, and (b) consider their own accountability. Everything you've told me suggests he won't do either. Close your mouth."

Lila waits as Eleanor applies the lipstick. "So he just gets away with it?"

"No. Not least because you tell Jessie. Oh, yes, that looks better." She leans back and nods with approval.

This is the weird bit. Lila wants to tell Jessie. She had liked her instinctively. She is clearly not to blame for any of this. She feels a kind of sisterly responsibility toward the fellow single mother, the fellow dupe. But when she thinks about starting the conversation, she feels clammy with anxiety. What if Jessie doesn't believe her? What if she blames Lila? She was clearly seeing Gabriel before Lila was. What if this creates yet another layer of drama in the school playground? The thought of everyone knowing this latest humiliation—the Philippa Grahams and the Marjas seeing she has been betrayed by yet another man— is too much to bear.

Eleanor turns Lila's seat so that she can see herself in the mirror. She looks, she thinks distantly, actually pretty good.

"I just . . . I just don't know if I can face it."

"Moody Blush? It's very subtle on you."

"No. Telling Jessie."

Eleanor rolls her eyes. "And this is how the patriarchy continues."

"So now I'm responsible for the oppression of all womankind?"

"If you don't tell her, you're responsible for the oppression of two."

"Ugh. Why are we somehow responsible for the fallout of men behaving like arseholes?"

Eleanor doesn't say anything.

"What?"

"I'm not sure you're *entirely* above blame right now."

"I did say sorry to Jensen."

Eleanor shrugs. "Sounded like a pretty flimsy apology to me."

"You think I should have said more?"

"Uh . . . yes?"

Lila thinks about this as they stroll back toward the tube station. This has been the worst thing about it all, and perhaps the reason why she hasn't felt as destroyed by the end of Gabriel as she might have expected. She had been so obsessed by the Shiny Object that had been Gabriel Mallory that she had completely failed to think about the far better man whose feelings she had trampled over. Every time she thinks about him picking up that typewritten chapter, the shock on his face, she feels a shame that ends up somewhere in her boots, a dreadful, chill thing, like the kind of damp cold that gets into your bones on the worst kind of winter day.

"I don't think he'll talk to me."

"Then you send him a long text explaining what an idiot you've been, and you absolutely take responsibility for all of it, and you say you hope that one day he can find it in himself to forgive you, especially as the book has been canceled." She turns to look at Lila and stops for a moment. "You did cancel it, right?"

Lila pulls a face.

"Oh, Lila. For God's sake."

THE THING IS, Lila cannot find a way round it. She knows she has to cancel the book. The contract had arrived in her inbox, followed a few days later by a cheerful digital reminder to sign. She had opened it, looked at the figure, with all its lovely zeros, and wanted to cry. She has no other way of earning money, not the kind she needs to support everyone. She has considered a thousand alternatives, but everything she thinks up sounds weak, even to her. Dan has cut her child support, her savings are down to an amount that would barely fill her car with petrol, and she has no idea what she and the girls will live on, once that is gone. She sent Jensen a payment for the last of the garden work the previous week. It was not acknowledged, and she was not surprised. But that was the last sizable chunk from her royalties, and she had not felt able to ask Bill for any of it, given he no longer even wanted to live with them.

There is nothing for it. She will have to sell the house. And somehow this fact mixes with the cold hard fury of the last few months, and finally propels her into action.

"Hi! I was wondering how you were."

Lila had pulled Jessie's number from the school WhatsApp, expressing interest in coming to her shop to buy some art supplies: a lie, but it sounded better than "I'd like to come and wrench your heart out through your ribcage with my bare hands." She has arrived forty minutes before she is due to pick up Violet, and stands in the little shop, stacked to the ceiling with tubes of paint, A3 cartridge paper, and crafting supplies, breathing in the faint smell of turpentine. "Much better, thanks," she says, trying to ignore the distinct sweatiness of her palms.

"You went so pale in that coffee shop! Does that happen to you often?"

Jessie is wearing an old-fashioned shop apron in navy blue. Her hair is clipped up and she looks young, fresh, and pretty. Lila gazes at her surreptitiously as she serves a customer: an old woman who counts out the price of two balls of wool with gnarled, arthritic fingers. It is easy to imagine how attractive she was to Gabriel. The mystery was why he wanted someone else at the same time.

"Would you like a cup of tea? I can nip out the back to make us one while it's quiet."

Lila declines. "Actually," she says. "I need to talk to you about something."

Jessie is apparently perceptive enough to detect the change in tone. She gazes warily at Lila for a minute, then walks out from behind the till. "What?" she says baldly.

"This is really awkward."

"Go on." Jessie's smile has disappeared.

"That headache I got when—when we met. It wasn't a headache. I was—" Lila swallows. "I was just shocked when you mentioned Gabriel Mallory. Because . . ." It's horrible what's happening on Jessie's face. It's as if she already knows, and her whole face is begging Lila silently not to say the thing. "I—I had been seeing him. I thought it was just me."

For a moment, everything in the shop grows still.

"Gabriel—Gabriel was seeing *you*?"

All the color has drained from Jessie's face. For a crazy moment Lila wonders if that was what she had looked like when Jessie had said the same to her. She suspects she hadn't looked quite so photogenic.

"You mean *seeing* seeing?"

"We had sex. And were talking most evenings."

Her mouth has dropped open. "Since when?"

"Well, two or three months ago, and the sex happened . . . in the last month."

They flinch as the bell rings at the door. As they turn, a man in a checked shirt and salmon-colored trousers walks in, holding a list. He squints at it, then looks up at them.

"I need some gouache. Is that how you pronounce it?" He says it "gwayche."

There is a short silence.

"Goo-arsh," says Jessie, numbly. "It's over here." She walks the man to the far corner of the shop, where all the paints are on display in little white tubes. "Don't go over as far as that bit. They're all watercolors." She turns back toward Lila, her face still rigid with shock.

"But what did he—"

"What's the difference?" The man's voice booms across the shop. He is staring at the tubes.

"I'm sorry?"

"Between goo-arsh and watercolors. Can you mix them? They're for my wife. I'm not really a painter. Come to think of it neither is she. She's trying to find something for her mental health. I told her Valium would be cheaper but apparently the GP disagrees. Haha!"

He's delighted with his own joke.

Jessie gives her head a tiny shake. "It's similar to watercolor but less opaque. It has a high percentage of chalk," she says, like someone reciting the words.

"Is it cheaper?"

"What?"

"Which is cheaper?"

"Depends." Jessie turns abruptly to Lila, her face incredulous. "Are you *sure*?"

"That I slept with him? Er, yes?"

"Which one?" the man repeats.

Jessie drags her attention back to him impatiently. "It depends on the brand. The prices are on the shelf." She stands there, her hands dangling at her sides, apparently still trying to digest Lila's news.

"I'm so sorry," says Lila. "Obviously if I'd known he was involved with someone else I wouldn't have gone near him."

"He didn't say anything about me?"

"Not a word." It is this that seems to wound Jessie more than anything. Lila can't help herself. She hesitates, then says: "I have to ask you something. Did he call you by a name? Other than your name, I mean?"

The man has taken two steps back toward them. "Can you tell me where I would find Burned Umber?"

Jessie screws up her eyes. "It's dark orange," she says, waving a hand behind her at the shelf. "They're all labeled. He called me 'carina.' It means 'cute.' It was our thing."

"He called me Bella. That was ours."

"Bella," she repeats.

"And Cadmium Orange?"

347

"*On the shelf*," Jessie says, louder this time. And then to Lila: "But I don't understand. I've been seeing him for almost a year!"

"I promise he didn't say a word. I thought—I thought he was still getting over the death of his wife."

"So did I!"

"I hate to interrupt your little conversation, but I need to find these colors."

"He was sleeping with both of us at the same time?"

"It looks like it."

"UGH!" Jessie's face is anguished.

"I just . . . I had to tell you. I mean obviously I'm never seeing him again so it's up to you what you decide, but I couldn't let you go on without knowing who you were dealing with."

"Oh, my God. He picked up *two mothers in the same school playground*?" Jessie's voice is lifting in pitch as the full horror sinks in.

"Cerulean Blue?" The man appears beside them.

Jessie turns, as if seeing him for the first time. She looks hard at his large, florid face, then whips the list out of his hand. She strides over to the shelf, and, almost without looking, plucks out twelve different colors, eliciting a muttered *I say* from the man. She walks back to the till, rings them up, and holds out her hand. "Fifty-nine forty-five."

"Fifty-nine pounds? That's an awful lot for a bunch of paints." He reaches reluctantly for his wallet.

"Think of it as investing in your wife's mental health. And, believe me, if it's that easy to keep her happy, you're a lucky man," Jessie says. She is not smiling.

He looks a little worried then. He hands over his credit card, accepts the proffered bag, and leaves. They stand in the little shop in silence, watching him stride briskly down the street, casting backward glances as he goes.

"Fucking hell," Jessie says, slumping. She looks like she wants to cry.

"I know."

"Does he know you know?"

"Not yet. But he will."

"Damn it. I can't leave the shop." Jessie presses her palms to her face. Her shoulders give a single shudder that seems to travel through her whole body. Lila feels a stab of sympathy. Then Jessie lowers her hands, and wipes briskly at her eyes. "Ugh. Ugh."

She looks up, and her face sags with disappointment. "You know the worst thing? I was doing fine before I met him. I was just rolling with my life, woke up happy most days, just me, the kid, my shop . . . We were doing okay. And he knocked me right off that perch. Made me ecstatic for about five minutes, then question myself all the time, made me feel empty when I wasn't with him. It was like I was living on a roller-coaster . . . happy, sad, anxious, ecstatic. Now . . . now I just feel like an idiot . . . And for what?"

SHE WILL WRITE a letter, Lila thinks. No, two letters. She will pick up Violet, then go home and write a letter to Jensen, with a much more abject and sincere apology. Then she will write to Gabriel, telling him what she knows, and laying bare the hurt he has caused to two decent women who had genuinely liked him and hadn't deserved any of it. She will write a letter so that she does not have to have this conversation in public, in full view of Philippa Graham and Marja and the rest of them, and then she will never acknowledge him again. But he will know what he has done, because she will not shy away from spelling out any of it: her hurt, Jessie's hurt, the horrible, insidious way he has made two women feel worse about themselves.

She walks the twenty minutes to the school, her thoughts lost in what she will say, the exact turn of phrase that will force him to look at his own behavior, cause him to question himself, in the way she and Jessie had done. She will channel Estella Esperanza—discreet, focused, deadly. She will make her move without anyone around her even being aware of what has happened. She is still thinking about the best way to express her disappointment when she does a double-take walking past the Crown and Duck, the gastropub beside the chemist, which has a sprinkling of tables outside. It is an overcast day, and at this time of year only half the tables are occupied. But it is the end table that draws her eye. Because there, sitting with a woman, his hand resting casually on the tabletop in front of him, is Gabriel Mallory.

Something in her solidifies, roots her briefly to the spot. She watches as they laugh at something. The woman is in her thirties, dark curly hair and a black polo-neck. Her large eyes are soft and adoring when she looks at him, and she reaches out and lightly touches his arm, as if she cannot bear to be that close and not make physical contact. He peers at his watch and says something, pointing in the direction of the school. It is the woman's expression as he speaks to her that makes Lila wince: her acquiescent smile, the slight ruefulness at their imminent separation. Lila crosses the road and walks over to the table. "Hello, Gabriel," she says brightly.

There is barely a flicker on his face. He looks as if he might be pleased to see her, in the slightly distant, pleasant way one might greet a neighbor. He half rises from his seat, puts a hand on her arm. He is wearing the blue cashmere jumper she had particularly loved. "Lila! How lovely to see you."

"On your way to school pickup?"

"Yup. Just finishing up a drink. I managed to get away early for once, so I thought I'd give Lennie a surprise."

The woman is gazing up at Lila, wearing the kind of bland smile someone wears when they're not sure what your relationship is to the person they're fixated upon.

"Lila's daughter is at Lennie's school," Gabriel says, turning to the woman, as if in explanation.

Lila considers this description of her presence for a moment. "Yes, I'm Lila. Lovely to meet you," she says, holding out a hand, which the woman takes. "And you must be . . . Divina?"

The woman's smile falters. "I'm sorry?"

"Hmm. Let me guess. Maybe Gorgeousa? Is that a word? Perhaps it's an English version. Beautiful? Sexy?"

The woman's gaze flickers toward Gabriel and back toward Lila. Gabriel's smile has fallen away.

"Oh. Sorry." Lila wiggles her head, like she's done something daft. "It's just that, according to Gabriel, I'm Bella. As in beautiful. And recently I accidentally ran into Gabriel's other special friend Carina—that means cute, by the way—and she and I exchanged notes and now we're just curious about who else is in our exclusive little gang. Perhaps a *little* less exclusive than either of us realized at the time. But hey-ho! Have a lovely rest of your drink."

She gives a cheerful little wave and starts to walk away. Then she stops and turns, holding up a finger. She drops her voice to a cartoon whisper. "Oh. And if you've made it past the intermittent texting stage, you might want to get tested. He's *really* bad at condoms. Bye!"

It turns out Lila cannot be bothered to write two bloody letters. There is only so much emotional labor a woman can be expected to handle.

Chapter Thirty-three

Jensen,

I've started this letter eight times and I'm still not sure I'm going to get it right. So I'm basically just going to say this: I'm so sorry. I made a huge error of judgment and lost sight of who I was, and I didn't mean to hurt you in doing those things, but I did, and that's something I'm going to have to live with. I get that you've moved on—and I truly hope you're happy—but I just wanted you to know that I won't be publishing what I wrote about you. None of it. I'm canceling the whole book. And I'm sorry if the flippant way I described a night that was actually very lovely caused you pain. You have shown me and my family nothing but kindness and I repaid you in the worst way possible.

I'm going to ask one thing: whatever you think of me, please don't end your relationship with Bill. He had nothing to do with any of it, and he's going through a rough time just now, and could really do with a friend. Your friendship especially.

I'm so sorry again.

Lila x

I t has taken Lila all day to write this letter. She has sat staring at her pen, working and reworking the words, and every one of them still feels inadequate. It feels like the world is full of people betraying each other, or doing each other wrong, and when she finally commits the words to paper, she does so wanting to feel like she is not one of those people. That she can at least own her faults, and shoddy behavior, and apologize for them. She tries not to think about the other reason: that she is still haunted by the way Jensen looked at her, the way she feels his absence all the time. The proprietorial way in which his new girl-friend took his arm and steered him firmly away from her. She feels like the dumbest person in the universe, not because Gabriel fooled her, but because she had been too stupid to see what was right in front of her: this kind, funny, honest man, who had looked at her as if she was some-thing great, and touched her as if she was revered. She keeps remember-ing the way it had been impossible to be anyone but herself when she was with him. The way he had made her laugh. The deep-rooted sense she had when he was around that everything was basically okay. What had she been thinking?

The wind has picked up during the day, and Lila walks to the post-box with her hair whipping around her face. The rain spits meanly from an angle that feels almost horizontal, and she puts her head down, feel-ing it reflects her mood. Now, without the distraction of her stupid, mis-guided infatuation, she is left with nothing but the knowledge of what she has done to a good man, and what she has thrown away.

She had read the letter to Eleanor before she sent it, and Eleanor had murmured, *Good, good*, in the way that a teacher might approve of a sat-isfactory piece of work. But a thought keeps nagging at her: why should Jensen trust her words when she has found it so easy to wound him with them before? Gabriel had found it easy to give her the words he thought she wanted—but they had been meaningless at best, misleading at worst. And this is the real reason she took so long to write a simple letter: she is no longer sure she trusts words either. They have become febrile, potentially inflammatory things. All that really matters is how someone makes you feel, and she has made Jensen feel terrible.

Dan had texted the previous evening saying that Marja had been admitted to hospital and he wouldn't be able to take the girls for the foreseeable. It was a bald text, with no detail, and Lila had sighed inwardly, realizing that this was just another example of how his first family was going to come second from now on. She will tell the girls that he is very busy at work. There is no point in them knowing the degree to which he no longer makes them a priority. She will protect them from that as far as she is able.

She puts the letter into the postbox, and turns to go home, Truant hunched at her heels. He does not like wet weather, and casts baleful glances from the end of the lead. "I know, sweetie," she murmurs to him, pulling up her collar. "You and me both." Gabriel, Dan, Gene. So much effort involved in clearing up the damage that their fragile egos have wrought.

There is something exhilarating about the wind, though, she realizes, as she keeps walking: a harbinger of change, or energy. Lila lifts her face to it, feeling her cheeks tingle, watching the leaves chase each other in circles, the umbrellas of passersby turning themselves inside out. She thinks suddenly of what she had said to Gabriel outside the pub, the woman's face when she had called her "Gorgeousa." She lets out an involuntary giggle. Eleanor had hooted at that story.

A plastic bin skitters across the pavement in front of her, and she and Truant pause to let it pass. She will make her way through this particular storm. She has been through worse. She will persuade Bill to come home. She will find another way to earn some money and a cheaper place for them to live. She will survive, as she has always done. If these few months have reinforced one thing, it is the knowledge that the only person you can truly rely on is yourself. Lila straightens her shoulders, takes a deep breath and, with renewed determination in her stride, heads toward home.

THE GIRLS ARE oddly peaceful that evening. Perhaps the storm raging outside makes their little home feel cozier, or perhaps they'd just had a reasonable enough day not to bring the usual complaints and cries of unfairness home with them. Celie, who seems relieved that she doesn't have to go to Dan's for the foreseeable, is working on some kind of cartoon drawing. She covers it with her arm when Lila brings a mug of cocoa to her room, then pulls it back almost reluctantly and says it's for Animation Club. Lila peers at the intricate line drawings and wants to punch the air with joy, but nods and says with a carefully calibrated level of approval that they look great, and tries not to be so enthusiastic that her daughter immediately changes her mind about them.

Violet is downstairs watching old episodes of *Star Squadron Zero* on YouTube. She has devoured a whole three seasons now, and Lila observes her from the corner of her eye while she cooks, hoping she's watching because she enjoys the show and not just because she misses her grandfather. Lila has not been in touch with Gene since he left. What's the point? She knows how this game goes—he will say sorry, charm the girls, worm his way back into the house for as long as it suits him, then up and leave again. They're all better off without him. She cooks a roast chicken with mashed potatoes—the girls' favorite—perhaps to reinforce the idea that they don't need anyone else around to lead a good life. They eat companionably round the table, listening to the rain spatter on the windows, and Celie manages to last at least half an hour before she gets up and retreats to her room.

Lila is just finishing the washing-up when the call comes. It's a number she doesn't recognize, and at first she stares at her phone screen, debating whether or not to pick up. "Hello?" she says, peeling off her rubber gloves.

Penelope's voice is breathless. "Oh, Lila. Thank goodness. You need to come to the hospital as quickly as you can. It's Bill."

LILA LURCHES HER way around the house, trying to gather bag, keys, a coat, tailed by Truant, who has picked up the shift in atmosphere and is now clearly convinced of imminent apocalypse. She manages to get everything together, knocks on Celie's door and opens it. Celie is still absorbed in her drawing and looks up as if she's been pulled from a trance.

"I—I've got to pop out for a bit. Can you mind Violet?"

"Why? Where are you going?"

She doesn't want to tell her daughter. She doesn't want to convey any of what she had heard in Penelope's voice—that undertow of dread and fear. A suspected heart attack, Penelope had said, a sob in her voice. She had gone round because he hadn't answered his phone all afternoon and found him. The ambulance had taken so long, too long, to get there.

"I just—"

"Mum." Celie is staring at her.

"It's Bill. He's not well. Penelope has gone with him to hospital. I didn't want to worry you."

She sees the fear in Celie's face. "Penelope is with him. But I need to be there too."

"Okay," she says. "You go. Call me when you get there."

There is something about her daughter's bravery, the immediate resolve in her expression, even while her eyes are wide with anxiety, that makes Lila's heart swell. She steps forward and gives Celie a swift, heartfelt hug, breathing in the scent of her hair, feeling her daughter's hands link briefly around her waist.

"And tell him I love him."

"I will. Of course I will. The moment I know anything I'll call you. Will you be okay by yourself?"

Celie pulls back. "Mum. I'm sixteen."

"I know. Just don't answer the door. To anyone. If there's a power cut, the fuse box is under the stairs. Call me and I'll talk you through it. Or if it's the whole street you'll have to check online. Oh, and there are candles in the box under the sink. And don't use the oven or light any-thing with a naked—"

"Mum. Go."

Lila goes. She will drive to the hospital. It will be impossible to get a taxi in this weather. She prays that the old Mercedes will start. She shuts the front door, feeling the wind lift her hair, hearing its whistle in her ears. Then, as she turns, she stops dead on the front steps. The large plane tree that had stood at the edge of her drive, the tree whose branches had elegantly framed her house and that Jensen had warned her was listing, is horizontal, completely blocking the entrance to her driveway. It's such an unlikely sight that at first she can barely take it in. Its longer branches are draped over the top of the Mercedes, obscuring the windows. Even to get to the pavement she will need to climb over the trunk.

Her brain is a blur. *Think*, she tells herself. *Think*. Dan is at the hospi-tal with Marja. He's not going to be able to help. Eleanor doesn't have a car. She calls for an Uber. The app tells her that nobody is available in her area but, helpfully, they are still searching. She feels panic rising in her chest, lets out a *fuck. Fuck!* She screws her eyes shut, and counts to five.

And then she makes the call.

"THANK YOU SO much for coming. I'm so sorry. I just . . . didn't have anyone else I could call."

"It's fine." Jensen doesn't look like it's fine. He doesn't look at her as he speaks, just keeps his eyes straight ahead, as the windscreen wipers move steadily backward and forward. He had arrived within seven minutes of her calling, climbed out of the pickup truck, gazed pointedly at the fallen tree, then opened the passenger door for her to get in.

"I should have got someone to look at it. I just—with everything—it kind of got away from me."

He doesn't say anything. She has rarely seen anyone so focused on their driving.

According to her phone, it will take seventeen minutes for them to get to the hospital. Her whole body is vibrating with anxiety. She keeps hearing the fear in Penelope's voice, pictures a thousand images behind the words "I found him."

Please be okay, Bill, she wills him silently. *Please just be okay. We can fix everything if you'll just be okay.*

"Where are the girls?" he says, as they approach the hospital.

"At home."

"Is anyone with them?"

"No. But they'll be fine. They have the dog. And Celie is under strict instructions not to open the door."

He nods, swinging the truck past the barriers toward the main entrance. It sits, glowing, like the portal to a world of pain. He slows the truck, and comes to a halt. He still stares resolutely ahead, as if he cannot bear even to look at her. It makes something in her contract. "Thank you. Thank you so much. Again, I'm so sorry to have to ask, especially after everything."

"Just let me know how he is," he says. "And call if you need a ride back from the hospital."

"I don't want to bother you again. I've already disrupted your—"

"Just call," he says shortly. He waits silently while she opens the door and climbs out of the truck. She runs in through the sliding doors, glancing back briefly to watch the tail lights disappear into the darkness.

• • •

BILL IS IN a room by himself on the third floor. It takes Lila a while to find it, jogging down the strip-lit corridors, weaving past the medics walking in groups or clutching folders to their chests. She finally locates him in Coronary Care, and sees him first through the small window on the door, lying immobile in a mask beneath a mass of wires, Penelope bent over at his side, her slim frame a question mark. She looks round as Lila walks in and Lila sees that she is holding Bill's hand in both her own. Lila registers the near-silence, the intermittent bleep of the monitors.

"How is he?"

"Stable. They've given him a cardiac . . . cardiac catheterization? He's having ECGs or EKGs or something. Oh, I can't remember. Just lots of drugs." Her voice is low and shaky.

Bill's exposed chest looks old and gray, plastered with sticky patches from which wires project in a spaghetti tangle, covered from the waist in a light blanket. His face is largely obscured by the mask and he seems sedated. His fingers twitch periodically in Penelope's, and she answers each twitch with a gentle squeeze.

"Oh, Lila. I thought I'd lost him." Penelope starts to cry, silent tears that fall onto her sleeves. "They won't even tell me if he's going to be all right because I'm not . . . I'm not family."

"Okay," says Lila, trying to keep her voice calm as she takes in the awful reality of it. "Okay."

Penelope straightens, struggles to pull herself together, gazing at Bill's face. "I know—I know that everyone loves him. But it just feels so cruel to find your person after all this time alone, the person you just love, such a *wonderful* man, and then to have them snatched away. I can't—I just can't—" She breaks off, then composes herself. "I'm so sorry. How terribly selfish of me. I'm just a newcomer in his life and you all have known and loved—"

Lila puts her hand gently on Penelope's shoulder. "Penelope. It's fine. You're allowed to feel the way you feel. We know you love him too."

Lila stoops and kisses Bill's forehead. He seems so removed from them, so far away, this man she has known almost her whole life. It is as if all the things that make him Bill, his upright stance, his air of purpose, the sense of safety he has always conveyed, have just evaporated, leaving this shell of an old, frail man. "I'll find a doctor. I'll—I'll go and find one. I'll be back."

Lila lets herself out of the room, closing the door gently behind her. She stands for a moment, feeling overwhelmed, and then she walks to the nurses' station. There are three women, one bent over a screen, entering something on a keyboard, the other two having a conversation in lowered voices.

"Hello," she says. "Would it be possible for me to talk to someone about Bill McKenzie? Heart attack in Room C3. He was admitted this evening." She pauses, then says firmly: "I'm his daughter."

LILA SPENDS SEVERAL hours at the hospital, long enough to ensure that Bill is stable, to learn that he has suffered a myocardial infarction, that the length of time he waited for treatment has possibly been offset by the fact that he had had the presence of mind to take aspirin when he first started having chest pains, that they are waiting on the results of a battery of tests, including one for brain hemorrhage, and that they will let Lila know if anything changes. Only one person is allowed to stay in the room overnight, and it feels wrong to evict Penelope, especially as Lila has to get back to the girls, so she finally leaves, with Penelope promising to stay in touch.

Lila arrives back shortly before one a.m., numb and drained of all feeling. She cannot think beyond each step of her journey: the front desk at the hospital has a hotline to a taxi company and she thanks them politely for ordering one for her, and sits silently in the back of the car when it comes, staring at nothing out of the window. The storm has abated, just the odd gust of wind gently causing the bushes to sway, and piles of leaves to scatter in skittish bursts across the pavements. It is only as she approaches her street that she remembers the tree, but it feels like a ridiculous cosmic joke on top of everything that has happened. She tells herself that it, like so much else, can wait until tomorrow. Because Bill, the man who has been a father to her for nearly her whole life, Bill, the kindest, most consistent, the best of men, is lying in a hospital bed with no guarantee of recovery, and she doesn't know what to say to her children, and that is all that matters.

"Just here, please," she says, when they reach her part of the street, and rummages in her bag for money to pay the driver. When she hands it to him and tells him to keep the change he swivels to her, gives her a sympathetic smile, and says: "I hope they're all right. Whoever it is."

She looks up at him.

"No one wants picking up from the hospital at a quarter to one in the morning unless it's bad news," he says. "Good luck to you, mate." A lump rises in her throat at the unexpected humanity. She manages to mutter a thank-you, and climbs out of the taxi. And it is then that she stops in confusion. The tree has gone. Her front door is in plain sight, as is her car. The enormous fallen tree has vanished so comprehensively that for a moment she wonders if she had imagined the whole thing. But, no, over to the right-hand side of her house, obscuring the garage doors, an enormous pile of logs bears the scars of a chainsaw. To the left a giant wigwam of branches. As she glances at the Mercedes, she can just detect a dent in the roof, visible in the glare of the sodium light from the lamp-post on the pavement. Lila stares at the three things, not quite able to take them all in, then lets herself in through the front door.

Truant is the first to greet her, racing down the stairs, his tongue lolling, leaping up at her in delight that she has, against all odds, returned.

She holds his soft face to hers for a moment, shushing him, but grateful for his presence in the too-still house. He follows her, bouncing with joy, as she goes to the kitchen, where she will make herself a cup of tea. It is the knee-jerk response to everything, she thinks distantly. Hot water and old leaves. Strange, really. But it's all she wants right now, and with a big teaspoon of sugar in it.

She jumps when Jensen scrambles up from the kitchen chair. "Sorry," he says, rubbing his face. "Didn't mean to startle you. I must have nodded off."

She's so shocked to see him there that she cannot speak. His expression is briefly unguarded.

"I—I didn't think the girls should be on their own. So I went home to pick up my chainsaw and just told Celie I'd be outside for the evening clearing the tree. Just, you know, so she had an adult around. And then when I finished she asked would I wait. I think she felt a little anxious, you know, with . . . everything."

"You did that. The tree."

He shrugs. "Well. It wasn't really the time for you not to be able to get in and out of your house. How is he?"

It is then that tears rise. She swallows hard, trying to contain them. "Um. Hard to say just now. But they're doing everything they can." She looks up at the ceiling, willing herself to keep it together. "Heart attack, it turns out. Big one. Penelope's still there with him."

She cannot look at him. She keeps staring at the ceiling, blinking, trying to hold back the tears.

"Damn. I'm sorry."

She shakes her head, mutely, compressing her lips.

There is a short silence.

"I—I'll get off, then," he says. He stands, and reaches for his jacket. "Just . . . didn't know how long you'd be and I didn't want . . ." She hears his voice and closes her eyes, suddenly too overwhelmed by his decency.

It is too much, the thing that has finally broken her. And she presses her hands against her face and starts to cry, the tears that have somehow been dammed for this whole wretched evening, perhaps this whole awful, awful month. She rams her knuckles into her eye sockets and lets out a long, low howl. She cannot hold it in, she cannot bear it all, because it is too much, always too much, all the bloody time.

And after a moment she feels Jensen's arm around her, at first tentative, and then more firmly, pulling her in, and she lets herself collapse onto the solidity of him, letting him hold her up as she cries, for Bill, for her daughters, for herself, for all of it. She cries and cries, her sobs hoarse in her ears, tears sliding unchecked down her cheeks, no longer even able to care what he might think, because it's all lost anyway, all broken. And Jensen holds her, until the sobs become shudders, and intermittent tremors, and then, an age later, when she has sat down on the chair, and wiped ineffectually at her face with a handful of tissues, he puts a mug of tea in front of her, nods an acknowledgment of her garbled apologies, says he'll be in touch about clearing the tree branches, and then quietly, so as not to wake the girls, he lets himself out.

Chapter Thirty-four

For the next few days Lila's life enters a new realm. She spends as many waking hours at the hospital as she can, and while she is at home she focuses solely on her daughters. She needs to: they have been knocked sideways by the news of Bill's illness. Celie retreats to her room, spending hours drawing, her face somber when she comes down to eat, but it is Violet who takes it hardest, fearful that she is about to lose the man she thinks of as her grandpa in the same abrupt, violent way she had lost her grandmother. She has night terrors, pads across the hallway in the small hours and climbs into Lila's bed, has become clingy, and blows up at the slightest excuse. It is as if the robustness she has always displayed has disappeared along with her peace of mind. Lila does her best to reassure them—Bill is awake, the prognosis hopeful—but she cannot give them the certainty they seek: Bill is old, and it turns out his heart is weakened, and nobody knows how well—or for how long—he will recover.

She had called Dan to let him know, relaying the news without emotion, wanting him, she supposes, to offer support, maybe to spend more time with his daughters when they need stability. But Marja is still in the maternity hospital. Apparently there is a problem with the placenta and he says, exhaustedly, that he is struggling to look after Hugo and manage his job. She finds herself hoping Marja's baby will be okay, not because she feels any great love for Marja, but because she just needs Dan to find some emotional energy for his girls. She just needs something to be normal, reliable.

Eleanor, like the best of friends, steps in. She has twice reorganized her work to pick Violet up from school, has walked Truant every morning and stops by in the evenings, bringing a takeaway supper or just her cheerful presence to break the unaccustomed stillness of their house. Jensen has returned on one of the days that Lila was at the hospital and cleared the tree branches so that all that is left is a neatly piled stack of logs. It is as if the tree had never existed. She sends him an effusive thank-you by text, explaining the many ways in which she is grateful for his generosity. He replies, *No problem.* He doesn't mention her letter. She would feel worse about it if she had any energy to feel worse about anything.

One afternoon, when she feels particularly low, she grabs her keys and takes the Mercedes out for a drive. She puts the roof down, and turns up her music, waiting for some alchemical change in her emotional state, but instead she feels exposed and stupid and gets as far as the high street before she puts the roof back up, then drives home.

Bill has a stent fitted. He will stay in hospital for a week, and will need to be on a variety of medications when he comes home—aspirin, anti-platelet treatment, beta-blockers, and something to lower his cholesterol. It seems insanely unfair that a man who has spent his whole life pursuing a healthy diet should suffer like this, but the fault may be genetic, the doctors tell her, and bodies are unpredictable, unknowable things. The consultant who tells her this smiles amiably, as if he is describing something magical. Bill will stay with her initially when he returns home—as much for his mental state as any physical risk: apparently it is common for those who have had a heart attack to go through a period of anxiety and depression. She accepts a sheaf of leaflets recommending self-help groups he can turn to, though she suspects this is as likely as him taking up heavy-metal guitar.

Lila's life has become completely binary. It boils down to two things: keeping her girls' spirits up, and helping keep Bill alive. It is almost a relief, this letting go of everything else. She moves through the requirements of her day with outward calm, taking healthy, home-cooked meals to Bill and Penelope (he is appalled by what they serve at the hospital), and bringing home encouraging reports to her daughters. *He complains that everybody on the ward watches daytime television. He thinks their brains will rot before their hearts give up.* There are periods of your life in which all that is really required is to keep putting one foot in front of the other. Lila wakes at six thirty every morning and does exactly this for sixteen hours before she climbs back into bed at ten thirty and sleeps a deep, exhausted sleep.

"DARLING! HOW BLISSFUL to hear from you! I was worried when you said you'd had a family emergency. Is everything okay?" Anoushka's voice booms out of the hands-free phone.

Lila is trying to tidy the kitchen before she goes out.

"Ah. Getting there. Bill—my stepdad—had a heart attack. It was pretty scary but he's on the mend, we hope." She can say these words with practiced ease now, as if they happened to someone else.

"Oh, how awful. Can we send flowers? *Gracie, can we organize some flowers for Lila? No carnations. Remember what we agreed.*"

"You don't have to. Really." Lila scrubs at a particularly stubborn piece of dried tomato on the hob.

"So do you need an extension? I'm sure we can arrange that. We don't even have to tell them the exact reason: family emergency is quite enough."

"Actually, that was what I needed to talk to you about."

Anoushka is unusually quiet as Lila takes a deep breath and explains that she needs to pull out of the contract. She tells Anoushka that she cannot write the book as planned because of the potential impact on her children, because her life has not worked out in the way that is needed for her to write about a woman's sexual escapades, that she feels the impact of it on the people she loves is too much.

"I'm so sorry," she says, into the resulting silence. "I really don't want to let everyone down. I should never have agreed to do it in the first place."

And this is the thing she has felt most braced for. She has misled Anoushka, misled the publishers. She has promised something she can't deliver, and pulling out will be as bad for Anoushka as it is for her: it may affect her reputation as an agent, future deals she may want to make with the same publishing house.

"And I'm especially sorry to you. I—I totally understand if you don't want to represent me any more. I should never have put you in this position."

She closes her eyes as she says this. Waiting for the outburst. But there is a tiny sliver of relief in it too: there is something liberating in simply telling the truth, in the black-and-white knowledge of what she can and cannot do.

"Oh. Darling," Anoushka says, after a moment. "Well, it is what it is. I'll get on to them. But please don't worry. You've got enough going on. No money has changed hands yet so no real harm done. We'll just say your family circumstances have changed and made writing the book impossible."

"Really?"

"And then we'll work out something else you can do. Of course I'm not going to take you off my list. We're friends, not just business associates. Goodness me. You just focus on your family for now. That's what's important after all."

"Oh, God, Anoushka, thank you. Thank you. I can't tell you how much I've dreaded making this call."

"Lila darling, you were an absolute trouper going through with the *Rebuild* publicity despite everything Dastardly Dan did at the time. You've just bitten off a bit more than you can chew with this one. Life happens. Put all this to one side, and let's speak when you're ready. We'll come up with something else."

THE MERCEDES IS worth seven thousand pounds less than Lila paid for it. It is partly the dent in the roof from the falling tree, but apparently the salesman who had assured her it would only ever increase in value had failed to account for the normal vicissitudes of the economy and right now people are just not buying vintage soft-tops. The salesman tells her this with the bland, unconvincing sympathy of a man who knows you are basically going to take what he gives you. Lila haggles a little, manages to get another eight hundred added to the price, and decides not to wonder whether her sex played a part in the total sum she was offered. Even with the loss, though, she walks away from the saleroom with a sense of relief. She will have some money in her account again. Plenty of people in the city survive without a car. It is all just stuff at the end of the day. And there is something about the Mercedes that just makes her sad now. She walks away from it without looking back.

THE DAY BEFORE Bill is due to return home, Lila goes for a massage. Eleanor has booked it for her as a treat at the parlor where she goes twice a week: a high-street place that Lila had previously assumed was probably a knocking shop, but turns out to be full of brisk, middle-aged Eastern European women who are unfazed by body types or inappropriate body hair and are uninterested in conversation. At midday, feeling the odd sense of subversion that comes with taking time out of a normal working day, she lies face down on the warmed, towel-covered bed and feels herself surrender for the first time in as long as she can remember. She's lulled by the pummeling and the hot oils, the low, ambient music interrupted only by the occasionally audible breath of Agnes, her masseuse, as she un-knots some particularly knotty part of Lila.

At first Lila's thoughts race, her self-consciousness about her body, and anxiety about Bill's return, what she will cook, how she will take care of him well enough, whether the girls are okay without her. And then, gradually, her mind slows, and she just lets it all happen, sinks into the human touch she has been missing for so long. And for a while it's blissful, having capable hands on her, feeling her body ease after months and months of tension, feeling long-tightened muscles start to let go. But somewhere in this relaxed state, something wells in her, an emotion unlocked by the reality of another human being touching her, listening to Lila's body, feeling its pain and its tensions and carefully remedying them. Suddenly, she feels a great swell of something overwhelming her. Grief? Gratitude? She isn't sure. She becomes aware that she is weeping, the tears running unchecked through the hole where her face is nestled, dropping onto the floor, her shoulders vibrating with an emotion she can no longer hold back. Agnes slows her hands as she becomes aware of what is happening. Lila pleads with her silently not to say anything because she cannot name what she is feeling. She cannot apologize. She cannot say anything. And perhaps Agnes, so attuned to the human body, understands. Because she simply places a hand on the space where Lila's neck meets her shoulders and lets it rest there, soft enough to be kind, firm enough to reassure her of its intention, perhaps just a silent message from another woman: I see you, I understand. The hand rests for some unknown length of time while Lila cries, a human connection in a world of complication and grief. When she finally dresses and leaves, twenty minutes later, and walks out into the blustery day, wrapped up again in her coat and scarf, Lila suspects that she will never forget it.

THERE IS A bewildering amount of procedure and paperwork involved in Bill being able to leave the hospital. Consultants must be consulted, forms must be signed off, pharmaceutical collections must be made and apparently involve waiting for interminable lengths of time until the appropriate pharmacist has returned from her scheduled break. Lila goes through these steps with one eye on the clock: Celie has Animation Club today and cannot pick up Violet, and Violet needs picking up from school at half past three. She had assumed she could collect Bill at lunchtime and go straight home, but so far the process has lasted almost two hours.

Not for the first time, Lila thanks God for Penelope, who has a car, and who has waited in the ward with Bill while all these errands are run. Penelope has taken to her new role as Bill's helpmate as if it is the one she has been waiting for her whole life. She has endless patience, positivity, and grace. When Bill fusses or worries about his clothing, she is there, holding up shirts she has pressed, the right socks and jacket; when he grows anxious about remembering the correct timings and dosages of his new medications, she has already written it down in a little red notebook with a panda on the cover, assuring him that everything is taken care of. She is just what their little family needs right now, and Lila is infinitely grateful.

Lila is just headed up to the ward again with a large white paper bag filled with bottles and packets of pills, when she realizes she is walking behind a familiar figure, taller than everyone else, with jeans that look like they may have been worn for days, and a leather jacket, his hair an unnatural shade of chocolate brown now. He pauses to look up at the signage, checking the numbers, then presses on the buzzer to be let in to C3. Lila has skidded behind him by the time the door clicks to let him in. "Gene?"

He turns and sees her, and it takes a moment too long for his smile to appear. "Oh, hey, sweetheart."

She pulls the door shut in front of him. "What are you doing here?"

"I—uh—I just came to see how Bill was doing. I heard, you know, about what had gone down. I just wanted to check—"

"That he was still alive? That you hadn't killed him?"

"Wha—"

"Why do you think Bill had a heart attack, Gene? Could it possibly have been related to the discovery that the love of his life had been seduced by her ex-husband? That you had made the last fifteen years of their marriage a sham?"

"Ah, Lila, c'mon . . ."

"No, *you* come on. Little test for you: who do you think is the exact last person that my father should see right now?"

That got him. He reels slightly at her use of the word, and blinks almost disbelievingly at her as if he hadn't realized her capable of such cruelty. But Lila is filled with blind rage at the sight of him, at his thoughtless audacity in thinking he could just turn up here, not even mindful of the potential harm he could cause.

"I just—I just wanted to make sure he was okay. We—we were pals, for a while at least, you know?"

"No. I don't know that. I know that you managed to get on for a couple of months until we all discovered that you were an even worse human being than we had previously thought. And that bar was pretty bloody low. I told you to stay away from my family, Gene. So now I'm going to tell you again, because you are clearly incapable of considering anyone else's opinions, or anyone else's needs. Bill needs peace and quiet—that's what the doctors have told us. He needs to stay calm. The last thing he needs is you walking in just as he's finally about to go home. So please just leave."

When he doesn't move, she adds: "Now."

Gene shakes his head. "Honey, it's not how you—"

But Lila cuts him off. "I'm not going to continue this conversation. I actually don't have the bandwidth for it. You've done enough. Just go."

Finally, he seems to hear her. Gene gazes at her for a moment, and then he compresses his mouth, as if he is trying not to say anything else. Finally he gives a small nod, turns, and starts to walk back along the hospital corridor. Lila watches, just to make sure he is not about to turn and try to come back, and when he goes round the corner, she buzzes the door of the ward. After taking a deep breath, she walks in.

Chapter Thirty-five

Francesca

Francesca McKenzie had spent her whole life trusting her body to make decisions for her. She felt things deep in her gut, she was fond of telling people. So many people were disconnected from the many wise ways in which a body could speak to the mind. From their earliest ages they were told to ignore it—*No, you can't be hungry. Give your uncle Don a hug. Go on, you're not scared, just jump into the water.* All those feelings of anxiety or resistance they were taught to override. She listened to her body as one would monitor a particularly finely calibrated compass, noting its tiny movements, trusting it to give an accurate picture of where she was. But as she awoke in the tiny hotel room in Dublin and gazed at the sleeping man beside her, Francesca McKenzie was forced to admit that on this occasion her body had been very wrong indeed.

• • •

SHE HAD FELT out of sorts for months, waking with a tight, nervous feeling in her chest, struggling to sleep, feeling a kind of existential bleakness settle over her, so at odds with her normal demeanor. *I don't feel like myself,* she had told her doctor, and he had seemed almost impatient with her, told her she had no medical symptoms, that it was probably hormonal given her age, that she should make sure she had a good exercise routine and a healthy diet, maybe take up a new hobby. He even uttered the dread phrase "Just go for a long walk." The implication ran under everything he said: *You're a middle-aged woman, probably still going through the change. Of course you don't feel like you used to.* Francesca had tried to count her blessings, had joined an outdoor swimming club (she found being cold utterly miserable), told herself she was just having an unsettled period, and tried to plow through it. She took long walks, supplements, hot baths, listened to her favorite music. She read books about psychology, replanted her garden, in the hope that watching things grow would bring her some ease with the notion of time passing. But the feelings of disconnection and vague unhappiness didn't seem to go away.

Bill, bless him, wasn't much help. He seemed so perfectly content with his life, and confused that what had satisfied her for so long now seemed not to be enough. "How about we take a holiday?" he had said, after she had yet again tried to articulate how she felt. "I hear Madeira is very nice at this time of year." But Bill was part of the problem: she did not want to visit flower gardens or go hiking in the hills. Bill was many things, but he was not capable of those moments of surprise, of the spontaneous joy of her younger years, and she felt its absence like a missing limb. He seemed suddenly so much older than her. *Is this it?* she kept asking herself. And then: *Why can't I just be satisfied?*

She didn't want to bother Lila with it: she and Dan were clearly having problems, and Lila was permanently overworked and stressed by trying to juggle her work with the baby. Her friends were busy with their own lives, and Francesca had always been the one they turned to for help: it seemed alien to her to ask them what she should be doing. But the unhappiness grew, as did her efforts to hide it, until she felt as if she was struggling to get through each day, to raise the necessary smiles, to feel what she was clearly supposed to be feeling.

It was the Week of No Sleep that did for her. Francesca who, for her whole life, had drifted off with ease had found for months that as soon as she put her head on the pillow her brain was racing like an out-of-control motor, whirring and spinning, her thoughts jumbling and looping. She would lie there for hours, increasingly enraged by Bill's peaceful slumbers beside her, despairing as she understood that tomorrow would be another day darkened by exhaustion and snappiness as she stumbled through it. It seemed to be a vicious circle: the less she slept, the more anxious she felt about going to bed. It culminated in a week where she barely slept at all.

That week she could hardly speak, felt hallucinatory and ill, could summon up none of the energy for the things that might make her feel better. She felt angry with Bill and angry with herself for feeling angry with Bill. He seemed helpless in the face of this new Francesca, tiptoeing around her and offering awkward platitudes that just made her crosser. She had nobody to turn to, no way of changing how she felt about it all. And then Gene had sent her a birthday greeting, Gene, who had barely remembered his daughter's birthdays, had, unexpectedly, sent a text message. Hey, sweetheart! I just remembered it's your special day! I'm filming in Dublin—God, these guys are crazy!—just a low-budget thing but it's great craic as they say here. Sending love and hope you're feeling great. You deserve it. Your old pal Gene x

"Your old pal." From the man who had broken her heart and destroyed her little family. A man who, for the longest time, she had thought she would never get over. At first it almost made her laugh, his absolute lack of self-awareness and reflection. Plus it wasn't her birthday: that had been the previous week. But the message had stuck in her head, its suggestions of fun and energy, a different place to be, perhaps even a different way to be. Francesca felt the pull to be somewhere else like a rope tied around her waist, urgent and inescapable, tugging at her through her days.

She told Bill she was going to see her old school friend Dorothy in Nottingham, and Bill had seemed almost relieved, as if this might change the dynamic and, more importantly, absolve him from the responsibility of having to work out how to do it. He had been so sweet about her "little break," making her snacks for the train journey, insisting on driving her to the station. She had told him she might not call—the signal at Dorothy's was terrible and, besides, she just wanted to forget everything for a few days—and he had accepted that with grace. "Just let me know when you want picking up," he had said. "Send a text and I'll be there."

That was the point at which she had almost changed her mind, but she was committed, as if a magnetic force was pulling her in this new direction. The change of momentum was almost inevitable: she couldn't stay where she was, not for another moment.

The minute he had driven out of the station car park she had bought her ticket to Heathrow.

She had met Gene at the Temple Bar, a short distance from her hotel. He had been thrilled when she messaged him to say that—coincidentally—she was due to be in Dublin visiting a friend so why didn't they meet up, and had suggested the bar, which had become a favorite in the three weeks the production had been there so far. They were all still with him when she arrived, and she had a sudden memory of how that had irritated her when they were together, his need always to be the center of any party. But the feeling disappeared almost as swiftly as it had come: she was relieved, confronted with the reality of him, of the actuality of her mad idea, that there were other people there to defuse the oddness of seeing him again.

He had spotted her almost immediately over the crowds of revelers in the pub, had thrown his arms wide, pushed forward, and swept her into a bear hug. He had always been the most tactile of men. Now he felt alien and utterly familiar at the same time. "Look at this!" he kept saying, so that she blushed. "This is my ex-wife! Francie! Look how gorgeous she is! How lucky was I, fellas, to be married to this girl?"

Francesca cannot remember the last time anyone called her a girl, but that is the beauty of seeing someone you knew in your youth. There will be a part of yourselves that only ever remembers each other in that way. "Lucky, but not smart enough to stay married to me," she had responded smartly.

Gene had clapped his hands over his heart. "Ouch! She's killing me already!" But it was said with warmth, and he had immediately turned to get her a drink. The more curious glances of his colleagues faded as they realized there was no drama, just two old friends enjoying a moment.

She had sat in the middle of the group for two hours. They were mostly crew: lighting technicians, sound men, gaffers, and runners. These were the people Gene had always felt most comfortable with, instead of the other actors (competition), directors, and producers (he had always had a problem with authority figures). She began to relax, nestled into the booth beside him, listening to the chatter around her as the drinks arrived again and again, the conversation flowed, funny stories were traded about other productions and badly behaved actors. Film gossip was always the best gossip, and Francesca was happy not to be the center of attention, just lodged neatly in another world, enjoying this holiday from her own, not having anybody's expectations or judgment around her.

There was a live band at nine, and they had ended up dancing to the Irish fiddle music, Gene swinging her round and round until she was dizzy, laughing, his large hands so familiar on her waist, his smile incessant, his enthusiasm joyous. She felt young again, silly, exchanging jokes with him about their life together, turning what had once been painful into performance. These people liked her, she could tell, leaning over the crowded table with their drinks, laughing with her as she told stories about Gene, against his vanity, his unreliability, and his chaos. He laughed the loudest, and without bitterness, no matter what she said. One of the things she had always enjoyed about him was his inability to either hide what he felt or bear a grudge. The past was the past, and all that mattered was that they were here now, two people who were once dear to each other, enjoying the moment.

The crew began to thin out at eleven, at a point when she was not drunk, but definitely merry, and he walked her a little way around Dublin to show her the sights, stopping under the sodium lights to acknowledge the people who recognized him, to share a joke or pose for a picture. It was as if performance was in his blood. Gene had always drawn his energy from the people around him, and Dublin suited him, because people met him where he was, with equal life, equal jokes, equal ready affection. He had handed her an envelope of money—proceeds from the film work—that he said he owed her. She didn't want to accept it but he insisted "I'm doing good just now. Put it in a savings account for her, if nothing else." He wanted to talk to her about Lila, about her baby, but she hadn't wanted to be reminded of that part of their lives together, so she had switched the conversation. Gratifyingly, it had been only a matter of minutes before another group of people leaving a pub had recognized him, and stopped to shoot the breeze and he had been distracted again. Perhaps that was the point at which she should have removed his arm from around her waist, but it was so pleasant just to lean into him, to remember the ghost of her youth. She felt giddy, adventurous. It was the shortest leap to suggest they go back to her hotel for a drink, the laughter of the evening still ringing in her ears. An even shorter leap for that to become two drinks. And then taking him into her bed hadn't felt like a decision at all. It was, after all, what her body wanted.

FRANCESCA LIES IN the hotel bed in the gray morning light and gazes at Gene's broad back, noting the slight sag in his skin, the gray coming through the dye in his hair, hearing his intermittent snores, and realizes, with the sickest of feelings, that she has made a colossal, colossal mistake. She could recall her reasoning: *If I was to have an adventure, who would be the best possible person to do that with?* Gene had been the obvious answer: who else did she know who was likely to offer her a night or two of fun and romance and walk away afterward without a backward glance? Gene had seemed like the safest possible option, the man-child of her twenties, the guy who was going to make her feel glorious and young again, then bounce happily onward from situation to situation for the rest of his life. And that was exactly how it had worked. The sex had been wonderful—he always was the most joyous and easiest of lovers—and she could remember the moment when she had felt she had occupied every inch of herself again, as if she had been restored to the person she once was. *I'm here*, she had wanted to shout, with surprise. *I'm still in here.*

And then Gene had ruined it.

She had climbed blearily out of bed and padded to the bathroom, brushing her teeth and already planning her escape. She would shower, hoping he would not be woken by the noise, leave him a note, and go out for breakfast, trusting he would be gone when she returned. And when she emerged, instead of being fast asleep as she had expected (he was always the type to drop off immediately after sex, and would stay soundly asleep until mid-morning), she had opened the bathroom door to find him sitting up and gazing directly at her. "I always wondered," he said, "and now I know."

He had this big, goofy grin on his face, and his expression was tender.

"Wondered what?" She had felt herself tense slightly. Some part of her already wanted to ask him to leave, but it seemed rude after what had happened.

"Whether we would find our way back to each other." He pulled back the covers, waiting for her to get in beside him. "I never dared hope after what I did. But when you texted me, it was like this little light came on—like a lighthouse in an ocean—and I felt like *Oh. Here it is. It's all going to be okay.*"

She climbed in, a little awkwardly. When she sat back against the headboard, she made sure her body was not touching his. "I'm not quite sure what you mean."

"Us. The old team. Back together." His eyes had grown soft, and he had taken her hand in his two enormous paws, and kissed it. "I was an idiot, Francie. I was young and impulsive and I think the reason I never managed to settle with anyone was because I was always still in love with you. I spent years thinking about it, how I had thrown away the best thing that ever happened to me."

"Don't be ridiculous," she had said, laughing, and pushing his hands away. "You're a free spirit. You always told me that."

"No. No. I know you think I'm an idiot who doesn't take anything seriously, but I never stopped loving you. When you got together with— with that guy, it killed me. I actually went a little nuts for a while. I knew that you and I were meant to be together. I never called you because I was trying to respect your decision. I knew how much I had hurt you,

WE ALL LIVE HERE

and I knew I didn't deserve another turn around the block. But when you said you were coming out here, it was like something in me that had died suddenly sprang to life again. I'm just . . . I'm just so happy you gave me—gave us—another chance."

Francesca started to feel a rising panic. "Gene, it's not like that."

"What do you mean, kiddo?"

"I—I'm still with Bill."

He paused to take this in. "You're still with Bill?"

"I came out here because—I don't know. I was stuck. I just—I wanted to feel something again. And it's been lovely. But . . . this is it. This stops here."

He had looked so shocked and hurt that something in her had keeled over.

"You—you . . . This didn't mean anything?"

She shook her head. "I didn't think for a minute you'd have real feelings for me."

There had been a long silence, his eyes never leaving her face, as if he was searching for evidence that what she had just said was wrong, that she was still joking.

"But—but what just happened with us. We're good together, Francie. It's our time."

"No, no, it's not."

She had looked at the slow dawning on his face and wanted to die. "I'm sorry," she said. "I made—I made a thoughtless mistake."

He had looked so uncomprehending. "I'm a . . . *mistake*?"

He had left not long after that. The worst part of it had been how gentlemanly he had been. He hadn't thrown a strop, or shouted at her, or accused her of misleading him. He had seemed so diminished, as if she had just sucked all the life out of him. She had watched him stumbling around the hotel bedroom picking up his things and climbing into them and half of her had wanted to hug him and tell him how sorry she was, but the other half just wanted him to go, as quickly as he could, so that she could begin the awful business of pretending this had never happened. She had thought he might try to hug her before he left, but instead he had just stood awkwardly at the door and reached out a hand, touching her lightly on the arm.

"It was lovely to see you, Francie," he had said, trying to raise a smile. "Be happy."

And then, as she watched him walk down the hotel corridor he had turned, and she thought she had never seen him look so raw, so vulnerable.

"You know," he said, "if you ever change your mind . . ."

She could have given him that. She could have just said, "I know." It would have meant nothing, after all. But she had moved her head slowly from left to right and said quietly and firmly, "I won't."

SHE HAD NEVER spoken to Gene again. She deleted his number from her phone, and spent the next day shopping almost manically, in an effort to persuade herself that she was the person she had been two days previously. She spent Gene's money—two jumpers for Bill, cashmere round-necks she could barely afford, and a dress for Lila's baby. She removed the bags and the price tags, so that nobody would guess they had come from Ireland, and the effort involved in this duplicity made her feel even worse. She ate alone downstairs in the hotel restaurant and watched television for the rest of the evening. By the time she flew home she had almost convinced herself she had been alone the whole time, that she had merely changed her planned location. And who could blame her for that?

But Francesca McKenzie was nothing if not a positive thinker. In those final hours in Dublin she told herself that sometimes it was necessary to make a mistake to persuade yourself of what was right and important. She told herself that the whole episode had only reinforced her love for Bill. She knew she would never make a mistake like that again. She would be the best wife to him. She would be with that sweet, kind, reliable man for the rest of her life.

And when she got home, she slept for eight hours straight.

Chapter Thirty-six

Lila

If having Bill live with them as a fully functioning adult had been a little challenging at times, living with Bill post-heart-attack is definitely tougher than Lila had anticipated. He is anxious about everything, what he eats, the state of the house, his medications, and whether he is taking them in the right order (he is: Lila has bought a selection of those days-of-the-week pill pockets from the local pharmacy and Penelope double-checks them every day). He is little trouble in that he asks for nothing, and does his best to help around the house, but Lila feels the cloud of anxiety settle over her home, like a permanent fog. If she offers to do things for him, he resists firmly, insisting that he is perfectly capable, thank you. But if she cleans the kitchen he cannot help but tidy up after her, and if she tells him to stop and rest, he sits uncomfortably, radiating discontent, or unable to help himself issuing instructions that she has missed a bit, or that Truant is hoovering up something unmentionable on the floor. She has done her best to warn the girls that Bill requires peace and quiet, but there is only so far that you can restrict an eight-year-old with a penchant for YouTube videos and loud rap music, and a teenage girl who believes all doors must be closed emphatically. Bill bears these incursions into what he clearly believes should be silence with a pained expression, or suggests to Penelope that they move upstairs to his bedroom "so I can hear myself think."

Penelope is equally anxious, fluttering around him, trying to anticipate his needs, while apologizing to Lila repeatedly for being in the way. The girls, having greeted Bill's homecoming with heartfelt, emotional hugs and kisses, have promptly forgotten it all, accepting his presence with the same benign lack of interest that they always had.

She suspects increasingly that they miss Gene. They do not talk about him, but he had a way of being around them that seemed to accept their chaos, their sudden emotions, and absorb it all. She hates to admit it, but there was also a cheeriness that is now absent in their domestic setting, and worsened by Bill's stay in hospital. Eleanor is busy at work again, and without her, Jensen, and Gene, the house is sorely missing the upbeat energy that they had brought with them.

Dan is still spending most of his time at the hospital. Apparently Marja will probably stay in until the birth. In the short phone calls he has made to tell her, he has sounded more stressed than Lila is. Lila feels it is probably beyond her to express sympathy for his predicament. She simply calls the girls downstairs to speak to him and tries not to note that their conversations with him last barely minutes too.

She cannot blame Bill for any of it—he has suffered a near-death experience—but juggling the needs of three very different generations is exhausting, and after a matter of days, Lila is beginning to flag.

Jensen has not responded to her letter. She hadn't really expected him to. She had sent a text thanking him again for his kindness, and for helping with the tree, but she daren't say anything beyond that because of his new girlfriend. She tells herself to let it go. To put him, as she has put Gabriel Mallory, into the past. It turns out that knowing something is entirely your fault does not necessarily help you get over it.

LILA HAD PROMISED Violet that she would pick her up from school that afternoon. Things at home have been so unsettled that it feels necessary to impose some order, some attempt at routine. She checks that Penelope can stay with Bill while she walks the short distance to school, trying to remember the things she has promised to buy on the way home: limescale remover (Bill apparently feels the bathroom has deteriorated in his absence), mackerel for heart health (the girls are going to love that), and a copy of the *Radio Times*, now that Bill has apparently adapted to daytime television (he enjoys the antiques shows and the general-knowledge quizzes, harrumphs at the panelists and criticizes their grammar). As she walks, she thinks about Jessie. She has not heard from her since that day in the art shop, and hopes she's okay. She would have liked to text her but she suspects further contact will be too weird after the circumstances of their meeting. Lila may well be someone that Jessie would prefer to forget. Lila sighs a little at the thought of yet more awkwardness at the school gates and feels another surge of irritation at Gabriel Mallory's ability to create problems for other people.

There is a queue at the supermarket and she is a little late so the playground is already busy with parents and children when she arrives. She stands on tiptoe, trying to spot Violet in the throng of brightly colored puffy coats and lunch boxes. She spies a couple of her classmates, then sees Violet at the far end of the playground, playing on the equipment, her turquoise and black anorak standing out above the metal bars. She begins to make her way through the playground, waving a hand and calling her name above the noise.

"I'm surprised *you* have the gall to show your face."

It takes Lila a second to realize that this is directed at her. She turns, and there is Philippa Graham, her mouth set in a thin line of judgment, her chin lifted. "I'm sorry?"

"Everyone else at this school does their bit. But not you. Oh, no. You just swan around behaving like you're somehow above it all, no matter the cost to everybody else."

Lila stops and blinks. "What are you talking about?"

"The costumes? The one thing you were asked to do? For the children's production? If you really couldn't manage them you could have told someone. Then one of us could have picked up the slack although, frankly, most of us are already covering several bases—as well as our regular reading slots with the year ones."

Oh, God. The bloody costumes.

"So now the production is going to be a laughing stock. All because you simply couldn't be bothered."

Lila opens her mouth to speak—even though she has nothing useful to say—but a male voice cuts in. "Back off, Philippa."

She spins round. Dan is standing behind her. At his hip stands Hugo, his coat buttoned under his chin, holding Dan's hand tightly.

"You have no idea what Lila has been dealing with. Her father had a massive heart attack. Lila has been in hospital with him, while trying to look after our girls. Sorting out costumes for a primary-school play would, I imagine, have been pretty low on her list of priorities."

Philippa looks awkward. She glances from Dan to Lila. "Well, I didn't know."

"Quite. You didn't know. You know very little about anyone's lives beyond what they choose to tell you. So, instead of attacking Lila, maybe a starting point might have been to ask if there was anything you could do to help. Anyway. As I understand it there are now other arrangements in place."

"Well, I had heard something." Philippa is the kind of woman who hates the suggestion that there is any element of school life she might not be aware of.

"In which case there is no need to attack my ex-wife, is there?" Dan's face is drawn, dark shadows circling his eyes. He looks exhausted.

Philippa's mouth opens and closes. She turns to look for support from other mothers, but they have drifted swiftly away. She softens her tone. "I just think it would have been helpful if we had known that Lila couldn't manage the costumes. I don't believe that the proposed alternatives can be—"

"It's a primary-school production of *Peter Pan*, for Chrissake, not *Uncle Vanya* at the Old Vic. I genuinely don't think any parent watching is going to give two shits what their kids are wearing." Clearly exasperated, Dan turns from Philippa's startled expression and touches Lila's arm. They walk a couple of steps away, feeling her gaze burning into them.

"How is he?" says Dan.

Lila is still stunned by his intervention, and it takes her a moment to gather her thoughts. "Uh—okay. I mean, not okay. But I think he's good for now."

"I'm sorry I haven't been able to pick up the slack with the girls. It's been—" He shakes his head and lets out a long breath before he speaks again. "This thing with the placenta. They are literally trying to keep the baby inside her day to day just to give it . . . to give it a chance."

Lila stares at him, at the tension in his jaw as he speaks, at Hugo's wide eyes as he gazes up at them both. "I'm so sorry," she says. "I didn't know it was so serious."

"Yeah. Well. It didn't feel like information you needed."

They stand beside each other, in silence, this man she had once loved, and the child of his lover. She feels a strange sensation, unfamiliar and half forgotten. She thinks, with surprise, it might be sympathy. And then Hugo tugs at Dan's hand. "Can we go home?"

Dan's eyes slide toward Lila's, perhaps braced for her reaction to that word, and when there is none, he nods, his mouth compressed. "Yeah," he says. "Sure." He forces his face into a smile that isn't really a smile, and starts to move away. "Give Bill my love, will you?" he says, turning his head, as he leaves.

She nods. "Thank you," she says suddenly. "For sticking up for me, I mean."

He lifts his shoulders in a brief shrug that could mean any number of things.

"I—I hope she's okay," Lila says. "And the baby."

He nods again, not speaking, and then he and Hugo make their way slowly toward the school gates.

Chapter Thirty-seven

Bill lasted twelve days before he moved back to the bungalow. He announced his plans gently on Sunday morning, while Violet sat on the sofa in her pajamas playing a video game that seemed to emit either bleeps or explosions every five seconds. He explained that, while he loved being with Lila and the children, right now his need for his own quieter space was paramount. "Penelope is going to stay with me for a while," he said, when Lila had opened her mouth to protest. She had experienced a strange swell of mixed emotions: grief, at not being able to give him what he needed, but also relief, because she couldn't give him what he needed, not without locking her girls in the shed.

"Penelope is going to keep an eye on me. And it's probably time I worked out what to do with that bungalow. It can't stay empty forever."

He had it all planned out. Jensen's Polish friends were going to come in two days' time and move Bill's things, so that all he needed to do was oversee the process. Penelope had already been in and thoroughly cleaned and warmed the house. He would visit them still, he assured her. Perhaps even cook dinner occasionally. Everything was going to be fine.

Except Lila didn't feel everything was fine. She felt as if she was being abandoned all over again.

"I'm so sorry," she had said, holding his hand. "I'm so sorry it turned out like this." She suspected she might be holding it a little too tightly, but she couldn't help herself.

"Not your fault, darling girl." He had placed his other hand over hers. And then he straightened. "Anyway, I'm getting back to my usual self. Doing my exercises. The doctors are most satisfied with how things are going. And, of course, Penelope is a blessing. She'll keep an eye on me."

And now here they are on Monday morning, and Lila is watching the three heavyset Polish men wrestle once again with the piano on a pair of dollies. (Penelope has removed Bill to the kitchen for this one, sensing correctly that watching his beloved instrument swaying precariously on the tiny wheeled trolleys will not be good for his blood pressure.) His wardrobe has already been carried downstairs, with boxes full of his clothes and books, and loaded into the battered white van. It is only now, as she watches his belongings leaving her house, that she sees how much had ended up here.

Lila helps him into Penelope's car when the van's tail lift rises with a whine for the last time, and after a final round of sweet tea, the Polish men are ready to go.

"I'll come and see you later," Lila tells Bill, hugging him. "Let me know if you need anything. Anything at all."

"I'm fine, darling," he says, and gives her a reassuring smile.

"It's all under control," says Penelope, brightly. It has become her constant mantra, this last few weeks, no matter what is going on around them. *It's all under control!* she says through gritted teeth, or from a slightly manic smile. *It's all under control!*

"You're still coming to Violet's school play next Friday, though, yes?" Violet had brought home six tickets. Apparently divorced parents got special dispensation, and hospitalized grandparents further special privileges from Mrs. Tugendhat. Lila hopes this means she is forgiven for the costume debacle.

"Wouldn't miss it for the world," he says, with the relaxed expression of someone who is no longer going to have to wear earphones to drown out the sound of Public Enemy or *America's Next Top Model,* atop the frantic barking of a neurotic dog. "Oh, and, darling, they couldn't fit the garden bench into the van, so someone will come for it later. I hope that's okay."

Lila watches Penelope pull her red Ford Fiesta out carefully into the quiet road, indicating and driving at a steady 15 mph all the way up to the junction with the main road, even though it is a 30 mph limit and no other traffic is visible. *Bill will be safe with her,* she thinks, and that's something.

It is only when Lila steps back inside her house that it really hits her. Where the piano had sat in the hallway there is now just a dusty patch on the rug. The bookshelves have thinned, and the semi-reclining easy chair he had brought from home is now an empty gap in the middle of the living-room floor. Truant walks around slowly, sniffing suspiciously at the floor space where these items have disappeared. In the kitchen, recipe books are missing from the side, along with some of Bill's kitchen equipment, his Roberts radio, the blue willow fruit bowl he tried to keep full in case it encouraged the girls to eat better. She moves a pile of paperwork and a couple of bottles of detergent into the gaps, just to make it look less empty.

That is not going to be possible in Bill's bedroom. There is now just a bare bed. All the accoutrements of Bill's life—his rug, slippers, bedspread, wooden towel rail, his piles of reference books, 1970s Teasmade, and old magazines all gone, along with the rest of the furniture. Lila stands in the doorway and folds her arms firmly around her middle, gazing at the many layers of absence in the room. This is life at this age, she muses, a million goodbyes, and you never know which are the final ones. You just absorb them, like little shocks, trusting with each one that you'll be able to keep moving forward.

The only thing Bill has left behind is the portrait of her mother, resting against the fireplace that has never been lit. Lila turns it slowly, gazing at her mother's face within the ornate frame, and tries not to think about the hole that has lodged inside her where Francesca's memory used to live. She asks the question she has asked a thousand times since the discovery of the letter: *Why did you let yourself be seduced by him, Mum? Did you not even care how much that would destroy?* She gazes at Francesca's smile, at the serene expression that will never give her an answer. And then she turns it back, closes the bedroom door behind her, and heads downstairs.

Celie is picking Violet up from school on her way home, and Lila has supper to prepare.

JENSEN APPEARS AS she is clearing up. Supper had been subdued: the girls are clearly affected by the shift in atmosphere that comes with the knowledge that it is now just the three of them again. They had stopped asking about Gene some time ago. Lila wonders if they had absorbed, as she has, the notion that Gene is someone who is only ever likely to be seen in fleeting visions, a grandparent who is as unlikely to stick around as Bill has been steadfast. They had picked at their spaghetti, and in truth she had little appetite either, and had let them go as soon as they asked. Violet had retreated into the living room with Truant, and Celie had disappeared upstairs.

Lila has just loaded the plates into the dishwasher when she jumps at the sound of knocking. Jensen's face appears at the French windows, his ears tinged with red in the cold.

"I've come for Bill's bench."

She puts down the plates, her heart thumping, and goes to let him in. He steps over the threshold, bringing with him a bracing gust of cold air.

"Oh. Of course. I—I didn't realize it was going to be you." She is discombobulated by Jensen's sudden appearance in her kitchen, aware that she is not wearing makeup, that she is in the jeans with the mud spatters on them.

"They're still moving stuff around over there. I said it would be easiest for me to just put it in the pickup."

Lila peels off her rubber gloves, trying not to look at him. "I'll give you a hand," she says.

The bench, it turns out, weighs a lot less than she had thought. It takes a matter of minutes for the two of them to lift it into the back of the pickup truck. He closes the back and the sound is horribly final. Lila folds her arms across her chest as he secures it with webbing straps. They stand for a moment on the street, not looking at each other. This might be the last time she sees him, she thinks, now that Bill has gone. And something in her cannot bear the thought that she will never be able to explain herself properly.

"I don't suppose you'd like a cup of tea?" she blurts out. "I—I was just about to put the kettle on."

He looks off to the left, his hands thrust deep in his pockets. And then his shoulders lower a fraction. "Sure," he says. "Why not?"

They walk into the house through the back, and Lila is confronted for the first time by the sight of the memorial garden without the bench in it. Somehow more seems to have disappeared from it than just a bench. It looks now like a hollow corner, an empty space, no longer the focal point of anything.

"I think I should probably get another bench," she says, her voice a little shaky.

"Yeah," says Jensen, pausing to study the space. "It definitely needs something."

She makes the tea in silence and they sit down at the kitchen table. Lila positions herself with her back to the garden, wanting suddenly not to look at any of it, as if the missing garden furniture now somehow symbolizes something so much greater. Jensen keeps his jacket on, as if he is primed to leave as quickly as possible. Perhaps he is just being polite by agreeing to the tea. She feels self-conscious now in his presence. She tries to work out how to open the conversation, but finds that she is already anticipating his every response, and it keeps stopping the words as they form in her mouth.

He asks a few questions about Bill, which eases things. She tells him the story of what had happened, of Penelope, and the girls, and her mixed feelings at him moving out. He tells her he'll be popping into the bungalow every day. That he often did even before the heart attack so Bill will see nothing unusual in it, and she is grateful for his diplomacy.

"So where's Gene?"

"Gone." She explains briefly about the letter in the attic. She wants to say more, about how she feels like she's lost her mother along with her father, how angry she feels with both of them, but it sounds stupid and childish and she, of all people, has probably forfeited the right to talk about how she feels in front of Jensen.

The tea is drained from their mugs. They sit in silence, watching Truant pace backward and forward. He does not like change either.

"I got your letter," he says.

She waits for a moment before she says: "It's all canceled. All of it. I'm not writing a book any more."

He gazes at his empty mug.

"It was a stupid idea. I've actually wanted to tell you that, and to say

I'm sorry in person too. So many times. I would have called . . . but after your girlfriend—"

He looks up sharply.

"I mean, she was right, obviously. I'm not trying to defend myself. But it was clear what she thought—the conversations you must have had about it . . . I guess. I didn't want to do or say anything that might cause you further . . ." Her words keep congealing in her mouth.

"What girlfriend?"

Lila blinks. "The one in the supermarket?" When he still looks blank she says, "Red hair?"

He pulls a face. "You mean my sister."

Lila stares at him.

"My sister. Nathalie. I told you about her. She—I was a bit knocked sideways by what happened. And she just, well, hung out with me for a couple of days. Just to make sure I was okay. I think they get worried after . . . you know . . ."

Lila wants to apologize again, to acknowledge her part in his hurt, but all she can think is *That's not your girlfriend.* "Oh," she says, and then, "Oh."

When she looks up he is gazing at her. "You thought I had a girl-friend."

"Well, I didn't think you'd hang around for long." She raises a smile. "You're clearly a catch."

"A catch." He raises his eyebrows. There is a sudden hint of a smile, and it's the loveliest thing she's seen for weeks, and suddenly she's talking, the words spilling out of her.

"Jensen, I'm so, so sorry. I just . . . I fucked everything up. I was still so messed up about Dan and Marja and a million other things and I was panicking about money and I just—I just didn't think things through properly. I know it was a hideous, hideous thing to even think of doing. I just—I'm not that person. I can see everything that was wrong with it now—I can see it all so clearly. I just hate that you think I'm this person, and all I can tell you is I'm doing everything possible to show you I'm not. I was for a moment, obviously, but that's not me. Not the real me. Maybe I don't even know who the real me is right now. But I'm trying to make sure it's someone better."

She stutters to a halt. "Oh, God, did that make any sense?"

"Am I allowed to therapize it?"

"No."

"Okay. Then it makes perfect sense."

"Can you forgive me? Even a bit?"

"I can forgive most of it." He rubs at a mark on the table. "Maybe not the reference to my 'homely body.'"

"You were the one who said you had a dadbod."

"Yeah, but the dadbod has an intimation of something sexy about it. A homely body is . . ." He pulls a face. ". . . sexless."

"Nope. You're wrong."

"I'm wrong."

"The—uh—evidence of that night would tell you that wasn't true. And, anyway, I told you I was disguising the truth. If I was going to write about you honestly as yourself, obviously I would have said I'd spent the night with a David Gandy lookalike."

He tilts his head. "Nice recovery."

"Anyway. I personally like a dadbod. It's . . . far sexier than a six-pack."

"Okay, now you've ruined it."

"I'm serious. I can't think of anything worse than some man prancing around displaying his abs. It would make me feel hopelessly inadequate."

"I don't know why. You have a fabulous body."

They both blush.

She gazes at his hands as they sit in silence, trying not to think about how those hands had felt on her, the capability of them, their reassuring strength. He looks as if he's about to speak, then changes his mind. Both of them fall back into silence.

"Well. Thanks for letting me apologize in person," she says, eventually. She thinks there is no point not being honest. What does she have to lose after all? "I—I just miss you being around. A lot."

When he doesn't speak she says, "I'm not trying to pressure you or anything. But I just needed you to know that. In case I never see you again."

"That's a bit dramatic."

"Well, you could be moving to South America for all I know."

"To get over my heartbreak?"

"Okay. Now you're being annoying."

He grins. He gazes into his mug. And then he looks up. "Do you want to go out Friday?"

It takes her a moment to make sure she heard him correctly. "Yes," she says. And then, with a big smile, "Yes." And then her smile disappears. "Oh, no. I can't. That's Violet's school play. Can we do Saturday?"

"I have to go back to Winchester. I've got another ten days' work down there."

"Thursday?"

"I've promised to see my parents."

She cannot let him go. She cannot. She thinks. "Then . . . would you . . . like to come to a particularly chaotic primary-school production of *Peter Pan*? Maybe we can grab a bite afterward? Bill can be your chaperone if you're worried I'm going to jump your bones."

"Can you make sure he sits between us at all times?"

"Penelope too. I'll have a whole human wall to prevent unnecessary touching."

"Then that sounds magical," he says.

He does not kiss her when he leaves, even though every bit of her wants him to. She understands that too much has passed between them for all but the most careful of steps forward. But he touches her hand fleetingly, and tells her he's glad they've spoken.

She stands on the front doorstep, her arms wrapped round her against the cold, trying not to beam as he climbs into his truck. He lifts his hand from the driver's seat, a salute, and she raises hers back. She waits for him to start the ignition. And then, abruptly, he climbs out and half walks, half jogs up the path and sweeps her into a big bear hug. And he says into her ear, quietly so that his voice is barely a murmur, "I really bloody missed you too."

Chapter Thirty-eight

Eleanor is packing in the swift, hyper-efficient way that she always packs: clothes rolled up in dry-cleaner's plastic covers, still on their hangers, to be pulled out and hung straight up in whatever locations she moves to, two pairs of flat shoes in shoe bags, a small bag of toiletries, all placed in the small case with the precision of a Japanese puzzle, and two enormous wheeled cases full of makeup. It would take Lila four hours to pack what Eleanor packs in twenty minutes. Years of practice, Eleanor always says cheerfully. She is off to Paris at four thirty the following morning for a six-week film shoot, and is brisk, focused, and a tiny bit distant, as she always is when she's about to head off on location.

"Well, I think it's great," she says, folding seven pairs of knickers and two bras into tissue paper.

"You do? Why tissue paper?"

"It's expensive lingerie. I don't want it touching anything else. Can you get me a toothpaste out of the bathroom cabinet?"

Lila goes to fetch it and hands her the tube. It's the same brand that Gene advertised not so long ago. She finds this faintly irritating, as if Gene has somehow got his tendrils into Eleanor too. "I told Jensen I'd missed him. And I did give him a massive apology."

Eleanor pulls a face. "I guess that's a start. But you'll have to do more than that. This is your time to have grown-up relationships, open communication." She closes her suitcase with a grunt and straightens. "Seriously. He's a good, straightforward man. Be good and straightforward back."

"Should I tell him what happened with Gabriel Mallory? Maybe I should."

Eleanor frowns, and lugs her suitcase toward the door. She stops and considers this for a minute. "I don't know. One massive lapse in judgment could probably be put down to misfortune. Two looks like . . . carelessness."

"In other words I'm the dickhead."

"You could be. I think you're going to have to judge that one for yourself. But, hey, it's lovely news! The only decent man in the whole of London is back!"

"And you're going to Paris!"

"To eat a ton of cheese and be flirted with inappropriately by French crew!"

"Living the dream, El." Lila hugs her friend fiercely. "Don't you dare decide to do an *Eat Pray Love* and not come back. You know I make terrible choices when you're not around." She's joking, but there's always an undercurrent of fear. Lila is not sure she would know who she was without Eleanor around. It's a constant revelation to her, the way these friendships become more important the older they get.

"You'll have to grow up one day, you know."

"I will when you will."

"When you put it like that . . ."

• • •

LILA RETURNS FROM Eleanor's flat to find Jane waiting on her front step, her long gray hair floating around her face in the gusty wind. She meets Lila with a beatific smile. She has come, she says, for Gene's things.

"Is he with you?" Lila opens the front door, shooing Truant inside.

"He has been. But Elijah—my partner—is growing a little weary of his energy, and I've told him he has to make alternative arrangements."

"So you've come to ask if I'll take him back."

"No, no, Lila. I've merely come to pick up two boxes of his. He says they're clearly marked. Could you show me where I might find the attic?"

Jane's serenity could be marketed and bottled. Lila cannot imagine any world event that would prompt more than a head tilt and a faint smile as Jane considered the implications. She does something called holistic massage, which apparently takes in the emotional and spiritual concerns of the client, and she takes care, she says, to stay contained, and not absorb other people's energy. "It would be overwhelming," she says, in the calm tones of one who is never remotely overwhelmed.

Lila pulls down the loft ladder and climbs up first, peering down to the end of the attic. There are only two boxes marked GENE still here; he must have taken the others when he left. She hauls them to the loft hatch and passes them out to Jane. "I think that's it," she says, as she makes her way back down the ladder.

She helps Jane carry the boxes to her car, placing them in the boot. They are bulkier than they are heavy. And now there is no remnant of either of her fathers left in her house. It's almost as if they have never been here at all. She resists the urge to ask how Gene is, what he is doing, but Jane tells her unprompted that Gene has been invited to take part in a Comic Con. She says the words carefully, enunciating each syllable, as if it is something strange and exotic. There has been retrospective interest in Captain Troy Strang and the cast of *Star Squadron Zero*—one of the streaming services has announced it will be broadcasting series one to three—and he is attending the fan convention in a couple of weeks to meet viewers and sign autographs. Apparently the queues go around the block. Lila wonders briefly if they do or if this is another of Gene's embellishments. And then she wonders if there even is a Comic Con.

"Thank you, Lila. Shall I give him your love? I know he'd love to see you."

Lila closes the boot. "No. Thanks, anyway."

Jane straightens and gazes at Lila. It is a slightly unnerving experience, like having someone see right through you. She smiles. "Don't be too hard on him. He loves you. And he really did love your mother."

"He had a funny way of showing it."

"Lila, we all like to think we know everything about our parents, but we don't. Your father learned a lot of lessons too late. Certainly too late for him and me, but I retain a great deal of fondness for him. He is a good person."

Lila fights the urge to roll her eyes. "Maybe. But he doesn't deserve to stay here, Jane. Not with us."

Jane stands very still for a moment, perhaps considering this. "One of the things I come up against often in my practice is the notion of forgiveness. Do you want to repeat the mistakes your parents made? Holding on to your grievances for the rest of your life? Or do you want to put that burden down?"

"Jane, with respect—"

"Oh, don't use that phrase. 'With respect' is what people say when they're spiky and defensive."

"Well, maybe I am spiky and defensive when it comes to my father. You don't know him like I know him."

"Darling girl, I lived with him on and off for fifteen years. That's probably more time than you spent with him. And I'm going to tell you something. You do not know what happened between him and your mother. Casual infidelity I could have let go. The degree to which he was in love with her, I couldn't." As Lila struggles to make sense of what Jane is saying, she adds: "Your mother was not a fragile flower, nor was she easily bidden to do anything she didn't want to do. She was a strong woman and she had agency. She made her own decisions." She holds up a long, strong finger. "And before you say it, that doesn't make her a terrible person either. Life is long and complicated, Lila, and we all make mistakes. What matters is what we do beyond them. But if you're going to hold up your mother and your father as villains of the piece it will be misguided and it is ultimately you who will suffer."

"So you just forgave him. For shagging my mother."

"Of course. I chose not to be romantically involved with him anymore, but I will always be fond of him, and glad that we're in each other's lives. Have you never made a mistake?"

Lila thinks about Jensen, about the awful discarded chapter. Jane seems to note her flicker of uncertainty. "Well, I hope, if you have, that you were forgiven. I hope the person understood that you're only human. You can hang on to anger and bitterness your whole life. But all you really do is prolong your own pain. Just think about it. Put that burden down. For you and your daughters."

Lila accepts the kiss that Jane plants on her cheek. She smells of lavender and patchouli.

"It was lovely seeing you, Lila. Love to the girls too."

Lila waits until she has started the car. "He's still not coming back here," she calls, as Jane pulls out of the driveway. "Definitely not."

Jane smiles back, one hand lifted in a cheerful wave, so that Lila is unsure whether she heard her. The wave would probably have been the same either way.

• • •

LILA IS MOVING furniture when Anoushka calls. She has decided a new start is needed, that perhaps moving the sofa and the easy chairs will disguise what is missing, and the rooms will look intentionally min-imalist or, at least, better for the estate agent, once the house goes on the market. She has puffed and tugged the furniture from one end of the room to the other, has dug an old vase and jug out of one of the removal boxes in the garage that was never unpacked, and placed them artfully on the kitchen surfaces to hide the absence of Bill's things. She has moved rugs and rehung pictures. She keeps telling herself that a house is just bricks and mortar. She will create a new home wherever they end up. They will be fine by themselves.

She is so busy dragging the television cabinet round to the far wall that she almost misses the call, and answers it breathless and a little sweaty.

"Darling. Have you got a minute?"

"Anoushka! Sure!" Lila glances up in the wall mirror and sees that she has a black smudge on her face. She rubs at it.

"I've had an idea. Just had a meeting with a new client—very success-ful actress. She wants to do a memoir. There's a huge appetite for memoir right now, especially the really spicy ones. I think it will be marvelous." She lets this dangle.

"I thought I'd already explained the reasons I can't do a memoir."

"Not your own, darling. I thought you could be her ghost."

"Her what?"

"Her ghost. She can't write for toffee. She tells you the stories, you turn it all into a wonderful book. We know you can write, and you're a marvel at shaping anecdotes. And I think it would be great fun—she's a namedropper *nonpareil*."

When Lila doesn't say anything, Anoushka adds: "It doesn't pay fan-tastically, I mean not like your advance for the other thing. There would be no royalties. But we can use the success of *The Rebuild* to demand a written credit. Some people quite like that, you know, especially if the writer has a bit of prestige. I think we could negotiate a fairly decent standalone sum."

"I would write someone else's memoir?"

"Exactly! It would keep you in the game until you know what you want to do next, and keep you employed for a few months. And if it does well, you'll be in demand for more of them. A nice little money-spinner and your personal life doesn't have to be anywhere near it. Shall I put your name forward?"

"Is she nice?"

"Darling, she doesn't have to be nice. She's a hoot. It's all good material."

This is Anoushka-speak for *She is an absolute nightmare.*

"Who is it?"

Anoushka whispers the name of a well-known soap actress, whose battles with alcohol and tempestuous relationships have been well documented in the tabloid press. You would not believe the sexual escapades, Anoushka says, in a voice that could be conveying shock or awed admiration, it is not clear which. She mutters something about Saudi princes, something else about an A-list movie star, and possibly the words "guinea pig."

"Uhh . . . maybe," says Lila, uncertainly, having decided not to ask for clarification. "I guess you could put my name forward. I'll think about it."

"Good-oh! I'll get on to her agent."

Lila thinks about the ghostwriting for the rest of the day while she's sorting out the house. She looks up a few interviews with the actress. The subtext of each is *absolute car-crash.* She tells the girls when they get home and they express mild interest, distracted by their various electronic devices, in the way that they usually do about her writing projects. But when she asks them over supper what they think about possibly moving house, their response is immediate and dramatic.

"Why? I don't want to move." Violet's eyes widen and she drops the iPad onto the table.

"I just thought . . . well, now that Bill has gone back to his house, and Gene has . . . Gene's going to be working elsewhere, maybe we could buy a smaller house. It would be more economical. And easier to look after. You know how things are always going wrong here."

"But where would we go?"

"We'd stay in the area, just get somewhere a little smaller. Maybe three bedrooms instead of five. Maybe something modern."

They glance at each other swiftly and Lila is not sure what passes between them. "It would be a nice change?" she says gamely.

"I like our house," says Violet.

"I don't want to go anywhere else," says Celie, scowling. "This is our home."

"I don't want any more change," says Violet. "There's been too much change."

Her voice wobbles and she looks so close to tears that Lila backs down, says it was just an idea, hugs her daughter and says it's fine, it's all fine, that they'll stay, that nothing is going to change.

And when Anoushka calls the next day to say the actress is absolutely delighted, that *The Rebuild* is one of her favorite books, and she would love to meet Lila to discuss it next week, Lila says, with as much enthusiasm as she can muster, that she's delighted too.

Right now, the girls' stability is the most important thing. The actress doesn't have to be nice. And hopes she misheard the thing about the guinea pig.

Chapter Thirty-nine

Celie

❦

Mum has spent at least an hour in the bathroom getting ready. She's done her hair in waves with the curling iron, like she used to do when she was getting interviewed for one of her books, and she is wearing her dark pink velvet trouser suit, the one she only wears for special things, mostly because Truant's hair sticks to it. She doesn't look like someone going to a primary school play, but when she casually mentions that Jensen is going to join them, Celie swiftly puts the pieces together. When he arrives, in smart jeans and a dark blue shirt, Mum keeps smiling shyly at him, and being weirdly over-animated, but pretending to Celie that nothing's going on. It's like she thinks Celie is actually blind. But Jensen is all right. He doesn't seem the kind of guy Martin's mum went out with before her current boyfriend, who made it clear he didn't like having her kids around, and always held the remote control so that Martin couldn't watch his own programs.

> My mum keeps doing this stupid fake
> laugh when Jensen says something funny.
> It's actually embarrassing.

Martin's response is immediate.

> My mum used to put on this posh voice. I
> used to call her Your Majesty when he
> was around just to wind her up.

They travel in Jensen's pickup truck. It has three seats in the front, which is actually quite cool, not that Celie is going to let them know she thinks that. Bill, Mum says, is going to meet them there with Penelope. When they get to the school Penelope is helping Bill out of the car, like he's an invalid or something. He's wearing his tweedy suit with the matching waistcoat and Penelope has dressed up in a sort of Chinese silk shawl with a big sparkly comb in her hair. It's kind of amazing that people that old even try.

Dad had texted to say he was coming to the play but told her he would be sitting with Marja's mother because Marja is still in the hospital and Hugo is "a bit wobbly." He still hasn't said anything about the perfumes. She thinks he's worried about the baby and a piece of her wants to thank the baby because she's secretly glad that it's keeping the attention off her. Celie mostly just hopes her mum and dad aren't going to start arguing, like they did at the Christmas pantomime.

The school is already packed with people, even though Celie thought they would be early. She spies a couple of her old teachers and ducks away so that she won't have to talk to them. People are helping themselves to glasses of wine from a long table at the back and taking their seats, dads looking like they'd rather be at the office, and mums trying to control small children. There are paper cups of squash and chocolate biscuits on the end table for the kids. Celie takes two and puts them into her pocket in case she gets hungry in the performance. She is a bit cross with Mum for insisting that she comes to the stupid play. She has to get her character studies finished for Animation Club, and they are going to take hours, and she still can't do hands that don't have sausage fingers. She spots her dad on the right-hand side of the seated area. When he stands and waves she makes her way over to say hello, hoping Mum won't notice because she and Jensen are finding seats with Bill and Penelope. Even though Mum would say it's fine to sit with Dad, she knows, but it would probably make Mum feel weird, and then she would hide it by being *über*-cheerful and acting like everything was totally fine, which sort of feels worse. Sometimes she feels exhausted by all the feelings going on in her family all the time.

It feels odd not having seen her dad for this long, like he doesn't even belong to her family anymore. He looks older than he did when she last saw him and he definitely needs a haircut. Marja's mother, who is very glamorous for an old woman, with thick blonde hair like Marja's, stands up to give her a hug and Celie accepts it, though it feels a bit uncomfortable. She's not like her actual grandmother or anything. But then, she observes, neither is Bill. Maybe her family is just going to be this endless bunch of not-quite-connected people from now on.

Dad seems grateful that she took the hug. He keeps touching her shoulder and saying it's good to see her and he's sorry he hasn't been around. Celie doesn't want to tell him she's been quite happy without him.

Then Dad asks her who Violet is playing and Celie says she doesn't know. He says Hugo has a big part and he's very nervous about remembering his lines, like Celie's meant to care, and Celie tries to look interested, because Dad always wants her to act like Hugo is her brother. Really all she wants to do is head back to her seat because she's worried that Mum won't save her one and then she'll have to sit next to people she doesn't know, so she says she has to go to the loo, walks around the back of the main hall, and comes in again on the other side just so it won't hurt his feelings.

Mrs. Tugendhat, who looks exactly the same as she did five years ago when Celie left, comes over and tells Celie she can't believe how much she's grown (why do old people always say this?), then takes Mum to one side and says her father is amazing, that he's been amazing. Everything is going to be amazing. Mum glances at Bill and looks a bit confused. Celie is watching them, trying to work out what is coming next, but then someone comes up and whispers something to Mrs. Tugendhat, who makes her apologies and hurries away backstage.

It turns out Mum has saved her a seat—right beside her, with Jensen on Mum's left, and Bill and Penelope beside them. They are four rows behind Dad and Marja's mother and Celie feels anxious because Mum will definitely be able to see them, though at least Marja isn't there. Penelope keeps fussing around Bill, asking if he's warm enough and checking he's happy with his water. Celie can tell he's a bit irritated by it, but he pats Penelope's hand and tells her she's very kind and really must stop worrying. So Penelope keeps pointing out kids she's taught piano to, then blushing, like she's boasting or something.

If my mum and dad have another fight here I am going to kill myself, she texts Martin.

Hey, at least it will get you out of watching a kids' play, he responds.

The wooden chairs are the exact same ones from when she was at school here. Celie has a weird flash of memory sitting in one: the feeling of boredom and safety that she always had at primary school, before everything went wrong, before her friendships evaporated and Mum and Dad split up.

And then it happens. She hears Mum say: "Ohhh, no." For a moment she thinks it's something to do with Dad and Marja and her stomach lurches, but when she looks up, following Mum's gaze, she sees Gene at the side of the hall, wearing his leather jacket and a really skanky T-shirt with a man smoking a joint on the front. He is making his way toward them. Mum looks at Jensen, and says something. She gets up, which is difficult because pretty much everyone else has sat down by now. Celie has not told Mum about Gene, and feels the knot of anxiety solidify inside her.

"Stay away. I've asked you to stay away. I do not want to risk anything happening to Bill. Why can't you see that?"

Celie is only four seats away from the end of the aisle and she can hear everything Mum is saying. She suspects all the other parents can hear it too, because everything has gone a bit quiet and people are definitely looking. She glances to her left. Jensen is watching Mum, and Bill is staring straight ahead but with the kind of tense look that says he knows Gene is there too.

"I just wanna talk to him." Gene's voice is always too loud.

"Absolutely not."

Oh, God, she texts Martin. My other granddad has turned up and he and Mum are fighting. Now I do want to die.

Martin doesn't respond for a minute and then he just says, Oh shit.

"Sweetheart," Gene is saying. "He needs to know the truth."

"He absolutely does not. You are not talking to him."

Everyone is looking now, heads swiveling, a low rumble of conversation rippling around the seats. Celie sinks in her chair. Why is her family literally the only family in the world who does this kind of thing? Why can't she just have a normal family where people turn up to stuff and get on with each other?

"Lila. Honey. Let me talk to him."

"Gene, I swear if you do not get out of my kid's school right now I am going to call the police and have you thrown out."

"Two minutes. That's all I'm asking."

Mum's face is pink and furious. She hisses at him. "Go home, Gene. I am going back to sit with Bill now, and you need to leave."

At the mention of the word "police," Jensen had risen and made his way past Celie toward Gene, meaning that the four people between have to stand up again. Oh, great. Now more people are involved. Someone in the chairs behind them is asking in a whiny voice what is going on. Celie wonders if she can just go and hide in the toilets. Mum comes and sits down beside her, and leans across, apologizing to Bill.

"We'll make sure he leaves. I'm so sorry."

Bill doesn't say anything.

Jensen is standing in front of Gene, pretty much blocking Gene's view of them. Gene puts his hand on Jensen's arm. "Jensen. Help me out here. I wanna sort this." As Celie watches, they have a whispered conversation. Jensen is leaning in close and nodding. Gene does not look like he's leaving any time soon. *Please just go*, Celie thinks, feeling the eyes of the whole school hall on her family. People in the front are actually turning round in their chairs to see what's going on.

Jensen makes his way back to Mum, which means that all the four people have to stand up and sit down again. They are starting to look a bit pissed off. Mum's face is all tight and furious. "Is he going?"

Jensen says quietly: "He wants to tell Bill something. He says he can tell him through me."

"What?"

"You don't want Bill to talk to him. But I can . . . pass it on via the phone? I actually think it might be helpful."

Lila looks at Jensen, disbelieving. "Oh, for Chrissake. How?"

"Just . . . just hear him out. And then he promises he'll leave."

Mum glances behind her at Bill, and then at Gene, who is hovering at the end of the aisle, watching them. She looks like she can't work out what to do. Her face softens a bit when she looks at Jensen and she lowers her voice. "Will you stop if you think it's going to make things worse? I don't want . . ."

Jensen puts a hand on hers. "I will be a very careful translator if necessary."

Mum thinks again, then sighs and turns to Bill. "Will you just hear what Gene has to say? Then he says he'll go."

Bill sort of harrumphs for a minute and then he glances sideways and says: "Well, he'd better hurry up. I don't want my granddaughter's performance interrupted."

The school orchestra has started filing in. There are tiny year threes with triangles and tambourines and bigger year sixes with guitars and a clarinet, all being shepherded into their red plastic seats at the front by a variety of teachers. Celie thinks that any minute this thing is going to start and her family will still be there bringing the drama. She sinks even lower in her seat. Jensen nods at Gene, and Celie watches Gene tap something into his phone. Jensen's phone rings with a disco tone, which causes a whole bunch of parents seated around them to tut and start shifting in their seats. Jensen holds up a hand in apology. He puts the phone to his ear and listens. Then he leans toward Bill.

"He wants to tell you there's been a big misunderstanding."

"I'm not interested in anything that man has to say." Bill looks straight ahead. Penelope is holding his hand tightly, running her thumb backward and forward over his knuckles.

Jensen looks at Bill, then holds the phone back to his ear. "He says he's not interested . . . Okay . . . okay." He listens, then leans toward Bill again. "He says you have the wrong idea about the time he and Francesca spent together. He realizes you think they had sex. They didn't. They just hung out."

"Had sex"? What is this? Now we're bringing old-people sex into this? Celie wants to throw up at the thought of people that old even *thinking* about having sex. She puts her face briefly into her hands. She is not sure this night could get any worse.

Jensen is still talking, his voice too loud, even though he's trying to be quiet. "He says she just wanted to party. To be young again. She hung out with Gene and the crew of the movie at a bar, she danced and had a good time, and the next day he didn't see her—he thinks she went shopping in Dublin. Or maybe to see her friend. But that was it."

Bill turns in his seat. "Then why on earth did he tell me he slept with her?"

"He didn't," says Mum, after a moment. "The letter just said she saw him."

Bill looks at Mum. "He didn't sleep with Francesca?"

Jensen says loudly into the phone: "Bill says you definitely didn't sleep with Francesca?"

They look at Gene, at the end of the row of parents. Gene shakes his head, and pulls a face. He says something into his phone. Jensen listens and says: "He says your mother would never have looked at another guy. This has all been a terrible misunderstanding."

Bill is clearly stunned. Almost as much as the parents around him, who cannot believe what they are listening to.

"You're absolutely certain?" says Bill.

Jensen speaks into the phone: "He says are you sure?"

Jensen nods at whatever Gene is saying. And then he puts his hand over the mouthpiece. "He says Bill, old pal, the drugs may have knocked out a good part of his gray matter, but he would definitely have remembered that. Sorry, Celie."

"Honestly, that is so not the worst part of this conversation."

Bill blinks. "Is he telling the truth?"

"Are you telling the truth?" Jensen nods again and turns back to Bill. "He says Scout's honor. He doesn't want to leave without you knowing the truth."

Something weird has happened to Bill. He is staring at his hands. And shaking his head to himself. And then he looks at Penelope. "Oh, my goodness," he says. "I feel rather foolish."

I feel sick, thinks Celie.

"You don't have to feel foolish, Bill," says Mum, her voice weird and sort of dull. "It was an easy misunderstanding to make."

Bill says again: "She didn't sleep with him."

Penelope is smiling at him in the gooey way she does. "Of course she didn't, darling. Of course there was an explanation for it."

Mum is staring at Gene. Bill is still in shock. "Oh, goodness," he says. "Oh, goodness. I seem to have caused a bit of a fuss."

No, they're telling him. No, no fuss. Not at all.

Someone has turned the overhead lights down. The school hall hushes. Jensen continues, whispering loudly as if nobody can hear him: "He says he's sorry for the misunderstanding and he realizes now he should have told you she'd visited Dublin but it was honestly such a small thing he didn't think anything of it at the time."

The orchestra has lifted their instruments. There is a music teacher Celie doesn't recognize standing in front of them, her hands raised like an actual conductor.

Bill looks at Gene. "Tell him thank you. Thank you for clearing that up. That's . . . very decent of him."

People have started to hiss around them now, telling them to be quiet, to please for goodness' sake stop talking. There are now about eight hundred reasons Celie wants to die. Jensen sits down beside Mum, leaning forward so that he can keep talking to Bill. "He says that's very decent of you . . . And he says any time you want to hang, he's down for it."

"Dear God." Bill rolls his eyes. "He never stops."

And then the music starts. Celie looks over but Gene has disappeared into the darkness. And when she turns back to her mother, Celie sees—with some surprise—that she looks like she's about to cry.

Chapter Forty

Lila

Lila cannot focus on the first few minutes of the performance. She is struggling to take in what has just happened, the way that Gene just lied to Bill. She keeps thinking about what Jane had said: *Infidelity I could have forgiven, the degree to which he was in love with her I could not.* There must be some ulterior reason Gene did what he'd done, she keeps telling herself. There always is with Gene.

Jensen, perhaps detecting her distance from proceedings, leans into her. "You okay?" he murmurs.

"That was so weird," she whispers back. "Because he definitely slept with Mum."

Jensen looks at her. "But why would he lie about it?"

"I have no idea." And then someone mutters, "*Do you mind?*" in an exasperated voice behind them, and Jensen shifts back toward his own seat. Violet has appeared on the stage. Violet, who is wearing an ill-fitting silver dress and is filled with the preternatural confidence she seems to have been born with, steps out without a moment's hesitation into the spotlight and begins narrating from a large paper scroll. The Darling children are in their bedrooms, their parents about to go out for the evening.

Lila lets out a breath, tries to push the last few minutes from her head, and settles into her hard wooden seat, just as she has settled into dozens of such school performances, braced for their odd mixture of poignancy and boredom, the way as a parent you can want these moments to last five minutes and a lifetime all at once. As Violet describes the scene before them, Lila's gaze flickers around the rest of the audience. Two rows in front, to the left, sits Philippa Graham, beside a balding man in a business suit, clearly just back from work. He has put an extra glass of red wine under his seat. She can just make out Gabriel Mallory down toward the front, seated beside his mother. He runs a hand through his floppy hair, checks his phone briefly, and then, perhaps aware he is being looked at, glances behind him. Lila makes sure her face is turned away. She feels almost nothing toward him now, oddly, except vague irritation that she will have to see him at the school gates for the next few years, like a bad meal repeating on you. A reminder of her vanity and stupidity, perhaps.

"He said I have to grow up and I don't want to grow up, Mother!" Wendy exclaims, on stage, scratching at her leg distractedly.

"Nobody wants to grow up, Wendy," says Mrs. Darling, in the exaggerated voice of a period-drama housekeeper. There is a low murmur of laughter in the audience.

And then, moments later, through a gap in the painted scenery, Peter Pan enters. Except Peter is not wearing green tights and a tunic. He is wearing . . . a burgundy two-piece uniform with silver epaulets and what looks like a ring of Saturn over his left breast. A low hum of surprise

422

ripples across the audience. The uniform is oddly familiar. Lila stares at it. And then she realizes: it is a *Star Squadron Zero* costume. It is one her father used to wear on the television show. A few minutes later the Lost Boys appear, and they are in *Star Squadron Zero* costumes too.

When Captain Hook comes on he is an alien, wearing a scaly head with a green elephant-like trunk. Lila knows it immediately: this was a television alien that terrified her during her childhood. It was the point at which Francesca insisted she stopped watching her father's show, blaming it for nightmares that lasted until Lila was almost ten. The entire production, she grasps now, is in *Star Squadron Zero* costumes. The script has been altered slightly—Captain Hook is an interplanetary villain, and the crocodile is a space lizard. The pirate ship is a space pirate ship and Neverland is now a planet, its backdrop one of those old-fashioned pictures of the moon's surface, with craters and a flag.

Around them the audience of parents laugh as the Lost Boys, in their oversized uniforms (if one looked closely it was just possible to make out the safety pins and rudimentary stitching holding them up), fight back against the space pirates. Tinkerbell is a flying astronaut, her hair a silver beehive similar to Troy Strang's once-recurrent love interest Vuleva.

Hugo is playing Michael, the youngest of the Darling children. Lila's heart always gives a reflexive lurch when she sees Hugo, as if he is the symbol of so much she has lost. He has no lines—or if he has he has forgotten them. His role seems to be to be propelled gently from one end of the stage to the other while the children declaim their lines around him, or are prompted by Mrs. Tugendhat from the side. Occasionally someone whispers in his ear but he seems utterly frozen.

The production staggers forward, through Neverland, the death by space lizard of Hook (which prompts good natured cheers from the audience), a slightly shambolic dance with what had been American Indians but are now space crew from another ship (their uniforms are gold Lurex with a definite seventies flare). There are songs, "You Can Fly!"

and "Following the Leader," taken from the film, the musical accompaniment comically raggle-taggle and only occasionally in tune, the tiny musicians shifting in their seats and periodically breaking off to wave surreptitiously at their parents. Beside her, Jensen keeps laughing, collapsing into giggles, apparently enjoying the chaos on the stage. He was so ready to come along and be part of it, happy to shape himself into her world, instead of expecting her to orbit around him. She finds herself sneaking glances at him, wondering that she had ever found him less attractive than Gabriel Mallory. She can barely sit beside him now without wanting to touch him, and as they watch, she reaches her hand across in the dark and slides it into his. His fingers close around hers unthinkingly, and he glances briefly toward her and smiles, as if this has surprised them both.

Around her Lila listens to the parents coo, or murmur to each other, the proud exclamations of grandparents as their child appears on cue, the soft mentions of names and surreptitious holding up of phones to take photographs, and feels something in her soften, some long-held tension start to evaporate, replaced instead by a sense of wonder, of the impermanence of things and how that, too, can be blissful and heartbreaking at the same time. Lila watches Violet as she emerges repeatedly from the wings to explain what is about to happen or to fill in some gap in the narrative, her voice clear and unwavering, and wonders what kind of young woman she will become. Will she hang on to that confidence? Or is life going to batter it out of her, squeeze her into a role she never asked for, in the way it does so many of us? *Stay the same, my darling*, she tells her silently. *Just stay who you are, fart jokes, inappropriate rap music and all.*

In the final scene Wendy, back in her nightie, is telling her mother about their adventures. "Look, Mother, see how well he sails the spaceship? Off to another galaxy!"

For once, it seems, "Michael" must speak. He turns and gazes out at the audience. The girl playing Wendy turns to Hugo. "Tell Mother—didn't we have an amazing adventure, Michael?" Mother waits attentively, Father hovering at her side, periodically adjusting his false mustache, which keeps slipping down the left of his face.

Nothing happens.

Wendy finally gives Hugo a vigorous nudge. Perhaps it is the reference to mothers that does for him. Perhaps it is the spotlight, or finally having to speak toward 150 rapt parents. But Hugo gazes out at the audience and his little face begins to crumple. Lila watches as, under the bright lights, a tear slides visibly down his face.

There is a certain kind of hush in a school hall that comes when it's clear that a child is actually traumatized on stage and nobody knows quite what to do. The small boy stands in the beam of light, unable to move. He gives a great, visible gulp. *Oh, no,* thinks Lila. *The poor child.* And then Celie stands up suddenly beside her. "Go, Hugo!" she calls to him. "You can do it!"

She starts to clap him, blushing furiously with anxiety even as she does. Hugo looks up, and he registers her. "Go, Hugo!" Celie says again.

Lila can see Dan in the half-light, making his way awkwardly along the line of chairs, other parents standing, shifting aside to let him through. He crouches at the side of the stage, trying to call something inaudible to Marja's son. The whole room is gazing at this small child for whom this night, perhaps these last few weeks, has clearly been too much.

"Yeah, Hugo!" says Celie. She glances anxiously at Lila, clearly afraid that this will be taken as a sign of her disloyalty. And something in Lila gives.

She finds she is on her feet beside her daughter.

"Yes, Hugo!" she says, and starts to clap. "Go on! You can do it!"

And suddenly a scattering of other parents are whooping and cheering, calling his name. A couple of the children step forward on the stage, encouraging him, murmuring at him, a swell of performative helpfulness rippling through the cast. Wendy steps forward and whispers in Hugo's ear. He nods then turns back to face the audience.

There is a hush. It feels as if the whole audience is holding its collective breath. His eyes widen, and for a moment he looks as if he's going to cry again. Then Hugo swallows, and his high child's voice breaks into the silence, wavering a little: "I—I knew Peter Pan would save us."

And suddenly Lila is clapping, and Celie is whooping, punching the air, and Jensen stands up beside her and shouts too. And the whole audience is clapping and cheering, so that whatever the last lines actually were are completely drowned in the applause. And Lila feels Jensen's fingers close around hers and something in her chest is bursting, tears are brimming in her eyes and with her other hand she takes Celie's, and their eyes meet, and Lila nods. *Good job*, she tells her daughter silently, and just for once, Celie smiles back, and takes it.

SHE IS ABOUT to head outside for some fresh air when Mrs. Tugendhat stops her, her face flushed, a hand pressed to her chest. "Oh, Lila, what a night. What an amazing job your father did. You know the children have adored working with him."

Lila doesn't need to ask what she means this time. She feels suddenly hollowed out from the evening's events. "I—It was an amazing production, Mrs. Tugendhat. Well done. I'm just so sorry I wasn't able to help more."

Mrs. Tugendhat is clearly giddy with relief that it has all gone off as planned. "Silver linings, my dear. Your father is a born teacher. The children were so enthusiastic to do it his way. They loved the costumes, even if some of them were a little full of moth! I don't think we've ever had a better production."

Lila is almost reluctant to ask. "How—how long has he been helping?"

"It must be four, five weeks now? It was very kind of you to suggest it,

Lila. Him bringing the costumes in was a blessing. But really it was the acting and the enthusiasm that brought it all to life. It's not often you get a genuine Hollywood star on your school production! And using actual Hollywood props! My old colleagues at St. Mary's are green with envy, I can tell you!"

She glances over the heads of the parents toward the back of the stage. "Now I must go and find Mr. Darling. Apparently there has been a little accident. Overexcitement, I think. Or maybe it was too much apple juice. Do excuse me."

BILL IS TIRED after the drama of the performance, and perhaps still digesting what he'd been told before the show, so after he and Penelope have made their way carefully to the end of the row of seats he tells Lila, clasping her arms, that they have had a lovely time but are going to head for home. "Please tell Violet I'm immensely proud of her. She was faultless. Faultless!"

Lila hugs him, breathing in his familiar old-man scent of tweed and soap. "I'll tell her, Bill. She'll be so happy that you came."

Around them people are making their way to the back of the room, grabbing final glasses of wine while their children change out of their costumes, comparing funny stories about the performance. Lila is grateful to have her family there. Just for once she doesn't feel like the awkward person who doesn't really fit, and she's shielded from the likes of Philippa Graham and Gabriel Mallory. She sees Dan, with Marja's mother, and he catches her eye and raises a hand, perhaps in thanks, perhaps just in greeting, she isn't sure. He looks, she thinks suddenly, like someone she doesn't really know anymore. Then she sees him register Jensen beside her, the faint flicker of something passing across his face, and realizes that perhaps, from now on, she is not the only one who is going to have to adapt.

Jensen has offered to take Bill and Penelope out to the car, just to make sure they're okay, and Lila tells him she's going backstage to find Violet. But it isn't just Violet she wants to see.

AS USUAL, YOU can hear him before you see him. He is in the backstage area, moving scenery with some of the bigger year sevens and eights. He's congratulating the children as they filter past, sporadically straightening up to give them high fives.

"Hamoud! My man! That was some guitar you were playing out there!" He stoops to pat a small alien shuffling past in an oversized costume, small trails of glitter in its wake. "Nancy? You were such a cool alien! I'll bet your parents didn't even know it was you in there!"

Lila stands and watches him, this man who can apparently be to other children what he never was to her. She has to move to the side as the pirate spaceship is carried past by two enormous boys and a caretaker, huffing slightly with the effort. And when it passes she sees Gene is looking at her, his expression a little wary, as if he's unsure what is about to happen. He fixes a smile on his face. "Hey, sweetheart. If you're looking for Violet, she's just getting out of her dress."

Lila takes a couple of steps closer to him. "You lied to Bill," she says.

"No, I didn't."

"I know you did. You're not that good an actor."

They stare at each other, like two prize fighters facing off.

And then Lila says: "It was . . . a nice thing."

Gene tilts his head, rubs at it with his right hand. He relaxes a little. "Huh." He shrugs. "Well, she did only want Bill. It seemed like the right thing to do."

"How long have you been seeing the girls? I'm guessing you've been coming here the whole time."

He grimaces. "Every day. Don't be hard on them. It's my fault. I

428

just . . . I knew you had your hands full. I didn't want them to think I'd deserted them. But I should've said. I'm sorry."

"Don't be." She stares at him, at his saggy, apologetic face. At his *I'm Sorry, I Was Probably High* T-shirt. At the way he clearly doesn't know what to do with any of his limbs.

"God, Dad." She throws up her hands. "Why can't you just let me hate you like a normal person?"

His face collapses a little. "Ah, don't hate me, Lila baby. You're killing me." He steps forward, and she feels his big arms surround her, the resoluteness of his hold on her. She feels, suddenly, as if she's four years old, before she knew he was leaving, before she felt that nothing would be reliable ever again. She stands and grips her father, ignoring the people moving stuff around them, the excited squeals of the children emerging from the changing rooms, Mrs. Tugendhat's urgent demands for kitchen roll from somewhere in the distance. She lets herself rest against him, holding him as tightly as he is holding her, wondering at the fact that finally, thirty-five years late, she may have been able to rely on her father more than she had realized. Finally she pulls back, and wipes at her face, trying to pull herself together.

"So. What's this about a Comic Con?"

Gene's face lights up. "Oh. Yeah. It's going to bring in some money, hopefully get my profile up again. First one's in Seattle in a couple of weeks."

"Seattle? America? You're going back to America?"

They gaze at each other awkwardly. And there it is, gone. Lila feels the familiar ice close around her, the shell once again taking hold.

"Well, yeah. I mean it's good money."

"Right."

Gene's eyes travel across her face. "Oh . . . no! But it's only a week. I'm—I'm going to need somewhere to stay when I come back." As Lila stares at him, he continues, "I mean, ideally, I'd want to keep on hanging with everyone . . . my family . . . I—It would feel pretty crappy to have got to know everyone just to disappear again."

Lila makes sure she has heard him right. "You're coming back?"

"Oh, sure. These fan conventions are only a few times a year. I'm going to have to find some work in between times. Ideally, right here."

Violet appears between them, beaming and wearing her normal clothes. She has located a packet of Walkers and is stuffing her face with cheese and onion crisps.

"Great job, kiddo!" Gene's voice is suddenly booming again, filled with confidence. "You rocked that narration! You carry on like that, and we're going to have to find you an agent!"

Violet, still chewing, accepts his praise as her due, and takes Gene's hand with casual possessiveness. She registers Lila standing there, and turns back to him. She waits until she has finished her mouthful then says, "Are you coming back with us?"

Gene looks at Lila. She sees her father's uncertain expression, Bill's relief, Violet's fingers inside her grandfather's hand, the whole familial mess of it all. "Yes," she says. "Gene is coming back with us."

Violet throws her arms around him. "Yay! We can watch that episode of *Star Squadron Zero* where you and Vuleva meet the sexy aliens! I found it on YouTube."

Gene's gaze flickers toward Lila. "Ah, maybe not that one, honey. I've seen that one too and that—that one was not, strictly speaking, a *Star Squadron* episode." And then he quickly changes the subject and starts sweeping up the excess glitter.

IT IS ALMOST half past eight when they walk out into the lobby area, where a multitude of parents are still milling around waiting for stray, overtired children and drinking the dregs of their wine. The air is thick with congratulations, exclamations, mothers trying to locate coats and bags, the odd father studying his watch and murmuring that they should go. She spies Celie, saying goodbye to Dan, who is carrying an exhausted Hugo, and Lila lifts her head, trying to see over everyone, to locate Jensen. "I think he must be still in the school hall," she tells Gene and Violet, but they are deep in conversation about Mr. Darling wetting his pants, and she isn't sure they hear her. She's just about to walk into the hall when she hears a sudden commotion behind her, a kind of collective *whoo!* Something makes her turn back.

She feeds her way through the thin crowd and there is Gabriel Mallory, bent over in a small semi-circle of people. He is wiping red wine from his face. Standing a few feet in front of him, Jessie is wearing a denim dress and a pair of orange Cuban-heeled boots. "You," she says, into the stunned silence, "are an absolute knob." She turns to his mother, who is staring at her, aghast. "Honestly, I hate to blame other women for the abysmal behavior of men but you *really* need to have a word with your son."

Jessie puts down her empty glass and starts walking back through the crowd, apparently oblivious to the shocked stares of the other parents. It is as she reaches the coat pegs that she spots Lila, who is standing open-mouthed. She does a small double-take, as if it is the nicest of surprises to find her there. "I hoped I'd see you. Want to go for a drink sometime?"

Lila closes her mouth. "Yes. Yes, I do," she says, nodding. "Definitely."

Jessie flashes her a grin, then reaches for her coat on the peg. "Great. I'll give you a call." And then she walks off backstage.

Chapter Forty-one

It is the oddest thing: Lila cannot stop smiling. It is as if a strange sense of joyousness has infected her little family; they had ridden home together in Jensen's pickup, Violet and Celie squashed between them in the front three seats, and Gene sitting in the open back, wedged against whatever is under the tarpaulin, pulling faces for the girls against the rear windscreen while they all prayed that no police would pass by. The girls keep singing "You Can Fly!" in one of those rare, unforced moments of sibling harmony. It makes Lila's heart swell, and she joins in, despite the fact that she knows only half the words, exchanging silent, amused looks with Jensen, even though she probably sounds like an idiot.

When they get back, Gene heads off to pick up his things from Jane's, possibly to make sure he has installed himself before Lila can change her mind again. He takes Celie, and she watches them head out of the front door, chatting companionably about animation, while Violet slumps on the sofa with a sandwich that Lila has made. Her energy has drained out of her like an empty battery, and she stares unseeing at the television screen, Truant waiting attentively for crumbs at her feet.

She tells Violet she's brilliant, that Bill thought she was faultless, that everyone is very proud of her, and Violet nods benignly, not really listening. She will need half an hour to decompress before she's ready for bed, and Lila finally leaves her to it, heading into the kitchen. When she looks outside, Jensen is carrying something bulky through the back gate. She walks out through the French windows, and as he removes the tarpaulin, she sees that it is a two-person oak Lutyens bench, silvered with age, and a little battered. He puts it carefully in the place where Bill's bench had been, adjusting it so that it is perfectly centered on the York stone.

"I got you a present," he says, standing back to show her.

Lila stares at him, at the bench, at the way the garden has a focus again. She walks up to it, running her hand over the grain, feeling the weathered surface under her fingertips.

"Some clients were going to throw it out. They're going modern. I thought it might work here. At least till you find something else. I know it's a bit scruffy."

It takes Lila a minute to find the words. "I love it," she says. "I don't like things that look new. It's perfect." She sits down on it in the cold night air and he sits beside her. This must have been the thing beneath the tarpaulin on his truck. She keeps running her fingers over it, feeling the gnarled wood, the age in its surface. She shakes her head disbelievingly. "You're always thinking about what I need."

"I know. I really need to stop that."

"Please don't."

They sit there for a while on the bench, and Lila feels herself gradually immersed in an unfamiliar sensation: peace. For months, perhaps years, she has been in permanent brace position, dipped low, her hands over her head, waiting for the next thing. The ups have been jagged, inconsistent, prone to turn abruptly into downs. Right now, for the first time she can remember, she just feels . . . level. As if calm is seeping into her bones. She sits back, gazing out at her garden, at the glowing kitchen at the end of the lawn, and lets out a long breath. "You know, the weirdest thing happened this evening. I was looking at Dan at the school play, and he just felt like someone I didn't know. Like I was watching him with Marja's son, and his hair and his clothes and the way he talks, and I looked at this man and I couldn't believe we were married for all that time. He just seemed . . . alien to me. And I thought about all those years we were together and it hit me that, if I'm honest with myself, for so much of it we weren't great."

She glances sideways at him, smiling ruefully. "We were always bickering, just a bit irritated by each other, but too busy with work or the girls to look properly at it. Because you're just meant to get through that stuff, right? And the love and connection is meant to somehow sit underneath it all like—I don't know—grass under a rock, a bit battered but ready to grow again when the rock lifts. And then he left and I was so hurt and angry he had done it that I never stopped to think about whether or not it was the right thing. I was so filled with self-righteousness, that he had abandoned us, made us all victims. That he had broken our family."

She shakes her head. "And tonight I looked at him and I thought maybe *we* broke our family. Because we had long stopped trying with each other. Or we stopped being curious about each other. We stopped being kind to each other. Or maybe we were two people who were never really a great match in the first place."

"I guess—I looked at him tonight and I just felt released. I felt like I could let him go, because he probably wasn't the right person for me anyway. And that just feels . . . weird."

"Good weird?"

Lila thinks. "Maybe. I haven't quite digested it yet." She stretches her arms above her head. "You know, I'm realizing every day that I know nothing. I'm nearly forty-three and I genuinely know nothing."

"That's the fun bit," says Jensen. "Working it out."

"Mm." She gives him a sideways look. "I'm a bit worried my family is going to be too much for you. I mean we are quite a lot."

"I like your family. It's all out there. My family look like the Waltons from outside but inside it's just a seething mass of resentments and insecurities."

"Really?"

"Yeah. I like my madness visible from the outside."

"Well, you certainly get that here."

And here it is, the decision she had made some days ago, after speaking to Eleanor. The thing she needed to get out in the open. She swallows. "I need to tell you something else. After our—our thing, I made a big mistake. Yup, another big mistake. I met this guy and I thought we had something going on. But I—"

Jensen stops her. "Lila. I don't need to know everything. We've been around the block enough to know that stuff happens."

"But you need to know what kind of a mess you're getting yourself into."

He screws up his face. "Yeah. I think I have a pretty good idea."

"And you still want to do this?"

"Apparently."

"Bloody hell. Your therapist clearly has work to do."

"So she tells me." He turns to her then, and his face is serious. "I just need to know one thing—"

She cuts him off. Her heart thumping, she takes his hand in hers and leans toward him. "Jensen, I really, really want to do this. I feel so lucky to have another chance with you. When I'm with you I keep thinking of things we could do together and I feel excited, because honestly? I've only ever really felt like I was on my own. I think my whole life I've felt I was on my own. And I know I can be on my own—I'm pretty good at it—but I just . . . I just want to do it all with you. You make me feel better about pretty much anything. You make me feel like who I am is basically okay. I think . . . you may actually be the best man I've ever met. So if you're in, I'm in. I'm definitely in."

She is gazing at him, waiting intently. He opens his mouth and closes it again.

"Too much?"

He blinks. "No. That's—um—lovely. I was just going to ask when we were going to eat something. Because I'm absolutely starving."

She stares at him. "Oh, my God. You're going to be really annoying, aren't you?"

"Yes. Yes, I am." And then he starts laughing, and then he is kissing her, pulling her in, smothering his laughter with his kisses until, despite herself, she is laughing too.

Postscript

Gene is, inevitably, a hit at the Seattle fan convention. On the first day he was delighted to find himself paired with Vuleva, who is apparently still a "stone-cold fox." She is divorced from the Chicago Bulls player, and lives on a ranch in Calabasas with a bunch of three-legged rescued animals and does not want a full-time relationship, though apparently she's still happy to partake in a bit of the old Gene magic. Violet tells Lila that Grandpa is annoyingly vague about what "the old Gene magic" involves. Lila tells Violet it's probably best not to think about it too much.

Gene spends three days appearing on panels, posing for and signing fan photographs, has the best time hanging with his old castmates (except for the director, who is, inevitably, a dick), and comes home with jet lag, a nasty cold, and thirty-four thousand dollars in his bank account, half of which he immediately transfers to Lila. "You take it, honey. You know it'll just disappear if I hold on to it."

He has already signed up to help out with the next school play. It will be a production of *A Midsummer Night's Dream* and Gene and Mrs. Tugendhat are already having heated discussions about how much he can rewrite the script to include references to hallucinogenics.

His new agent, a fiercely ambitious twenty-eight-year-old Californian called Glenn, has signed him up for three future fan conventions, but he and all his remaining belongings are now installed in what was Bill's room. Lila enjoys the periods when he is back, bringing his irrepressible energy, his bad jokes, and his rapturous adoration of their company, and enjoys equally the period when he goes again, and it's just her and the girls.

She doesn't even mind the school run anymore. Gabriel sends his mother most days, and Jessie comes much more often than she used to. It's always nice to have someone to talk to in the playground.

BILL IS MOVING in with Penelope, into her three-bedroomed house six doors down from Lila's. He knows things have moved rather swiftly, but he says, at his stage of life, what is the point in hanging around? He arranges for the Poles to bring the piano back to Lila's, as Penelope has her far superior Yamaha (as well as a baby grand in her dining room). Lila watches the delivery of the piano on the wobbly piano dollies and thinks the Poles are now very much over bringing the old Steinway backward and forward between the houses and will probably decline to answer the call if they ever have to move it again.

Penelope is pretty much vibrating with happiness. She calls in to give Violet free piano lessons, and whenever Lila passes the hallway she bursts out with breathless snippets of information about the move. Bill is making new doors for her fitted wardrobes! It's too lovely—they're exactly what she would have wanted! Bill is the most marvelous cook— did they know? She has put on at least half a stone. Bill has found a remarkable piano tuner and she doesn't think her Yamaha has ever had a better tone. Lila listens and smiles and lets Penelope's happiness spill out where it will. There is something lovely about someone being so unapologetically and unexpectedly happy in their sixties. It suggests hope for them all.

PERHAPS AIDED BY Bill's general sense of romantic contentment, Bill and Gene seem to have formed a new diplomatic relationship, which mostly manifests itself in Gene teasing Bill about his healthy diet ("Should've stuck to the doughnuts, pal! I told you all those lentils weren't going to do you any good!") and Bill sighing good-naturedly, and occasionally retorting: "If you looked after yourself a little better, Gene, you might manage to attract a lovely young lady, like I have," which always makes Penelope a little fluttery.

On Wednesdays Bill cooks for everyone, and it's a shambolic, but cheerful event, one of the few evenings that Gene can be relied upon to be home from the pub in time, and Celie can be drawn down from her room. These days she seems to be drawing pictures rather than hiding out with her phone, so Lila tries not to take it personally. They have done it four times now, and everyone seems to be on their best behavior, even if that involves Bill making the occasional veiled comment about the cleanliness of the pans (one should really clean the outside of the pan with the same vigor that one addresses the inside) and Gene adding ketchup to whatever Bill has concocted (possibly just to wind him up: Lila can't believe anyone really enjoys tomato sauce on coconut rice pudding), and being just a few degrees too flirtatious with Penelope.

Lila sits at the head of the table and just enjoys it all, eating the food that has been cooked for her and watching the invisible threads reattach the different sides of her family, at first fragile, but then swiftly growing in strength, like an enormous silken web. Sometimes she thinks about her mother, and wonders what she would have made of it all. She's pretty sure it would be something along the lines of *"Isn't it the most fun, Lils? Aren't we all just ridiculously modern?"*

LILA HAS MET Nella, the actress for whom she is ghosting a memoir, twice. Both times the two-hour meetings have stretched to a full day, partly because the actress talks so much and veers off so chaotically that Lila struggles to keep her on track, and has to keep making sure she has fleshed out the half-told stories, but also because, to her surprise, she likes her. Nella is glamorous, filthy and funny, bursts frequently into impromptu laughter, is terrifyingly unforgiving of her enemies and prone to announcing: *Fuck them all, darling. Fuck every last one of them.* There is going to be a lot of editing. But Lila is well-used to dealing with actors, is oddly energized every time she meets her, and there is something about her robust survivor mentality that invigorates her. So far Nella has tried to press on her a fur coat, a bottle of tequila, and a jeweled bracelet from a Saudi sheikh that turned out to be fake. "Fake, darling, can you believe that? And I'd sent him a whole portfolio of nude pictures of myself, at his request. The third time I went out with him I nicked one of his Rolex watches. Oh, he won't have noticed, he had about thirty of them. That wasn't fake, I can tell you. I sold it at Bonhams and used the money to get my roof insulated."

Lila tells Anoushka that the book is going to be great and she's up for any further ghosting work that comes along. There have been no references to guinea pigs. So far.

JENSEN LEAVES FOR Winchester, and is gone for ten days. He calls her twice a day for every one of them. Lila thinks afterward that it was probably quite good for them both, having the enforced separation at a time when she could quite easily have panicked about over-committing herself. She had, somehow, said an awful lot to him for someone she had barely dated. He tells her stories of how his day went, which plants he put where, which machinery played up, and the erratic decisions of the owners (the Winchester people are nice but flaky) and Lila listens to it all carefully, making sure he knows she is entirely focused on the call, and not distracted by anything else. Sometimes this involves locking herself into the bathroom and sending Violet surreptitious texts on the iPad that read:

> Just give me ten minutes
> I know it's been ten. Okay twenty
> Put Truant in the garden. If it's solid, use
> kitchen roll and put it down the loo. If it's
> runny, I'll deal with it when I come
> downstairs
> Yes, you can do it. I'm on the phone

When Jensen had finally come home she had left Gene in charge and spent the night at his flat—he has been sweet about her family, but there is only so much chaos a man can be expected to deal with—spraying herself with perfume and wearing a new button-down dress she had bought with Gene's convention money. Jensen's flat was nice: a little rustic, with airy rooms and a large low sofa. None of the furniture was cream-colored. Jensen cooked dinner—nothing fancy, just something with chicken and wild mushrooms and rice—and they had both admitted to feeling oddly nervous, as if the tension that had built up during his absence was now threatening to collapse on them, like an overinflated balloon.

Lila had felt herself growing self-conscious as they ate, her conversation faltering as she worried whether this could possibly match what she had created in her mind, whether she was about to make yet another terrible mistake. She wanted to sleep with him again, and she was terrified of what that might mean. She told him apropos of nothing that she had read a statistic that said 60 percent of all second marriages failed, and that was especially likely if one side had children. She added, only half joking: "They didn't mention the statistics if you have a pair of eccentric fathers too." And then she had added hurriedly: "I'm not saying I want us to get married." And then she had said, in case that sounded cold: "I mean, I'm not saying that if I did want to get married you wouldn't be the kind of person that I would want to marry."

Jensen had looked at her carefully, put down his knife and fork, and said: "Right. I can see I'm going to have to take charge of this." He had walked out of the room, dimmed the lights a little, then walked back in a few minutes later wearing only his boxer shorts, saying, as Lila stared in shock: "This has got way too serious and weighty. Let's treat the first go as a fun test run. We can get that out of the way and just enjoy the next time."

He had lifted his arms to the sides and beamed at her. He may have said *ta-dah!* She can't remember. She had been momentarily transfixed. He looked an awful lot fitter than the last time she had seen him undressed. There was nothing homely about Jensen's body anymore.

Lila put her empty plate on the coffee-table. When she could speak, she said: "I'm impressed that you think there's going to be a next time."

His eyes locked on hers. He was still smiling. "Oh," he said. "There's going to be a next time."

There was, indeed, a next time. But the test run, she told him afterward, as they lay in bed laughing at his bravery and sharing a bowl of the mango pudding they had forgotten to have with the dinner, had been an excellent start.

ESTELLA ESPERANZA FINALLY murders her husband in episode thirty-seven. She shoots him at a fairground, the sound muffled by the screams of the passengers on the big wheel, and the never-ending *rat-a-tat-tat* of the rifle range nearby. He turns, sees who is pointing the gun, and sinks to his knees, clutching his bloodied chest. It is at this point that Estella seems to have a change of heart, and cries bitter tears over the body as he expires extravagantly. When he dies, she announces that everything she has done has been a mistake, that it was all for love, that she had been blinded by her need for revenge, and that her life is no longer worth living.

Lila frowns at the screen for a while and decides she is not going to watch any more. It's a stupid program. She thinks she might start reading a book instead.

THE PORTRAIT OF Francesca hangs once again in the living room. Lila had put it back in its space above the television after Gene moved back in (he preferred to have framed posters of himself in various roles in his bedroom—*Talking Dog III*, *Terror Teacher*, and *In the Land of the Space Cowboys*). Lila feels in her bones that it is time to restore Francesca's presence to the household, to be reminded that her mother had been, above all, the most caring, attentive, and enthusiastic of parents. She has started having conversations with her in her head again, asking her advice and working out how her mother would have responded. Lila has chosen not to think too hard about any mistakes Francesca may have made—who is she to judge, after all?—and to focus only on how lucky they all were to have had that vibrant, loving woman in their lives for as long as they did.

It has been there three days before Lila notices one of the girls—presumably Celie—has carefully painted a pair of dark blue knickers over what Violet still refers to as Grandma's pocket book.

"ARE WE READY?" Lila has packed the big beach basket, and is looping the long leather straps over her shoulder. She wraps up in a scarf—today is cold and blustery—and waits while Violet locates her coat, complaining bitterly about being dragged away from her computer game at a point when she is apparently about to hit "boss level." Gene is out with Truant for the afternoon. He has forced the dog to love him, of course, and likes to have the company when he leaves the house. Occasionally Truant comes back smelling suspiciously like the carpet at the Red Lion, but he seems happy, so Lila chooses to enjoy the fact that he is not spending most of his life being neurotic in the house. It is costing her a lot less in wine for the neighbors.

Celie has cut her hair short and dyed it a vibrant shade of pink. Lila was a little shocked at first, but it's nice not to have her daughter's face permanently obscured by a cloud of dark hair, and she secretly admires the determined autonomy that comes with Celie's new look. She has just observed that it looks great, and thanks God privately that Celie is not at a school where they mind that kind of thing.

Celie has acquired a quiet, ginger-haired friend called Martin, who appears periodically with a huge folder of drawings. They sit upstairs going through their work, or making stop-go animation stills on the computer in the front room. When Lila asked Celie casually if there was anything going on between them, Celie had looked at her as if she was a dinosaur and said: "God, Mum, boys and girls are allowed to be friends you know." Lila suspects that Martin may not see things in quite the same way, but that will be their mess to deal with.

"Violet, come *on*." Celie is standing at the door, impatient to leave, probably so that she can come back again.

"Stop hassling me," Violet whines. "You're being really annoying."

Dan's baby had been born two weeks previously, a boy named Marius. He had been premature, underweight, and jaundiced, and spent the first ten days of his life in an incubator in the pediatric intensive care unit, while Marja and Dan sat for hours at the side of the clear Perspex box like a hyper-vigilant tag team. He had been finally allowed home, with a clean bill of health, yesterday—ten days before Christmas. Dan's voice, when he had called, had been giddy with relief: "He's feeding fine. Filled a couple of disgusting nappies, and kept us up all night, but it's all good."

Jessie had spotted Marja at the supermarket four days ago and said she looked properly wrecked, an exaggerated version of how all new mothers look, but with added exhaustion, anxiety, and greasy hair. "God, I couldn't go through that again, could you?"

"No," Lila had said. "Probably not."

Lila and the girls let themselves out of the house and start walking down the road. It is a windy day and they button their coats as they walk, pulling up their collars. Lila knows enough about these early days to have the timeline worked out in her head already. In the basket, along with the overpriced Babygro from the posh French shop in Hampstead, she carries a packet of expensive biscuits, a fruit cake, and a box of chocolates. New mothers rarely get enough treats. They will deliver the gifts, stay long enough for one cup of tea and to admire the baby, and then they will wash up their own cups (new parents have enough to do without extra washing-up) and leave. It may feel a little weird—there may be the odd twinge of pain or poignancy—but it's important to do it, and important that the girls see their parents do it. Because they are all part of this family now, uneven shape, frayed edges, half-built or rebuilt parts and all. And they will be, for decades to come.

"You ready, Mum?" Celie looks at her, her gaze holding a faint question, and Lila observes with distant surprise that her daughter's eyes are now level with Lila's own.

"I certainly am, lovely."

Celie, unexpectedly, slides her arm through Lila's. Lila takes a breath, adjusts the basket on her shoulder, and with Violet skipping ahead, they set off together toward Dan's house.

Acknowledgments

This has probably been my least heavily researched book, but that doesn't mean there aren't a whole bunch of people I need to acknowledge. Even this, the most solitary of professions, requires a team of people in every corner.

Thank you, as ever, to my agent, Sheila Crowley, and my publisher Louise Moore for their continuing faith and endless support. Thanks to the many talented people at Penguin Michael Joseph who help turn a raw draft into something worthy of people's bookshelves, particularly: Maxine Hitchcock, Hazel Orme, Clare Parker and Ellie Hughes, and Maddy Woodfield.

Thank you to my US publisher, Pamela Dorman at Pamela Dorman Books, and to Brian Tart and Marie Michels at Penguin Random House. Thank you also to Katharina Dornhöfer, Dr. Marcus Gärtner, Anne-Claire Kühne, and Nicola Bartels at Rowohlt in Germany. I am so grateful for your continued backing, as I am to all my publishers across the globe.

Huge gratitude to everyone at Curtis Brown, especially Katie Mc-Gowan, Tanja Goossens, and Aoife MacIntyre in foreign rights, Nick

Marston, Katie Battcock, and Nick Fenwick in TV/film. Thank you also to my legendary Los Angeles representative, Mr. Bob Bookman.

Nearer home, thank you to my support network of writers—truly one of the most generous-natured professions there is. Thank you to Kate Weinberg, Maddy Wickham, Jenny Colgan, Lisa Jewell, Jodi Picoult, and Lucy Ward. Thank you to my most youthful of old friends, Cathy Runciman, for endless advice, usually while one or the other of us is trying to locate a dog on Hampstead Heath. Gratitude also to Thea Sharrock, Caitlin Moran, and John Niven for helping me with my psychological research (that's what we're calling it, anyway) and Sarah Phelps and Sarah Harvey for help and adventures in the screen trade.

Thanks to everyone who provides the practical help that allows me to do what I do—my longtime friend and assistant, Jackie Shapley, and Maria D. Otero Menoya. I appreciate you both more than I can say. Likewise Susy Wheeler, Isabelle Russo, and Gaby Noble.

Lots of love to my family, who bear absolutely no resemblance to anyone in this book. To my dad, Jim Moyes, and my stepdad, Brian Sanders, as well as my three excellent offspring—Saskia, Harry, and Lu—who are now teaching me so much more than I ever taught them. Last but not least to John, for emotional support, bag-carrying, plot dissection, and dinner. Yes, turns out it *is* usually just me being hungry.

Finally, thanks to three people who have generously supported two charities in return for having their names in this book. Thank you to Jorg Roth and Tricia Philips for their donation to Park Lane Stables in London, a charity that offers riding for the disabled and was recently saved by crowdfunding, and to Davinia Brotherton for her support of the Speakers Trust, a charity that helps young people find their voice.

And thank you to everyone who has read, borrowed, or supported my books in any way, or who I have connected with on social media. You're not the only reason we do what we do, but we'd look pretty silly if you weren't there.